Smoke!' ordered Karras as he threw his first grenade. Rauth discarded the detonator and did the same. Two, three, four small canisters bounced onto the ship's bridge, spread just enough to avoid redundancy. Within two seconds, the whole deck was covered in a dense grey cloud. The ork crew went into an uproar, barely able to see their hands in front of their faces. But to the Astartes, all was perfectly clear. They entered the room with bolters firing, each shot a vicious bark, and the greenskins fell where they stood.

More Space Marines from Black Library

DEATHWATCH
Steve Parker

SPACE MARINES
Edited by Christian Dunn, Nick Kyme and Lindsey Priestley

WARHAMMER 40,000
SPACE MARINE BATTLES

DAMNOS
Nick Kyme

ARMAGEDDON
Aaron Dembski-Bowden

DEATH OF INTEGRITY
Guy Haley

THE DEATH OF ANTAGONIS
David Annandale

THE SIEGE OF CASTELLAX
C L Werner

WRATH OF IRON
Chris Wraight

ARCHITECT OF FATE
Edited by Christian Dunn

LEGION OF THE DAMNED
Rob Sanders

THE GILDAR RIFT
Sarah Cawkwell

BATTLE OF THE FANG
Chris Wraight

THE PURGING OF KADILLUS
Gav Thorpe

HUNT FOR VOLDORIUS
Andy Hoare

RYNN'S WORLD
Steve Parker

A WARHAMMER 40,000 ANTHOLOGY

BLACK LIBRARY

A Black Library Publication

'Headhunted' first published in the Heroes of the Space Marines anthology.

'Exhumed' first published in the Victories of the Space Marines anthology.

'Last Watch' appears in print for the first time.

First published in 2012.
This edition published in Great Britain in 2014 by
Black Library,
Games Workshop Ltd.,
Willow Road,
Nottingham, NG7 2WS, UK.

10 9 8 7 6 5 4 3 2 1

Cover illustration by Cheol Joo Lee.

A CIP record for this book is available from the British Library.

UK ISBN 13: 978 1 84970 608 7
US ISBN 13: 978 1 84970 615 5

See Black Library on the internet at

www.blacklibrary.com

Find out more about Games Workshop
and the world of Warhammer 40,000 at

www.games-workshop.com

Printed and bound by CPI Group (UK) Ltd, Croydon, CR0 4YY

It is the 41st millennium. For more than a hundred centuries the Emperor has sat immobile on the Golden Throne of Earth. He is the master of mankind by the will of the gods, and master of a million worlds by the might of his inexhaustible armies. He is a rotting carcass writhing invisibly with power from the Dark Age of Technology. He is the Carrion Lord of the Imperium for whom a thousand souls are sacrificed every day, so that he may never truly die.

Yet even in his deathless state, the Emperor continues his eternal vigilance. Mighty battlefleets cross the daemon-infested miasma of the warp, the only route between distant stars, their way lit by the Astronomican, the psychic manifestation of the Emperor's will. Vast armies give battle in His name on uncounted worlds. Greatest amongst his soldiers are the Adeptus Astartes, the Space Marines, bio-engineered super-warriors. Their comrades in arms are legion: the Imperial Guard and countless planetary defence forces, the ever-vigilant Inquisition and the tech-priests of the Adeptus Mechanicus to name only a few. But for all their multitudes, they are barely enough to hold off the ever-present threat from aliens, heretics, mutants – and worse.

To be a man in such times is to be one amongst untold billions. It is to live in the cruellest and most bloody regime imaginable. These are the tales of those times. Forget the power of technology and science, for so much has been forgotten, never to be re-learned. Forget the promise of progress and understanding, for in the grim dark future there is only war. There is no peace amongst the stars, only an eternity of carnage and slaughter, and the laughter of thirsting gods.

CONTENTS

MACHINE SPIRIT

NICK KYME

'Tracking...'

The gruff voice issued through a mouth grille, reverberating inside the warrior's battle-helm. Gauntleted fingers rimed with dried blood, the black ceramite chipped from hand-to-hand combat, twisted a dial on the magnoculars.

'Wait...'

A slew of data came through the scopes. The myopic visual of a white, trackless desert was augmented by a scrolling commentary describing wind speed and directionality, mineral composition, temperature and atmospherics in truncated rune-script. The most salient piece of intel was revealed in the hazy image return, however.

Squalls of armour-abrading calcite were whipping across endless dunes farther out, presaging another storm. The more dangerous hazard had yet to reveal itself, but Zaeus knew it was there.

He grunted, annoyed and trying to marshal his temper.

'Any sign, Brother Zaeus?' asked another voice, one partially obscured by the rising wind. What began as a zephyr had developed into a gale.

The more cultured speaker was crouched below Zaeus in a shallow calcite basin where the rest of the kill-team had taken refuge. He looked up expectantly at the Brazen Minotaur through the burning coals of his eyes. An orange drake head upon a black field on his right shoulder guard marked him as a Salamander, and he was supporting a third warrior who carried the sigil of the Imperial Fists. A fourth knelt in silent vigil beside them both, head bowed, while the last of their group was laid in still repose nearby.

'Weather's impeding visual feed,' Zaeus muttered, careful to mask his fatigue. He adjusted the dials again, using small movements that looked too delicate for such a hulking brute.

Despite their power armour, he was more broad-shouldered than the others and his chin jutted as if set in a challenge, even encased by a battle-helm.

Distant shadow figures, like patches of blurred ink on a canvas, resolved through the growing blizzard. The grain and rock whipped about within it *plinked* against Zaeus's shoulder guards. It wore at the gold trim and cracked the black bull icon against its field of flaking white.

Some of the shadow figures were larger than the others, gene-bulked by carapace and outfitted with forearm blades. Zaeus's stomach clenched, as did his jaw, as he remembered the fate of Brother Festaron. The former Star Phantom had killed a swath of the creatures before they'd gutted him. A greater mass of the less developed aliens moved slowly behind the hulks, bowed against the wind. Their avian war-cries, altered slightly by the hybridisation of the thorax, were just audible.

Zaeus counted at least fifty, but he knew there were more. He made a mental note of the ammunition left in his cache. Thirteen hellfire, four kraken rounds, three metal storm and two tangle-web. Including two clips of standard mass-reactive, it wasn't much.

'They have our spoor now,' he told the others.

He reckoned on over three hundred. The kill-team's present condition removed 'combat engagement' as a mission option. It only left 'harass and retreat'. That irritated the Brazen Minotaur like a thorn under a nail and he growled.

'I feel it too, brother,' said Ar'gan, the Salamander. 'The desire to burn them to ash.'

Zaeus lowered the magnoculars and headed back down into the basin where the others were waiting.

'Carfax will be expecting us,' he said, referring to their pilot.

The kneeling warrior, Vortan, looked up from his litany as Zaeus's shadow fell across him.

'How many?' he asked, voice grating, getting to his feet. Vortan was of the Marines Malevolent, and carried a winged bolt of lightning against a yellow background on his guard. He was also a miserable bastard, but hard as adamantium.

Zaeus stopped, racked his bolter's slide, but didn't turn. He wore a bulky armature fitted to his power pack, a servo-arm that flexed in simpatico with his body's movements.

'We will be meeting the Emperor if we stay to find out,' he said.

Vortan sneered, hefting a belt feed around his waist and attaching it to his heavy cannon. 'Fleeing from xenos scum…' He shook his head. 'It's beneath us.'

The Brazen Minotaur sniffed noncommittally, 'Then I shall see you again at the foot of the Golden Throne, brother.' He checked his ammo gauge. 'My count is low,' he muttered, stooping to grab a length of chain looped around Festaron's torso.

Zaeus grunted, and began to heave the body. The trail left by the dead Star Phantom was quickly absorbed by the drifts of calcite. At least his blood wouldn't give them away. Not that it really mattered.

'We should move. Use the storm as cover,' he said, increasing his pace. 'Ar'gan?'

The Salamander was helping up Captain Polino. Both went without battle-helms, and Ar'gan's red eyes flared like hellfires in the blizzard. His face was like a slab of onyx. It stuck out, but then they all did, wearing Deathwatch black.

'So much for the line of Dorn,' Polino rasped, flecking his ashen lips with blood. The Imperial Fist turned moribund, and as he leaned heavily against Ar'gan's shoulder said, 'I'm sorry, brother… I led us to this.'

Hunters had become the hunted, their elite kill-team in danger of extermination by the very filth they were supposed to have already neutralised.

Ar'gan's tone was conciliatory. 'None of us, not even you, Captain Polino, could have anticipated what we found in that nest, their immunity to the nerve toxin.' He nodded to the armoured corpse of Festaron and the fist-sized puncture wound in his breastplate. The Deathwatch had sealed it with a binding solution that kept what was inside dormant. 'But soon the truth here will be exposed and end the Imperium's treaty with the tau by unleashing the wrath of the Inquisition.'

'Only if we escape this Throne-forsaken desert before we share the same demise as our eviscerated comrade,' said Vortan.

Zaeus kept his own counsel. War with the tau had been ongoing for months with no sign of inroads on either side. Negotiation was sought, but certain interested parties within the Inquisition were keen to avoid that. A single kill-team had been dispatched to eliminate the bulk of the alien's forces – a faction of avian mercenaries designated *krootis aviana* by Imperial taxonomers – through the utilisation of an Ordo Xenos nerve toxin that would remove them as a threat. Without their mercenary horde, the tau would be unable to match the Imperium on a war footing. That the nerve toxin had proven less than efficacious grated on the Brazen Minotaur, even if its failure did mean he and his comrades had unearthed a greater threat in their midst.

The Marine Malevolent was still venting. 'We should have broken into that council session and executed every single one of those grey-fleshed dung-eaters.'

'The Imperial officers would have resisted us,' said Zaeus.

'They would have been next before my guns.'

Zaeus believed him. The Marine Malevolent was a singular warrior, driven and harsh to the point of brutality, but he saw only in absolutes and so his view was oft narrow.

Vortan glanced at the Imperial Fist, whispering to Ar'gan, '*He slows us*,' before he looked at the Star Phantom being dragged by Zaeus. '*They both do*.'

As if to make Vortan's point, Captain Polino staggered and would have fallen if not for Ar'gan. Pain reduced his voice to a rasp between clenched teeth.

'Keep moving...'

Ar'gan gave Vortan a dark look that was both a reproach and suggested their captain wasn't going to last much longer. They needed to find Carfax and the gunship before the hunters found them.

Vortan shrugged, engaging the suspensors on his heavy bolter that allowed him to move as fast as the others in his kill-team, even whilst encumbered.

He marched ahead to take point. 'Give me a bearing, Zaeus.'

It was tough to get a reading with so much environmental interference. The retinal lenses of all the helmeted Space Marines were fraught with static, and ghosted with false returns and feedback.

Heat signatures were non-existent and visual confirmation of landmarks, geography or enemies was reduced to almost point-blank. The data stream through scopes or retinal feed was scrambled, useless. But the Brazen Minotaur possessed much better auspex than his brothers, and could cut through the fog of static easily. He sub-vocalised the coordinates of the rendezvous point relative to their position and ex-loaded them to Vortan's lens display.

'I have it,' said the Marine Malevolent. 'Advancing.'

Ar'gan's voice came through Zaeus's comm-feed, low and full of distaste.

'He would sacrifice them both for the mission.'

'As would I, son of Vulkan,' Zaeus replied, 'as should you.' He half-glanced over his shoulder at the Salamander.

'But he is callous to a sharpened edge, brother. We all must be pragmatic, but what Vortan suggests is disrespectful.'

'He is of the Marines Malevolent, and therefore practical to the point of being an utter bastard. I thought your Chapter was familiar with their ways?'

Ar'gan's tone grew darker and there was a scowl in his words, 'That we are, but I cannot condone–'

'Hsst!' Zaeus raised a clenched fist for silence. 'Stop.' It was an order to the entire kill-team, even Captain Polino. The Imperial Fist was all but incapacitated; as Techmarine, the Brazen Minotaur was next in command.

'Brother?' Vortan asked warily through the feed.

Intensifying storm winds were making it tough to hear, but Zaeus had reacted to something.

The Brazen Minotaur's entire left side, all the way down to his abdomen, was cybernetic, sacrificed to the Machine-God and the glory of the Omnissiah. As well as granting phenomenal strength and endurance, his augmentations also included superlative hearing courtesy of a bionic ear.

Zaeus arched his neck towards the skies. After four seconds, he shouted out, 'Incoming!'

Kraken rounds scudded through the storm-drift, chewing off pieces of carapace that fell in chunks. Vortan heard the creature bleat before it ditched into a nearby dune. Ar'gan was already moving low with his combat-blade drawn. It was acid-edged, fashioned to slice through hardened xenos-chitin like air. The creature was bleeding, one wing broken, the other shredded and incapable of flight when he found it. A jet of caustic bile spewed from its maw, but the Salamander warded it off with his vambrace before ramming the blade into the insect's throat. It shuddered once and was still.

From the shallow ridge, Vortan bellowed, 'More coming!' The *dug-dug* staccato of armour-piercing heavy bolter rounds joined a muzzle flash that spat from the cannon's smoke-blackened mouth. Two of the flyers were cut apart, exploding in a shower of viscous gore that coated Ar'gan's armour.

The Salamander scowled at his battle-brother, but the Marine Malevolent was laughing, loud and raucously. When the cannon *chanked* empty and the belt feed ran slack, his humour evaporated as he went for his sidearm. Before he could slip the pistol from its holster, a stingwing arrowed towards him, flesh-hooks extended. Vortan used the heavy bolter like a club and smacked the creature head-on, crushing its snout and most of its skull. He stamped on its neck, finishing it off.

Zaeus stayed at Polino's side, and also watched over the corpse of Festaron, who would be like carrion to the flyers. The injured captain was doing his best to keep upright, and snapped off loose shots with his bolter.

'Herd them to me if you can, brother-captain,' said Zaeus, eyes keen as he discerned a jagged shape arcing through the drifts. An ululating challenge, foul with alien cadence, resonated from a stingwing's throat as it dived hungrily.

'Here, filth!' Zaeus spat, and swung his servo-arm. The mechanical clamps seized the creature's neck in mid-flight, piling on the pressure until the reinforced chitin buckled and its head came off with a snap. Gore spewed across the Brazen

Minotaur's battle-plate, scoring the metal and acid-burning it down to raw grey. Through his bionic, he performed a split-second analysis.

'High concentrations of sulphuric and hydrochloric acid,' he related to the data-corder in his helmet. 'Trace elements of alkali, potential hydrogen levels fourteen or greater. Extremely corrosive, and inconsistent with the bio-strains in-loaded to the kill-team mission brief.'

This he catalogued whilst bringing down another stingwing with a snap shot from his bolter. The designation came from the xenos datacore identified: *tau*. Countless others filled the hard-wired cogitator arrays of the Iron Fortress watch station where Zaeus and his comrades were currently barracked. Interrogating the data from the mission brief and cross-referencing it with previous engagements, he noticed an inter-species correlation with a second organism class.

Tyrannic.

The xeno-form, 'stingwing', was a mutated strain corrupted by genetic hybridisation. It could explain why the nerve toxin had failed, and why the kill-team were running for their lives.

'They're still coming,' breathed Polino.

Zaeus gave him a glance. The Imperial Fist was flagging, his left hand perpetually pressed against his torso. Dark blood flowed freely from the wound through Polino's fingers as his Larraman cells lost the battle against whatever anti-coagulating agents were rife in his dead attacker's bodily juices.

'Hold on,' snarled Zaeus, 'we're almost through them.'

Despite their initial frenzy, the stingwings were peeling off and returning to the larger herd now lost in the sandstorm.

Tracer rounds from Vortan's heavy bolter followed the creatures and a miniature sun erupted from the hellfire shell the Marine Malevolent had loaded, streaking flame across the choked sky. The red dawn was short-lived, however, though Vortan grunted his satisfaction as he watched the burning carcasses of a pair of stingwings spiral earthwards.

'Slightly profligate, brother?' Zaeus suggested upon Vortan's return.

The Marine Malevolent grunted, almost a verbal shrug as he continued on the marked route that would take them back to Carfax and exfiltration.

Ar'gan was farther out and ran to catch up to the rest of the kill-team, who were already moving again.

'How is he?'

Zaeus shook his head, trying to be surreptitious. He need not have bothered. Polino was putting one foot in front of the other, but his eyes were glazed, his expression slackening by the minute.

'We need to get back to Carfax,' the Salamander urged. He spoke through a comm-bead built into his gorget.

'Aye,' Zaeus agreed, taking up the chains wrapped around Festaron. The Brazen Minotaur's eyes were fixed on the hulking ammo hopper attached to Vortan's back. 'But we won't make it.'

'What?' Ar'gan turned swiftly. 'Explain, Techmarine.'

'Those flyers didn't attack us for no reason,' he said. 'They were gauging our strength and our foot speed. Across this terrain,' he gestured to the raging sand storm, 'and in these conditions, we will be fortunate if we get halfway to Carfax before the herd catches us. And then…' He paused to draw his hand across his throat in a cutting motion.

'I didn't mark you for a fatalist, Zaeus.' There was some reproach in the Salamander's tone that the Brazen Minotaur ignored.

'I'm not. I'm a realist, as I thought you Nocturneans were supposed to be.'

Hooting cries, the bleating battle-cant of the hunters, followed them on the breeze.

'Hear that?' said Zaeus, 'They are sending another vanguard to slow us down. It'll be more flyers, but this time with support. This desert is theirs, Ar'gan. In it they are faster, cleverer and more deadly. Make no mistake, we are prey here and our head start has almost been eroded.'

Ar'gan kept up the pace, just less than ten metres behind Vortan and in lockstep with Zaeus. He felt the urge to increase it but Polino was at the edge of his endurance already. He recalled what the Marine Malevolent had said about leaving the Imperial Fist, and dismissed the idea as unworthy.

'How can you know what they're planning, or did they teach you xeno-lexography on the red world too?'

'It's what any hunting pack would do,' Zaeus replied. 'Trammel us with lesser forces to give the horde time to arrive. Once they've encircled us, we will make a last stand and die before we've destroyed even half their number.'

Zaeus had stopped to manipulate a panel affixed to one of his armour's cuffs.

He called out, 'Vortan.'

The Marine Malevolent only half-turned, barely slowing his

determined march in the direction of the Thunderhawk and extraction.

'What are you doing? We need to move! I'm not dying on this dust bowl world.'

A minuscule hololith projected from a node attached to the Brazen Minotaur's wrist. There was a small focusing dish appended to it. As he swept his arm around, the landscape was revealed in grainy green, undulating contours.

'I'm mapping the region, searching for weaknesses, a fissure, anything we can use.'

Ar'gan's expression remained concerned as his eyes flicked from the injured Captain Polino to the storm belt now behind them. Somewhere in its depths, the herd were coming.

'Whatever it is you are planning, Zaeus, do it swiftly.'

'Madness. We need to move!' Vortan reasserted, having now come to a dead halt. 'If we march hard we can still reach Carfax and the gunship.'

'And what about our injured and dead?' It sounded more like a suggestion, even coming from Ar'gan's lips. So conflicted was he that the Salamander could not bring himself to face Vortan.

The Marine Malevolent's solution was brutally simple. 'We leave them behind. Both.'

Though he was largely incoherent now, Polino caught enough of the conversation to weigh in himself. He nodded. 'I will make the sacrifice for the rest, and take a heavy toll of the alien filth.'

'Stoic to the end, captain,' said Zaeus, letting a little machine edge grate his voice, 'but you can barely lift your weapon.'

Polino tried, but his entire arm was shaking.

'And, besides,' Zaeus added, 'it wouldn't matter. We still wouldn't reach the gunship. We have a further problem.'

Vortan snarled. 'This Throne-forsaken mission has been fraught with them.'

'Such as?' asked Ar'gan, raising his eyebrow in inquiry.

Zaeus's eyes narrowed behind his retinal lenses as he found what he needed, but his answer had nothing to do with this discovery.

'I have heard nothing from Brother Carfax in over an hour. The Angel Vermillion is likely already dead.'

'Without the ship, so are we,' snapped Vortan. He stomped to where Ar'gan was watching the storm belt. 'So are we to wait here for the end then? Kill as many as we can?'

'You don't sound displeased with that scenario,' suggested the Salamander.

'I want to live, but if doomed then I will at least decide the manner of my destruction.'

Zaeus asked, 'How many charges do you have?'

'A pair of krak grenades and a melta bomb, why?' Ar'gan replied, turning to see Zaeus aiming the focusing dish at a point in front of them. A fractured script beneath the hololith display read: 5.3 km.

'All of you,' Zaeus corrected, looking down at Polino. 'Festaron too, someone check his wargear.'

Vortan did, offering up another krak grenade. 'I have four incendiaries,' he said of his own cache.

'Two melta bombs,' said Polino, still struggling.

'And with mine that makes four, plus the krak grenades.' Zaeus shut down the scanner.

More avian war-cries knifed the air, louder now as the herd slowly emerged from the storm.

'You have a plan, Techmarine?' asked Vortan.

'I do.' Zaeus pointed. 'Ahead, about three kilometres, there is a tectonic imperfection. It's little more than a crack in the desert basin at the moment but with the correct explosive encouragement, I think we can broaden it into a chasm. The fault line is long, easily wide enough to impede the entire herd.'

'And what of the stingwings? A chasm will be no impediment to them,' said Vortan.

'I doubt they'll attack without reinforcement, especially given what we did to them last time.'

The Marine Malevolent grunted in what could have been either derision or approval. 'Which way?' he asked, revealing the truth of his first response.

'North.'

They went north.

Thunder erupted across the desert as a line of explosions obliterated the edge of the basin behind them, plunging it into a deep sinkhole many metres wide and many more across.

It was, as Zaeus had promised, a chasm.

'All our grenades went into making that pretty hole,' remarked Vortan bitterly.

Ar'gan ignored the Marine Malevolent, asking, 'How long will it take them to navigate around it?'

'An hour, maybe two if the Throne is merciful.'

Zaeus was transfixed, his eyes on the vast clouds of expelled earth spewing into the air in dirty white geysers of calcite.

'And what mercy do you think the Throne has shown us so far?' asked Vortan, the sneer half-formed on his face when Zaeus struck him.

The Marine Malevolent crumpled under the blow, like he'd just been charged down by a raging bull.

In many ways, he had.

'A second blow will shatter your collarbone, and you won't be able to lift that cannon of yours any more,' snarled the Brazen Minotaur. 'Don't think because I am of the Omnissiah now that I forget my heritage. You have been shown mercy. If any of my brothers had been present here instead of me, you would be dead by now for your constant dissent.'

Retaliation crossed Vortan's mind for a split second, Zaeus saw it in the near-perceptible tremor of his fingers, but the Marine Malevolent recognised the error in that and his conduct thus far, so relented.

'We the Watchers, though divided in brotherhood, are as one in our calling,' he said, uttering one of the many catechisms of the order.

Zaeus nodded.

'Accord is preferable to conflict, is it not brother?'

Vortan slowly bowed his head.

'Especially a conflict you would lose. Now,' said Zaeus, 'we make for the ship and hope that Carfax yet lives.'

Brother Carfax was dead. Slumped over the command console, the glacis of the gunship shattered by several dozen bullet holes, the Angel Vermillion had tried to take off when the snipers ventilated him.

Vortan was in the cockpit and placed a gauntleted hand against the dead warrior's brow, closing his eyes, which were still etched with futile anger.

'No way for a warrior like Carfax to pass,' muttered Ar'gan, solemn as the Marine Malevolent murmured a benediction.

'Aye, he was a bloody bastard,' Vortan agreed, lifting his eyes from the corpse. 'Do you remember when he gutted that clade of psykers?'

Ar'gan smirked ferally, giving a glimpse of the fire in his heart, 'The eldar barely had a moment to consult their skeins of fate before Carfax had weighed in with bolter and blade to cut them.'

Vortan laughed warmly at the memory, but Zaeus returning from his inspection curtailed his humour.

'The gunship's inoperable, but I can repair it,' the Techmarine informed them. An icon was flashing on his vambrace.

Abruptly, the mood turned grim.

'How far out is the herd?' asked the Salamander.

'Too close for me to repair the damage and for us to take off.'

'And what is that on your arm?' Vortan gestured to Zaeus's vambrace.

'Carfax engaged the gunship's distress beacon before he died.' When the Techmarine's eyes met the gaze of the others, they were bright and shining behind his retinal lenses. 'It has picked up a signal.'

...the Emperor's name, here all true servants of the Throne will find sanctuary. In the Emperor's name, here all true servants of the Throne will find sanctuary. In the Emp–

Zaeus killed the feed.

'There are coordinates, and from what I could discern when I interfaced with the ship's long range augurs, they lead to a stronghold.'

Ar'gan had been crouched listening to the looped message, but now he sat up.

'A bastion? Reinforcements?'

'At the very least a way off this rock and back to the Watch.'

The two of them were sitting in the ship's hold. Festaron was laid out in front of them, hands folded across his chest in the sign of the aquila. Polino was resting against a bulkhead, his eyes fluttering. In the dull lambency of the internal lighting, the captain's skin looked sallow and waxy. He gave no indication he had heard either of them.

Ar'gan remained sceptical. 'There was nothing in the mission brief that mentioned an Adeptus Astartes garrison on this world.'

'Perhaps it wasn't relevant. Perhaps it had simply been forgotten. Either way, we must investigate.'

After a moment's thought, Ar'gan nodded.

Vortan was outside, keeping watch through the scopes from a vantage on top of the fuselage.

Three hard raps against the hull was the signal that he had seen something.

Wordlessly, Zaeus and Ar'gan went outside.

The Marine Malevolent handed the magnoculars to Zaeus who augmented the view with his bionic eye.

'It's them, isn't it,' said Vortan.

'Yes,' Zaeus confirmed, checking the internal chrono on his

lens display. 'Less than an hour. Mercy wasn't on our side after all.'

'I want to kill them,' the Marine Malevolent declared.

Ar'gan was casting around the ship. Carfax had set it down in a narrow defile, high cliffs on either side that were tough to reach from the ground. It was a good extraction point: hidden, defensible with only two bottlenecks at either end of the valley as realistic points of ingress.

'Zaeus has found a bastion, potential reinforcement,' announced the Salamander. He was still appraising their surroundings when he added, 'We could hold here. Maintain a defensive perimeter until your return.' He looked at the Brazen Minotaur, who looked back impassively through his retinal lenses.

'Three of these turrets are still functional,' Vortan weighed in. 'I can liberate the cannons, set them up behind a makeshift emplacement with the cargo from the hold.' He thumbed towards Ar'gan. 'Salamander takes one, I the other. Both ends of the valley covered. A pity you used all our grenades,' he added wryly. 'We could have mined them too.'

'And Captain Polino?' Zaeus asked.

Now the Marine Malevolent gave a short, snorted laugh. 'He takes the third gun, squeezes the trigger until the moment his fingers give out. He's close to suspended animation coma as it is, but at least this way his contribution might count for something.'

'Agreed,' said Zaeus, giving the scopes to Ar'gan so the Salamander could take a look at the opposition.

'How far's the bastion?' he asked, tweaking the focus. 'Or

should I ask how long we need to hold them for?'

'Taking into account the return journey, one hundred and thirty-seven minutes. But the ident-marker on that message was Adeptus Astartes in origin, so reinforcement will be substantial and battle-winning.'

Vortan clapped Zaeus on the shoulder. 'Then bring back angels on wings of screaming death for our salvation, brother.'

'You always were the poet,' said Ar'gan.

The Marine Malevolent corrected him, 'You're mistaking poet for zealot, Salamander.'

Whilst his brothers made ready the defences outside, Zaeus was left alone to explore the hold. Captain Polino was in there too, but inert. Eyes closed, his skin the colour of wax, he might well have been dead. Only the slight murmur of his neck as he breathed fitfully betrayed the ruse.

'Rest easy, brother,' said Zaeus, lifting a hand from the Imperial Fist's shoulder as he went deeper into the hold. It was dark, most of the internal lume-strips shorted out or simply destroyed in the attack that had claimed Carfax's life. If the ambushers were still around they had yet to announce their presence, but Zaeus suspected not. Some of the gunship's contents had been stripped, only that which could easily be carried and reappropriated. It was why the heavy cannon still remained.

Zaeus mouthed a silent prayer of binaric to the Omnissiah that something else had proven too cumbersome for the xenos scavengers and smiled when he saw the cargo crate at the very back of the hold, still unopened.

A luminator attached to his battle-helm snapped on, revealing a dusty access panel. There were no runes upon it in which to punch a code. Instead there was a simple vox-corder. A blurt of binaric from the Brazen Minotaur's mouth grille turned the red lume on the panel to green. Escaping pressure hissed into the cabin and the door to the cargo crate, which was easily as tall again as the Techmarine, opened.

Within, Zaeus found what he sought and quickly set to work.

The low, angry squeal of a rotating belt-track interrupted the defence preparations around the gunship.

Ar'gan looked up from fitting a drum mag into one of the cannons he'd liberated from the Thunderhawk's wing. Vortan was stripping sections of the gunship's ablative armour to form makeshift barricades behind which the Salamander would set up the guns.

'In the name of the Throne…' said Vortan, setting down a chunk of scrap he'd been hammering into shape.

Ar'gan simply stared.

'What did you do?'

'Removed the torso and organics,' Zaeus told them. 'It's crude but will provide much greater land speed across the desert.' He was squatting on the hard metal frame of a track bed, two wide slatted belts of vulcanised rubber grinding either side, providing locomotion. The Techmarine's haptic implants were connected to the simple motor engine that had once been slaved to the cyborganic body of a servitor. Through them, he controlled the vehicle's speed and directionality.

It had taken him approximately four minutes to affect the

modification, engage the machine-spirit and drive from the gunship's hold.

'I have a revised estimate for my return,' said Zaeus. 'Eighty-eight minutes. Think you can last that long?' he asked.

'Be on your way, brother,' said Ar'gan.

Vortan finished for the Salamander. 'The chrono's already running.'

Another xenos coming over the ridge line exploded, and Vortan revelled in the destructive fury of the gunship's weapons.

'Yes! Come and taste the wrath!' he bellowed, stitching a line across the narrow aperture into the defile. With a jerk and a grunt, he aimed the cannon upwards to strafe the dwindling swarm of stingwings attempting to attack from above. 'Watch the skies,' he warned his comrades through the comm-feed.

Ar'gan nodded, but had his own problems. His autocannon's drum mag was empty but locked. He couldn't free it to slam home another. Polino's support fire was desultory but no better than that. The captain skirted oblivion now and couldn't be relied upon to hold down a trigger, let alone cover one side of the ravine.

Creatures were spilling into the gorge, a mutant soup of alien limbs, chitinous appendages and snapping mandible claws. They were *krootis aviana* but they were also something else, something altogether more abhorrent.

Aspects that were distinctly avian persisted about the kroot, their long sloping beaks and spine quills protruding from the backs of their heads. Long limbed, they had sharp claws and hooves, capable of impressive foot speed with the ability to wield semi-complex weapons. Natural armour was not one of the kroot's usual traits but these creatures wore a sheath of chitin over their bodies that provided some protection. Others had additional limbs that ended in scything talons. Some were malformed facially, possessing glands not unlike gills through which they could project flesh barbs or trailing hooks.

Despite their evolutionary advantages, an autocannon could render them down into bio-matter easily enough, but only if it could actually fire.

Ar'gan railed at his misfortune, eager to cut them and trying to resist the urge to draw blades and do just that. He was adept at close combat, more so than any of his kill-team brothers. In one sheath he carried a Nocturnean drake-sabre, fashioned from sa'hrk teeth honed to a monomolecular edge, and in the other a Kravian fire-axe. The heavy bladed weapon was a rare specimen of the Kravian machine-cult, a faction of xeno-artificers with obscure ties to the jakaero. A third blade, his back-up or culling knife, was strapped to his thigh.

Against a horde of fifty something kroot-hybrids, its use had limits.

In the end, it was his boot not his blades that prevailed as a swift kick dislodged the drum. Though quick to slam in a replacement, Ar'gan was already overrun.

The creatures had advanced almost to the edge of the gunship's perimeter and the Salamander engaged the cannon's fully automatic fire mode, yanking back the alternator slide and lighting up the muzzle with a roar of star fire.

Swathes of the kroot died, malformed carapaces yielding to the aggressive fury of the high-calibre shells. Organs were pulped, limbs ripped off and bodies transformed into visceral mist. A clutch made it through the barrage, wounded but determined. Ar'gan wedged the trigger down and leapt over the barricade. He took a solid slug to the left shoulder; it scored his guard but left no lasting damage. A second hit mashed against his breastplate, blunted by adamantium. The kroot sniper lined up a third but Ar'gan's combat-knife had left its sheath and was lodged in the creature's throat. It bleated once before crumpling into a wretched heap of quivering mandibles.

The autocannon was still eating through its explosive payload when Ar'gan blocked the claw swipe of a second assailant, seizing its wrist and throwing it into the fusillade. Ululating screaming told the Salamander the threat was neutralised. A third and fourth he killed with two strikes, one an elbow smash to the thorax, the second a pile-driving follow up with his clenched fist that broke the fifth creature's clavicle and went on going into its ribcage. When Ar'gan withdrew his forearm it was steaming with gore and intestinal acids.

Only when the fifth kept coming did the Salamander draw the drake-sabre. It flensed flesh and bone in an eye blink, leaving two halves of a kroot bifurcated along its breastbone. A rapid lunge, like an assassin would use with a punch-dagger but which Ar'gan employed with a full blade, speared another through the heart. The last he decapitated, just as the autocannon was rattling close to empty, having shred the ravine opening to rubble and corpses.

The alien head was still falling as he turned, looking for further prey, his other hand hovering near the hilt of his fire-axe. It remained undrawn – the kroot were slain, but Polino was down.

Ar'gan was already running to the captain when he cried out, 'Vortan!'

The Marine Malevolent was finishing off some dregs with snapshots from his bolter. He was an excellent marksman. Vortan looked up, breathless but exultant from the carnage he had wrought, but rushed over to Polino.

A ragged line of flesh barbs was lodged in the Imperial Fist's upper chest and neck. Fortunately, his armour had borne the brunt of the attack and the cuts weren't deep, but they were envenomed. Polino was fading, descending into full cardiac shock.

'Keep a watch,' Vortan snapped at the Salamander, working at the Imperial Fist's armour clasps so he could remove the front half of his cuirass.

Ar'gan nodded, his gaze returning constantly to the stricken captain, trying to fight off the guilt threatening to impair his ability to follow orders. Mercifully, both sides of the ravine were clear and swamped with settling white dust.

'It was my fault,' he said, surrendering to dismay. 'The drum was jammed. I took too long to–'

'Forget that!' snapped the Marine Malevolent, wrenching off a chunk of Polino's battle-plate and noisily casting it aside. 'Are we still under attack or not?'

'No,' Ar'gan regained his composure, 'the gorge is clear for now.'

'They'll be back.' Vortan stepped back to regard the mess of Polino's bodyglove beneath his armour. It was bloody and it stank like a gretchin had just taken a shit in his breastplate. 'I knew we should have left him.'

Ar'gan scowled, not at the stench but at the wound. 'Putrefaction. It must have been like this for a while. There's a narthecium in the hold,' he said, meeting Vortan's gaze.

'Get it. Quickly.'

Ar'gan returned a few seconds later with a small medical kit. It was rudimentary with gauze, unguents, oils and a small set of tools. It wasn't exactly apothecarion standards but it was still a useable field kit. Vortan had some experience as a field medic and rummaged through the few phials and philtres, ampules and other medicines.

They had resisted its usage until that point, not knowing when it would be most needed. That time had arrived.

'Excise those flesh barbs,' Vortan barked, taking a tube of briny-looking liquid.

Ar'gan had left his shorter combat-blade in the kroot sniper's neck, so took a scalpel from the kit instead and began removing the barbs.

'These things...' he swore, slicing the skin around the wounds carefully so as not to aggravate more of the poison and further envenom it. 'Abominations.'

Vortan's reply was curt, 'All xenos are abominations, fit for extermination and nothing else.' He licked his finger, tasting a droplet of the liquid in the tube before spitting it out with a grimace. 'Should bring him around.' The Marine Malevolent waved the Salamander back, who was done with his improvised surgery anyway.

Vortan had fitted a syringe to the tube and was squeezing out any air bubbles when he said, 'This needs to go into his primary heart. Immediately.'

Polino looked weak, murmuring incoherently, a pained expression gripping his face.

Using a clean scalpel, Ar'gan cut away the section of body-glove over the Imperial Fist's primary heart to reveal skin. It looked pale and unhealthy.

'How will you pierce the bone?' asked the Salamander, glancing sidelong at either entrance to the ravine. Mercifully, a second wave wasn't coming. Not yet.

'With as much brute force as I can muster.' Vortan rammed the syringe, two-handed, into Polino's chest and depressed the trigger.

Enhanced adrenaline surged into the captain's arteries, flooding his heart with the equivalent of a chemical electro-shock. It was dangerous, especially for someone in the captain's condition. But they were desperate. Polino's eyes snapped open like shutters and he roared, smashing Vortan off his feet with a backhand and kicking Ar'gan in the chest, doubling the Salamander over. Bolt upright, he jerked to standing position and then sagged, breathing heavily.

'Sword of Dorn,' he gasped, spitting blood. 'What did you do to me?' He looked up at Vortan, who was only just now rising, eyes wild.

'I got you back in the fight, sir,' he growled, removing his battered helmet. Polino had dented it and cracked one of the retinal lenses with his punch.

The Imperial Fist looked around.

'Where is Zaeus?'

'Off fetching reinforcements.' Ar'gan grimaced, clutching his bruised chest. Straightening up, he glared at the spent autocannon. Smoke was rising from the ammo feed where it had overheated. Part of the metal was fused and had seized the mechanism.

'It's scrap,' he said, cursing inwardly, 'be more use as a club now.'

'Do we have any other weapons?' asked Polino, trying to get a handle on the tactical situation. Despite his enhanced strategic acumen, he was having trouble focusing.

Vortan spread his arms to encompass the gunship and the makeshift defences.

'This is it. Everything you see.'

Ar'gan looked down at the chrono readout in his vambrace.

'How long?' asked Vortan.

'Eighteen minutes.'

They had lasted only eighteen minutes so far, and already they were down one autocannon and Polino was unlikely to last the duration of the next engagement.

'And the estimated arrival of Zaeus with our reinforcements?' asked Polino.

Shadows were gathering at the edges of the ravine again, heralded by the tell-tale cries of the kroot. A deeper strain joined the shrilling chorus this time, as something larger at the periphery of the kill-team's defences lumbered into view.

Vortan was already on his way back to the autocannon, 'Not soon enough.'

At the edge of the crash site, the kroot had been waiting for him. Zaeus had barely left the ravine when the creatures attacked. He killed them quickly, using up the last of his kraken and hellfire rounds to leave a mess of destroyed carcasses in his wake. The ambush was predictable, Zaeus reasoning that the kroot would have drawn a loose perimeter around the gunship and were using it to bait a trap. It was one the kill-team had gladly fallen into. If nothing else, the Thunderhawk was the only defensible position in the desert and their only means of exfiltration, but only if Zaeus could repair the damage done to the gunship, and then only if they could defeat the horde pursuing them to enable the Techmarine to do it. Kilometres clicked by in the Brazen Minotaur's retinal lens display, as did data describing fault lines, contours, temperature fluctuations and calcite density in the air. Beyond the ravine where he had left his brothers, the storm had not fully abated. It carved shallow grooves into his armour and wore at his Deathwatch black.

He remembered the day he had repurposed it, painted over the colours of his Chapter and taken the sacred oaths of moment of the xenos hunters. Back then, he had barely known the other warriors in his kill-team.

Carfax, so full of choler, his blood always up, had seemed ill-suited as a pilot; the quiet depths of Ar'gan hid a deadly bladesman; Vortan, the bitter and moribund priest, who cradled a heavy bolter like a favoured pet; Polino, the Fist, was as rigid as any son of Dorn but a strong captain; but Festaron, gifted as a field medic, was more open than any Star Phantom Zaeus had known or heard of. Their cultures and ways of war were strange, even anathema to the son of Tauron at first. Giving up the black lion pelt had been hard during that time, but the bond with his new-found brothers made it a worthy sacrifice. Respect and synchronicity had grown between them, and their differences became as boons that strengthened and united rather than weakened the group.

Now they were one, but they were dying and Zaeus raged at the fates that had brought them to this mortal place. He could not fail them.

A chrono counted down in his other retinal lens. It was over twenty-six minutes old already, the harsh terrain adding precious minutes to his arrival at the bastion or whatever was broadcasting the signal. It looped in his helmet vox, repeating the same message over and over. Recently, it had become a taunt rather than a promise of reinforcement.

Zaeus fed more power into the half-track, ignoring the whine of its sand-clogged engine as he pushed the servitor unit to its limit.

'Emperor, make me swift…'

Slowly a bulky structure began to resolve through the storm. Cycling through the optical spectra of his bionic eye, Zaeus discovered it was indeed a fastness, isolated but ironbound with thick buttresses and high, sloping walls.

He resisted the natural urge to charge straight at it, demand audience and bring back warriors to help save his beleaguered brothers.

Common sense tempered his Tauron desires and he eased his speed.

The bastion was dark green, much of its militaristic stencilling eroded by the desert, so he could only guess at its provenance. There was no mistaking the Adeptus Astartes ident-code of the signal. Zaeus switched to a corresponding frequency and spat a blurt of simple binaric that even the most rudimentary codifier could interpret.

I am an ally in need of aid. Cycle down your defences.

The half-track growled the last few kilometres to the installation, slowing as Zaeus approached the shadow of its defence towers.

No answer came from his hails, but the tell-tale muzzles of heavy bolters jutting from lofty firing slits looked threatening. The gun nests sat in a pair of watchtowers, which flanked an open gate. A quick biometric analysis suggested they were unmanned but could be auto-slaved.

Zaeus decided on the direct approach.

'Archeval Zaeus, of the Emperor's Adeptus Astartes,' he declared, letting the engine idle. If there was a data-corder or pict-feeder located in the gate somewhere it would have logged his presence.

Silence.

Time lapsed so loudly Zaeus could almost hear the seconds ticking over on the chrono in his retinal lens. The lion within him stirred, demanding action.

Zaeus looked through the gate but could find no evidence of habitation. The cannons were still, not even auto-tracking.

He snorted, a deep nasal exhalation that speckled the inside of his battle-helm with sputum. Caution was not a trait his Chapter held in much regard. He risked approaching the entryway. Like the walls it was thickly armoured, but gaped wide enough to fit the half-track. Easing down further on the speed to preserve the engine for the return journey, Zaeus passed through but met no resistance.

He met no signs of life or occupation at all.

Stretched in front of him was a large square plaza delineated by what he assumed were barracks or stores. Zaeus examined the signal data again and determined it was emanating from a large blocky structure at the end of the plaza.

Flurries of calcite were drifting across the ground, scuffing the Brazen Minotaur's boots after he had ditched the half-track at the gate to rest its protesting mechanics. He crossed the square of metal plates quickly, trying to banish the itch that the back of his head was in crosshairs, but reached the blocky structure without incident.

Up close, he realised it was some kind of workshop or forge. Perhaps the Chapter here had a Techmarine as part of its garrison. Zaeus prayed to the Omnissiah he was right. It would make repairing the gunship much easier if there were a second pair of mechadendrites devoted to the task.

A heavy door barred access but a simple chain and pulley would open it. Taking the partially corroded links in both hands, Zaeus grunted and heaved. After some initial resistance the chain spilled through his fingers, but the gate was obviously broken and only slid aside halfway to partially reveal the darkness of the workshop within.

He muttered, 'No time for this.' Taking a back step, Zaeus barged the gate using his head and shoulder like a battering ram. It crumpled inwards with a squeal of wrenched metal, and he snarled at his achievement, some of the old Tauron warrior emerging through his Martian conditioning. He could have torn it off its hinges with his servo-arm but old habits were tough to break, and he was feeling pugnacious.

Zaeus ventured into the darkness, his hand on the grip of his bolter.

'Hail, brothers.'

The machine growl of his voice echoed back at him.

In such a large installation, it was possible the warriors who had sent the message were deeper in its confines. It was also possible that a single Space Marine acted as its garrison warden. Such postings were not uncommon. Perhaps their alarums were malfunctioning too, as the Brazen Minotaur's violent entry would certainly have tripped more than one warning klaxon. He penetrated further, but still nothing. From the condition of the ragged machines in the workshop it certainly appeared as if the bastion had suffered from several years of neglect. He found a heavy switch and threw it, igniting a bank of flickering halogen strips above, but the dim light revealed little else but more mechanised decrepitude.

Zaeus's bionic eye added little to that analysis. There were no heat traces, biological or otherwise, but he did detect the hidden Icon Mechanicus inlaid into the back wall. It was only revealed through specific data-interrogation, the likes of which only an adept of the Mechanicus could perform. Whoever had hidden this chamber did not want it found by a casual inspection.

A glance at his bolter confirmed his low ammo count. Zaeus mentally shrugged – hand-to-hand would do just as well if it came to that. Already, he could feel his enhanced physiology priming him for the eventuality of close combat, fuelling his body, heightening his senses and reactions, incrementally increasing his strength and adrenaline levels with every step.

For now, Zaeus kept himself in check. Closer inspection of the Icon Mechanicus suggested it might occlude a second gate leading further into the compound.

A quick glance at the chrono showed almost forty-eight minutes had elapsed. Over half his time had passed. He needed to move faster.

A patina of age and a veil of gossamer-thin cobwebs enshrouded ranks and ranks of ancient welders, rivet-punchers, machine lathes and furnaces. As he walked through the graveyard of extinct machines a theory formed. Much of the desert was overrun by the kroot-hybrids. Whilst the high walls of the bastion would keep most casual predators at bay, they might not be proof against a hardier, more adaptive strain of xenos. From his research of the kroot carnivore, Zaeus knew they were a race that had the ability to absorb the traits and characteristics of creatures through ingestion of biological matter. He balked at what species of xenos would evolve through a fusion of kroot and tyranid. So far, the kill-team had seen little of its potential but perhaps in the deeper desert the old garrison of the bastion knew more of such horrors.

Regardless of any possible danger, it was too late now to do anything other than press on. Zaeus had reached the concealed gate and shone a beam of binaric-filled decoding light onto the Icon Mechanicus. It responded instantly, illuminating, the light spreading to a data wire that ran up to the top of the gate describing a hexagonal portal limned in magnesium white.

Gears and motors, extant servos and half-forgotten engines grumbled into life from somewhere below. Zaeus felt the great machine beneath kilometres of rockcrete stirring like a leviathan awakened in an ocean trench. The gate cracked, split into four, each fissure running to a nodal point in the exact centre of the Icon Mechanicus. Monolithic in sheer size, the portal dwarfed Zaeus and he had to crane his neck just to see how far up it would open.

A vast hangar was revealed beyond the gate, immense and echoing. Dust motes thronged the air, which was musty and dryer than the desert. Zaeus's helmet sensorium detected mould spores and the activity of dormant insect life disturbed by his sudden entrance.

But there was no life beyond that, and no death either. He had feared there would be bodies, the empty carcasses of slain battle-brothers and the genetic soup of dead xeno-forms. Neither greeted him, but something else did – something he did not expect.

And as the gloom within was lit up like a firmament of a thousand crimson stars, Zaeus raised his bolter.

He'd been wrong, so wrong about everything. The kroot-hybrids had not come here. Something else had happened to the bastion. Possibly, something even worse...

'Omnissiah,' he breathed, taking up a firing stance.

The gorge was almost overrun. For over an hour and a half they had held the line with just the weapons salvaged from the gunship and inhuman determination. But after ninety-seven minutes of near relentless assault, ammunition was low and hope with it. Only wrath remained and the fervent desire to sell their lives at the cost of their enemies'.

For Vortan, the price could not be high enough.

He roared, a righteous expression of anger and defiance that merged with the ballistic shout of the cannon punching solid shot into the kroot beast's torso. The Marine Malevolent could hardly miss such a gargantuan creature. Slab-snouted, with two bulky forelimbs that were more simian than avian, it was broad-backed with much shorter rear legs and loped towards Vortan in the manner of an ape. Underneath its ribbed torso were paired rending claws, jutting forward like tusks.

It snorted and snarled, its chitinous body wracked by cannon-fire, then bleated as Vortan found more tender flesh.

'Hate is the surest weapon!' the Marine Malevolent raged, chanting his Chapter's battle-cry as zealous indignation washed over him. 'Suffer not the alien to live!'

The beast was slowing. Blood oozed from its nostrils, foaming with its heavy breath. But it wasn't done, not even close. A half glance at Polino during the barrage revealed the Imperial Fist was in worse shape. He sagged at the gun emplacement, the adrenaline fuelling his system almost spent, his finger locked against the trigger through sheer force of will. He strafed the gorge but his fire was only seventy per cent effective.

'Keep them off me,' Vortan spat down the comm-feed.

A horde of the lesser kroot were scurrying through the narrow aperture of the gorge, abandoning rifles in favour of the deadly gifts granted them through their hybridisation with the tyranid. A swarm of champing tooth and claw was descending on the survivors of the kill-team and only Captain Polino could stop it.

The Imperial Fist barely nodded.

'By Dorn's blood...' It came out as a rasp, strained by fatigue.

'I'll kill them all if I have to,' Vortan snarled through clenched teeth, putting a three-round burst through the kroot beast's skull. It grunted once, spitting up more blood and acid-bile, before slewing to a halt. Momentum carried it forwards, its bulk carving a deep furrow in the calcite.

Polino was down. Hoping to share in his triumph, Vortan only saw the Imperial Fist's gauntleted fingers slipping off the gun before he disappeared behind the barricade. He opened up the feed to Ar'gan.

They needed to retrench, head back towards the gunship and try to mount some kind of defence. Hold and repel. Victory through attrition – that was the Salamander way.

'Vulkan's fire beats in my breast.' Ar'gan uttered the mantra known and honoured by every fire-born son of Nocturne. With his death so imminent he found comfort in this small act of remembrance.

'Ar'gan.'

The comm-feed crackled in his ear. He didn't risk a glance behind; his side of the gorge was filling up with xenos. Staccato bursts of heavy bolter-fire had turned into an unceasing salvo that would eventually reach its terminus. Ar'gan smiled. When that happened, he would turn to his blades.

For now, he squatted on the gunship's nose cone. He'd stripped off much of the armoured fuselage to gain access to the prow-mounted heavy bolter. The weapon was underslung, half-buried in the dirt, but made for a good makeshift deterrent to ward off the attackers. As he fired, it spat out clods of calcite and mass-reactives. He kept up the punishment.

'Ar'gan.' The comm-feed sounded insistent.

'Speak.'

There was a short pause. Behind him, Ar'gan knew the Marine Malevolent was as hard pressed as he was.

'Polino's not getting back up.'

Something large and hulking bullied its way through a crowd of lesser creatures. Kroot were crushed to paste and broken limbs. It didn't seem to concern the beast.

It was a little way off, tough to discern through the drifts and the swell of alien bodies. But definitely monstrous. It filled the end of the gorge, spined shoulders scraping rock, the suggestion of a tail lashing in irritation behind it... a beak, eye clusters hooded by sheaths of nictitating chitin. Ar'gan absorbed the details, his brain analysing them for potential weaknesses even as he listened to the *chug-chank* of the cannons and heard the tell-tale hollow report of a rapidly diminishing ammo supply.

Vortan was speaking again. It sounded like he was moving.

'We need to retreat.'

'Where?'

'The gunship. We get inside, defend it.'

'We'd be besieged.' Though the Salamander acknowledged he'd considered the same tactic.

A spray of shells cut down a cluster of kroot that had approached the twenty metre mark. *Nothing breaches that line.*

That rule was about to be broken. The fire-axe practically hummed in its scabbard.

Soon... It was like talking to an old friend.

'Have you not noticed, Salamander,' said Vortan, with an edge of irritation, 'we already are.'

Ar'gan could not disagree. He tried to see beyond the horde, for evidence of Zaeus's coming.

Vortan read his thoughts. 'The Techmarine's dead. We're on our own.'

'Meet you inside,' Ar'gan replied as the underslung mount ran dry.

'Where are you going?'

He was already up, leaping off the nose cone, twisting the fire-axe out of its scabbard.

'To kill something.'

The beast was struggling through the neck of the gorge. Everything around it was dead or dying. A landslide would make a poorer bung. A pity they had used up their grenades or he would've already collapsed the rock face to achieve just that.

Instead, he had a beast, some fusion of one monster with another to create a fresh abomination more terrible than both.

Ar'gan was running at it. The fire-axe came alive in his hand, bright as sun-flare.

Eight pairs of milk-white sclera alighted on the Salamander. Nasal pits opened in the monster's neck, drinking in his scent but not finding prey.

+You are the hunted+, Ar'gan told it, his mind cast back to gutting sa'hrk on the Scorian Plain when he was just a boy, when he was mortal.

He had transformed, just as this beast had. The strength of the evolution of both was about to be tested in a bloody survival of the fittest.

Recognising a threat, the monster opened its maw and a

barbed proboscis lashed out like a whip. It caught Ar'gan's shoulder, piercing the armour and sending a jolt of pain which his advanced nervous system rerouted so he felt it as a pinch, a slow spread of numbness through his upper arm.

He whirled the fire-axe, severing the monster's proboscis tongue. Left it flopping like a drowning fish in his wake. Ar'gan rolled, ducking under a thick flesh hook that would have impaled him like a sauroch on a Themian's spear. He came up with an arc of fire clenched in his fist. It seared the monster's beak, which snapped like a bird's at the Salamander. Snarling, Ar'gan dug his blade into its snout. It jerked spasmodically, hurt, and wrenched the weapon from his grasp. In a nanosecond, he'd drawn the sa'hrk knife and proceeded to stab it into the creature's neck and face. Acid-bile ruined the blade but Ar'gan kept going, knowing that sometimes frenzy was as valid as any finessed sword tactic.

The monster thrashed against the gorge, squirming and fighting. It managed to angle a shoulder in Ar'gan's direction and released a cluster of dagger-thick spines. Three lodged in the Salamander's vambrace and one struck his chest, went through battle-plate, the epidermis of his bodyglove and scraped into flesh. He was wracked by convulsion, enhanced biology struggling to retard the sudden rush of poison.

Fingertips brushed the hilt of the fire-axe as it came back within reach. Ar'gan lurched forward and took it, ripping the blade free and swinging it two-handed against the monster's neck. The head came off at an awkward angle, spilling gore and bile all over him. Kroot were crawling to get over the corpse. One had crested its back, clinging on despite the monster's last shuddering motions.

Ar'gan disengaged. Poison was turning his limbs to lead, stealing away his vitality and endurance, replacing it with agony. He took it. He was a son of Vulkan, fire-born. It would take more than alien venom to stop him.

The edges of the gunship looked blurred as he turned. He could no longer run. It was a half-limp, half-stagger.

Shrieking, avian noises behind him told Ar'gan he needed to be faster.

'Vortan.' His voice did not sound like his own as opened up the feed. A few minutes and his organs would counteract the poison, dilute it, neutralise it. He didn't have one minute. 'Vortan...' They were almost upon him. Engaging them was suicide. His Lyman's implant picked out eight distinct tonal arrangements. And that was just the first wave.

The feed crackled in his ear.

'Get down!'

Three metres from the gunship, Ar'gan hit the dirt.

Overhead, the air was lit by muzzle fire.

Through a haze of slowly fading poison, Ar'gan saw the Marine Malevolent braced on the roof of the gunship. He carried an autocannon, one hand on the grip at the top of the stock, holding it like a scythe; the other on its trigger. He dampened the recoil by jamming the butt into his stomach. His armour's servos did the rest, steadying his aim.

Eight kroot vanished in the metal storm.

Ar'gan was dragging himself up to his knees, thumbing the release clamp off a grenade from his weapons belt. He rolled it behind him, hard so it would travel, then pitched into the gunship.

A few seconds later, Vortan swung in beside him. The

auto-cannon was gone, empty and discarded on the roof. He had Polino's bolter instead.

The captain was lying in the hold along with Festaron. Both were of equal use now.

'Holding out on us, brother?' he asked as the tangle-web grenade exploded behind Ar'gan, filling a five-metre wide area with deadly razor-wire.

'Only for emergency,' the Salamander replied. 'I didn't think it was worth wasting on collapsing that chasm.'

Vortan laughed. It sounded like metal scraping metal.

'Got one of those for me?' Ar'gan pointed to the bolter. Sensation was returning, his body's advanced immune systems finally counteracting the poison.

The Marine Malevolent shook his head. 'Only half a clip, anyway. Not enough to kill all of them.'

'Fortune I kept hold of this then.' Ar'gan brandished the fire-axe.

'You'll have to tell me one day how you came upon that brutal weapon.'

Outside, the horde had recovered from their blooding and was advancing. High pitched war-cries echoed from several directions, colliding in a deafening welter of noise that told the Space Marines they were surrounded.

'One day.'

Ar'gan glanced at the various points of ingress around the gunship.

'The hold has only three access points,' he observed.

'I can probably watch the roof and left side,' said Vortan, racking the bolter's slide.

'Then the right side is mine.' Ar'gan swung the fire-axe in a languid arc to relieve some of the stiffness in his shoulder from the proboscis wound. 'Bet you're wishing we'd have left the others now, eh?'

'No,' said Vortan. 'I like it better that we'll all die together.' He smiled. It was like a dagger slit across his mouth. 'Seems some of your compassion is rubbing off on me.'

Ar'gan met the Marine Malevolent's gaze across the length of the hold. 'I doubt that. Any last words, brother? A benediction perhaps, before we go before the Throne?'

Vortan tapped the bolter's stock, 'This,' he said, then nodding to the Salamander's fire-axe, 'and that are the only words we need now. Kill as many as you can.'

'Would you like to wager on the outcome?' Ar'gan asked.

More grating laughter from the Marine Malevolent cut through the cacophony from the kroot. 'Bolter versus blade? Very well.'

'Good hunting,' said Ar'gan.

Vortan didn't respond, and went to guard the left side of the fuselage.

Embracing the sheer fatality of it all, Ar'gan turned his back on him and took up a ready stance on the right. Through the side hatch a torrent of aliens were swarming towards the stricken gunship.

The chrono on his vambrace was broken, damaged by the spine attack. It stood frozen but flickering, close to two hours.

'Zaeus,' the Salamander said to the air. 'I hope you died well.'

Thunder filled the gorge. It echoed off the walls, rebounded and amplified by the natural close confines. Lightning followed, rippling in flashes along the high, rocky flanks right at the summit.

It wasn't a storm, at least not any natural one. It was fire and it was fury, wrath distilled into an unremitting barrage that tore into the alien horde and savaged it. Missile strikes provided a different tone to the war chorus, dense *fooms* of exhalation ending in a crescendo of earth-trembling impacts and flame.

Kroot bodies were thrown into the air like leaves.

The larger beasts mewled like cattle as their bodies were ripped apart by incendiaries.

'Vortan…' Ar'gan said down the feed.

'I see it! It's on this side of the gorge too.'

A broad smile split the Salamander's lips apart. 'Zaeus isn't dead.'

'If he is, I salute his undead corpse.'

Gunfire rained down from either side of the gorge, angling into a kill box where the kroot were advancing. Ar'gan noticed it wasn't accurate. As the xenos died they began to disperse, gaps appeared in their ranks that the massed fire from above failed to adapt to. Space Marines would not be so profligate.

Straining, Ar'gan tried to ascertain the nature of their saviours, but all he caught were snatches of silhouettes through split-second breaks in the continuous muzzle flare.

The kroot brayed and hooted at their unseen attackers. It took less than three minutes for their resolve to fail. Howling, they fled the gorge, spilling out in a tide in both directions.

They still numbered in the hundreds but the herd was spooked and sought the safety of the desert where the harsh flashes couldn't sting them further.

Slowly, the muzzle flashes faded one by one. Ar'gan detected the harsh *clank* of weapons on empty, the impotent *clack* of vented rocket tubes. Their saviours hadn't stopped firing because the enemy was dead or running; they'd stopped because there was nothing left for them *to* fire.

'What is this?' Ar'gan stepped out from the confines of the gunship.

There was a morass of sundered alien corpses outside.

Vortan joined him from the other side.

'I approve of the massacre, but what just happened?'

The Salamander shook his head. Craning his neck he saw a figure appear at the summit of one of the high walls of the gorge.

Zaeus gave a clipped salute.

'Thought you were dead,' said Vortan through the feed, having followed Ar'gan's gaze.

'You sound disappointed,' the Brazen Minotaur replied.

'Where are the rest of our brothers? Why don't they show themselves?' asked Ar'gan.

Zaeus stepped back from the edge as he manipulated something on his gauntlet the Salamander couldn't see. 'Because they are not exactly our brothers.'

After a few seconds the grind of machine servos resonated throughout the now silent gorge as a host of pallid faces emerged from the shadows.

Most were on tracks, but some stomped forward on piston-like legs or tottered on reverse-jointed stilts. Others still were not like men at all, but merely automated weapon platforms slaved to the Techmarine's will. They were servitors, dozens of them, armed with stubbers and autolaunchers, heavy bolters and shot cannons. Zaeus had found his reinforcements; he had recruited an entire force of dead-eyed cybernetics to his will.

They stared, unthinking, unfeeling at the pair of warriors looking up at them.

'I am sorry I was late,' said Zaeus, 'but as you can see, I was busy.'

The Brazen Minotaur vaulted the edge of the gorge and slid down the sharp incline, grinding a furrow down the rock with his back and shoulders. In a few minutes he was standing with his brothers again.

'Climbing up wouldn't have been so easy,' Vortan griped, but gave a nod of thanks.

Ar'gan clasped the Brazen Minotaur's forearm in a warrior's grip, which Zaeus returned.

'Your arrival was timely, brother.'

Vortan eyed the servitors warily. 'Still need to repair the ship. I assume they aren't coming with us.'

Zaeus gestured to the edges of the gorge where a small cadre of servitors had begun to encroach. Unlike the warrior caste above, these cybernetics were equipped with tools.

'We can be airborne in under an hour.'

'So there was no garrison, no Space Marine bastion,' said Ar'gan. 'The signal was fake?'

'No,' Zaeus replied, 'just a little out of date. Our brothers were long gone but they left an army behind.'

Above, the weapon servitors began to retreat from the edge of the gorge and were lost to the shadows again.

'I thought they were hostile but most were simply dying out.

I accessed the doctrina programming of the functional ones, inloaded some new imperatives and led them here.'

'You did all that with ones and zeros, brother?' asked Vortan.

Zaeus snorted, pugnacious. 'It was slightly more complicated than that. But now the protocol I gave them is complete they will revert to their default settings and return to dormancy inside the bastion.'

Vortan laughed again, he had never been so mirthful. 'For the next beleaguered survivors to find.'

Zaeus shook his head. 'This world dies, brother. I have already contacted Inquisitor Vaskiel and provided my report. I am certain her response will be Exterminatus.'

'How soon until we're wings up?' asked Vortan.

'We have ample time. The chrono is no longer running.'

'Do you think they know?' asked Ar'gan, staring at the blank space above them at the edge of the gorge.

'Know what?' Zaeus was directing the remaining servitors in the repairing of the gunship.

'That they saved us but doomed a world.'

'This world was already doomed, but I think perhaps a mote of cognitive recognition remains. A machine-spirit, if not in the literal sense.'

Ar'gan nodded.

'Well, praise the Omnissiah,' said Vortan.

'Praise the Omnissiah,' echoed Ar'gan.

Zaeus stayed silent. Polino would live, so too Vortan and Ar'gan. Carfax and Festaron would be returned to their Chapters with the highest honours, their legacies could live on.

Though he would never forget his Tauron heritage, Zaeus

knew he was of the Machine-God now. Flesh or machine, he would serve the Throne and his brothers until duty ended in death. Even in that bleak thought he took comfort as he looked to the horizon.

A train of soldiers were marching. Their hearts still pumped, their limbs still moved, their lungs still drew air, but their minds were empty tombs only filled with what their masters put into them.

Zaeus saluted them as they faded into the storm.

It would rise higher and swallow the entire world in cyclonic death, a million souls consigned to the grave so a trillion more would live on. Then the Deathwatch would come to their worlds too – Zaeus had seen it happen countless times before, and the same thing would repeat.

Without an iota of remorse, he turned his back on the servitors and went to the gunship.

This world had only hours left to it, but there were thousands more in need of purgation. The task of the Deathwatch was endless, their victories unsung.

As he watched his brothers return to the ship, he wondered where they would be bound for next and what they would have to kill.

None of it really mattered. The mission could always be broken down to a single universal truth: suffer not the alien to live.

THE INFINITE TABLEAU

ANTHONY REYNOLDS

One of them was about to die.

They stood at the epicentre of the battle, beneath a sky that was burning, and it seemed as though time stood still. The black-armoured paragon of humanity brought a golden-winged power sword around in a crackling two-handed killing strike. His pale face was twisted in hatred, and his eyes were tinged red with blood-rage. Despite the thickness of his enemy's bull-like neck, the blow was perfectly timed, delivered with all his genhanced and armour-augmented strength.

His opponent was a hulking, green-skinned monster that stood over two and half metres tall. It lived only for battle and knew – nay, cared for – nothing else. It roared as it swung its chugging chain-glaive around in a brutal arc, a blow that could carve the Space Marine clean in two.

Either blow would be mortal if it landed. Both would land within a single heartbeat.

One of them was about to die.

His rage was a vile, black thing dwelling deep within him. His force of will kept it coiled and bound for now, but it was growing stronger day by day, year by year. He knew that there would come a day when it *would* overcome him. All that would be left was the beast within.

Today would not be that day.

He repeated it to himself silently, like a mantra. *Today is not that day.* He forced himself to unclench his fists, and took a deep breath. The anger always came when he felt trapped, or when he felt that his fate was not his own to direct.

The gunship shuddered, but not from incoming fire. The native-born called the scouring winds that whipped across the ice floes the *skree-tha* – the witch-howling. He could understand why. Even enclosed within the ceramite-reinforced shell of the gunship, the roar of the straining engines was drowned out by the screaming, banshee wail outside.

The winds buffeted them hard, slamming the craft from side to side as they hurtled over the vast, empty expanse of ice. It lifted them sharply, threatening to rip the gunship's wings off, before pulling them down, dragging the nose towards the ice floe below.

'Cassiel,' said a voice behind him. It was Tanaka. 'Will you not sit?'

Cassiel did not reply. Nor did he make to return to his restraint harness. He could feel the White Scar's reproachful gaze upon his back, but he ignored it. Had he remained seated, his anger would have blossomed.

He filled the doorway of the gunship's cockpit, his already oversized frame made more massive still by his black power armour. One shoulder pad was dull silver and bore the Inquisition's iconography. The other was blood red, and had the heraldry of his Chapter – the Blood Angels – sculpted in bas-relief upon its curved surface.

Cassiel peered over the shoulder of the ship's pilot, his expression dark. He had taken up the position as soon as they had entered the moon's atmosphere. He'd been unable to bear being restrained any longer.

'We are nearing the distress beacon, sir,' said the gunship pilot, his voice crackling through into Cassiel's earpiece. Despite their close proximity, the howling gale made the vox necessary.

'How long?' said Cassiel.

'Two minutes.'

Cassiel looked over his shoulder, back into the red-lit gloom of the gunship's hold. Twelve black-clad storm troopers were seated back there, strapped in tightly. They were elite soldiers, trained from childhood to serve the Ordo Xenos. Their bodies had been enhanced, making them bigger, stronger and faster than regular humans. Nevertheless, they were dwarfed by Cassiel and the other two members of his kill-team.

'Two minutes to touchdown,' Cassiel said, his words being relayed into the ear of every soldier onboard. 'Be ready.'

'We should be able to see the ship any moment now,' said the pilot. 'There.'

Cassiel leaned forward, brushing a strand of dark blond hair back from his eyes. The storm made it almost impossible to see anything at all beyond the ice-fogged cockpit. Everything was a swirling wall of white.

Then he saw what the human pilot's augmented vision had picked out a moment earlier: a dark, bug-like shuttle crouched low on the ice. It was just a shadow at first, but solidified as the gunship drew in close. It was half-buried in ice and snow. Another few hours, and it would be completely hidden.

Beside the ship, he could see a dark fissure in the ice: a massive crack that extended out into the storm.

'We're here,' Cassiel said.

Cassiel was the first to step onto the ice, his black armour a stark contrast to his surroundings. How many worlds had he set foot upon now? How many foes had fallen beneath the long golden-winged blade, *Aruthel*, that he wore slung across his back? He had stopped counting long ago.

His face was as pale and cold as his surroundings. He might have resembled a classical statue, carved from pale marble, but for the trio of parallel scars that crossed his face, twisting his lips and puckering his skin; a memento of his encounter with a chameleonic xenos beast two years past.

The gale whipped at Cassiel's shoulder-length hair and the tabard draped across his armour. Ice slashed at his cheeks, and he was forced to narrow his eyes against the biting gale. He breathed in deeply. The cold was as sharp as a knife in his lungs. Without a sealed enviro-suit, an unaugmented human would have been dead within a minute in these conditions. Cassiel was far from unaugmented, however, and he made a point of breathing the air of every planet he visited, even if only for a moment.

A pair of large, black-clad figures clomped out onto the ice behind him.

Tanaka, hefting his heavy bolter, and Var'myr of the Mortifactors, his boltgun held across his chest. These were his adopted battle brothers, his kill-team.

He had fought alongside Tanaka for over a decade – they had both started their tenure with the Deathwatch at the same time. Var'myr was a newcomer, having joined the ranks of the Ordo Xenos fewer than six months ago. There had been others before him, but they were gone now: Svorgar of the Space Wolves had been decapitated by a clawed fiend on the nightworld of Jar'Mun'Gar; Ryzmor of the Carcharodons had been ripped limb from limb by the magicks of eldar witches in the ruins of Delthasur; Titus Constantine of the White Consuls had been released back to his Chapter with honour after the successful purging of Alanthus.

As much as Cassiel yearned to return to his Chapter, it was a privilege to fight alongside such esteemed warriors.

'Var'myr, scan the area.'

A servo-skull hovered at the Mortifactor's shoulder, its mechanical left eye blinking red. Once, that skull had belonged to one of his battle-brothers. They were a morbid Chapter, a fact reinforced by the bones strung across Var'myr's armour.

'Go. Seek,' the Mortifactor said, his voice deep and sombre. The servo-skull swung out into the storm, as ordered. The winds buffeted it – Cassiel heard Tanaka chuckle at the sight – but the device compensated swiftly, gyros buzzing. It commenced a wide sweep of the area, scanning and recording.

He glanced at the White Scar. Tanaka met his gaze, his dark obsidian eyes glinting with humour. His face was gnarled and weathered, the colour of tanned leather.

'I like this place,' Tanaka said, shouting to be heard above the gale and the dying whine of the gunship's engines.

'I see nothing redeemable about it,' said Var'myr.

'Bah!' said Tanaka. 'You know nothing! This cold is good. It lets you know you are still alive.'

'I know I'm alive because I *am* alive,' said Var'myr. 'I don't need the cold to tell me that.'

Var'myr assessed the skull's findings, reading from the auspex built into his left forearm. The entire arm was bionic from the shoulder down.

'The scan is clear,' he said. He snapped the data-screen back into his vambrace, and the armoured plate clicked into place around it like a shell. 'There is nothing living within a hundred kilometres, nor any heat signature or radiation. This is a dead world.'

'Lieutenant, secure a perimeter,' Cassiel ordered over the vox, and the storm troopers who had been standing by moved out onto the ice, flowing around the three Space Marines with their hellguns at the ready.

As they took up support positions, Cassiel and his brothers marched towards the silent shuttle squatting upon the ice. It was a bulbous, ugly ship resembling a fat-bodied insect. Its six articulated legs clung to the ice, and a pair of large eye-like portal-windows were positioned at the front of its 'head'. Through them, Cassiel could see three vacant seats, where the pilot, co-pilot and navigator would normally be seated. There were no lights inside.

With crisp orders, Cassiel directed Var'myr and a pair of storm troopers to search the ship while Tanaka checked the ravine.

Cassiel pulled on his helm; the slicing storm was stinging his eyes. Once he had worn a helmet of shining gold, but since his indoctrination into the Deathwatch he had worn nothing but their traditional black. Among the Blood Angels, the only warriors who wore black were the holy Chaplain-wardens of the Chapter, and the damned warriors of the Death Company.

He walked around the exterior of the shuttle, scrutinising it for signs of battle damage. The nose and wingtips were blackened, but this looked like charring from orbital entry; it had not been brought down by weapons-fire. Var'myr stepped down from the explorator vessel just as he finished his circuit.

'Nothing,' said the Mortifactor, shaking his head. His servo-skull had returned to him, and was once more hovering at his shoulder.

Var'myr fell in beside Cassiel, and the pair trudged into the wind to join the vague figure of Tanaka, standing some way off and staring into the storm. The White Scar was almost completely hidden by swirling ice that seemed to confuse even the advanced sensory arrays of Cassiel's battle plate.

'Speak your mind,' said Cassiel. Var'myr was taciturn at best, silent and sullen at worst, but in the brief time they had known each other, Cassiel felt he was beginning to learn how to read those silences.

'We should never have been sent here,' said Var'myr. 'We

ought to have joined the other strike teams in the final assault. We earned that, at least.'

'Watch-Commander Haldaron felt that our presence was needed here,' said Cassiel, keeping his voice neutral. 'It is no smear on our honour.'

'It is,' said Var'myr. 'The greenskin warlord's head should have been ours to claim. By now, someone else will probably have it.'

In truth, Cassiel tended to agree, but that was not helpful.

'I would hope so,' he said, 'else the brute still lives. Put it from your mind, brother. We are here now, and we have been given our duty.'

They joined the heavy bolter wielding White Scar, standing on the edge of the immense ice fissure. Steam was rising from the gaping rift, making it impossible to gauge its depth. It was narrow, little more than two metres across at any point, and extended further than the eye could see.

'You think they went down there?' asked Cassiel.

'Where else?' replied Tanaka.

'Then that is where we shall go too.'

Var'myr sent his servo-skull down into the crack, red beams of light from its sensors scanning and documenting.

'Seismic activity opened this crack twelve days ago,' said Var'myr, tapping his data-slate. 'The whole area is unstable. There are… seventeen active volcanic rifts within an eighty-kilometre radius of this location.'

'How deep is it?' said Cassiel.

'Nine metres, here,' said Var'myr, reading the output upon his forearm screen. 'Deeper… *much* deeper further along.'

'Is the ground solid at the bottom of the fissure, just here?'

'It is.'

'Good,' said Cassiel.

'It is unstable, however,' said Var'myr. 'Another tremor could seal this crack at any moment. You are not thinking of–'

Before the Mortifactor could finish, Cassiel stepped off the ice floe, dropping silently down into the gaping fissure.

The sound of wind down in the narrow defile was even more unearthly than it was up on the ice floe, though it was out of the worst of the gale. The sheer walls of ice were a brilliant, luminous blue – the first real colour that he had seen on this moon – and almost completely transparent in places where the ice was near flawless. Steam vented up from narrower cracks underfoot.

A flurry of ice and snow fell down around him, and Tanaka landed in a crouch a half-second later. He grinned at Cassiel as he rose to his feet. Var'myr landed a moment later, amid a small avalanche of ice.

'You took your time, brother,' said Cassiel.

The Mortifactor did not deign to answer. Up above, the storm troopers were readying their rappelling lines.

'They went this way,' said Tanaka, pointing. 'But they did not come back.'

'Did your ancestors tell you that?' said Var'myr.

'The tracks on the ground tell me that.'

Cassiel led the way. In places the ice canyon was so narrow that their shoulder plates scratched deep furrows in the ice. Their progress was not swift, but after a time they came to a low opening in one of the canyon walls. Hot steam spewed from the gap.

Var'myr's servo-skull disappeared into the steam. It reappeared a moment later, its red eye blinking impatiently. Tanaka scowled at it, and it darted back into the steam like a rebuked hound. It reappeared a moment later, hanging just behind Tanaka's shoulder, and Cassiel smirked. The White Scar caught sight of it, and swore in his own, guttural dialect.

'Irritating thing,' he said, swatting at it. 'Away!'

It darted back, just out of reach. Cassiel wondered how much sentience remained within the skull – it seemed to delight in taunting the White Scar whenever possible. 'Var'myr, control your creature,' he said.

'It's just a machine,' replied the Mortifactor mildly.

'Here,' Tanaka muttered, pointing out the tell-tale marks in the ice. 'They widened the entrance with chainblades.'

'Not enough, though,' said Var'myr. Though the aperture was large enough for a regular human to get through, there was no chance that any of the three Deathwatch brothers could pass.

'Move aside,' Cassiel ordered. He would not sully *Aruthel*'s blade with such a mundane duty, nor did he need to. With a grunt he struck the ice with his gauntleted fist, dislodging a massive chunk. Within the space of a minute he had cleared an opening that he and his team could negotiate, followed a few moments later by the storm troopers.

Cassiel once again took up the lead, ice grinding against his armour. The steam made rivulets of condensation run down the lenses of his helm. Some way on, the passage opened up into an irregular cave formation, its floor at a steep angle.

Ice-crystals formed by the volcanic updrafts filled the space. It was easy to see which path the explorators had taken – they merely had to follow the path of crushed crystals.

There was a surprising amount of light within the caves, even as they clambered, slid and crawled deeper beneath the ice floe. It was a diffuse, cold glow, which seemed to radiate from the very ice itself. A rumble of seismic activity shook the ground underfoot, ice fell from the slanted roof, and spider-web cracks appeared in the walls around them.

'We do not want to be here any longer than necessary,' said Cassiel, brushing melt-water from his shoulders.

Eighty metres below the ice floe, having traversed more than a kilometre from their starting point, the Space Marines came upon what the explorator team had been sent to find.

Cassiel dropped down into a large cavern, ice crunching underfoot. He was decidedly conscious of the millions of tonnes of glacier hanging above him, even more so as another ice-quake rumbled. It was groaning like a ship in the void. The walls seemed to close in, shifting and altering their position as the ice floe shuddered, and fresh cracks inched their way across the walls, clouding their previously transparent surfaces. Cassiel forced himself to breathe calmly, controlling his inner rage.

Tanaka and Var'myr joined him, dropping down into the cavern after him. It was as large as the embarkation deck of a battle-barge. The floors were uneven, rising and falling at acute angles, almost meeting the jagged ceiling in places and falling away into sheer deadfalls that sank hundreds of metres further down in others. Traversing the chamber was slow, and a clear line of sight from one side to the other was difficult, for pillars of crystal linked floor to roof and clusters of needle-like ice fanned out from wall and floor.

The storm troopers descended into the cavern in the kill-team's wake. At a silent signal from their lieutenant, they broke off into pairs, each advancing via a different route. Their training was obvious; they moved swiftly but silently, covering each other and scanning constantly for threats.

It was Var'myr who first saw it.

'Cassiel,' he said, drawing his sergeant's attention.

It was located towards the back of the cavern, jutting some four metres from the ice. The exposed section was curved and gleaming black, as if made from obsidian: a four-sided arc, like part of a large, incomplete ring. Judging by the curve of it, Cassiel guessed that the whole thing could have a diameter of over twenty metres, most of which appeared to be embedded in the ice, a dark shadow that curved away beneath their feet.

The cavern darkened considerably around it, as if the black stone were absorbing the light. Strange symbols marked its surface.

Tanaka swore in his guttural tongue.

'What is it?' asked Var'myr.

'I don't know,' said Cassiel. 'A weapon of some kind, but not one made by any human hand. Who knows how long it's been down here. Can you get a reading on it?'

'No,' said Var'myr, fingers sliding through the data relaying across his forearm-mounted auspex. 'This glacier is more than one hundred and fifty thousand years old, however.'

Cassiel shook his head. Such a timeframe was unfathomable.

'We know the Adeptus Mechanicus got this far,' he said. 'What happened to them?'

No answer was forthcoming.

The kill-team circled around the curved structure, keeping their weapons ready. There was something about it that made Cassiel's skin itch. Its geometry was somehow abhorrent; its glossy surfaces made him uneasy.

'There are some mysteries that humanity was not meant to know,' said Tanaka. 'This thing should have remained buried.'

'The entire region is becoming increasingly unstable,' said Var'myr. 'It will probably soon be buried beneath another fifty million tonnes of ice, regardless of what we do.'

'It is not enough,' said Cassiel. 'Even if it were buried at the centre of this moon, the Adeptus Mechanicus would come looking for it again, now they know it is here. They wouldn't be able to help themselves. We have to destroy it.'

'Destroy it?' said Var'myr. 'It's been down here for Guilliman knows how many tens of thousands of years. What danger can it pose?'

'Where is the explorator team, Mortifactor?' Tanaka asked, by way of an answer.

'We have to destroy it,' Cassiel said. 'We cannot trust the Mechanicus to leave this undisturbed.'

'Then let us do so, and be on our way,' said Var'myr. 'Those rumblings are becoming more frequent.'

'I thought your Chapter did not fear death, Mortifactor,' said Tanaka.

'Death, we do not fear,' said Var'myr, his voice cold. 'That does not mean that we invite it. Dying pointlessly, before one's duty is done, is a blasphemy.'

Cassiel opened up a vox-channel to the storm trooper lieutenant. 'I need the melta-charges brought forward,' he said. Even with his helm on, it was clear that Var'myr was glaring at Tanaka. And Cassiel knew the White Scar well enough to guess that he was smiling behind his own faceplate at having riled the Mortifactor.

'Tanaka,' Cassiel said. 'Help me with the charges. Var'myr, determine where to place them. I want nothing to remain of this thing.'

Cassiel turned away, paused, and turned back. 'And don't touch it.'

The White Scar fell in beside Cassiel, and the two of them clambered down towards the storm troopers picking their way through the chamber.

'Why antagonise him, brother?' Cassiel said via a closed channel. 'Is it really necessary?'

'Mortifactors,' Tanaka replied. 'They take themselves so seriously. And this one's ignorance offends me.'

'We were young once ourselves, my brother,' said Cassiel.

Tanaka laughed. 'You sound like an old man,' he said. 'Me? I'm in my prime!'

Cassiel smiled. Tanaka was one hundred and twenty-two years older than him, and looked it, with his weathered face and grey-streaked hair. His smile slipped however, and he paused, narrowing his eyes.

The ice dropped steeply away to the side of the ridge they were traversing, disappearing into a hollow. Steam billowed up from below, obscuring his sight.

'What is it?' said Tanaka, suddenly serious.

'Probably nothing,' said Cassiel. 'Go ahead. Collect the melta-charges. I'll be with you in a moment.'

Tanaka shrugged, and continued on down to meet the storm troopers. Cassiel eased himself off the side of the ridge, and climbed down into the steam, finding adequate handholds in the ice wall.

The descent was short, and soon his feet met the ground once more. Steam billowed around him, and moisture that would turn to ice as soon as he was away from the volcanic updraft beaded upon his armour.

He advanced, stepping gingerly, ensuring that the ground would take his weight before moving forward. He squinted, peering through the fog and steam.

'Blood of Sanguinius,' he breathed as the vapours parted.

A dozen bodies were scattered before him, half buried in the ice. Each corpse had been skinned, exposing frozen, dripping musculature. It appeared as though something had fed upon them: chunks of flesh had been torn from the bone, and entrails lay scattered. It was clear to Cassiel from the tortured poses, silent screams and anguished expressions on skinless faces that these horrors had been enacted while these people were still alive.

He saw an iron cog-wheel embedded in the forehead of one of the tortured bodies – the holy symbol of the Adeptus Mechanicus. He'd found the missing explorators.

That was when the screaming began.

* * *

Cassiel was up the sheer cliff in an instant, barely touching it. His long blade *Aruthel* was unsheathed, humming with power. He didn't even remember drawing it.

Two detonations echoed through the cavern. Bolter fire.

'Lieutenant, pull your soldiers back and regroup,' he ordered. 'Kill-team, to me.'

Another scream. Cassiel broke into a run, drawing his ornate bolt pistol as he rushed towards the piteous cry. He saw blood spray across an angled wall of ice. More than one of the storm troopers was down. Cassiel strained to locate a target as he ran.

There. Target lock.

A hunched thing of tortured flesh and blood, hands ending in half-metre talons slick with gore. It ripped open the throat of a storm trooper, unleashing a fresh torrent of red. It pressed its face into the gushing fountain – drinking, or perhaps just revelling in the sensation.

It was an easy mark, even at a run.

Cassiel's bolt pistol barked. Two shots struck the target, one in the back, one at the base of the neck. Those detonations should have ripped the creature – man? – to pieces, but they did not. Its flesh was torn, exposing dark metal bones.

Sprawling, the creature righted itself and swung towards him with a snarl. Its face was a dull metal skull draped in dead flesh. Its eye sockets were hollow pits, dark and fathomless, but tiny pinpricks of light lay deep within them, like cold green stars glinting in the void. Gore caked its jaw. Viscera dripped from its hollow ribcage.

A necron warrior, then, but like none that Cassiel had ever encountered before.

More of the creatures were among the storm troopers spread throughout the cavern, ripping and tearing. Shouts and screams echoed in the gloom. Hellguns whined as they powered up, then barked as their power was unleashed, sending angry red beams cutting across the open space. He heard Var'myr open fire again, and Tanaka incanting a tribal war-chant before his heavy bolter ripped across the cavern in a ceaseless stream of fire.

Cassiel quickly closed the distance with his foe. It was edging towards him, moving on all fours like a beast. He fired on it again as he ran. The bolt slammed it onto its back – its chest was a blackened ruin, but its metallic ribcage still held. Cassiel sprang off an uneven ice-boulder, leaping high, *Aruthel* humming in his hands. He came down on top of the deathly creature, landing with one knee upon its chest, buckling it inwards. He drove his blade into the beast's cranium, forcing it deep. It gargled a death rattle, and the pinpricks of light in its empty sockets faded.

A scream came from nearby and he spun, whipping *Aruthel* free. A storm trooper had fallen to one knee, and blood was pooling beneath him. Another of the skeletal creatures draped in dead, frozen flesh was hauling itself up from the ice beneath the Ordo Xenos soldier, its talons hooked into the man's leg.

Sheathing his blade, Cassiel took two bounding steps and grabbed the bloodied necron around its neck, hauling it off the stricken trooper. It thrashed like a feral beast, lashing at Cassiel with its talons.

Using his forward momentum, Cassiel slammed it against an ice wall, sending out a spread of cracks across its surface. He forced the creature's head back and sent a bolt from his pistol up into its metallic brainpan. He released his hold on it, and it flopped to the ground, broken, its skull a ruin of twisted metal.

He turned away, scanning for fresh targets.

He made to re-enter the fray when one of the creatures leapt onto his back, spitting and snarling, its talons slashing at his collar. While it could not breach his armoured plates, the flexible fibre-bundles at his joints – and his neck – were not so well protected. Razored claws sliced through to his flesh, carving deep into his shoulder.

Cassiel threw it off with a curse, warning icons flashing before his eyes. He didn't feel any pain. All he felt was the urge to kill – the urge to taste blood, though the creature had none to shed.

It was the one that he had just put down: its ruptured skull was reknitting itself, flowing like liquid silver back into its original form. Cassiel gripped *Aruthel* in both hands and carved the blade in at its neck. It raised its bladed claws to ward off the blow, but all it achieved was to lose both hands, along with its head. Cassiel kicked the metal cranium away.

'Beware,' he said across an open channel. 'They are self-repairing. Their fallen rise again.'

The foul creatures were setting upon the corpses of the storm troopers – and those who were not yet dead – ripping and tearing. Their talons eagerly sliced away the soldiers' carapace armour, exposing the flesh within, and they tore into it with relish, expertly flensing skin from muscle and bone. Others buried their faces in stomach cavities and throats, snapping and jerking. They snarled and spat at each other, like wild animals fighting over the spoils.

Cassiel snapped off a pair of angry shots, smashing two of the feeding beasts back. The others seemed oblivious or uncaring of the danger, intent on gorging themselves… though they were creatures of little more than metal and malice, with no flesh to feed. Every chunk of meat they swallowed simply flopped, wet and glistening, from their hollow ribcages to the ice, yet they seemed driven by an insatiable, ravenous hunger. It was obscene.

The ice cracked beneath his feet, and a taloned hand shot up and locked around his leg. Swivelling *Aruthel* in one hand into a downward grip, Cassiel thrust the blade down into the ice, skewering the creature's head even before it had emerged.

More of the creatures were appearing, and those that fell simply rejoined the savage attack moments later, their mortal injuries repaired. The storm troopers were being butchered. The survivors had formed a tight knot of defiance in the centre of the cavern, dragging the wounded with them. The storm trooper lieutenant was at their centre, barking orders and snapping off shots with her hellpistol. Cassiel saw her die a moment later, yanked to the ground with her throat torn out, and he cursed.

Cassiel felt torn. Part of him desperately wanted to pull his team out, to save those soldiers who still drew breath. Duty was his life, however. It had been built into his genes. The mission was paramount.

'We must finish this,' he barked.

The Blood Angels sergeant moved through the slaughter with a grace that belied his size. Spinning, wielding his blade in a two-handed grip, he cut the legs from beneath one of the deathly creatures rushing at him frenziedly. Still turning, he sliced the blade through the torso of another, carving it neatly in two. *Aruthel* sang a keening wail as it sliced through the air.

Briefly free of assailants, Cassiel joined the knot of storm troopers and took up a position at their fore. Tanaka joined him, walking steadily backwards, his heavy bolter coughing death. Each controlled burst of fire smashed the enemy backwards, and Cassiel saw metal limbs shorn from bodies, yet even that damage was being repaired.

'Something is happening,' said Tanaka, in between bursts.

'I see it,' growled Cassiel.

Beneath their feet, green light was glowing up through the ice. It was coming from the black xenos structure that curved underneath them.

One of the creatures leapt at Cassiel from a ledge above, talons extended to impale him. Before he could raise his weapon, a kraken bolt struck it from the side and its skull disintegrated into shards of metal. Cassiel looked up to see Var'myr staring down his smoking bolter from his position up at the curved black obelisk. He nodded his thanks, and the Mortifactor inclined his head in acknowledgement. Cassiel saw several fallen creatures around Var'myr's position, and another pinned beneath his boot, thrashing wildly. The Mortifactor had not been idle.

Cassiel's gaze was drawn to the black obelisk behind Var'myr. Green light was spilling from the glyphs and symbols upon its surface.

'Var'myr,' said Cassiel. 'Fall back.'

The Mortifactor bent down towards the screeching, flailing creature trapped beneath his boot. He grasped its skull in one huge hand and, with a violent wrench, tore it loose.

'A keepsake,' he declared as he stood upright.

Then he shuddered, and the metal skull slipped from his fingers.

A glowing blade of green light emerged from Var'myr's chest, transfixing him. Then the blade was sharply retracted, and Var'myr slid to his knees.

A towering being stood behind the fallen Mortifactor. It was as different from the hunched, flesh-wearing creatures as night was from day. Tall and broad-shouldered, it would have loomed over even Cassiel and the tallest of his Chapter brothers. Its skeletal limbs were a gleaming silver and it was decked in heavy plates of black obsidian. It carried a three-metre halberd ending in a humming blade of pure energy. With a swift motion, it brought the weapon around in a lethal arc, and took off Var'myr's head.

'No!' bellowed Cassiel.

The air behind the deathly metal being shimmered and distorted, and more armoured figures materialised. The nature of the curved obelisk was now clear. It was not a weapon, as Cassiel had suspected at first, but something far worse.

It was a *gateway.*

Five of the elite, armour-clad beings stood up there now. They bore a mix of energy-bladed halberds and one-handed axes, though their blades were similar, made of nothing more than crackling energy.

Var'myr's servo-skull hovered just above the Mortifactor's

corpse, its red eye flickering. Then it too was cut down, carved in two by an energy blade.

The air shimmered, like silver-dust catching the light, and a final figure appeared, materialising within their protective cordon. It was a creature of alien, yet undeniably regal, bearing.

This newcomer was stooped, and its protectors towered over it, yet it exuded a palpable aura of dominance. It wore a cloak of golden scales and a gleaming cowl, and its ribcage was armoured in polished ebony. Its skeletal limbs were bound in circlets of gold and obsidian and covered in xenos hieroglyphs, and it leaned upon a golden staff topped with a flaring winged icon pulsing with viridian radiance.

It stared around its surroundings, craning its neck one way then the other, like a vulture. Its gaze swept across the ice cavern before settling upon Cassiel. It held his gaze, eyes burning with deathless, pitiless fire. It croaked something indecipherable, speaking in a language that had already been dead a million years before the birth of humanity. It was the voice of the crypt, conjuring images of dust and dry sands. This was no unthinking automaton, Cassiel realised. This was an impossibly ancient being, filled with bitterness and anger, bound within a shell of metal.

The creature jabbed a skeletal finger in the Blood Angel's direction, and spoke again in its dead language. Tall shields of glowing green light sprang to life upon the off-weapon arms of the axe-wielding guardians, and they stepped to the fore, forming a protective shield wall.

Then, as one, the necrons began to advance.

Cassiel's rage was threatening to overwhelm him, and he struggled to control it. It would be so easy to give in…

His vision began to cloud, a reddish tinge over everything he saw, and the pounding of his hearts – his secondary beating now, too – drowned out all else. His lips curled back, and had he not been wearing his black-painted helm, his elongated canines would have been exposed.

Var'myr's blood, spreading from his headless corpse, was almost painfully bright. Everything else was as nothing… except for his foes. He glared at the advancing xenos warriors, and a shameful, animal growl rumbled from his vox-grille. His grip tightened on the haft of his blade as he prepared to attack.

No.

He must remain in control. His duty demanded it.

He forced himself to breathe deeply, and forcibly loosened his grip on the blade. The red haze began to clear, though it hung around the fringes of his vision, ready to descend again at any moment. The black tendrils of his hatred recoiled, temporarily, and once more it retreated to its lair. Its time would come.

'Storm troopers,' he growled. 'Be ready. My brother and I will hold them. Split, and get around behind them. Use the charges. Destroy that gateway.'

'How do we hold them?' asked Tanaka.

'We kill them.'

'Yes. That would do it.'

At Cassiel's direction, the storm troopers divided into two groups, each carrying a case of demolition charges, and they peeled off to each flank.

Cassiel glanced over at his White Scar brother, the last of his kill-team.

'Ready?' he said.

In answer, the White Scar planted his feet wide and brought his heavy bolter around to bear, the built-in suspensors steadying his aim. Squeezing and holding the trigger, he unleashed a blazing torrent of fire. It was virtually a solid stream of large-calibre bolts he sent roaring across the ice cavern, and the sound was deafening.

Tanaka's onslaught tore across the enemy, but their advance did not slow. The shield bearers at their fore tightened their formation, shields interlocking as the heavy bolter fire hammered into them. The shimmering barrier flashed brightly as each heavy bolter round struck, absorbing their energy, creating a flickering strobe as shot after shot rained upon them. Each shot rebounded off this seemingly impenetrable wall, hurled away with the same velocity as it was delivered. Heavy bolter rounds ricocheted across the ice cavern, filling the air.

One round skimmed just over the rim of one of the shields and took one of the foes in the head. The resultant detonation demolished its skull, and it fell heavily. Its brethren gave it no mind, simply stepping over the body to continue their relentless march. A moment later, it rose again.

The necrons altered the angle of their shields, and the warriors of the Ordo Xenos suddenly found Tanaka's stream of bolter fire being redirected back at them.

Cassiel was struck in the shoulder, half spinning him, and other rounds screamed by him, missing by scant centimetres.

He turned his head instinctively, registering an incoming

bolt a fraction of a second before it took him between the eyes. It still struck a glancing blow, and the resulting detonation ruined his vision in a haze of grainy static, and kicked his neck to one side.

He tore his helmet off. The whole left hemisphere was a mess of torn metal and fractured ceramite, and his left eye lens was shattered. He could feel blood trickling down his temple. He cast the ruined helm aside.

The head of one of the storm troopers disappeared in a red mist, and another was torn bodily in two as a stream of fire cut through his midsection.

Tanaka cut off his volley with an anguished cry, aghast at the carnage he had wrought. No storm trooper had been left standing. Their blood was sprayed across the ice.

One of the flesh-wearers took its opportunity, leaping upon the White Scar as he stared in horror at the dead. He tried to raise his weapon, but he was too slow and the creature too close. It thrust its talons into his faceplate. Two of the blades smashed straight through his visor lenses, driving deep into his brain. He died instantly, slumping to the ground.

Cassiel roared, his fury surging to the surface, and this time he made no attempt to quash it. He hurled his bolt pistol aside and hacked into Tanaka's killer with his blade. His lips drew back in a snarl, exposing his dagger-like canines and he tasted blood on his lips. His blade rose and fell, hacking and slicing. Only when the creature was rendered into a dozen separate sections did he stop. Even then, those parts quivered on the ice, pulling themselves back together, but Cassiel gave it no more thought. He lifted his reddened gaze, breathing heavily, and focused on the xenos lord and his phalanx of guardians.

He closed the distance quickly, his fury lending him speed. Twenty metres. Fifteen. Ten. He gripped his long blade in a double-handed grip, drawing it back for a powerful strike.

He sprang lightly off one foot, angling his leap to take him slightly to the side and past the closest guardian's shield. He turned in the air as he leapt, and rather than bringing his blade around in arc, he drove it down in a powerful two-handed thrust. It sank deep, driven down behind his enemy's armoured ribcage. Cassiel swiftly withdrew the blade, pulling it free even before his feet had touched the ground.

He instantly threw himself into a roll as a glowing-bladed halberd swung out, humming through the air. It passed harmlessly above him, and he rammed *Aruthel* up into his would-be killer as he rose. The blade punched up under the ribcage, thrusting up through its body. The tip burst from the top of its metal cranium, green sparks dancing wildly along its length. He yanked the blade free and the creature collapsed.

He lifted the sword in a horizontal parry, sensing rather than seeing a blow coming at him from behind. His blade crackled and gave off the smell of ozone as it met the downward strike of an energy halberd. The force of the blow drove him to his knees, but he was up in a second, snarling and spitting, stepping in close.

Still holding his blade two-handed, he slammed its pommel up into his opponent's skull twice in quick succession, jerking its head back but doing little real damage. It backhanded him across the side of his face, sending him sprawling.

With an animalistic snarl, Cassiel rose, swinging his blade

around in a lethal arc. One of the warriors that he had already dropped was rising once more, its damage self-repairing. He chopped its legs out from under it and rammed *Aruthel* down into its skull as it toppled to the ground. An energy shield slammed into him, shocking him and sending him stumbling. An overhead blow came crashing down upon him. Cassiel took it upon his blade before ripping around in a screaming arc, neatly cutting the creature in two.

He stood before the xenos lord now, having fought his way in behind its guardians. It glared at him with its baleful green orbs. A burst of mechanised sound emerged from its throat. It took a moment for Cassiel to realise that it was laughing at him.

It stepped forward, thrusting its staff at his chest. Cassiel batted the blow aside and lunged, the move perfectly timed. His blade slid between the lord's slit of a mouth, silencing its ugly laughter. With a roar, he pressed forward, using all his strength and weight to ram *Aruthel* home until the hilt struck its face, a full metre and a half of blade protruding out from the back of its neck.

Even as the light died in the xenos being's eyes, its appearance changed. Its body grew larger in stature, heavy armoured plates appearing on its shoulders and chest, and the shape of its cranium altering. Before Cassiel's eyes, its metal physiology had morphed into that of one of its bodyguards.

'What–' he began, startled by this unexpected transformation.

He felt the hairs on the back of his neck stiffen, and there was a crackling sound behind him.

A blow struck him squarely in the back, accompanied by a sound akin to a thunderclap.

He was slammed flat, twitching involuntarily. Green-tinged lightning danced across his armour. He struggled to push himself to his feet, but his muscles were convulsing uncontrollably, and he could not rise.

The xenos lord stood behind him. It had taken over the body of another of its bodyguards and stood now in its place, looking down upon him, croaking its ugly laughter.

One of the guardians, newly reformed from the damage Cassiel had wrought upon it, stepped forward with its blade ready. The xenos lord barked something in its indecipherable dead language, and the guardian halted, warily. Hunched and cowled, the lord shuffled in, leaning over Cassiel, regarding him closely.

It was so close that he could see the intricate circuitry behind its armoured ribcage, and smell its repugnant stink, a strange mix of battery acid, oil and dust. *Aruthel* lay on the ice, just half a metre away. He could kill this abomination in an instant, he was sure, and he strained to regain control of his body. The convulsions were passing. His fingers twitched, and the veins in his neck bulged.

With a roar, he shot his hand out and grabbed the blade.

He was too slow, however. The ancient xenos placed its hand upon his chest, skeletal metal fingers spread wide. A pulse of energy passed into Cassiel's body. He gasped, his eyes wide – in that instant, Cassiel's twin hearts ceased to beat, and his breathing halted.

'You… are… *mine*,' the necron lord said, his hand still upon the fallen Space Marine's chest.

* * *

One of them was about to die.

They stood at the epicentre of the battle, beneath a sky that was burning, and it seemed as though time stood still. The black-armoured paragon of humanity brought a golden-winged power sword around in a crackling two-handed killing strike. His pale face was twisted in hatred, and his eyes were tinged red with blood-rage. Despite the thickness of his enemy's bull-like neck, the blow was perfectly timed, delivered with all his genhanced and armour-augmented strength.

His opponent was a hulking green skinned monster that stood over two and half metres tall. It lived only for battle and knew – nay, cared for – nothing else. It roared as it swung its chugging chain-glaive around in a brutal arc, a blow that could carve the Space Marine clean in two.

Either blow would be mortal if it landed. Both would land within a single heartbeat.

But that heartbeat would never come.

Trazyn the Infinite stepped between the two frozen combatants, inspecting his latest acquisition. He peered into the Space Marine's eyes. Life blazed there, along with a frenzied, insane fury. He knew that the enhanced human creature could see him. He knew that its conscious mind still remained, trapped forever within the prison of its own body. If it were not so, then his display would be lacking.

Satisfied, he shuffled across the battlefield, past hundreds more frozen statues, each carefully positioned as per his grand design. Some were firing weapons or swinging blades. Others were dying, trapped forever in the moment of their deaths. It was glorious.

The holographic burning sky and the red-sanded earth flickered as he reached the edge of the display. Once again he stood upon the gleaming obsidian deck of his infinite gallery.

Trazyn strode away, his staff clicking sharply with each step. He walked his halls, past countless other displays with primitive creatures of every description, breed and race; all arrayed and carefully posed; all living, trapped until the end of time. He passed beings that had died out half a million years earlier – some whose loss was mourned by the galaxy at large, and others that had simply disappeared without note.

There were hundreds of displays on this deck alone, many of them far grander than his latest, humble effort. Thousands more decks lay above and below.

Trazyn gave them no more thought. His mind was already moving on to his next project.

He rubbed his metal hands in glee. It would be a masterpiece.

Something vast, dark and brutish moved across the pinpricked curtain of space, blotting out the diamond lights of the constellations behind it as if swallowing them whole. It was the size of a city block, and its bulbous eyes, like those of a great blind fish, glowed with a green and baleful light.

It was a terrible thing to behold, this leviathan – a harbinger of doom – and its passage had brought agony and destruction to countless victims in the centuries it had swum among the stars. It travelled, now, through the Charybdis Subsector on trails of angry red plasma, cutting across the inky darkness with a purpose.

That purpose was close at hand, and a change began to take place on its bestial features. New lights flickered to life on its muzzle, shining far brighter and sharper than its eyes, illuminating myriad shapes, large and small, that danced and spun in high orbit above the glowing orange sphere of Arronax II. With a slow, deliberate motion, the leviathan unhinged its massive lower jaw, and opened its mouth to feed.

At first, the glimmering pieces of debris it swallowed were mere fragments, nothing much larger than a man. But soon, heavier, bulkier pieces drifted into that gaping maw, passing between its bladelike teeth and down into its black throat.

For hours, the monster gorged itself on space-borne scrap, devouring everything it could fit into its mouth. The pickings were good. There had been heavy fighting here in ages past. Scoured worlds and lifeless wrecks were all that remained now, locked in a slow elliptical dance around the local star. But the wrecks, at least, had a future. Once salvaged, they would be forged anew, recast in forms that would bring death and suffering down upon countless others. For, of course, this beast, this hungry monster of the void, was no beast at all.

It was an ork ship. And the massive glyphs daubed sloppily on its hull marked it as a vessel of the Deathskull clan.

Re-pressurisation began the moment the ship's vast metal jaws clanged shut. The process took around twenty minutes, pumps flooding the salvage bay with breathable, if foul-smelling, air. The orks crowding the corridor beyond the bay's airlock doors roared their impatience and hammered their fists against the thick metal bulkheads. They shoved and jostled for position. Then, just when it seemed murderous violence was sure to erupt, sirens sounded and the heavy doors split apart. The orks surged forward, pushing and scrambling, racing towards the mountains of scrap, each utterly focused on claiming the choicest pieces for himself.

Fights broke out between the biggest and darkest-skinned. They roared and wrestled with each other, and snapped at each other with tusk-filled jaws. They lashed out with the tools and weapons that bristled on their augmented limbs. They might have killed each other but for the massive suits of cybernetic armour they wore. These were no mere greenskin foot soldiers. They were orks of a unique genus, the engineers of their race, each born with an inherent understanding of machines. It was hard-coded into their marrow in the same way as violence and torture.

As was true of every caste, however, some among them were cleverer than others. While the mightiest bellowed and beat their metal-plated chests, one ork, marginally shorter and leaner than the rest, slid around them and into the shadows, intent on getting first pickings.

This ork was called Gorgrot in the rough speech of his race, and, despite the sheer density of salvage the ship had swallowed, it didn't take him long to find something truly valuable. At the very back of the junk-filled bay, closest to the ship's great metal teeth, he found the ruined, severed prow of a mid-sized human craft. As he studied it, he noticed weapon barrels protruding from the front end. His alien heart quickened. Functional or not, he could do great things with salvaged weapon systems. He would make himself more dangerous, an ork to be reckoned with.

After a furtive look over his shoulder to make sure none of the bigger orks had noticed him, he moved straight across to the wrecked prow, reached out a gnarled hand and touched the hull. Its armour-plating was in bad shape, pocked and cratered by plasma fire and torpedo impacts. To the rear, the metal was twisted and black where it had sheared away from the rest of the craft. It looked like an explosion had torn the ship apart. To Gorgrot, however, the nature of the ship's destruction mattered not at all. What mattered was its potential. Already, visions of murderous creativity were flashing through his tiny mind in rapid succession, so many at once, in fact, that he forgot to breathe until his lungs sent him a painful reminder. These visions were a gift from Gork and Mork, the bloodthirsty greenskin gods, and he had received their like many times before. All greenskin engineers received them, and nothing, save the rending of an enemy's flesh, felt so utterly right.

Even so, it was something small and insignificant that pulled him out of his rapture.

A light had begun to flash on the lower left side of the ruined prow, winking at him from beneath a tangle of beams and cables and dented armour plates, igniting his simple-minded curiosity, drawing him towards it. It was small and green, and it looked like it might be a button of some kind. Gorgrot began clearing debris from the area around it. Soon, he was grunting and growling with the effort, sweating despite the assistance of his armour's strength-boosting hydraulics.

Within minutes, he had removed all obstructions between himself and the blinking light, and discovered that it was indeed a kind of button.

Gorgrot was extending his finger out to press it when something suddenly wrenched him backwards with irresistible force. He was hurled to the ground and landed hard on his back with a snarl. Immediately, he tried to scramble up again, but a huge metal boot stamped down on him, denting his belly-armour and pushing him deep into the carpet of sharp scrap.

Gorgrot looked up into the blazing red eyes of the biggest, heaviest ork in the salvage bay.

This was Zazog, personal engineer to the mighty Warboss Balthazog Bludwrekk, and few orks on the ship were foolish enough to challenge any of his salvage claims. It was the reason he always arrived in the salvage bay last of all; his tardiness was the supreme symbol of his dominance among the scavengers.

Zazog staked his claim now, turning from Gorgrot and stomping over to the wrecked prow. There, he hunkered down to examine the winking button. He knew well enough what it meant. There had to be a working power source onboard, something far more valuable than most scrap. He flicked out a blowtorch attachment from the middle knuckle of his mechanised left claw and burned a rough likeness of his personal glyph into the side of the wrecked prow. Then he rose and bellowed a challenge to those around him.

Scores of gretchin, the puniest members of the orkoid race, skittered away in panic, disappearing into the protection of the shadows. The other orks stepped back, growling at Zazog, snarling in anger. But none dared challenge him.

Zazog glared at each in turn, forcing them, one by one, to drop their gazes or die by his hand. Then, satisfied at their deference, he turned and pressed a thick finger to the winking green button.

For a brief moment, nothing happened. Zazog growled and

pressed it again. Still nothing. He was about to begin pounding it with his mighty fist when he heard a noise.

It was the sound of atmospheric seals unlocking.

The door shuddered, and began sliding up into the hull.

Zazog's craggy, scar-covered face twisted into a hideous grin. Yes, there *was* a power source on board. The door's motion proved it. He, like Gorgrot, began to experience flashes of divine inspiration, visions of weaponry so grand and deadly that his limited brain could hardly cope. No matter; the gods would work through him once he got started. His hands would automatically fashion what his brain could barely comprehend. It was always the way.

The sliding door retracted fully now, revealing an entrance just large enough for Zazog's armoured bulk to squeeze through. He shifted forward with that very intention, but the moment never came.

From the shadows inside the doorway, there was a soft coughing sound.

Zazog's skull disintegrated in a haze of blood and bone chips. His headless corpse crashed backwards onto the carpet of junk.

The other orks gaped in slack-jawed wonder. They looked down at Zazog's body, trying to make sense of the dim warnings that rolled through their minds. Ignoring the obvious threat, the biggest orks quickly began roaring fresh claims and shoving the others aside, little realising that their own deaths were imminent.

But imminent they were.

A great black shadow appeared, bursting from the door Zazog had opened. It was humanoid, not quite as large as the orks surrounding it, but bulky nonetheless, though it moved with a speed and confidence no ork could ever have matched. Its long adamantium talons sparked and crackled with deadly energy as it slashed and stabbed in all directions, a whirlwind of lethal motion. Great fountains of thick red blood arced through the air as it killed again and again. Greenskins fell like sacks of meat.

More shadows emerged from the wreck now. Four of them. Like the first, all were dressed in heavy black ceramite armour. All bore an intricate skull and 'I' design on their massive left pauldrons. The icons on their right pauldrons, however, were each unique.

'Clear the room,' barked one over his comm-link as he gunned down a greenskin in front of him, spitting death from the barrel of his silenced bolter. 'Quick and quiet. Kill the rest before they raise the alarm.' Switching comm channels, he said, 'Sigma, this is Talon Alpha. Phase one complete. Kill-team is aboard. Securing entry point now.'

'Understood, Alpha,' replied the toneless voice at the other end of the link. 'Proceed on mission. Extract within the hour, as instructed. Captain Redthorne has orders to pull out if you miss your pick-up, so keep your team on a tight leash. This is *not* a purge operation. Is that clear?'

'I'm well aware of that, Sigma,' the kill-team leader replied brusquely.

'You had better be,' replied the voice. 'Sigma, out.'

It took Talon squad less than sixty seconds to clear the salvage bay. Brother Rauth of the Exorcists Chapter gunned down the last of the fleeing gretchin as it dashed for the exit. The creature stumbled as a single silenced bolt punched into its back. Half a second later, a flesh-muffled detonation ripped it apart.

It was the last of twenty-six bodies to fall among the litter of salvaged scrap.

'Target down, Karras,' reported Rauth. 'Area clear.'

'Confirmed,' replied Karras. He turned to face a Space Marine with a heavy flamer. 'Omni, you know what to do. The rest of you, cover the entrance.'

With the exception of Omni, the team immediately moved to positions covering the mouth of the corridor through which the orks had come. Omni, otherwise known as Maximmion Voss of the Imperial Fists, moved to the side walls, first the left, then the right, working quickly at a number of thick hydraulic pistons and power cables there.

'That was messy, Karras,' said Brother Solarion, 'letting them see us as we came out. I told you we should have used smoke. If one had escaped and raised the alarm...'

Karras ignored the comment. It was just Solarion being Solarion.

'Give it a rest, Prophet,' said Brother Zeed, opting to use Solarion's nickname. Zeed had coined it himself, and knew precisely how much it irritated the proud Ultramarine. 'The room is clear. No runners. No alarms. Scholar knows what he's doing.'

Scholar. That was what they called Karras, or at least Brothers Voss and Zeed did. Rauth and Solarion insisted on calling him by his second name. Sigma always called him Alpha.

And his battle-brothers back on Occludus, homeworld of the Death Spectres Chapter, simply called him by his first name, Lyandro, or sometimes simply Codicier – his rank in the Librarius.

Karras didn't much care what anyone called him so long as they all did their jobs. The honour of serving in the Deathwatch had been offered to him, and he had taken it, knowing the great glory it would bring both himself and his Chapter. But he wouldn't be sorry when his obligation to the Emperor's Holy Inquisition was over. Astartes life seemed far less complicated among one's own Chapter-brothers.

When would he return to the fold? He didn't know. There was no fixed term for Deathwatch service. The Inquisition made high demands of all it called upon. Karras might not see the darkly beautiful crypt-cities of his home world again for decades… if he lived that long.

'Done, Scholar,' reported Voss as he rejoined the rest of the team.

Karras nodded and pointed towards a shattered pict screen and rune-board that protruded from the wall, close to the bay's only exit. 'Think you can get anything from that?' he asked.

'Nothing from the screen,' said Voss, 'but I could try wiring the data-feed directly into my visor.'

'Do it,' said Karras, 'but be quick.' To the others, he said, 'Proceed with phase two. Solarion, take point.'

The Ultramarine nodded curtly, rose from his position among the scrap and stalked forward into the shadowy corridor, bolter raised and ready. He moved with smooth, near-silent steps despite the massive weight of his armour. Torias Telion, famed Ultramarine Scout Master and Solarion's former mentor, would have been proud of his prize student.

One by one, with the exception of Voss, the rest of the kill-team followed in his wake.

The filthy, rusting corridors of the ork ship were lit, but the electric lamps the greenskins had strung up along pipes and ducts were old and in poor repair. Barely half of them seemed to be working at all. Even these buzzed and flickered in a constant battle to throw out their weak illumination. Still, the little light they did give was enough to bother the kill-team leader. The inquisitor, known to the members of Talon only by his call-sign, Sigma, had estimated the ork population of the ship at somewhere over twenty thousand. Against odds like these, Karras knew only too well that darkness and stealth were among his best weapons.

'I want the lights taken out,' he growled. 'The longer we stay hidden, the better our chances of making it off this damned heap.'

'We could shoot them out as we go,' offered Solarion, 'but I'd rather not waste my ammunition on something that doesn't bleed.'

Just then, Karras heard Voss on the comm-link. 'I've finished with the terminal, Scholar. I managed to pull some old cargo manifests from the ship's memory core. Not much else, though. Apparently, this ship used to be a civilian heavy-transport, Magellann class, built on Stygies. It was called *The Pegasus*.'

'No schematics?'

'Most of the memory core is heavily corrupted. It's thousands of years old. We were lucky to get that much.'

'Sigma, this is Alpha,' said Karras. 'The ork ship is built around an Imperial transport called *The Pegasus*. Requesting schematics, priority one.'

'I heard,' said Sigma. 'You'll have them as soon as I do.'

'Voss, where are you now?' Karras asked.

'Close to your position,' said the Imperial Fist.

'Do you have any idea which cable provides power to the lights?'

'Look up,' said Voss. 'See those cables running along the ceiling? The thick one, third from the left. I'd wager my knife on it.'

Karras didn't have to issue the order. The moment Zeed heard Voss's words, his right arm flashed upwards. There was a crackle of blue energy as the Raven Guard's claws sliced through the cable, and the corridor went utterly dark.

To the Space Marines, however, everything remained clear as day. Their Mark VII helmets, like everything else in their arsenal, had been heavily modified by the Inquisition's finest artificers. They boasted a composite low-light/thermal vision mode that was superior to anything else Karras had ever used. In the three years he had been leading Talon, it had tipped the balance in his favour more times than he cared to count. He hoped it would do so many more times in the years to come, but that would all depend on their survival here, and he knew all too well that the odds were against them from the start. It wasn't just the numbers they were up against, or the tight deadline. There was something here the likes of which few Deathwatch kill-teams had ever faced before.

Karras could already feel its presence somewhere on the upper levels of the ship.

'Keep moving,' he told the others.

Three minutes after Zeed had killed the lights, Solarion hissed for them all to stop. 'Karras,' he rasped, 'I have multiple xenos up ahead. Suggest you move up and take a look.'

Karras ordered the others to hold and went forward, careful not to bang or scrape his broad pauldrons against the clutter of twisting pipes that lined both walls. Crouching beside Solarion, he realised he needn't have worried about a little noise. In front of him, over a hundred orks had crowded into a high-ceilinged, octagonal chamber. They were hooting and laughing and wrestling with each other to get nearer the centre of the room.

Neither Karras nor Solarion could see beyond the wall of broad green backs, but there was clearly something in the middle that was holding their attention.

'What are they doing?' whispered Solarion.

Karras decided there was only one way to find out. He centred his awareness down in the pit of his stomach, and began reciting the Litany of the Sight Beyond Sight that his former master, Chief Librarian Athio Cordatus, had taught him during his earliest years in the Librarius. Beneath his helmet, hidden from Solarion's view, Karras's eyes, normally deep red in colour, began to glow with an ethereal white flame. On his forehead, a wound appeared. A single drop of blood rolled over his brow and down to the bridge of his narrow, angular nose. Slowly, as he opened his soul fractionally more to the dangerous power within him, the wound widened, revealing the physical manifestation of his psychic inner eye.

Karras felt his awareness lift out of his body now. He willed it deeper into the chamber, rising above the backs of the orks, looking down on them from above.

He saw a great pit sunk into the centre of the metal floor. It was filled with hideous ovoid creatures of every possible colour, their tiny red eyes set above oversized mouths crammed with razor-edged teeth.

'It's a mess hall,' Karras told his team over the link. 'There's a squig pit in the centre.'

As his projected consciousness watched, the greenskins at the rim of the pit stabbed downwards with cruelly barbed poles, hooking their prey through soft flesh. Then they lifted the squigs, bleeding and screaming, into the air before reaching for them, tearing them from the hooks, and feasting on them.

'They're busy,' said Karras, 'but we'll need to find another way through.'

'Send me in, Scholar,' said Voss from the rear. 'I'll turn them all into cooked meat before they even realise they're under attack. Ghost can back me up.'

'On your order, Scholar,' said Zeed eagerly.

Ghost. That was Siefer Zeed. With his helmet off, it was easy to see how he'd come by the name. Like Karras, and like all brothers of their respective Chapters, Zeed was the victim of a failed melanochromic implant, a slight mutation in his ancient and otherwise worthy gene-seed. The skin of both he and the kill-team leader was as white as porcelain. But, whereas Karras bore the blood-red eyes and chalk-white hair of the true albino, Zeed's eyes were black as coals, and his hair no less dark.

'Negative,' said Karras. 'We'll find another way through.'

He pushed his astral-self further into the chamber, desperate to find a means that didn't involve alerting the foe, but there seemed little choice. Only when he turned his awareness upwards did he see what he was looking for.

'There's a walkway near the ceiling,' he reported. 'It looks frail, rusting badly, but if we cross it one at a time, it should hold.'

A sharp, icy voice on the comm-link interrupted him. 'Talon Alpha, get ready to receive those schematics. Transmitting now.'

Karras willed his consciousness back into his body, and his glowing third eye sealed itself, leaving only the barest trace of a scar. Using conventional sight, he consulted his helmet's heads-up display and watched the last few per cent of the schematics file being downloaded. When it was finished, he called it up with a thought, and the helmet projected it as a shimmering green image cast directly onto his left retina.

The others, he knew, were seeing the same thing.

'According to these plans,' he told them, 'there's an access ladder set into the wall near the second junction we passed. We'll backtrack to it. The corridor above this one will give us access to the walkway.'

'If it's still there,' said Solarion. 'The orks may have removed it.'

'And backtracking will cost us time,' grumbled Voss.

'Less time than a firefight would cost us,' countered Rauth. His hard, gravelly tones were made even harder by the slight distortion on the comm-link. 'There's a time and place for that kind of killing, but it isn't now.'

'Watcher's right,' said Zeed reluctantly. It was rare for he and Rauth to agree.

'I've told you before,' warned Rauth. 'Don't call me that.'

'Right or wrong,' said Karras, 'I'm not taking votes. I've made my call. Let's move.'

Karras was the last to cross the gantry above the ork feeding pit. The shadows up here were dense and, so far, the orks had noticed nothing, though there had been a few moments when it looked as if the aging iron were about to collapse, particularly beneath the tremendous weight of Voss with his heavy flamer, high explosives, and back-mounted promethium supply.

Such was the weight of the Imperial Fist and his kit that Karras had decided to send him over first. Voss had made it across, but it was nothing short of a miracle that the orks below hadn't noticed the rain of red flakes showering down on them.

Lucky we didn't bring old Chyron after all, thought Karras.

The sixth member of Talon wouldn't have made it out of the salvage bay. The corridors on this ship were too narrow for such a mighty Space Marine. Instead, Sigma had ordered the redoubtable Dreadnought, formerly of the Lamenters Chapter but now permanently attached to Talon, to remain behind on Redthorne's ship, the *Saint Nevarre*. That had caused a few tense moments. Chyron had a vile temper.

Karras made his way, centimetre by centimetre, along the creaking metal grille, his silenced bolter fixed securely to the magnetic couplings on his right thigh plate, his force sword sheathed on his left hip. Over one massive shoulder was slung the cryo-case that Sigma had insisted he carry. Karras cursed it, but there was no way he could leave it behind. It added twenty kilogrammes to his already significant weight, but the case was absolutely critical to the mission. He had no choice.

Up ahead, he could see Rauth watching him, as ever, from the end of the gangway. What was the Exorcist thinking? Karras had no clue. He had never been able to read the mysterious Astartes. Rauth seemed to have no warp signature whatsoever. He simply didn't register at all. Even his armour, even his bolter for Throne's sake, resonated more than he did. And it was an anomaly that Rauth was singularly unwilling to discuss.

There was no love lost between them, Karras knew, and, for his part, he regretted that. He had made gestures, occasional overtures, but for whatever reason, they had been rebuffed every time. The Exorcist was unreachable, distant, remote, and it seemed he planned to stay that way.

As Karras took his next step, the cryo-case suddenly swung forward on its strap, shifting his centre of gravity and threatening to unbalance him. He compensated swiftly, but the effort caused the gangway to creak and a piece of rusted metal snapped off, spinning away under him.

He froze, praying that the orks wouldn't notice.

But one did.

It was at the edge of the pit, poking a fat squig with its barbed pole, when the metal fragment struck its head. The ork immediately stopped what it was doing and scanned the shadows above it, squinting suspiciously up towards the unlit recesses of the high ceiling.

Karras stared back, willing it to turn away. Reading minds and controlling minds, however, were two very different things. The latter was a power beyond his gifts. Ultimately, it wasn't Karras's will that turned the ork from its scrutiny. It was the nature of the greenskin species.

The other orks around it, impatient to feed, began grabbing at the barbed pole. One managed to snatch it, and the gazing ork suddenly found himself robbed of his chance to feed. He launched himself into a violent frenzy, lashing out at the pole-thief and those nearby. That was when the orks behind him surged forward, and pushed him into the squig pit.

Karras saw the squigs swarm on the hapless ork, sinking their long teeth into its flesh and tearing away great, bloody mouthfuls. The food chain had been turned on its head. The orks around the pit laughed and capered and struck at their dying fellow with their poles.

Karras didn't stop to watch. He moved on carefully, cursing the black case that was now pressed tight to his side with one arm. He rejoined his team in the mouth of a tunnel on the far side of the gantry and they moved off, pressing deeper into the ship. Solarion moved up front with Zeed. Voss stayed in the middle. Rauth and Karras brought up the rear.

'They need to do some damned maintenance around here,' Karras told Rauth in a wry tone.

The Exorcist said nothing.

* * *

By comparing Sigma's schematics of *The Pegasus* with the features he saw as he moved through it, it soon became clear to Karras that the orks had done very little to alter the interior of the ship beyond covering its walls in badly rendered glyphs, defecating wherever they pleased, leaving dead bodies to rot where they fell, and generally making the place unfit for habitation by anything save their own wretched kind. Masses of quivering fungi had sprouted from broken water pipes. Frayed electrical cables sparked and hissed at anyone who walked by. And there were so many bones strewn about that some sections almost looked like mass graves.

The Deathwatch members made a number of kills, or rather Solarion did, as they proceeded deeper into the ship's belly. Most of these were gretchin sent out on some errand or other by their slavemasters. The Ultramarine silently executed them wherever he found them and stuffed the small corpses under pipes or in dark alcoves. Only twice did the kill-team encounter parties of ork warriors, and both times, the greenskins announced themselves well in advance with their loud grunting and jabbering. Karras could tell that Voss and Zeed were both itching to engage, but stealth was still paramount. Instead, he, Rauth and Solarion eliminated the foe, loading powerful hellfire rounds into their silenced bolters to ensure quick, quiet one-shot kills.

'I've reached Waypoint Adrius,' Solarion soon reported from up ahead. 'No xenos contacts.'

'Okay, move in and secure,' Karras ordered. 'Check your corners and exits.'

The kill-team hurried forward, emerging from the blackness

of the corridor into a towering square shaft. It was hundreds of metres high, its metal walls stained with age and rust and all kinds of spillage. Thick pipes ran across the walls at all angles, many of them venting steam or dripping icy coolant. There were broken staircases and rusting gantries at regular intervals, each of which led to gaping doorways. And, in the middle of the left-side wall, an open elevator shaft ran almost to the top.

It was here that Talon would be forced to split up. From this chamber, they could access any level in the ship. Voss and Zeed would go down via a metal stairway, the others would go up.

'Good luck using that,' said Voss, nodding towards the elevator cage. It was clearly of ork construction, a mishmash of metal bits bolted together. It had a bloodstained steel floor, a folding lattice-work gate and a large lever which could be pushed forward for up, or pulled backwards for down.

There was no sign of what had happened to the original elevator.

Karras scowled under his helmet as he looked at it and cross-referenced what he saw against his schematics. 'We'll have to take it as high as it will go,' he told Rauth and Solarion. He pointed up towards the far ceiling. 'That landing at the top; that is where we are going. From there we can access the corridor to the bridge. Ghost, Omni, you have your own objectives.' He checked the mission chrono in the corner of his visor. 'Forty-three minutes,' he told them. 'Avoid confrontation if you can. And stay in contact.'

'Understood, Scholar,' said Voss.

Karras frowned. He could sense the Imperial Fist's hunger for battle. It had been there since the moment they'd set foot on this mechanical abomination. Like most Imperial Fists, once Voss was in a fight, he tended to stay there until the foe was dead. He could be stubborn to the point of idiocy, but there was no denying his versatility. Weapons, vehicles, demolitions… Voss could do it all.

'Ghost,' said Karras. 'Make sure he gets back here on schedule.'

'If I have to knock him out and drag him back myself,' said Zeed.

'You can try,' Voss snorted, grinning under his helmet. He and the Raven Guard had enjoyed a good rapport since the moment they had met. Karras occasionally envied them that.

'Go,' he told them, and they moved off, disappearing down a stairwell on the right, their footsteps vibrating the grille under Karras's feet.

'Then there were three,' said Solarion.

'With the Emperor's blessing,' said Karras, 'that's all we'll need.' He strode over to the elevator, pulled the latticework gate aside, and got in. As the others joined him, he added, 'If either of you know a Mechanicus prayer, now would be a good time. Rauth, take us up.'

The Exorcist pushed the control lever forward, and it gave a harsh, metallic screech. A winch high above them began turning. Slowly at first, then with increasing speed, the lower levels dropped away beneath them. Pipes and landings flashed by, then the counterweight whistled past. The floor of the cage creaked and groaned under their feet as it carried them higher and higher. Disconcerting sounds issued from the cable and the assembly at the top, but the ride was short, lasting barely a minute, for which Karras thanked the Emperor.

When they were almost at the top of the shaft, Rauth eased the control lever backwards and the elevator slowed, issuing the same high-pitched complaint with which it had started.

Karras heard Solarion cursing.

'Problem, brother?' he asked.

'We'll be lucky if the whole damned ship doesn't know we're here by now,' spat the Ultramarine. 'Accursed piece of ork junk.'

The elevator ground to a halt at the level of the topmost landing, and Solarion almost tore the latticework gate from its fixings as he wrenched it aside. Stepping out, he took point again automatically.

The rickety steel landing led off in two directions. To the left, it led to a trio of dimly lit corridor entrances. To the right, it led towards a steep metal staircase in a severe state of disrepair.

Karras consulted his schematics.

'Now for the bad news,' he said.

The others eyed the stair grimly.

'It won't hold us,' said Rauth. 'Not together.'

Some of the metal steps had rusted away completely leaving gaps of up to a metre. Others were bent and twisted, torn half-way free of their bolts as if something heavy had landed hard on them.

'So we spread out,' said Karras. 'Stay close to the wall. Put as little pressure on each step as we can. We don't have time to debate it.'

They moved off, Solarion in front, Karras in the middle, Rauth at the rear. Karras watched his point-man carefully, noting exactly where he placed each foot. The Ultramarine moved with a certainty and fluidity that few could match. Had he registered more of a warp signature than he did, Karras might even have suspected some kind of extrasensory perception, but, in fact, it was simply the superior training of the Master Scout, Telion.

Halfway up the stair, however, Solarion suddenly held up his hand and hissed, 'Hold!'

Rauth and Karras froze at once. The stairway creaked gently under them.

'Xenos, direct front. Twenty metres. Three big ones.'

Neither Karras nor Rauth could see them. The steep angle of the stair prevented it.

'Can you deal with them?' asked Karras.

'Not alone,' said Solarion. 'One is standing in a doorway. I don't have clear line of fire on him. It could go either way. If he charges, fine. But he may raise the alarm as soon as I drop the others. Better the three of us take them out at once, if you think you can move up quietly.'

The challenge in Solarion's words, not to mention his tone, could hardly be missed. Karras lifted a foot and placed it gently on the next step up. Slowly, he put his weight on it. There was a harsh grating sound.

'I said *quietly*,' hissed Solarion.

'I heard you, damn it,' Karras snapped back. Silently, he cursed the cryo-case strapped over his shoulder. Its extra weight and shifting centre of gravity was hampering him, as it had on the gantry above the squig pit, but what could he do?

'Rauth,' he said. 'Move past me. Don't touch this step. Place yourself on Solarion's left. Try to get an angle on the ork in the doorway. Solarion, open fire on Rauth's mark. You'll have to handle the other two yourself.'

'Confirmed,' rumbled Rauth. Slowly, carefully, the Exorcist moved out from behind Karras and continued climbing as quietly as he could. Flakes of rust fell from the underside of the stair like red snow.

Rauth was just ahead of Karras, barely a metre out in front, when, as he put the weight down on his right foot, the step under it gave way with a sharp snap. Rauth plunged into open space, nothing below him but two hundred metres of freefall and a lethally hard landing.

Karras moved on instinct with a speed that bordered on supernatural. His gauntleted fist shot out, catching Rauth just in time, closing around the Exorcist's left wrist with almost crushing force.

The orks turned their heads towards the sudden noise and stomped towards the top of the stairs, massive stubbers raised in front of them.

'By Guilliman's blood!' raged Solarion.

He opened fire.

The first of the orks collapsed with its brainpan blown out.

Karras was struggling to haul Rauth back onto the stairway, but the metal under his own feet, forced to support the weight of both Astartes, began to scrape clear of its fixings.

'Quickly, psyker,' gasped Rauth, 'or we'll both die.'

'Not a damned chance,' Karras growled. With a monumental effort of strength, he heaved Rauth high enough that the Exorcist could grab the staircase and scramble back onto it.

As Rauth got to his feet, he breathed, 'Thank you, Karras... but you may live to regret saving me.'

Karras was scowling furiously under his helmet. 'You may not think of me as your brother, but, at the very least, you are a member of my team. However, the next time you call me psyker with such disdain, you will be the one to regret it. Is that understood?'

Rauth glared at him for a second, then nodded once. 'Fair words.'

Karras moved past him, stepping over the broad gap then stopping at Solarion's side. On the landing ahead, he saw two ork bodies leaking copious amounts of fluid from severe head wounds.

As he looked at them, wailing alarms began to sound throughout the ship.

Solarion turned to face him. 'I told Sigma he should have put me in charge,' he hissed. 'Damn it, Karras.'

'Save it,' Karras barked. His eyes flicked to the countdown on his heads-up display. 'Thirty-three minutes left. They know we're here. The killing starts in earnest now, but we can't let them hold us up. Both of you follow me. Let's move!'

Without another word, the three Astartes pounded across the upper landing and into the mouth of the corridor down which the third ork had vanished, desperate to reach their primary objective before the whole damned horde descended on them.

'So much for keeping a low profile, eh, brother?' said Zeed as he guarded Voss's back.

A deafening, ululating wail had filled the air. Red lights began to rotate in their wall fixtures.

Voss grunted by way of response. He was concentrating hard on the task at hand. He crouched by the coolant valves of the ship's massive plasma reactor, power source for the vessel's gigantic main thrusters.

The noise in the reactor room was deafening even without the ork alarms, and none of the busy gretchin work crews had noticed the two Deathwatch members until it was too late. Zeed had hacked them limb from limb before they'd had a chance to scatter. Now that the alarm had been sounded, though, orks would be arming themselves and filling the corridors outside, each filthy alien desperate to claim a kill.

'We're done here,' said Voss, rising from his crouch. He hefted his heavy flamer from the floor and turned. 'The rest is up to Scholar and the others.'

Voss couldn't check in with them. Not from here. Such close proximity to a reactor, particularly one with so much leakage, filled the kill-team's primary comm-channels with nothing but static.

Zeed moved to the thick steel door of the reactor room, opened it a crack, and peered outside.

'It's getting busy out there,' he reported. 'Lots of mean-looking bastards, but they can hardly see with all the lights knocked out. What do you say, brother? Are you ready to paint the walls with the blood of the foe?'

Under his helmet, Voss grinned. He thumbed his heavy flamer's igniter switch and a hot blue flame burst to life just in front of the weapon's promethium nozzle. 'Always,' he said, coming abreast of the Raven Guard.

Together, the two comrades charged into the corridor, howling the names of their primarchs as battle-cries.

* * *

'We're pinned,' hissed Rauth as ork stubber and pistol fire smacked into the metal wall beside him. Pipes shattered. Iron flakes showered the ground. Karras, Rauth and Solarion had pushed as far and as fast as they could once the alarms had been tripped. But now they found themselves penned-in at a junction, a confluence of three broad corridors, and mobs of howling, jabbering orks were pouring towards them from all sides.

With his knife, Solarion had already severed the cable that powered the lights, along with a score of others that did Throne knew what. A number of the orks, however, were equipped with goggles, not to mention weapons and armour far above typical greenskin standards. Karras had fought such fiends before. They were the greenskin equivalent of commando squads, far more cunning and deadly than the usual muscle-minded oafs. Their red night-vision lenses glowed like daemons' eyes as they pressed closer and closer, keeping to cover as much as possible.

Karras and his Deathwatch Marines were outnumbered at least twenty to one, and that ratio would quickly change for the worse if they didn't break through soon.

'Orders, Karras,' growled Solarion as his right pauldron absorbed a direct hit. The ork shell left an ugly scrape on the blue and white Chapter insignia there. 'We're taking too much fire. The cover here is pitiful.'

Karras thought fast. A smokescreen would be useless. If the ork goggles were operating on thermal signatures, they would see right through it. Incendiaries or frags would kill a good score of them and dissuade the others from closing, but that wouldn't solve the problem of being pinned.

'Novas,' he told them. 'On my signal, one down each corridor. Short throws. Remember to cover your visors. The moment they detonate, we make a push. I'm taking point. Clear?'

'On your mark, Karras,' said Solarion with a nod.

'Give the word,' said Rauth.

Karras tugged a nova grenade from the webbing around his armoured waist. The others did the same. He pulled the pin, swung his arm back and called out, 'Now!'

Three small black cylinders flew through the darkness to clatter against the metal floor. Swept up in the excitement of the firefight, the orks didn't notice them.

'Eyes!' shouted Karras and threw an arm up over his visor.

Three deafening bangs sounded in quick succession, louder even than the bark of the orks' guns. Howls of agony immediately followed, filling the close, damp air of the corridors. Karras looked up to see the orks reeling around in the dark with their great, thick-fingered hands pressed to their faces. They were crashing into the walls, weapons forgotten, thrown to the floor in their agony and confusion.

Nova grenades were typically employed for room clearance, but they worked well in any dark, enclosed space. They were far from standard-issue Astartes hardware, but the Deathwatch were the elite, the best of the best, and they had access to the kind of resources that few others could boast. The intense, phosphor-bright flash that the grenades produced overloaded optical receptors, both mechanical and biological. The blindness was temporary in most cases, but Karras was betting that the orks' goggles would magnify the glare.

Their retinas would be permanently burned out.

'With me,' he barked, and charged out from his corner. He moved in a blur, fixing his silenced bolter to the mag-locks on his thigh plate and drawing his faithful force sword, Arquemann, from its scabbard as he raced towards the foe.

Rauth and Solarion came behind, but not so close as to gamble with their lives. The bite of Arquemann was certain death whenever it glowed with otherworldly energy, and it had begun to glow now, throwing out a chill, unnatural light.

Karras threw himself in among the greenskin commandos, turning great powerful arcs with his blade, despatching more xenos filth with every limb-severing stroke. Steaming corpses soon littered the floor. The orks in the corridors behind continued to flail blindly, attacking each other now, in their sightless desperation.

'The way is clear,' Karras gasped. 'We run.' He sheathed Arquemann and led the way, feet pounding on the metal deck. The cryo-case swung wildly behind him as he moved, but he paid it no mind. Beneath his helmet, his third eye was closing again. The dangerous energies that gave him his powers were retreating at his command, suppressed by the mantras that kept him strong, kept him safe.

The inquisitor's voice intruded on the comm-link. 'Alpha, this is Sigma. Respond.'

'I hear you, Sigma,' said Karras as he ran.

'Where are you now?'

'Closing on Waypoint Barrius. We're about one minute out.'

'You're falling behind, Alpha. Perhaps I should begin preparing death certificates to your respective Chapters.'

'Damn you, inquisitor. We'll make it. Now if that's all you wanted…'

'Solarion is to leave you at Barrius. I have another task for him.'

'No,' said Karras flatly. 'We're already facing heavy resistance here. I need him with me.'

'I don't make requests, Deathwatch. According to naval intelligence reports, there is a large fighter bay on the ship's starboard side. Significant fuel dumps. Give Solarion your explosives. I want him to knock out that fighter bay while you and Rauth proceed to the bridge. If all goes well, the diversion may help clear your escape route. If not, you had better start praying for a miracle.'

'Rauth will blow the fuel dumps,' said Karras, opting to test a hunch.

'No,' said Sigma. 'Solarion is better acquainted with operating alone.'

Karras wondered about Sigma's insistence that Solarion go. Rauth hardly ever let Karras out of his sight. It had been that way ever since they'd met. Little wonder, then, that Zeed had settled on the nickname '*Watcher*'. Was Sigma behind it all? Karras couldn't be sure. The inquisitor had a point about Solarion's solo skills, and he knew it.

'Fine, I'll give Solarion the new orders.'

'No,' said Sigma. 'I'll do it directly. You and Rauth must hurry to the command bridge. Expect to lose comms once you get closer to the target. I'm sure you've sensed the creature's incredible power already. I want that thing eliminated, Alpha. Do not fail me.'

'When have I ever?' Karras retorted, but Sigma had already cut the link. Judging by Solarion's body language as he ran, the inquisitor was already giving him his new orders.

At the next junction, Waypoint Barrius, the trio encountered another ork mob. But the speed at which Karras and his men were moving caught the orks by surprise. Karras didn't even have time to charge his blade with psychic energy before he was in among them, hacking and thrusting. Arquemann was lethally sharp even without the power of the immaterium running through it, and orks fell in a great tide of blood. Silenced bolters coughed on either side of him, Solarion and Rauth giving fire support, and soon the junction was heaped with twitching green meat.

Karras turned to Rauth. 'Give Solarion your frags and incendiaries,' he said, pulling his own from his webbing. 'But keep two breaching charges. We'll need them.'

Solarion accepted the grenades, quickly fixing them to his belt, then he said, 'Good hunting, brothers.'

Karras nodded. 'We'll rendezvous back at the elevator shaft. Whoever gets there first holds it until the others arrive. Keep the comm-link open. If it goes dead for more than ten minutes at our end, don't waste any time. Rendezvous with Voss and Zeed and get to the salvage bay.'

Solarion banged a fist on his breastplate in salute and turned.

Karras nodded to Rauth. 'Let's go,' he said, and together, they ran on towards the fore section of the ship while Solarion merged with the shadows in the other direction.

* * *

'Die!' spat Zeed as another massive greenskin slid to the floor, its body opened from gullet to groin. Then he was moving again. Instincts every bit as sharp as his lightning claws told him to sidestep just in time to avoid the stroke of a giant chainaxe that would have cleaved him in two. The ork wielding the axe roared in frustration as its whirring blade bit into the metal floor, sending up a shower of orange sparks. It made a grab for Zeed with its empty hand, but Zeed parried, slipped inside at the same instant, and thrust his right set of claws straight up under the creature's jutting jaw. The tips of the long slender blades punched through the top of its skull, and it stood there quivering, literally dead on its feet.

Zeed stepped back, wrenching his claws from the creature's throat, and watched its body drop beside the others.

He looked around hungrily, eager for another opponent to step forward, but there were none to be had. Voss and he stood surrounded by dead xenos. The Imperial Fist had already lowered his heavy flamer. He stood admiring his handiwork, a small hill of smoking black corpses. The two comrades had fought their way back to Waypoint Adrius. The air in the towering chamber was now thick with the stink of spilled blood and burnt flesh.

Zeed looked up at the landings overhead and said, 'No sign of the others.'

Voss moved up beside him. 'There's much less static on the comm-link here. Scholar, this is Omni. If you can hear me, respond.'

At first there was no answer. Voss was about to try again when the Death Spectre Librarian finally acknowledged. 'I hear you, Omni. This isn't the best time.'

Karras sounded strained, as if fighting for his life.

'We are finished with the reactor,' Voss reported. 'Back at Waypoint Adrius, now. Do you need assistance?'

As he asked this, Voss automatically checked the mission countdown.

Not good.

Twenty-seven minutes left.

'Hold that position,' Karras grunted. 'We need to keep that area secure for our escape. Rauth and I are–'

His words were cut off in mid-sentence. For a brief instant, Voss and Zeed thought the kill-team leader had been hit, possibly even killed. But their fears were allayed when Karras heaved a sigh of relief and said, 'Damn, those bastards were strong. Ghost, you would have enjoyed that. Listen, brothers, Rauth and I are outside the ship's command bridge. Time is running out. If we don't make it back to Waypoint Adrius within the next twelve minutes, I want the rest of you to pull out. Do *not* miss the pick-up. Is that understood?'

Voss scowled. The words *pull out* made him want to smash something. As far as his Chapter was concerned, they were curse words. But he knew Karras was right. There was little to be gained by dying here. 'Emperor's speed, Scholar,' he said.

'For Terra and the Throne,' Karras replied then signed off.

Zeed was scraping his claws together restlessly, a bad habit that manifested itself when he had excess adrenaline and no further outlet for it. 'Damn,' he said. 'I'm not standing around here while the others are fighting for their lives.' He pointed to the metal landing high above him where Karras and the others had gotten off the elevator. 'There has to be a way to call that piece of junk back down to this level. We can ride it up there and–'

He was interrupted by the clatter of heavy, iron-shod boots closing from multiple directions. The sounds echoed into the chamber from a dozen corridor mouths.

'I think we're about to be too busy for that, brother,' said Voss darkly.

Rauth stepped over the body of the massive ork guard he had just slain, flicked the beast's blood from the groove on his shortsword, and sheathed it at his side. There was a shallow crater in the ceramite of his right pauldron. Part of his Chapter icon was missing, cleaved off in the fight. The daemon-skull design now boasted only a single horn. The other pauldron, intricately detailed with the skull, bones and inquisitorial 'I' of the Deathwatch, was chipped and scraped, but had suffered no serious damage.

'That's the biggest I've slain hand-to-hand,' the Exorcist muttered, mostly to himself.

The one Karras had just slain was no smaller, but the Death Spectre was focused on something else. He was standing with one hand pressed to a massive steel blast door covered in orkish glyphs. Tiny lambent arcs of unnatural energy flickered around him.

'There's a tremendous amount of psychic interference,' he said, 'but I sense at least thirty of them on this level. Our target is on the upper deck. And he knows we're here.'

Rauth nodded, but said nothing. *We?* No. Karras was wrong in that. Rauth knew well enough that the target couldn't have sensed him. Nothing psychic could. It was a side effect of the unspeakable horrors he had endured during his Chapter's selection and training programmes – programmes that had taught him to hate all psykers and the terrible daemons their powers sometimes loosed into the galaxy.

The frequency with which Lyandro Karras tapped the power of the immaterium disgusted Rauth. Did the Librarian not realise the great peril in which he placed his soul? Or was he simply a fool, spilling over with an arrogance that invited the ultimate calamity. Daemons of the warp rejoiced in the folly of such men.

Of course, that was why Rauth had been sequestered to Deathwatch in the first place. The inquisitor had never said so explicitly, but it simply had to be the case. As enigmatic as Sigma was, he was clearly no fool. Who better than an Exorcist to watch over one such as Karras? Even the mighty Grey Knights, from whose seed Rauth's Chapter had been born, could hardly have been more suited to the task.

'Smoke,' said Karras. 'The moment we breach, I want smoke grenades in there. Don't spare them for later. Use what we have. We go in with bolters blazing. Remove your suppressor. There's no need for it now. Let them hear the bark of our guns. The minute the lower floor is cleared, we each take a side stair to the command deck. You go left. I'll take the right. We'll find the target at the top.'

'Bodyguards?' asked Rauth. Like Karras, he began unscrewing the sound suppressor from the barrel of his bolter.

'I can't tell. If there are, the psychic resonance is blotting them out. It's... incredible.'

The two Astartes stored their suppressors in pouches on their webbing, then Rauth fixed a rectangular breaching charge to the seam between the double doors. The Exorcist was about to step back when Karras said, 'No, brother. We'll need two. These doors are stronger than you think.'

Rauth fixed another charge just below the first, then he and Karras moved to either side of the doorway and pressed their backs to the wall.

Simultaneously, they checked the magazines in their bolters. Rauth slid in a fresh clip. Karras tugged a smoke grenade from his webbing, and nodded.

'Now!'

Rauth pressed the tiny detonator switch in his hand, and the whole corridor shook with a deafening blast to rival the boom of any artillery piece. The heavy doors blew straight into the room, causing immediate casualties among the orks closest to the explosion.

'Smoke!' ordered Karras as he threw his first grenade. Rauth discarded the detonator and did the same. Two, three, four small canisters bounced onto the ship's bridge, spread just enough to avoid redundancy. Within two seconds, the whole deck was covered in a dense grey cloud. The ork crew went into an uproar, barely able to see their hands in front of their faces. But to the Astartes, all was perfectly clear. They entered the room with bolters firing, each shot a vicious bark, and the greenskins fell where they stood.

Not a single bolt was wasted. Every last one found its target, every shot a headshot, an instant kill. In the time it took to draw three breaths, the lower floor of the bridge was cleared of threats.

'Move!' said Karras, making for the stair that jutted from the right-hand wall.

The smoke had begun to billow upwards now, thinning as it did.

Rauth stormed the left-side stair.

Neither Space Marine, however, was entirely prepared for what he found at the top.

Solarion burst from the mouth of the corridor and sprinted along the metal landing in the direction of the elevator cage. He was breathing hard, and rivulets of red blood ran from grape-sized holes in the armour of his torso and left upper arm. If he could only stop, the wounds would quickly seal themselves, but there was no time for that. His normally dormant second heart was pumping in tandem with the first, flushing lactic acid from his muscles, helping him to keep going. Following barely a second behind him, a great mob of armoured orks with heavy pistols and blades surged out of the same corridor in hot pursuit. The platform trembled under their tremendous weight.

Solarion didn't stop to look behind. Just ahead of him, the upper section of the landing ended. Beyond it was the rusted stairway that had almost claimed Rauth's life. There was no time now to navigate those stairs.

He put on an extra burst of speed and leapt straight out over them.

It was an impressive jump. For a moment, he almost seemed to fly. Then he passed the apex of his jump and the ship's artificial gravity started to pull him downwards. He landed on the lower section of the landing with a loud clang. Sharp spears of pain shot up the nerves in his legs, but he ignored them and turned, bolter held ready at his shoulder.

The orks were following his example, leaping from the upper platform, hoping to land right beside him and cut him to pieces. Their lack of agility, however, betrayed them. The first row crashed down onto the rickety stairs about two thirds of the way down. The old iron steps couldn't take that kind of punishment. They crumbled and snapped, dropping the luckless orks into lethal freefall. The air filled with howls, but the others didn't catch on until it was too late. They, too, leapt from the platform's edge in their eagerness to make a kill. Step after step gave way with each heavy body that crashed down on it, and soon the stairway was reduced almost to nothing.

A broad chasm, some thirty metres across, now separated the metal platforms that had been joined by the stairs. The surviving orks saw that they couldn't follow the Space Marine across. Instead, they paced the edge of the upper platform, bellowing at Solarion in outrage and frustration and taking wild potshots at him with their clunky pistols.

'It's raining greenskins,' said a gruff voice on the link. 'What in Dorn's name is going on up there?'

With one eye still on the pacing orks, Solarion moved to the edge of the platform. As he reached the twisted railing, he looked out over the edge and down towards the steel floor two-hundred metres below. Gouts of bright promethium flame illuminated a conflict there. Voss and Zeed were standing back to back, about five metres apart, fighting off an ork assault from all sides. The floor around them was heaped with dead aliens.

'This is Solarion,' the Ultramarine told them. 'Do you need aid, brothers?'

'Prophet?' said Zeed between lethal sweeps of his claws. 'Where are Scholar and Watcher?'

'You've had no word?' asked Solarion.

'They've been out of contact since they entered the command bridge. Sigma warned of that. But time is running out. Can you go to them?'

'Impossible,' replied Solarion. 'The stairs are gone. I can't get back up there now.'

'Then pray for them,' said Voss.

Solarion checked his mission chrono. He remembered Karras's orders. Four more minutes. After that, he would have to assume they were dead. He would take the elevator down and, with the others, strike out for the salvage bay and their only hope of escape.

A shell from an ork pistol ricocheted from the platform and smacked against his breastplate. The shot wasn't powerful enough to penetrate ceramite, not like the heavy-stubber shells he had taken at close range, but it got his attention. He was about to return fire, to start clearing the upper platform in anticipation of Karras and Rauth's return, when a great boom shook the air and sent deep vibrations through the metal under his feet.

'That's not one of mine,' said Voss.

'It's mine,' said Solarion. 'I rigged the fuel dump in their fighter bay. If we're lucky, most of the greenskins will be drawn there, thinking that's where the conflict is. It might buy our brothers a little time.'

The mission chrono now read eighteen minutes and forty seconds. He watched it drop. Thirty-nine seconds. Thirty-eight. Thirty-seven.

Come on, Karras, he thought. What in Terra's name are you doing?

Karras barely had time to register the sheer size of Balthazog Bludwrekk's twin bodyguards before their blistering assault began. They were easily the largest orks he had ever seen, even larger than the door guards he and Rauth had slain, and they wielded their massive two-handed warhammers as if they weighed nothing at all. Under normal circumstances, orks of this size and strength would have become mighty warbosses, but these two were nothing of the kind. They were slaves to a far greater power than mere muscle or aggression. They were mindless puppets held in servitude by a much deadlier force, and the puppeteer himself sat some ten metres behind them, perched on a bizarre mechanical throne in the centre of the ship's command deck.

Bludwrekk!

Karras only needed an instant, a fraction of a second, to take in the details of the fiend's appearance.

Even for an ork, the psychic warboss was hideous. Portions of his head were vastly swollen, with great vein-marbled bumps extending out in all directions from his crown. His brow was ringed with large, blood-stained metal plugs sunk deep into the bone of his skull. The beast's leering, lopsided face was twisted, like something seen in a curved mirror, the features pathetically small on one side, grotesquely overlarge on the other, and saliva dripped from his slack jaw, great strands of it hanging from the spaces between his tusks.

He wore a patchwork robe of cured human skins stitched together with gut, and a trio of decaying heads hung between his knees, fixed to his belt by long, braided hair. Karras had the immediate impression that the heads had been taken from murdered women, perhaps the wives of some human lord or tribal leader that the beast had slain during a raid. Orks had a known fondness for such grisly trophies.

The beast's throne was just as strange; a mass of coils, cogs and moving pistons without any apparent purpose whatsoever. Thick bundles of wire linked it to an inexplicable clutter of vast, arcane machines that crackled and hummed with sickly green light. In the instant Karras took all this in, he felt his anger and hate break over him like a thunderstorm.

It was as if this creature, this blasted aberration, sat in sickening, blasphemous parody of the immortal Emperor Himself.

The two Space Marines opened fire at the same time, eager to drop the bodyguards and engage the real target quickly. Their bolters chattered, spitting their deadly hail, but somehow each round detonated harmlessly in the air.

'He's shielding them!' Karras called out. 'Draw your blade!'

He dropped the cryo-case from his shoulder, pulled Arquemann from its scabbard and let the power of the immaterium flow through him, focusing it into the ancient crystalline matrix that lay embedded in the blade.

'To me, xenos scum!' he roared at the hulking beast in front of him.

The bodyguard's massive hammer whistled up into the air, then changed direction with a speed that seemed impossible. Karras barely managed to step aside. Sparks flew as the weapon clipped his left pauldron, sending a painful shock along his arm. The thick steel floor fared worse. The hammer left a hole in it the size of a human head.

On his right, Karras heard Rauth loose a great battle-cry as he clashed with his own opponent, barely ducking a lateral blow that would have taken his head clean off. The Exorcist's short-sword looked awfully small compared to his enemy's hammer.

Bludwrekk was laughing, revelling in the life and death struggle that was playing out before him, as if it were some kind of grand entertainment laid on just for him. The more he cackled, the more the green light seemed to shimmer and churn around him. Karras felt the resonance of that power disorienting him. The air was supercharged with it. He felt his own power surging up inside him, rising to meet it. Only so much could be channelled into his force sword. Already, the blade sang with deadly energy as it slashed through the air.

This surge is dangerous, he warned himself. *I mustn't let it get out of control.*

Automatically, he began reciting the mantras Master Cordatus had taught him, but the effort of wrestling to maintain his equilibrium cost him an opening in which he could have killed his foe with a stroke. The ork bodyguard, on the other hand, did not miss its chance. It caught Karras squarely on the right pauldron with the head of its hammer, shattering the Deathwatch insignia there, and knocking him sideways, straight off his feet.

The impact hurled Karras directly into Rauth's opponent, and the two tumbled to the metal floor. Karras's helmet was torn from his head, and rolled away. In the sudden tangle of thrashing Space Marine and ork bodies, Rauth saw an opening. He stepped straight in, plunging his shortsword up under the beast's sternum, shoving it deep, cleaving the ork's heart in two. Without hesitation, he then turned to face the remaining bodyguard while Karras kicked himself clear of the dead behemoth and got to his feet.

The last bodyguard was fast, and Rauth did well to stay clear of the whistling hammerhead, but the stabbing and slashing strokes of his shortsword were having little effect. It was only when Karras joined him, and the ork was faced with attacks from two directions at once, that the tables truly turned. Balthazog Bludwrekk had stopped laughing now. He gave a deafening roar of anger as Rauth and Karras thrust from opposite angles and, between them, pierced the greenskin's heart and lungs.

Blood bubbled from its wounds as it sank to the floor, dropping its mighty hammer with a crash.

Bludwrekk surged upwards from his throne. Arcs of green lightning lanced outwards from his fingers. Karras felt Waaagh! energy lick his armour, looking for chinks through which it might burn his flesh and corrode his soul. Together, blades raised, he and Rauth rounded on their foe.

The moment they stepped forward to engage, however, a great torrent of kinetic energy burst from the ork's outstretched hands and launched Rauth into the air. Karras ducked and rolled sideways, narrowly avoiding death, but he heard Rauth land with a heavy crash on the lower floor of the bridge.

'Rauth!' he shouted over the link. 'Answer!'

No answer was forthcoming. The comm-link was useless here. And perhaps Rauth was already dead.

Karras felt the ork's magnified power pressing in on him from all sides, and now he saw its source. Behind Bludwrekk's mechanical throne, beyond a filthy, blood-spattered window of thick glass, there were hundreds – no, thousands – of orks strapped to vertical slabs that looked like operating tables. The tops of their skulls had been removed, and cables and tubes ran from their exposed brains to the core of a vast power-siphoning system.

'By the Golden Throne,' gasped Karras. 'No wonder Sigma wants your ugly head.'

How much time remained before the ship's reactors detonated? Without his helmet, he couldn't tell. Long enough to kill this monstrosity? Maybe. But, one on one, was he even a match for the thing?

Not without exploiting more of the dangerous power at his disposal. He had to trust in his master's teachings. The mantras would keep him safe. They had to. He opened himself up to the warp a little more, channelling it, focusing it with his mind.

Bludwrekk stepped forward to meet him, and the two powers clashed with apocalyptic fury.

Darrion Rauth was not dead. The searing impact of the ork warlord's psychic blast would have killed a lesser man on contact, ripping his soul from his body and leaving it a lifeless hunk of meat. But Rauth was no lesser man. The secret rites of his Chapter, and the suffering he had endured to earn his place in it, had proofed him against such a fate. Also, though a number of his bones were broken, his superhuman physiology was already about the business of reknitting them, making them whole and strong again. The internal bleeding would stop soon, too.

But there wasn't time to heal completely. Not if he wanted to make a difference.

With a grunt of pain, he rolled, pushed himself to one knee, and looked for his shortsword. He couldn't see it. His bolter, however, was still attached to his thigh plate. He tugged it free, slammed in a fresh magazine, cocked it, and struggled to his feet. He coughed wetly, tasting blood in his mouth. Looking up towards the place from which he had been thrown, he saw unnatural light blazing and strobing. There was a great deal of noise, too, almost like thunder, but not quite the same. It made the air tremble around him.

Karras must still be alive, he thought. He's still fighting.

Pushing aside the agony in his limbs, he ran to the stairs on his right and, with an ancient litany of strength on his lips, charged up them to rejoin the battle.

Karras was failing. He could feel it. Balthazog Bludwrekk was drawing on an incredible reserve of power. The psychic Waaagh! energy he was tapping seemed boundless, pouring into the warlord from the brains of the tormented orks wired into his insane contraption.

Karras cursed as he struggled to turn aside another wave of roiling green fire. It buckled the deck plates all around him. Only those beneath his feet, those that fell inside the shimmering bubble he fought to maintain, remained undamaged.

His shield was holding, but only just, and the effort required to maintain it precluded him from launching attacks of his own. Worse yet, as the ork warlord pressed his advantage, Karras was forced to let the power of the warp flow through him more and more. A cacophony of voices had risen in his head, chittering and whispering in tongues he knew were blasphemous. This was the moment all Librarians feared, when the power they wielded threatened to consume them, when user became used, master became slave. The voices started to drown out his own. Much more of this and his soul would be lost for eternity, ripped from him and thrown into the maelstrom. Daemons would wrestle for command of his mortal flesh.

Was it right to slay this ork at the cost of his immortal soul? Should he not simply drop his shield and die so that something far worse than Bludwrekk would be denied entry into the material universe?

Karras could barely hear these questions in his head. So many other voices crowded them out.

Balthazog Bludwrekk seemed to sense the moment was his. He stepped nearer, still trailing thick cables from the metal plugs in his distorted skull.

Karras sank to one knee under the onslaught to both body and mind. His protective bubble was dissipating. Only seconds remained. One way or another, he realised, he was doomed.

Bludwrekk was almost on him now, still throwing green

lightning from one hand, drawing a long, curved blade with the other. Glistening strands of drool shone in the fierce green light. His eyes were ablaze.

Karras sagged, barely able to hold himself upright, leaning heavily on the sword his mentor had given him.

I am Lyandro Karras, he tried to think. Librarian. Death Spectre. Space Marine. The Emperor will not let me fall.

But his inner voice was faint. Bludwrekk was barely two metres away. His psychic assault pierced Karras's shield. The Codicer felt the skin on his arms blazing and crisping. His nerves began to scream.

In his mind, one voice began to dominate the others. Was this the voice of the daemon that would claim him? It was so loud and clear that it seemed to issue from the very air around him. 'Get up, Karras!' it snarled. 'Fight!'

He realised it was speaking in High Gothic. He hadn't expected that.

His vision was darkening, despite the green fire that blazed all around, but, distantly, he caught a flicker of movement to his right. A hulking black figure appeared as if from nowhere, weapon raised before it. There was something familiar about it, an icon on the left shoulder; a skull with a single gleaming red eye.

Rauth!

The Exorcist's bolter spat a torrent of shells, forcing Balthazog Bludwrekk to spin and defend himself, concentrating all his psychic power on stopping the stream of deadly bolts.

Karras acted without pause for conscious thought. He moved on reflex, conditioned by decades of harsh daily training rituals.

With Bludwrekk's merciless assault momentarily halted, he surged upwards, putting all his strength into a single horizontal swing of his force sword. The warp energy he had been trying to marshal crashed over him, flooding into the crystalline matrix of his blade as the razor-edged metal bit deep into the ork's thick green neck.

The monster didn't even have time to scream. Body and head fell in separate directions, the green light vanished, and the upper bridge was suddenly awash with steaming ork blood.

Karras fell to his knees, and screamed, dropping Arquemann at his side. His fight wasn't over. Not yet.

Now, he turned his attention to the battle for his soul.

Rauth saw all too clearly that his moment had come, as he had known it must, sooner or later, but he couldn't relish it. There was no joy to be had here. Psyker or not, Lyandro Karras was a Space Marine, a son of the Emperor just as he was himself, and he had saved Rauth's life.

But you must do it for him, Rauth told himself. You must do it to save his soul.

Out of respect, Rauth took off his helmet so that he might bear witness to the Death Spectre's final moments with his own naked eyes. Grimacing, he raised the barrel of his bolter to Karras's temple and began reciting the words of the *Mortis Morgatii Praetovo*. It was an ancient rite from long before the Great Crusade, forgotten by all save the Exorcists and the Grey Knights. If it worked, it would send Karras's spiritual essence beyond the reach of the warp's ravenous fiends, but it could not save his life.

It was not a long rite, and Rauth recited it perfectly.

As he came to the end of it, he prepared to squeeze the trigger.

War raged inside Lyandro Karras. Sickening entities filled with hate and hunger strove to overwhelm him. They were brutal and relentless, bombarding him with unholy visions that threatened to drown him in horror and disgust. He saw Imperial saints defiled and mutilated on altars of burning black rock. He saw the Golden Throne smashed and ruined, and the body of the Emperor trampled under the feet of vile capering beasts. He saw his Chapter house sundered, its walls covered in weeping sores as if the stones themselves had contracted a vile disease.

He cried out, railing against the visions, denying them. But still they came. He scrambled for something Cordatus had told him.

Cordatus!

The thought of that name alone gave him the strength to keep up the fight, if only for a moment. To avoid becoming lost in the empyrean, the old warrior had said, one must anchor oneself to the physical.

Karras reached for the physical now, for something real, a bastion against the visions.

He found it in a strange place, in a sensation he couldn't quite explain. Something hot and metallic was pressing hard against the skin of his temple.

The metal was scalding him, causing him physical pain. Other pains joined it, accumulating so that the song of agony his nerves were singing became louder and louder. He felt again the pain of his burned hands, even while his gene-boosted body worked fast to heal them. He clutched at the pain, letting the sensation pull his mind back to the moment, to the here and now. He grasped it like a rock in a storm-tossed sea.

The voices of the vile multitude began to weaken. He heard his own inner voice again, and immediately resumed his mantras. Soon enough, the energy of the immaterium slowed to a trickle, then ceased completely. He felt the physical manifestation of his third eye closing. He felt the skin knitting on his brow once again.

What was it, he wondered, this hot metal pressed to his head, this thing that had saved him?

He opened his eyes and saw the craggy, battle-scarred features of Darrion Rauth. The Exorcist was standing very close, helmet at his side, muttering something that sounded like a prayer.

His bolter was pressed to Karras's head, and he was about to blow his brains out.

'What are you doing?' Karras asked quietly.

Rauth looked surprised to hear his voice.

'I'm saving your soul, Death Spectre. Be at peace. Your honour will be spared. The daemons of the warp will not have you.'

'That is good to know,' said Karras. 'Now lower your weapon. My soul is exactly where it should be, and there it stays until my service to the Emperor is done.'

For a moment, neither Rauth nor Karras moved. The Exorcist did not seem convinced.

'Darrion Rauth,' said Karras. 'Are you so eager to spill my blood? Is this why you have shadowed my every movement for the last three years? Perhaps Solarion would thank you for killing me, but I don't think Sigma would.'

'That would depend,' Rauth replied. Hesitantly, however, he lowered his gun. 'You will submit to proper testing when we return to the *Saint Nevarre*. Sigma will insist on it, and so shall I.'

'As is your right, brother, but be assured that you will find no taint. Of course it won't matter either way unless we get off this ship alive. Quickly now, grab the monster's head. I will open the cryo-case.'

Rauth did as ordered, though he kept a wary eye on the kill-team leader. Lifting Bludwrekk's lifeless head, he offered it to Karras, saying, 'The machinery that boosted Bludwrekk's power should be analysed. If other ork psykers begin to employ such things…'

Karras took the ork's head from him, placed it inside the black case, and pressed a four-digit code into the keypad on the side. The lid fused itself shut with a hiss. Karras rose, slung it over his right shoulder, sheathed Arquemann, located his helmet, and fixed it back on his head. Rauth donned his own helmet, too.

'If Sigma wanted the machine,' said Karras as he led his comrade off the command bridge, 'he would have said so.'

Glancing at the mission chrono, he saw that barely seventeen minutes remained until the exfiltration deadline. He doubted it would be enough to escape the ship, but he wasn't about to give up without trying. Not after all they had been through here.

'Can you run?' he asked Rauth.

* * *

'Time is up,' said Solarion grimly. He stood in front of the open elevator cage. 'They're not going to make it. I'm coming down.'

'No,' said Voss. 'Give them another minute, Prophet.'

Voss and Zeed had finished slaughtering their attackers on the lower floor. It was just as well, too. Voss had used up the last of his promethium fuel in the fight. With great regret, he had slung the fuel pack off his back and relinquished the powerful weapon. He drew his support weapon, a bolt pistol, from a holster on his webbing.

It felt pathetically small and light in his hand.

'Would you have us all die here, brother?' asked the Ultramarine. 'For no gain? Because that will be our lot if we don't get moving right now.'

'If only we had heard *something* on the link...' said Zeed. 'Omni, as much as I hate to say it, Prophet has a point.'

'Believe me,' said Solarion, 'I wish it were otherwise. As of this moment, however, it seems only prudent that I assume operational command. Sigma, if you are listening–'

A familiar voice cut him off.

'Wait until my boots have cooled before you step into them, Solarion!'

'Scholar!' exclaimed Zeed. 'And is Watcher with you?'

'How many times must I warn you, Raven Guard,' said the Exorcist. 'Don't call me that.'

'At least another hundred,' replied Zeed.

'Karras,' said Voss, 'where in Dorn's name are you?'

'Almost at the platform now,' said Karras. 'We've got company. Ork commandos closing the distance from the rear.'

'Keep your speed up,' said Solarion. 'The stairs are out. You'll have to jump. The gap is about thirty metres.'

'Understood,' said Karras. 'Coming out of the corridor now.'

Solarion could hear the thunder of heavy feet pounding the upper metal platform from which he had so recently leaped. He watched from beside the elevator, and saw two bulky black figures soar out into the air.

Karras landed first, coming down hard. The cryo-case came free of his shoulder and skidded across the metal floor towards the edge. Solarion saw it and moved automatically, stopping it with one booted foot before it slid over the side.

Rauth landed a second later, slamming onto the platform in a heap. He gave a grunt of pain, pushed himself up and limped past Solarion into the elevator cage.

'Are you wounded, brother?' asked the Ultramarine.

'It is nothing,' growled Rauth.

Karras and Solarion joined him in the cage. The kill-team leader pulled the lever, starting them on their downward journey.

The cage started slowly at first, but soon gathered speed. Halfway down, the heavy counterweight again whooshed past them.

'Ghost, Omni,' said Karras over the link. 'Start clearing the route towards the salvage bay. We'll catch up with you as soon as we're at the bottom.'

'Loud and clear, Scholar,' said Zeed. He and Voss disappeared off into the darkness of the corridor through which the kill-team had originally come.

Suddenly, Rauth pointed upwards. 'Trouble,' he said.

Karras and Solarion looked up.

Some of the ork commandos, those more resourceful than their kin, had used grapnels to cross the gap in the platforms. Now they were hacking at the elevator cables with their broad blades.

'Solarion,' said Karras.

He didn't need to say anything else. The Ultramarine raised his bolter, sighted along the barrel, and began firing up at the orks. Shots sparked from the metal around the greenskins' heads, but it was hard to fire accurately with the elevator shaking and shuddering throughout its descent.

Rauth stepped forward and ripped the latticework gate from its hinges. 'We should jump the last twenty metres,' he said.

Solarion stopped firing. 'Agreed.'

Karras looked down from the edge of the cage floor. 'Forty metres,' he said. 'Thirty-five. Thirty. Twenty-five. Go!'

Together, the three Astartes leapt clear of the elevator and landed on the metal floor below. Again, Rauth gave a pained grunt, but he was up just as fast as the others.

Behind them, the elevator cage slammed into the floor with a mighty clang. Karras turned just in time to see the heavy counterweight smash down on top of it. The orks had cut the cables after all. Had the three Space Marines stayed in the cage until it reached the bottom, they would have been crushed to a fleshy pulp.

'Ten minutes left,' said Karras, adjusting the cryo-case on his shoulder. 'In the Emperor's name, run!'

Karras, Rauth and Solarion soon caught up with Voss and Zeed. There wasn't time to move carefully now, but Karras dreaded getting caught up in another firefight. That would surely doom them. Perhaps the saints were smiling on him, though, because it seemed that most of the orks in the sections between the central shaft and the prow had responded to the earlier alarms and had already been slain by Zeed and Voss.

The corridors were comparatively empty, but the large mess room with its central squig pit was not.

The Space Marines charged straight in, this time on ground level, and opened fire with their bolters, cutting down the orks that were directly in their way. With his beloved blade, Karras hacked down all who stood before him, always maintaining his forward momentum, never stopping for a moment. In a matter of seconds, the kill-team crossed the mess hall and plunged into the shadowy corridor on the far side.

A great noise erupted behind them. Those orks that had not been killed or injured were taking up weapons and following close by. Their heavy, booted feet shook the grillework floors of the corridor as they swarmed along it.

'Omni,' said Karras, feet hammering the metal floor, 'the moment we reach the bay, I want you to ready the shuttle. Do not stop to engage, is that clear?'

If Karras had been expecting some argument from the Imperial Fist, he was surprised. Voss acknowledged the order without dispute. The whole team had made it this far by the skin of their teeth, but he knew it would count for absolutely nothing if their shuttle didn't get clear of the ork ship in time.

Up ahead, just over Solarion's shoulder, Karras saw the light of the salvage bay. Then, in another few seconds, they were out of the corridor and charging through the mountains of scrap towards the large piece of starship wreckage in which they had stolen aboard.

There was a crew of gretchin around it, working feverishly with wrenches and hammers that looked far too big for their sinewy little bodies. Some even had blowtorches and were cutting through sections of the outer plate.

Damn them, cursed Karras. If they've damaged any of our critical systems…

Bolters spat, and the gretchin dropped in a red mist.

'Omni, get those systems running,' Karras ordered. 'We'll hold them off.'

Voss tossed Karras his bolt pistol as he ran past, then disappeared into the doorway in the side of the ruined prow.

Karras saw Rauth and Solarion open fire as the first of the pursuing orks charged in. At first, they came in twos and threes. Then they came in a great flood. Empty magazines fell to the scrap-covered floor, to be replaced by others that were quickly spent.

Karras drew his own bolt pistol from its holster and joined the firefight, wielding one in each hand. Orks fell before him with gaping exit wounds in their heads.

'I'm out!' yelled Solarion, drawing his shortsword.

'Dry,' called Rauth seconds later and did the same.

Frenzied orks continued to pour in, firing their guns and waving their oversized blades, despite the steadily growing number of their dead that they had to trample over.

'Blast it!' cursed Karras. 'Talk to me, Omni.'

'Forty seconds,' answered the Imperial Fist. 'Coils at sixty per cent.'

Karras's bolt pistols clicked empty within two rounds of each other. He holstered his own, fixed Voss's to a loop on his webbing, drew Arquemann and called to the others, 'Into the shuttle, now. We'll have to take our chances.'

And hope they don't cut through to our fuel lines, he thought sourly.

One member of the kill-team, however, didn't seem to like those odds much.

'They're mine!' Zeed roared, and he threw himself in among the orks, cutting and stabbing in a battle-fury, dropping the giant alien savages like flies. Karras felt a flash of anger, but he marvelled at the way the Raven Guard moved, as if every single flex of muscle and claw was part of a dance that sent xenos filth howling to their deaths.

Zeed's armour was soon drenched in blood, and still he fought, swiping this way and that, always moving in perpetual slaughter, as if he were a tireless engine of death.

'Plasma coils at eighty per cent,' Voss announced. 'What are we waiting on, Scholar?'

Solarion and Rauth had already broken from the orks they were fighting and had raced inside, but Karras hovered by the door.

Zeed was still fighting.

'Ghost,' shouted Karras. 'Fall back, damn you.'

Zeed didn't seem to hear him, and the seconds kept ticking away. Any moment now, Karras knew, the ork ship's reactor would explode. Voss had seen to that. Death would take all of them if they didn't leave right now.

'Raven Guard!' Karras roared.

That did it.

Zeed plunged his lightning claws deep into the belly of one last ork, gutted him, then turned and raced towards Karras.

When they were through the door, Karras thumped the locking mechanism with the heel of his fist. 'You're worse than Omni,' he growled at the Raven Guard. Then, over the comm-link, he said, 'Blow the piston charges and get us out of here fast.'

He heard the sound of ork blades and hammers battering the hull as the orks tried to hack their way inside. The shuttle door would hold but, if Voss didn't get them out of the salvage bay soon, they would go up with the rest of the ship.

'Detonating charges now,' said the Imperial Fist.

In the salvage bay, the packages he had fixed to the big pistons and cables on either side of the bay at the start of the mission exploded, shearing straight through the metal.

There was a great metallic screeching sound and the whole floor of the salvage bay began to shudder. Slowly, the ork ship's gigantic mouth fell open, and the cold void of space rushed in, stealing away the breathable atmosphere. Everything inside the salvage bay, both animate and inanimate, was blown out of the gigantic mouth, as if snatched up by a mighty hurricane. Anything that hit the great triangular teeth on the way out went into a wild spin. Karras's team was lucky. Their craft missed clipping the upper front teeth by less than a metre.

'Shedding the shell,' said Voss, 'in three... two... one...'

He hit a button on the pilot's console that fired a series of explosive bolts, and the wrecked prow façade fragmented and fell away, the pieces drifting off into space like metal blossoms on a breeze. The shuttle beneath was now revealed – a sleek, black wedge-shaped craft bearing the icons of both the Ordo Xenos and the Inquisition proper. All around it, metal debris and rapidly freezing ork bodies spun in zero gravity.

Inside the craft, Karras, Rauth, Solarion and Zeed fixed their weapons on storage racks, sat in their respective places, and locked themselves into impact frames.

'Hold on to something,' said Voss from the cockpit as he fired the ship's plasma thrusters.

The shuttle leapt forward, accelerating violently just as the stern of the massive ork ship exploded. There was a blinding flash of yellow light that outshone even the local star. Then a series of secondary explosions erupted, blowing each section of the vast metal monstrosity apart, from aft to fore, in a great chain of utter destruction. Twenty thousand ork lives were snuffed out in a matter of seconds, reduced to their component atoms in the plasma-charged blasts.

Aboard the shuttle, Zeed removed his helmet and shook out his long black hair. With a broad grin, he said, 'Damn, but I fought well today.'

Karras might have grinned at the Raven Guard's exaggerated arrogance, but not this time. His mood was dark, despite their survival. Sigma had asked a lot this time. He looked down at the black surface of the cryo-case between his booted feet.

Zeed followed his gaze. 'We got what we came for, right, Scholar?' he asked.

Karras nodded.

'Going to let me see it?'

Zeed hated the ordo's need-to-know policies, hated not knowing exactly why Talon squad was put on the line, time after time. Karras could identify with that. Maybe they all could. But curiosity brought its own dangers.

In one sense, it didn't really matter *why* Sigma wanted Bludwrekk's head, or anything else, so long as each of the Space Marines honoured the obligations of their Chapters and lived to return to them.

One day, it would all be over.

One day, Karras would set foot on Occludus again, and return to the Librarius as a veteran of the Deathwatch.

He felt Rauth's eyes on him, watching as always, perhaps closer than ever now. There would be trouble later. Difficult questions. Tests. Karras didn't lie to himself. He knew how close he had come to losing his soul. He had never allowed so much of the power to flow through him before, and the results made him anxious never to do so again.

How readily would Rauth pull the trigger next time?

Focusing his attention back on Zeed, he shook his head and muttered, 'There's nothing to see, Ghost. Just an ugly green head with metal plugs in it.' He tapped the case. 'Besides, the moment I locked this thing, it fused itself shut. You could ask Sigma to let you see it, but we both know what he'll say.'

The mention of his name seemed to invoke the inquisitor. His voice sounded on the comm-link. 'That could have gone better, Alpha. I confess I'm disappointed.'

'Don't be,' Karras replied coldly. 'We have what you wanted. How fine we cut it is beside the point.'

Sigma said nothing for a moment, then, 'Fly the shuttle to the extraction coordinates and prepare for pick-up. Redthorne is on her way. And rest while you can. Something else has come up, and I want Talon on it.'

'What is it this time?' asked Karras.

'You'll know,' said the inquisitor, 'when you need to know. Sigma out.'

Magos Altando, former member of both biologis and technicus arms of the glorious Adeptus Mechanicus, stared through the wide plex window at his current project. Beyond the transparent barrier, a hundred captured orks lay strapped down to cold metal tables. Their skulls were trepanned, soft grey brains open to the air. Servo-arms dangling from the ceiling prodded each of them with short electrically-charged spikes, eliciting thunderous roars and howls of rage. The strange machine in the centre, wired directly to the greenskins' brains, siphoned off the psychic energy their collective anger and aggression was generating.

Altando's many eye-lenses watched his servitors scuttle among the tables, taking the measurements he had demanded.

I must comprehend the manner of its function, he told himself. Who could have projected that the orks were capable of fabricating such a thing?

Frustratingly, much of the data surrounding the recovery of the ork machine was classified above Altando's clearance level. He knew that a Deathwatch kill-team, designation *Scimitar*, had uncovered it during a purge of mining tunnels on Delta IV Genova. The inquisitor had brought it to him, knowing

Altando followed a school of thought which other tech-magi considered disconcertingly radical.

Of course, the machine would tell Altando very little without the last missing part of the puzzle.

A door slid open behind him, and he turned from his observations to greet a cloaked and hooded figure accompanied by a large, shambling servitor who carried a black case.

'Progress?' said the figure.

'Limited,' said Altando, 'and so it will remain, inquisitor, without the resources we need. Ah, but it appears you have solved that problem. Correct?'

The inquisitor muttered something and the blank-eyed servitor trudged forward. It stopped just in front of Altando and wordlessly passed him the black metal case.

Altando accepted it without thanks, his own heavily augmented body having no trouble with the weight. 'Let us go next door, inquisitor,' he said, 'to the primary laboratory.'

The hooded figure followed the magos into a chamber on the left, leaving the servitor where it stood, staring lifelessly into empty space.

The laboratory was large, but so packed with devices of every conceivable scientific purpose that there was little room to move. Servo-skulls hovered in the air overhead, awaiting commands, their metallic components gleaming in the lamplight. Altando placed the black case on a table in the middle of the room, and unfurled a long mechanical arm from his back. It was tipped with a las-cutter.

'May I?' asked the magos.

'Proceed.'

The cutter sent bright red sparks out as it traced the circumference of the case. When it was done, the mechanical arm folded again behind the magos's back, and another unfurled over the opposite shoulder. This was tipped with a powerful metal manipulator, like an angular crab's claw but with three tapering digits instead of two. With it, the magos clutched the top of the case, lifted it, and set it aside. Then he dipped the manipulator into the box and lifted out the head of Balthazog Bludwrekk.

'Yes,' he grated through his vocaliser. 'This will be perfect.'

'It had better be,' said the inquisitor. 'These new orkoid machines represent a significant threat, and the Inquisition must have answers.'

The magos craned forward to examine the severed head. It was frozen solid, glittering with frost. The cut at its neck was incredibly clean, even at the highest magnification his eye-lenses would allow.

It must have been a fine weapon indeed that did this, Altando thought. No typical blade.

'Look at the distortion of the skull,' he said. 'Look at the features. Fascinating. A mutation, perhaps? Or a side effect of the channelling process? Give me time, inquisitor, and the august Ordo Xenos will have the answers it seeks.'

'Do not take *too* long, magos,' said the inquisitor as he turned to leave. 'And do not disappoint me. It took my best assets to acquire that abomination.'

The magos barely registered these words. Nor did he look up to watch the inquisitor and his servitor depart. He was already far too engrossed in his study of the monstrous head.

Now, at long last, he could begin to unravel the secrets of the strange ork machine.

RACKINRUIN

BRADEN CAMPBELL

Jerrell had confronted the xenos threat for more than half his life. For the sake and safety of the Imperium, he had staged pre-emptive strikes on eldar pirates, set drahken hatchlings aflame, and ripped the cybernetic limbs from dozens of jorgall. He had faced off against entire platoons of tallerian dog-soldiers. He had been shot with vespid neutron blasters, burned by hrud fusils, and nearly crippled by a chuffian armed with one of their trademark power mauls. The missions had been tough, no doubt, but that was why they were assigned to him. Only he and the specially trained Space Marines who served under him could be trusted to get the job done, and each and every time he had succeeded. His current prey, however, was proving difficult.

Jerrell looked up from the display table upon which he was leaning and took stock of his team. Carbrey, the Sentinel, was double-checking his storm bolter and muttering a litany of hate. Launo, the last remaining Ultramarine, stood with his arms crossed, awaiting his commander's decision. Archelaos, the Dark Angel, stooped his bulk across the opposite side of the display and traced its surface with a beefy, ceramite-plated finger. His face was hidden by a cavernous hood.

The Inquisition unimaginatively called their target 'the jump ship'. Carbrey, on the other hand, had christened it *Rackinruin*, after a mythological void whale said to prowl the segmentum his Chapter called home. Unlike other greenskin spacecraft, *Rackinruin* was able to attain speeds so fantastic as to propel it through the warp. It was covered with ablative amour and shrugged off damage that would have gutted other ships. It had cut a swath across half the galaxy, performing devastating hit-and-run attacks on one forge-world after another. *Rackinruin* had evaded every ambush and defeated every fleet the Imperial Navy had sent up against it.

Jerrell believed all that was about to change. 'Launo,' he barked. 'Prep the boarding torpedo.'

Carbrey looked up from his prayers. 'We'll nay be teleportin' then?' he enquired in his unique dialect.

'Too many variables,' Jerrell replied. *Rackinruin* had evaded the Space Marines thus far because it could accelerate faster than their small cruiser. However, in their last encounter, as the orks had barrelled towards the forge-world of Paskal, they had passed directly through the planet's glittering rings of ice and metallic rock. For precious moments, *Rackinruin*'s speed had dropped dramatically. Following a furious exchange of fire between the two vessels, the orks had sped off again.

Behind them they had left a blizzard in space, kilometres long. Whatever kind of engine was powering *Rackinruin* generated a magnetic field so intense that it had caused tons of rock to stick to its sides. It might also scatter their atoms across the void if they tried to materialise near it.

They now hurtled towards the forge-world of Chestirad, famous not only for the weaponry it produced but for its natural satellite. Chestirad's moon was titanic and contained vast deposits of ferrite-236. Jerrell was certain that it would interfere with *Rackinruin*'s power source. Once again it would slow, and as it did, they would attack.

'Coordinates, watch-captain?' Launo asked.

'We'll hit them just below the bridge.'

Archelaos righted himself. 'No. Wait,' he snapped.

Jerrell ground his teeth. Of course, the Dark Angel had some objection. He always did. 'What is it?' he growled.

'I disagree with your choice,' Archelaos said.

Carbrey shook his head, and returned his attention to his weapon. Launo shifted his weight in strained patience.

After a moment, Archelaos added, 'Respectfully.'

Jerrell's eyes narrowed. 'I am tired of having conversations like these,' he said in a low voice. 'I am the watch-captain, and I give the orders.'

Archelaos pulled back his hood. 'I am your Second, and your technical advisor. It's my duty to present you with the best course of action.'

'And what would you have us do?'

Archelaos tapped the display for emphasis. The blue and white schematic they had been studying was suddenly replaced by a pict-capture of *Rackinruin*. 'We board here. Aft quarter. It's the shortest route to their primary engineering core.'

Jerrell shook his head. 'The hull plating is too thick on the rear sections. A torpedo will never be able to punch through.'

'We go in through the engine bell.'

Jerrell was incredulous. 'Are you mad? They are moving at full thrust. Their plasma trail would disintegrate us before we even got near them.'

'I've given this no little amount of thought,' Archelaos said. 'I believe the heat shielding on the torpedo will hold.'

'If you're going to suggest a course of action then make it a plausible one. We'll board them just below the bridge, fight our way in, and slay their leader.'

'We should go in through the engines,' Archelaos repeated. 'We can exit directly into the master control room and eliminate their technical experts.'

'In half an hour that ship will have passed Chestirad's moon and will accelerate beyond our range. We have only this one chance to stop it.'

'Yes,' Archelaos nodded, 'and my plan will do that. Orks can't maintain their ships or weaponry without their engineers.'

'Orks fight less effectively without a commander.'

'Our mission is to is discern why *Rackinruin* can travel the way it does, and then stop it from ransacking more Imperial worlds. We don't need to seek out the ork leaders in order to do that.'

A tense silence suddenly filled the briefing chamber. Jerrell's voice was little more than a growl. 'That almost sounds like cowardice.'

Archelaos's eyes flared. 'What it sounds like,' he said slowly, 'is the recommendation for a surgical strike as opposed to a sledgehammer blow. It is tactically sound, given the time constraints and our low squad strength.'

'Is it what the Dark Angels would do?' he asked.

'Without hesitation.'

'But you are not in your home Chapter any more,' Jerrell said pointedly.

The members of the Deathwatch were drawn from a wide variety of Chapters, and during his term of enrolment, each member was expected to don the sombre battle colours of the Ordo Xenos and work wholeheartedly with those he might not otherwise get along with. It was only natural for everyone to keep some small reminder of home, be it a trinket or pre-battle prayer, a salute or heraldic symbol. Jerrell himself wore a red clenched fist on the left pauldron of his otherwise matt-black Terminator armour that he would never paint over or disgrace.

Archelaos, on the other hand, had dyed his suit as black as space, but it seemed his immersion stopped there. His shoulder plate bore the white winged sword of Caliban. A cluster of pale feathers hung from the hilt of his power sword. He continued to wear the long beige robe and deep hood that were the hallmarks of his Dark Angels brethren.

'The previous order stands.' Jerrell picked up his helmet and stomped heavily out of the room. Launo and Carbrey followed without a word. Behind them, there was a cracking sound as Archelaos slammed his fist down on the display in frustration.

* * *

The boarding torpedo was a windowless, narrow tube. The forefront was occupied by a pilot servitor: the emaciated upper half of a heretic whose punishment was to serve the Ordo Xenos even unto a fiery, crushing death. Behind that five alcoves were recessed into each wall. Jerrell, Launo, and Carbrey each backed into one. Restraints automatically sprung around their feet, waist and shoulders.

Archelaos entered and closed the hatch. He performed a final check on the pilot, and then locked himself into place beside Jerrell.

'Synchronise countdown on your displays,' Jerrell ordered, and in each of their helmets a timer appeared, frozen at ten seconds.

'Ready,' Launo grunted.

'Aye,' Carbrey replied.

'Synched,' Archelaos muttered.

A massive bulkhead slammed down, separating the Space Marines from the pilot. Then, the torpedo rocketed forward with an intensity that would have liquefied the bones of a normal man. The numbers in their displays began to race towards zero, counting off the time until they smashed through *Rackinruin*'s armoured skin.

The actual impact came and went in a heartbeat. From where they were ensconced, Jerrell and the others felt only a single, wrenching lurch. There was a dull thump from behind the blast door, and a staccato clacking as their restraints let go.

'Five seconds!' Jerrell announced. He hoisted his shield in front of him with his left arm, and drew his sword from its scabbard. Both were highly polished and crackled with destructive power.

Launo slid into place behind Jerrell and to his left. The assault cannon mounted to his right arm hummed softly. Carbrey took up position opposite him. Archelaos filled in behind. His storm bolter was decorated in an outlandish pattern of red and green, typical of the Dark Angels.

No one spoke. They simply waited until the bulkhead detonated outwards in a hail of thick shrapnel, and then, as one, they rushed forward.

They emerged into a humid scrapyard that apparently served as a spare parts storage facility. Tall piles of rusted metal and broken machinery, salvaged from countless different planets, lay everywhere. Each pile was being tended to by a multitude of tiny, pale green creatures. They had spindly limbs and grossly oversized noses, and in the dim light looked almost like ork children. Several dozen of them had been turned into gristly chunks by the torpedo's explosive arrival. The rest stood frozen in shock, mouths agape and watery eyes wide. They were alien rabbits caught in the glare of the Emperor's purifying light.

Jerrell pointed towards them wordlessly. The others opened fire, filling the chamber with thunder. Launo's assault cannon, in particular, produced a deafening roar as it swept back and forth. The pathetic little creatures flew apart in droves, or tried to bury themselves under the scrap. A few who were either too brave or too stupid to accept the inevitable tried to fire back with clunky revolvers. The slugs impacted futilely against the Space Marines' Terminator armour. It was over in moments.

Archelaos kicked away a pile of the dead creatures, reached into the folds of his cassock, and produced a bulky scanner. He turned in a slow circle before pointing down a dark corridor to their left.

'This way,' he said.

Jerrell took the lead with Launo and Carbrey by his sides. The walls of the passageway were typically ork: a haphazard collection of metal plates, salvaged over the years from the wreckage of other civilisations, welded together in a slapdash fashion. Everything had the look of refuse about it, broken and corroded.

'Fifty metres,' Archelaos reported, 'then a large open area. There's a shaft or lift of some kind. Should take us straight up to the bridge.'

Behind his faceplate, Jerrell smirked in anticipation. 'That's where it will start,' he said needlessly. They had all received extensive lessons in xeno-behaviour as part of their Deathwatch indoctrination, but Jerrell knew the greenskins well. Nothing was more pleasing to a mob of orks than a close-quarters brawl in which they could dogpile their opponents. It sustained their barbaric natures, but it also required a lot of space.

The 'open area' was two storeys tall and lined with discoloured metal and sparking cables. A large set of double doors was directly opposite them. Three more corridors branched off at odd angles. There was a catwalk above them where several more of the diminutive scrap-tenders cowered. At the Space

Marines' approach, they screamed and began to flee. Archelaos aimed his storm bolter at them when a piercing trumpet blast suddenly rang twice, followed by a booming, metallic voice. Its staccato words were harsh and clipped, and in a language familiar to none of them. It cut through their armour's sound filters, and left a ringing in their ears.

Launo spoke in the stillness that followed. 'What was that?'

'*Rackinruin*'s voice,' Carbrey replied.

'You jest?' Launo asked.

The auspex began to chirp before Carbrey could answer. Archelaos glanced down to see clusters of illuminated dots closing in on them from all sides. The wet air was filled with the rushing sound of innumerable, iron-clad boots.

Launo turned down the closest corridor, steadied himself, and let the assault cannon roar. Orks flew apart, dismembered. Archelaos and Carbrey each positioned themselves in a doorway, and emptied the clips of their storm bolters into the rushing throng. The muzzle flashes were blinding in the dank light. Discarded casings piled around their feet. The orks bellowed and cursed and died in droves, but still they came on, pushing closer, closer. They trampled over the bodies of the fallen. Their eyes were as red as blood. Their screaming maws were filled with razor fangs.

In the midst of it all, Jerrell stood smiling. The part of him that would always belong to the Crimson Fists could have stayed there for an eternity. If he could have fought nothing but greenskins from now until death, he would have counted his life well spent. Still, there was a Deathwatch mission to complete. They had to press on.

'Archelaos! Carbrey!' Jerrell thundered. 'Set your charges!'

He ploughed his fist through the lift door and shoved it aside. There was an open platform beyond, large enough to hold the four of them. Immense chains vanished into the black shaft above. Behind him, Launo was firing down one corridor, then another, covering Archelaos and Carbrey as they released the safety locks on the melta bomb each was carrying. They set them for the shortest possible delay, dropped them to the floor, and then backed into the lift. Finally, Launo joined them.

The orks were pressing within melee distance. Carbrey ejected his spent magazine and slapped a fresh one into place. He fired several bursts into the orks at a range so short that blood and brains splashed across his chestpiece and soaked Archelaos's robe. On one side of the platform there was a heavy switch which Jerrell slammed down. The platform made a grinding sound, and began to slowly ascend. Below, they could hear the orks screaming with ferocious bloodlust as their prey escaped.

The bombs the Space Marines had left behind were designed primarily to penetrate thick armoured targets with a concentrated burst of thermal energy. When they detonated seconds later, their power was such that they literally set fire to the air. The orks' flesh was blacked into ash even as their lungs combusted. The walls, floor and ceiling glowed red-hot and liquefied in several places. A roiling, orange fireball raced up the shaft and washed around them. They paid it no heed.

'Report,' Jerrell said.

'No apparent injuries, watch-captain,' Archelaos replied.

'Materiel?'

'Two melta bombs left,' Carbrey answered. 'I'd say fifty per cent ammunition remaining.'

Jerrell turned to Launo. 'Special weapons?'

Wisps of smoke curled from the end of the cannon. 'I used two-thirds of my munitions, but the mechanics are still sound.'

Jerrell nodded, satisfied. 'Then ready yourselves.'

The lift trundled to a stop at *Rackinruin*'s laughably primitive bridge. It was square and cluttered with a mismatched array of cogs, levers, oversized buttons and cranks. There were no view-screens or cogitators, only pipes spouting steam and rusty boxes filled with blinking lights. A massive window dominated one entire wall. A series of piloting chairs were set before it, as was a raised platform featuring a steering wheel of some kind. Scores of the little green creatures milled about, carrying wrenches and hammers and tending to the machinery.

Towering over them were eight hulking orks. Their skin was a deep green hue and their faces meaty. They sported exotic melee weapons and thick sheets of metal plating on their shoulders and chests. Pistons and gears were embedded throughout their bodies at seemingly random points: the greenskin version of bionic augmentation.

Things happened very quickly then. Reacting instinctually, the burly orks moved to close the distance between themselves and the Space Marines. They fired their oversized pistols as they went. Jerrell exited the lift first holding his shield before him. Huge, heavy bullets slammed into it and fragmented. A lucky shot shattered part of his helmet and he noted with cold detachment that he was now blind in his left eye. It mattered little. The other three Space Marines fanned out and opened fire around him. The eight ork lieutenants screamed defiantly and surged forward. The little gretchin, buoyed by the presence of their massive overseers, also gave cackling battle-cries and ran forward. They took no notice as two of them were torn in half by bolter-fire, and crashed into the Space Marines with the force of an avalanche.

The little ones posed no threat, but Jerrell noted that the ork weapons were surrounded by crackling power fields. They would be slow to hit with them, but when they did, they would be enough to test even a Terminator's redundant layers of protection. He had to strike first. He threw his full weight against the orks, shoving two of them back a few paces, and squashing a half dozen of the little runts beneath his foot. He slashed out with his sword, lopping a limb off one and a head from another. Through a red haze, he wondered if Archelaos was doing likewise. He parried two more blows against his shield, and glanced to his left.

The Dark Angel's hood had fallen back off of his helmet. His blade was indiscernible amidst a whirlwind of parries, but even he couldn't stop them all. A rough-hewn claw, mounted to one of the ork's forearms, punched straight through his armour and embedded itself in his chest.

Carbrey and Launo had moved up to reinforce their leaders. They each bore a crushing mechanical glove on their left hands. The servos in their armour groaned as they wound back and drove them into the foe. Launo punched clear through one of the orks, and sprung back into a riposte. Carbrey, however, swung his entire arm downwards like a lumberjack cleaving logs. He ripped his opponent in half from shoulder to hip, but overextended himself in doing so. A pair of greenskin claws hammered down, catching him between the shoulders. He convulsed, and dropped face first onto the blood-soaked deck plates.

Jerrell roared in anger and came at them like a thing possessed. He chopped and bludgeoned, and before Archelaos or Launo could even react the orks were dead. The remaining gretchin, bereft of their protectors, scrambled and hid, diving for cover behind machinery banks or wriggling up through ventilation shafts. Jerrell stood amidst the carnage, his chest heaving. He stuck his sword into the floor and peeled off his ruined helmet.

Launo dropped to one knee, and rolled Carbrey over. His teeth were clenched as he gave a thick, gurgling sound.

'Easy, brother,' Launo said softly. 'Easy.'

Archelaos looked down. The wound was obviously fatal, and without an Apothecary there was nothing to be done. They had taken the bridge, but at a terrible cost. Now there were only three of them. 'Captain?' he called.

Jerrell didn't respond. He was preoccupied with surveying the dead orks.

'Jerrell!' Archelaos yelled.

Jerrell's head snapped up. His augmented biology was already at work. The gush of blood that had been pouring from his shattered eye socket had reduced to a trickle.

'He isn't here,' Jerrell muttered.

Archelaos stormed over to him. 'What?'

'The ork leader. He's not among them.'

Archelaos looked about quickly. 'You're certain?'

'These bodies are all the same size,' Jerrell sighed. 'Bigger than regular orks, but not one of them larger than the rest.'

Archelaos sheathed his sword. He put his hands on his hips, shook his head, and walked away to scrutinise the crude control panels. Launo appeared beside Jerrell. He had a helmet in his free hand, and held it out.

'Carbrey?' Jerrell asked hopefully.

Launo's posture was supremely rigid. 'Fallen in the service of the Emperor,' he said proudly. 'The watch-captain has need of a new helmet. It would honour our brother if you take his.' Jerrell reached out and took it with a heavy solemnity.

Archelaos cursed and stared out the window. A mottled grey and brown planet was looming large. 'We're well past Chestirad's moon,' he announced, 'and still under full thrust. This ship is preparing for a low orbital raid.'

'Sir, how can that be?' Launo said to Jerrell. 'We're in control now.'

Archelaos shook his head. The ork machinery made absolutely no sense to him. 'I'm not certain that we are,' he said. 'There might well be controls hidden amongst all this refuse, but it would take weeks to discern them.'

The watch-captain did not reply at first. He was still gazing down at Carbrey's helmet, cradled in his massive hands. 'I should have seen it before. A drive that lets the greenskins leap across space? What could be more valuable? What could be more rare?'

The tilt of Launo's faceplate said that he wasn't following.

'Orks are incapable of building such a thing,' Jerrell elaborated. 'They must have pillaged or stolen it from somewhere.

The ork commander would want to stay near it, the better to keep an eye on his treasure.'

Jerrell turned back to Archelaos. His brow was furrowed. 'You were correct. Knocking out *Rackinruin*'s power source would have been far more efficient than trying to usurp command of it. I let my hatred of the orks cloud my tactical sense. Coming to the bridge has not only cost us precious time, but the life of a battle-brother as well.' He swallowed hard. 'I cry your pardon. Both of you.'

'You weren't wrong,' Archelaos corrected. 'We simply come from different Chapters. There were two options, and as watch-captain, you chose the one you thought best.'

Jerrell pointed to their fallen comrade. 'And Carbrey...'

'Will not have died in vain.' Archelaos finished. 'We still have time.'

They left their second-to-last melta bomb behind them, set three minutes later to turn the bridge to slag. The Space Marines would either shut down the engines, or they would ride down to Chestirad's surface atop a cataclysmic fireball. Either way, *Rackinruin*'s pillaging would come to an end this day.

Their journey towards engineering was eerily uneventful. They could hear the little green monstrosities scrabbling about behind the walls and in the shadows, but none of them dared come forth. Jerrell walked in between his remaining two men. 'A ship this size,' he said, 'should be carrying several hundred full-sized orks.'

'Then where are they?' Archelaos asked. He had his sword

drawn. The auspex was secured atop his storm bolter using strips torn from his robe.

Finally, they came to a thick blast door seemingly built by giants. It towered above the Space Marines and was covered with crudely painted glyphs.

Archelaos pulled a heavy wall switch, and it rumbled aside like a rusty curtain. Beyond was a cavernous chamber. The floor was covered ankle-deep with huge bones and fanged, lantern-jawed skulls. Amidst the charnel sat a machine that was of neither greenskin nor Imperial manufacture. It was a perfect sphere, etched in intricate patterns and lit from within by a bright yellow glow. From deep within it came a thrumming sound, like a heart beating in overdrive. Arranged around it stood five enormous orks. Their bodies were covered in layer upon layer of metal armour and cybernetic attachments. Each of them had a large-calibre cannon mounted on one arm. The opposing hand had been replaced by an unwieldy claw. Rusty cables protruded from their heads and torsos. Their faces were gaunt and starved. They stared blankly at the alien sphere as if in a trance.

'Emperor protect us.' Launo's voice was uncharacteristically hoarse. 'It ate them.'

Two sharp notes cut the air, and again came the thundering, alien voice of *Rackinruin*. The orks snapped awake and turned to face the Space Marines. One of them, larger and more heavily plated than the rest, gave a bellow. Then they began trundling forward simultaneously, unleashing a torrent of oversized shells.

Jerrell lifted his shield reflexively. Even so, he felt a massive impact in his right knee. Another tore clean through his right shoulder.

Launo stood his ground, answering back with his assault cannon. When he blew the midsection out of one of the augmented orks, wires and mechanical parts spilled forth where blood and guts should have been. The monstrosity fell over dead. When the greenskins fired at him again, chunks of his Terminator armour spalled inwards, puncturing his organs. He spat blood, went to one knee and fell to the floor.

Archelaos dashed back next to Jerrell, spraying the storm bolter as he went. The rounds sparked and ricocheted off the orks' armour. He glanced at Jerrell, who nodded. They would die in moments if they did not shorten the range of this fight.

Together they rushed forward. Jerrell collided, shield first, into the biggest of the orks and brought his weapon down in a humming arc. There was a fountain of sparks and a screaming of rent metal. The powerful leg servos in Archelaos's suit launched him into the air and he came crashing down, sword first, amongst the rest. A mechanical limb went flying.

Their foes' armour made them slow but their massive claws had enough force to cleave either of the Space Marines in half. Archelaos and Jerrell ducked and parried, moving wholly on instinct. They swept at legs and lopped off heads. The biggest of the orks was the last to go down, and did so only with a combined effort. Jerrell drove his sword into the beast's chest with all his might, as Archelaos slashed it deeply through a hip joint. The deck plating shook as it collapsed.

* * *

Archelaos's breathing came in shallow, rapid gasps. His armour was filled with ragged, fist-wide bullet holes. 'We have to... stop the... ship.'

'You've been injured,' Jerrell said.

'Yes, but we've no time for that.'

Together, they turned towards the alien sphere. The orks had obviously tried, in their crude way, to integrate the device into their own mechanical systems. Thick, rusting cables formed a nest at its base, and ran off in all directions. Red paint had been splashed across every surface. Gears and corrugated metal were piled everywhere. There was a cracked display screen recessed into a square box and surrounded by levers and buttons. Archelaos kneeled down and removed his helmet. He leaned in close to examine it. His face was covered with beads of sweat. He saw Chestirad in the foreground, a massive moon in the distance, and two bright dots that obviously represented their cruiser and this abomination of a ship. Alien hieroglyphs scrolled by at a furious rate.

'I've served three enrolments in the Deathwatch.' Jerrell said, slowly reaching out to touch the silver ball. 'I've never seen the like.'

'I have,' Archelaos panted. He began pressing lightened buttons. 'This is khrave technology.'

Jerrell pulled back. 'The mind eaters?' he said, referring to them by their more common name.

'They're really more like... mind copiers,' Archelaos managed. 'They steal memories. Imprint themselves with... personalities that... aren't their own.'

'Are you certain?'

'Quite.' Archelaos smiled grimly to himself. Although he was now certain that he would die in the service of the Deathwatch, he would always be a Dark Angel. Secrets were his forte. 'The orks must have… found this. Tried to use it…'

'And it ended up using them.' Jerrell was suddenly very glad that Archelaos had been assigned to his team. 'Can you disable it?' he asked hopefully.

'Let's pray,' Archelaos muttered, 'that this is… main drive.' He indicated a particular knob and pulled.

The air was cut once again by a piercing alarm that rang on and on. The metallic, alien voice that followed was deafening in its volume.

'Forget it,' Jerrell shouted. He grabbed the final melta bomb in both hands and moved to clamp it on to the metal sphere.

'No, Jerrell!' Archelaos screamed, but it was too late. The moment the bomb made contact, the watch-captain felt a cold presence swirl around inside his skull, rifling through every thought he'd ever had.

The room shook. The alarm became a scream, and the thrumming heartbeat of the khrave machine turned into a single, gut-wrenching tone. A pulse of energy threw the Space Marines across the room to land among the bones. Jerrell felt himself turned inside out for a moment, a tell-tale sign of travel through the warp. Terrible forces pressed around him. Then, as quickly as it had begun, it was over.

Jerrell was still holding the now charred and useless melta bomb. He got up, cast it aside, and walked back to the machine. The image on the screen had changed. Chestirad and its moon were no longer hanging there, replaced instead by a distant star.

Ten planets orbited around it. The fourth one was highlighted. Hundreds of bright dots, other starships, were scattered nearby. He knew this beleaguered system. It was home to one of the largest concentrations of orks in the known galaxy; the focal point in three full-scale wars between the Imperium and the greenskins.

'Armageddon, Archelaos,' he laughed. 'Of course it would take us to Armageddon. It brought me to where I'd most like to be.'

Archelaos lay in a motionless, crumpled heap. He was no longer breathing. Jerrell hauled his body into a sitting position against Launo's corpse, and placed the feather crested pommel of his sword into his hand. Then he picked up his own weapons and stood facing the entryway of the chamber.

'We'll take them together,' he said. There was a glint of madness in his eye. 'You and I, brothers at the end.'

Within moments, he knew, this ship would begin filling up with filthy, swearing, murderous orks. They would come in the hundreds, the thousands, and they would find him blocking their way. He couldn't wait to get started.

WEAPONSMITH

BEN COUNTER

Brother-Sergeant Chrysius grabbed a handful of filthy hair and rammed the peon's face into the side of the fuel tank. Bone crunched under the impact. He threw the dead man aside and backed up against the huge cylindrical tank.

His squad hurried into place alongside him. They were his battle-brothers, men he had fought alongside for decades: Vryksus, who had been bested at the Tournament of Blades seven years ago and still wore a black stripe down the centre of his faceplate as a mark of shame; Myrdos, whose study of the Imperial Fists' past heroes made him the tactical brain of the squad; Helian, the monster and Gruz, who treated combat as an art. Assault Squad Chrysius, ready to kill.

The sound of their ceramite soles on the deck was drowned out by the noise of machinery. This level of the station was a fuel depot, where enormous stirring mechanisms churned the vats of starship fuel to keep it from separating and congealing. Between the vats laboured the peons, marked by brands on their faces. They all had the same raised scar blistered up across their lips and crushed noses. Only someone who knew of their allegiance beforehand would recognise the shape of it – a stylised skull with a grille for a mouth, like the face of a steel skeleton. Chrysius had estimated thirty peons held this floor, all of them armed, none of them ready for the wrath of the Imperial Fists.

Twenty-nine, he corrected himself. The body of the man he had just taken down slid to the floor beside him, leaving a glistening slick of blood on the side of the fuel tank.

'Chrysius to command,' he whispered into the vox, for he habitually fought with his helmet removed and did not want his voice to carry. He went into battle bare-headed because the facial tattoos of his youth, acquired in a half-remembered previous life among the hive gangers of the Devlan Infernus, were his personal heraldry and it was cowardice not to display it. 'In position.'

'The assault has begun,' came the reply from Captain Haestorr. 'Execute, Squad Chrysius.'

Chrysius gave the signal, a clenched fist punched forwards, and his squad charged from their hiding place.

The peons had no idea they were about to be attacked. Even when the Imperial Fists stormed into the open, bolt pistols hammering, the enemy took several seconds to realise it. In those seconds half a dozen men were dead, pinpoint shots blasting heads from shoulders or ripping holes through torsos.

'Helian, Gruz, go high!' ordered Chrysius, pausing amid the

carnage to take stock of the situation. A foot ramp led to a series of walkways circling the upper levels of the fuel cylinders. Enemies might be up there, and they would have excellent positions to fire on the Imperial Fists. Brother Helian was first up – half a metre taller than some of the other Imperial Fists, his armour had been altered to fit his frame and even Gruz looked small compared to him.

Chrysius spun around to see three peons taking up firing positions behind a bank of machinery. They had solid projectile guns of simple but effective design, perhaps even capable of putting a hole in power armour at close enough range. Chrysius did not intend to find out.

He ran right at them. It was not the natural reaction for a *human* being faced with a gun, and the peons reacted with shock when they should have blazed every bullet they had at the charging Imperial Fist. But Chrysius was post-human and not afraid of being shot. That was the first thing the hypnodoctrination had weeded out of him.

He vaulted the machinery and crashed down onto the first peon. This one's face was so disfigured by the brand he seemed to have no nose or lips at all, just a torn snarl of blistered flesh that failed to cover his broken teeth. His eyes were yellow, and they rolled back into his head as Chrysius's weight crunched into his ribcage.

Chrysius thrust his chainsword into the belly of the next peon, squeezing the charging stud as he stabbed. The chain teeth chewed through the stomach and spine with a spray of blood and smoke. Chrysius barely even had to look to fire in the opposite direction, into the last peon, leaving three holes in his chest so huge that his upper body flopped away, the centre of the torso completely gone.

'Report. Sound off!' ordered Chrysius. More than ten seconds had passed since battle had been joined. It would be a good way towards its conclusion by now.

'Helian. Nothing up here.' Helian sounded disappointed.

'Myrdos. Four down, am holding.'

'Vryskus. Under fire. Five have fallen to me!'

'Gruz,' voxed Chrysius. 'Gruz, report!'

The reply was the yellow-armoured body of Brother Gruz slamming into the floor ten metres from Chrysius's position. Chrysius ran up to him, grabbed his wrist and hauled him into the cover of the machinery. Gruz's pistol and chainsword lay where he had fallen, the teeth of the chainsword stripped away.

Chrysius glanced at the panel on the forearm of Gruz's armour, where the power armour's sensors read off the user's life signs. His battle-brother was alive.

'Helian!' yelled Chrysius into the vox. 'Helian, what's up there?'

Chrysius saw Helian running along the walkways above. He was firing at something out of sight and return fire, heavier, was hammering back at him.

Chrysius saw a ramp leading up to the tank behind him. It might take him up behind the unseen enemy. He ran for it, bolt pistol held up ready to snap off shots at anything that wasn't Brother Helian. Gunfire stuttered from below him – he would have to leave Myrdos and Vryskus to deal with the peons below.

The great dark shape that barrelled towards him, around the

curve of the fuel tank, was too big to be one of the peons. It moved too fast. Chrysius jammed the trigger down by instinct but the shot didn't fell it, and a great weight slammed into him.

It was a Space Marine in battered power armour the colour of smoke-stained steel. The faceplate of the helmet was like the visor of a feudal knight, with dark red eyepieces and a grille over the nose and mouth like a jaw full of steel fangs. That same shape, the stylised, skull-like image, was emblazoned in silver on one black-painted shoulder pad.

An Iron Warrior.

The traitor's weight was on Chrysius and he could barely move. His chainblade was pinned down by his side and his bolt pistol was jammed under the Iron Warrior's torso, the barrel pointing down.

The Imperial Fists had suspected the Iron Warriors had a hand in the taking over of the orbital habitats around Euklid IV, but here was proof. Proof that would kill Chrysius in a matter of seconds if he could not fight like a Space Marine when it counted.

Chrysius let go of his chainsword and forced his arm out, feeling muscles wrenching. He grabbed the back of the Iron Warrior's helmet and yanked it back, forcing the enemy's head back and taking some of the weight off. He drove a foot into the walkway below him and rolled over, throwing the Iron Warrior off.

'Did you think you could hide here like vermin?' gasped Chrysius. 'Hide from the sons of Rogal Dorn?'

'Brave words, whelp of Terra,' replied the Iron Warrior. His voice was a metallic grind, distorted through the helmet filters.

He tried to draw a bolter from a scabbard on his waist but Chrysius grabbed his wrist and the two grappled there, face to face, a test of strength with each trying to throw the other down.

The Iron Warrior won.

Chrysius toppled off the walkway, the railing parting underneath him. He slammed hard into the top of the fuel tank amid a tangle of cables and pipes. The Iron Warrior's bolter was out and he snapped off a rattling volley of shots. Chrysius rolled to make himself a moving target as explosive shells hammered home around him. Blooms of flame erupted as fuel lines were ruptured. A ball of fire rushed up, masking Chrysius for the second it took him to get onto his feet.

Chrysius fired blindly through the flames. He counted off the shells in his bolt pistol's magazine, knowing he was outgunned and outmuscled by the enemy.

But this was not just an enemy. This was an Iron Warrior, a Traitor Marine who had engaged the Imperial Fists in battle after bloody battle to test their strength against the scions of Rogal Dorn. Between the two, there was nothing but hate.

Enough hate to propel the Iron Warrior through the fire, closing with Chrysius in a couple of seconds, a combat knife in one hand and the bolter in the other. Chrysius just had time to turn to face his assailant before the knife stabbed home.

Chrysius had earned his laurels through an expertise in hand to hand combat that few Imperial Fists could better. He recognised the strike: a low one to the relatively vulnerable joints between the abdomen of his power armour and the chest plate. Chrysius drove the heel of his hand down, knocked the combat blade off target, and blasted off the remaining shells in his pistol into the Iron Warrior.

One shot rang off the Iron Warrior's shoulder guard, doing nothing more than adding another scar to the pitted paintwork. One hit the chest, blowing a crater in the ceramite but nothing more. A third, the last, punched into the Iron Warrior's thigh, ripping through his thigh joint and blasting muscle and bone apart.

The Iron Warrior bellowed in pain and dropped to one knee. Chrysius was on him. His chainblade was left up on the walkway, but he still had the hands of an Imperial Fist.

He smashed his pistol into the Iron Warrior's face. The weapon shattered but the faceplate buckled, one eye lens popping out.

'There are ten thousand of us,' growled the Iron Warrior as he tried to fend off Chrysius. 'The future is ours. Every–'

Chrysius didn't let the Iron Warrior finish. He drove his fist into his face, feeling nothing but hatred. It was as if there were nothing in the galaxy but Chrysius's fist and the Iron Warrior's steel face, which every blow crumpled and split.

Chrysius's fist pistoned over and over again until the faceplate came apart and he was able to rip the helmet away. He looked into the Iron Warrior's face.

Brother Hestion reached the walkway overlooking the fuel tank. By the time he had vaulted down and reached Chrysius, the Iron Warrior's face had been reduced to a crimson pulp. Chrysius let the body fall, and it clattered limply to his feet.

Hestion handed Chrysius the chainsword he had left on the walkway. 'Good kill, sergeant,' he said.

* * *

The edge of night passed across the surface of Euklid IV. The gas giant's upper atmosphere was, in daytime, a mass of firestorms. As night passed the flames became dark, replaced with a grey-black caul of ash speckled with islands of glowing embers.

People had lived here once – humans, citizens of the Imperium, living on the dozens of space stations orbiting the planet. Now whoever lived here could not be described as people at all.

Against the scale of Euklid IV, those orbital stations seemed so tiny and delicate they could barely be thought of as existing at all. And compared to the void that lay beyond it, the planet was an insignificant, infinitesimally tiny fragment of nothing. Even Euklid, the system's star, meant nothing compared to the galaxy. And the galaxy meant nothing compared to the universe.

It was good, thought Chrysius, that a Space Marine rarely had the luxury of time to think about such things.

'Chrysius!' came a familiar voice behind him. Chrysius turned to see another Space Marine entering the observation deck. This one wore the White Scars' livery on one shoulder pad but the rest of his armour was black with silver lettering inscribed. His face was familiar too, half the scalp a metallic shell, one eye a bionic, contrasting with a mouth that smiled easily. His skin, battered and tanned like beaten bronze, was typical of the horse nomads from which his Chapter drew their recruits.

'Kholedei!' said Chrysius. 'My brother. It has been too long!'

The two clasped hands. 'It has,' said Kholedei. 'For all the honour of the Deathwatch, it is good to fight alongside old friends again.'

The last time Chrysius had seen Kholedei, it had been as a joint White Scars and Imperial Fists strike force lifted off from the shattered remains of Hive Mandibus. The city had fallen to a xenos plague which turned the inhabitants into walking incubators for wormlike aliens. The mission had been nothing short of a cull, exterminating every living thing they found. It was a foul, grim business, a merciless grind, when even a Space Marine had been in need of friends. The two had fought alongside each other, their squads merged into one and taking strength from their new comrades.

'I had heard the Deathwatch had sent a kill-team to Euklid IV,' said Chrysius. 'I did not know you would be among them.'

'When I knew we would be in support of the Imperial Fists, I ensured that I would be in the kill-team,' said Kholedei. 'I would not miss the chance to fight alongside the Sons of Dorn again. What news of your squad?'

'Venelus fell at Thorgin,' said Chrysius. 'A shot from an eldar sniper. And Koron at the Fallmarch Expanse, when the *Eternal Sacrifice* was lost.'

'They were fine brothers, Chrysius. We are all diminished by their loss.'

'It is the way of war to take our best,' said Chrysius. 'Vryskus has yet to atone for his defeat at the tournament, though to everyone else but him he has redeemed himself a dozen times over. Myrdos is on his way to taking his own squad. Helian's just the same, of course.'

'Good to know. I hear that you killed an Iron Warrior yourself.'

'That is so,' said Chrysius. 'I was fortunate.'

'A kill that I have not equalled, sergeant,' said Kholedei. 'Aliens aplenty have fallen to me and my team, but an Iron Warrior is something else. I would dearly love to shed the blood of such a traitor. I know of the dishonours they have done to the Imperial Fists.'

'Gruz was wounded,' said Chrysius. 'I am proud to have taken the kill, but not that my battle-brother suffered for it.'

'Then you will avenge him. Just as we avenge our fallen every time we fight. And the next fight will be soon. I have spoken with Captain Haestorr. Given the intelligence the Inquisition gathered on this mission, the enemy will be concentrated in the science facility. We strike there, and strike hard, and the Iron Warriors will be thrown off Euklid IV before they have the chance to mount a defence.'

'What interest does the Ordo Xenos have in Euklid IV?' asked Chrysius.

Kholedei smiled. 'Believe me, the ordo wants the Iron Warriors extinct just as much as we do. They might specialise in hunting the alien, but an enemy is an enemy.'

'Well, that's why we are here. Why are the Iron Warriors here?'

Kholedei looked out through the viewing port. Once this station had been a beautiful place, where the citizens could gather and reflect on the majesty of Euklid IV. Now the place was decaying, the walls spotted with rust and damp, the port smeared with condensation. 'This was an intellectual colony,' said Kholedei. 'Artists, philosophers. Perhaps their meditations uncovered or woke something. A moral threat. Perhaps the Iron Warriors want it. Perhaps they built a science station of enough sophistication to make it valuable to the enemy. It matters little as long as it gives us a time and a place to kill them.'

'I am glad the Inquisition and the Chapter made common cause here,' said Chrysius. 'It is good to have you back, brother.'

'It is good to be back,' said Kholedei. Chrysius recognised that smile, which his old friend only broke out when the chance for competition showed itself. 'I get another chance to show you how a Space Marine really fights.'

Captain Haestorr ascribed to the tactical philosophy that a Space Marine was not a soldier. A soldier could lose his nerve. A soldier would not just walk into the fury of the enemy – he had to be corralled like an animal or cajoled like a child.

A Space Marine was more like a bullet fired from a gun. He went wherever he was pointed, and needed no convincing to inflict fatal damage on anything he hit.

The Imperial Fists' boarding torpedoes slammed into the side of the station. By the lettering stencilled on its side, this station was called the *Enlightenment*. The hull plates came apart under the reinforced prows of the Caestus-pattern boarding rams, as the assault vehicles drove through the multiple levels of protective plating.

Space Marine power armour was proof against the vacuum that ripped everything out of the station's outer hull spaces. After a few seconds to let the gases vent, the prows of the boarding rams opened up and the Imperial Fists emerged, the assault squad first into the breach. They forged into the tangled labyrinth of ventilation ducts and fuel coolant pipes that encased the station's interior.

The enemy knew they were there. Even without any sensors left on the station, the impacts of the rams would have rung throughout the *Enlightenment*. Every Imperial Fist, and the Deathwatch kill-team members who accompanied them, knew this would be a contested boarding. That meant a close quarters fight, a butcher's battle.

It would be against the most hated enemy the Imperial Fists had ever made. They couldn't wait.

The first sight Chrysius had of the enemy was a blurred, half-glimpsed shape leaping between the laboratory benches. The lab floor was choked with machinery: wires and ducts hanging from the ceiling. An enormous cylindrical structure, an electron microscope, loomed like a monumental sculpture. The enemy had lots of places to hide and the one Chrysius saw, jumping from one piece of cover to the next, was humanoid in a way that was fundamentally wrong. It trailed fronds of skin and its limbs were too long, jointed in the wrong places.

Mutants.

Chrysius's immediate objective was to close with the enemy. It was the first principle of The Doctrines of Assault, sleep-taught to Chrysius during his training. He crashed through the lab equipment, kicking through the bench in front of him, scattering chemical beakers and glassware everywhere. Gunfire was already starting – the staccato thunder of the Imperial Fists' boltguns, and the red flashes of laser fire in return. Chrysius could see more of them now behind barricades of overturned benches and toppled lab gear, dressed in ragtag uniforms of black and yellow, and sporting different mutations. He saw in that glimpse vividly coloured and patterned skin, claws and stinger tails, tattered wings, scorched and blistered skin.

Hestion was ahead of Chrysius, dropping a shoulder and crashing through a bank of cogitator screens. He slammed into the mutant sheltering behind it and yanked the thing off its feet as the mutant tried to wrench the Imperial Fist's head off with its tentacles. Hestion dashed the mutant against the ground, splitting its head open against the white-tiled floor, and impaled a second mutant through the chest with his chainsword. The whirr of the teeth screeched even above the dying scream and the gunfire, and it was the sound of imminent victory.

Chrysius jumped a barricade of furniture, shooting one of the mutants behind it through the chest before he even landed. It had huge compound eyes and mouthparts like an insect. He swept his chainblade and cut another in two at the waist, his backswing ruining the leg of a third. He barely had time to register what manner of uncleanness had been marked on their flesh before they died, fresh blood spraying across the golden yellow of his armour, the vibrations of cracking bone running up through his feet as he stamped down on them.

More mutants were running into the fray, brought by the screams of their brothers. They were armed with las-weapons and autoguns. Bullets and las-blasts pinged off Hestion's armour as he stood proud, battering down a mutant who charged at him with gun blazing. Hestion was wounded often, and Chrysius had often lectured him on a Space Marine's duty to preserve himself and his wargear as well as destroy the enemy, but Hestion did not have a self-preserving cell in his huge body.

There were hundreds of mutants pouring onto the laboratory deck. Radios were blasting orders and exaltations to kill. Chrysius's squad paused for a moment, the first line of the enemy dead and the next line rushing towards them.

'Hestion! Hold the line and charge on my mark,' ordered Chrysius. 'And get down!'

'Behold the enslavers!' came a braying voice over a vox-caster with speakers mounted on the lab ceiling. 'The heralds of order! The enslavers of your kind! Watch them fall, and revel in their death-cries!'

Chrysius glanced over the cover. The mutants were close. He could see their faces, and the ones with expressions he could read were glassy-eyed, as if they had been hypnotised or mind-wiped.

Dogs, thought Chrysius. Animals, conditioned to attack. The Imperium's malcontents lied to and indoctrinated, and loosed like a pack of dogs.

'Now!' yelled Chrysius, and leapt into the front rank of mutants, into the storm of claws and blades.

Even against this fanatical horde there was glory to be won. The brutal rhythm of violence came easily to Assault-Sergeant Chrysius. They thrust, he parried, reversed and cut, blasted another few bolt shells into them and let them close again, near enough for the pattern to repeat. He saw Brother Myrdos clamber onto the cylinder of the microscope and hack down those who tried to reach him, as if he were a flag planted at the summit of a mountain and the mutants were competing to see who could pull it down first. Somewhere in the thick of it was Hestion, hurling the enemy in every direction, some even clattering against the coolant ducts running across the ceiling.

The enemy relented. They had to – there were only so many of them. As they broke off in twos and threes they were shot down by the bolters of the Imperial Fists behind, directed by Captain Haestorr. The kill-team were there too, firing with lethal precision, each bolter shell shredding a mutant's central mass in a spray of gore.

'Squads, respond!' came the vox on Haestorr's command channel. 'Report all sightings of the Iron Warriors!'

'None here,' replied Chrysius. 'They sent in the fodder. They thought we'd be softened up before we reached them.'

'None yet,' came a voice Chrysius recognised as Kholedei's. 'Squad, free target at will, don't waste your kraken shells. Watch for the Weaponsmith.'

Chrysius dropped to one knee behind a bullet-riddled lab bench. 'Kholedei? Brother Kholedei, can you repeat that?'

There was no answer. The second part of the vox had sounded like it was directed to the Deathwatch kill-team and not the rest of the force. Perhaps it had been a mistake, Kholedei momentarily forgetting to switch channels.

But Chrysius was quite sure of what he had heard. And so had the rest of his squad.

'Sergeant,' said Brother Hestion, who emerged from a bank of machines to join Chrysius. Hestion was covered from head to toe in blood. His bolt pistol was still in its holster, and he had probably killed as many with his bare left hand as with his chainsword. 'Did he say that? About the Weaponsmith?'

'Focus on the enemy, Brother Hestion,' said Chrysius.

'But he did,' said Brother Vryskus, who approached wiping

the blood from the blade of the duellist's sabre he used in place of a chainsword. 'We all heard him. I think, sergeant, we all know now why we are here.'

According to the collators of the Imperial Fists' lore – those battle-brothers responsible for recording battle legends and old grudges –Weaponsmith Gurlagorg had been one of the first Iron Warriors ever to break the greatest taboo of the Space Marines. This Iron Warrior, a commander of his Legion, had taken an Imperial Fist prisoner at a long-ago battle, cut open his body and removed the gene-seed organs. The gene-seed, the organ that regulated all the many augmentations of a Space Marine's body, without which he could simply not exist. The gene-seed, created after the genetic pattern of the Primarch Rogal Dorn himself who had in turn been made in the image of the Emperor. A shred of the divine that every Space Marine carried inside him.

Gurlagorg had sought a way to create more Iron Warriors, and had struck upon the idea of harvesting the gene-seed from Imperial Space Marines, corrupting and debasing it, and creating new battle-brothers of his own. It was as blasphemous a concept as ever existed among the Chapter of the Space Marines. Some had even thought that the Traitor Legions, heretics and sworn enemies of mankind though they were, would at least respect the principles of their own creation. But no – Gurlagorg had created a new Iron Warrior from the first gene-seed he took, and set about seeking more to defile with his corrupted sciences.

It was a dangerous story to tell, and the Chapter Masters

condemned its spreading. But it was told, hushed and always changing. Gurlagorg was the worst of the worst, as deadly an enemy as the Imperial Fists had. If ever a roll of the Imperial Fists' deadliest enemies were drawn up, Weaponsmith Gurlagorg would be near the top. Few and powerful would be the names ahead of his.

And now he was orbiting Euklid IV. The Deathwatch knew, and presumably Captain Haestorr and the Chapter's leaders did, too. That was why the Inquisition had sent the kill-team to assist the Imperial Fists in wiping out the Iron Warriors there – because the Inquisition knew that Gurlagorg was a hated enemy of mankind, and that his death would make the galaxy that one degree more sacred.

They had found him. After thousands of years they had found him. And now, after thousands of years, they would kill him.

The deck beyond the laboratory bled from its walls. Where there had once been panels of steel, there was now a blackened biomechanical covering of skin, the rotting metal blistered up with pulsing steel veins. Drops of acid pattered from the sagging ceiling and a silver-black ooze bubbled up underfoot. Every warning rune was lit up on the retinas of the Imperial Fists as they warily moved into the science station's core, the filters of their armoured faceplates capturing the worst of the pollutants that turned the air thick and hazy.

Even Assault-Sergeant Chrysius wore his helmet here. The Imperial Fists force spread out through the deck, which stretched most of the rest of the way to the station's centre. The deck was badly warped, forming slopes and hills as it rose and fell, and in places it shuddered underfoot as if ready to give way into the fuel cells and thruster arrays on the station's underside.

'It's a miracle the gravity still works,' voxed Brother Vryskus.

'Speak not too soon, brother,' replied Myrdos. 'Think to the Battle of the *Dark Ascension*. The Night Lords there deactivated their flagship's gravity just as battle was joined, hoping to spread confusion through the Imperial Fists' ranks.'

'Did it work?' asked Vryskus.

'If you were minded to read anything our forefathers wrote, Vryskus, you would know the Imperial Fists were stern and resolute, and were victorious,' said Myrdos testily. 'Our brethren there were ready. So must we be.'

Before Chrysius was a blistered section of the deck where the biomechanical substance was stretched thin. Beneath the surface, suspended in greyish translucent fluid, was an object that looked like a boltgun of an ancient mark. Its lines were undeveloped and its details indistinct, as if it had been moulded from clay. 'They're growing their wargear here,' he said.

'Truly,' said Vryskus, 'no tech-heresy is beyond the Iron Warriors.'

Other blisters held segments of power armour and more weapons, all in various stages of growth. 'We can destroy this on the way out,' voxed Captain Haestorr. 'The Iron Warriors are the objective here.'

'And Weaponsmith Gurlagorg,' replied Chrysius over the command vox. 'If he is here. You cannot deny us that knowledge, captain.'

'Discipline,' replied Haestorr. 'Focus, sergeant. The mission above all else.'

'If the Weaponsmith is on this station then our mission is to kill him,' replied Chrysius. 'As it has been the mission of the Imperial Fists to kill all enemies of mankind.'

'You are ahead of yourself,' voxed Haestorr. 'There is no sign the Weaponsmith is here.'

'The Deathwatch think otherwise,' said Chrysius. He could see Kholedei and the rest of his kill-team moving carefully through the unstable chamber, on one flank of the Imperial Fists' formation. Chrysius could see, along with Kholedei's own White Scars livery, the heraldry of other Space Marine Chapters on the shoulder pads of the kill-team members – a Praetor of Orpheus, a Black Dragon, a Scimitar Guard. Chrysius wondered what it would mean to fight alongside Space Marines whose way of thinking came from the doctrines of a different Chapter, men who might be his brothers as the Emperor's finest but not brothers raised together in war.

'We're closing on the Hazardous Materials Lab,' voxed Sergeant Moxus, whose squad held the opposite flank. 'It's shielded and fortified, if the original blueprints still hold true. If the Iron Warriors make a stand on this station, they will make it there.'

'Captain Kholedei!' ordered Haestorr. 'Bring your demolitions charges forth. We'll blast our way in.'

The kill-team headed to the front where a great bulkhead, the spine of the station, met the corrupted deck. Chrysius saw now the Praetor of Orpheus had the servo-harness and artificer armour of a Techmarine. He attached three large steel canisters to the bulkhead wall and keyed in a command sequence as the kill-team retired beyond the blast zone.

'If the Weaponsmith didn't know we were coming,' said Vryskus bleakly, 'he will soon.'

'Lesser men would call us the forlorn hope,' said Chrysius. 'The first into the breach. A Space Marine calls it the place of the greatest honour, for to us will fall the first blood of the enemy.' Chrysius drew his chainsword. 'To us will fall the Weaponsmith.'

A trio of rapid explosions shuddered the chamber. The cysts burst, spilling half-formed wargear across the floor in a flood of greasy filth. The bulkhead shattered in a blast of red light and flame, and black smoke filled the air.

Through the gloom, Chrysius's auto-senses cut a path through the interior of the Hazardous Materials Lab. Whatever it had once been, it now resembled nothing so much as a temple ripped from whatever dimension had birthed it and transplanted into this space station. Chains hung across the void in the heart of the station, hung with festoons of mangled corpses impaled on the spiked links. Shafts of black steel fell down through the darkness, impaling great altars of carved stone. The laboratory floor had been turned into a maze of altars, the spaces between them choked with bodies and forming a charnel house labyrinth. Statues of monstrous gods and daemons – a dog-headed representation of the Blood God Khorne, a sagging monstrosity of grey stone that was surely Nurgle, the Plague Lord – glowered over the scene, the gemstones in their eyes watching for bloodshed about to begin.

The only remnants of the original lab were the cells. They were of polished steel and now stood on the top of black stone pillars, each one holding a specimen of a different xenos species. Chrysius recognised a genestealer of the Ymargl strain, the harbinger species who moved ahead of the tyranid hive fleets. Another cell held the filth-encrusted mass of a hrud, spacebound scavengers who clothed themselves in exoskeletons of other species' detritus. There was a snake-bodied, four-armed creature among them whose ornate armour suggested ownership by a more sophisticated species who likely used it as a bodyguard or foot soldier. On many of the altars were the corpses of other xenos, some cut open with their innards spread as fodder for soothsayers, other dissected as if for study, their body parts laid out as neatly as a watchmaker's cogs on the sacrificial slabs.

Chrysius took all this in as he led the charge. Half his mind was that of a student of war, sizing up every aspect for cover and fields of fire. The other half saw only the tell-tale shapes of ancient power armour among the heaps of bones and let the recognition of them fill him with hate,

The Iron Warriors. They were here, making their stand in this grand temple to the warp's own gods.

If anyone had asked Chrysius, in that moment, to recite the principles of warfare that had been implanted in his mind in hypno-doctrination, he could not have done so. The glories of Rogal Dorn. The legends of his Chapter. His own name. They were all gone from his mind, replaced by a raw and burning hatred.

Because he had seen the Iron Warrior's face. The one he had killed in the fuel depot. And the image of that face filled his mind, an icon of hatred without equal.

Bolter fire hammered against the shattered bulkhead as Chrysius vaulted the twisted wreckage. Shots burst against his chestplate and greave, but his momentum carried him on.

He passed into the dense shadow between two altars, his feet crunching through xenos skeletons.

Black power armour loomed in front of him. The shape was that of a Space Marine but deformed with bulky bionics. One arm was an industrial claw, more suited to carving up slabs of metal in a manufactorum than for using as a hand. Half the head was a metallic skull, crowned with a circle of bronze horns. The single eye in the centre of the faceplate glowed green as it played targeting lasers across Chrysius's body.

Chrysius never gave the Iron Warrior the opportunity to shoot. He closed the gap in two strides and hit the traitor square in the chest.

But it held firm. It was heavier and stronger than Chrysius. It slammed its claw against Chrysius's midriff in a colossal backhand, throwing the Imperial Fist into the black stone of the altar behind him.

Chrysius kicked out, forcing open the gap between himself and the Iron Warrior. It was just enough to bring the point of his chainsword up and drive it forward. The tip sheared through the pistons of the traitor's bionic shoulder, slicing through cables and hoses.

The Iron Warrior laughed. It was a hateful, metallic sound. Chrysius tried to wrench his chainblade back out and the Iron Warrior held up his claw, slamming its blades together as if in mockery, to show Chrysius the weapon that would cut him in half in a handful of seconds.

Another shadow fell against the darkness, black against black. It was Brother Vryskus, his duelling blade arrowing down at the Iron Warrior.

The blade punched into the Iron Warrior's chest. The pressure came off Chrysius for a second and he was free, rolling out from under the Iron Warrior.

The Iron Warrior ignored the injury, pivoting and catching Vryskus between the blades of his claw. Steam spurted from its damaged shoulder as the twin blades slammed closed, slicing Brother Vryskus in half at the waist.

Chrysius felt as if he had been immersed in ice. His blood seemed gone, replaced with freezing gas. He cried out and stabbed his chainblade forward again, this time aiming at the back of the Iron Warrior's head.

The chainsword caught the Iron Warrior in the neck, where the spine joined the skull. The traitor tensed rigid as the chain teeth sawed through the top of his spine and brain stem, pulping the inside of the cranium. The single eyepiece popped and spurted viscous gore down the front of its black armour.

It had taken less than a second. One moment Vryskus had been alive, the next he was dead. Chrysius had seen thousands of deaths, but the death of a brother, of a squad mate, was never the same.

Brother Myrdos, who had bickered with Vryskus minutes before, crunched through the corpses underfoot and stopped dead when he saw Vryskus's helmet, with the black stripe painted down its faceplate, down among the broken bodies. He saw instantly that Vryskus was dead.

'We will mourn him when the Weaponsmith has fallen,' gasped Chrysius.

Myrdos could only nod his agreement before Chrysius stepped over the two dead Space Marines, one traitor and one loyal, and struck further into the altar labyrinth.

The hate had been hot a moment ago. Now Chrysius was filled with ice, and it seemed twice as fierce. He had to be rid of it, this awful freezing pressure building up in his chest, and the only way was to fight on through, kill and maim and avenge with every stroke.

Revenge. He would have revenge. He would carve every unspoken syllable of his hate onto the Weaponsmith's body.

Gunfire streaked from an altar above. Chrysius vaulted up onto the top and saw another Iron Warrior, this one with both hands altered with mutation and bionics into multi-barrelled bolters. It was spraying out the firepower of four or five Imperial Fists, filling the air with burning chains of shrapnel. Chrysius slashed down at one of the Iron Warrior's legs, knocking it onto its back. Myrdos was beside him and leapt on the downed Iron Warrior, stabbing down at its heart. Myrdos's chainsword threw a shower of sparks as it bit into ceramite.

The Iron Warrior threw Myrdos off and, before Chrysius could even swing a return stroke at it, fired a volley at him. One shot caught Chrysius full in the leg and he felt the bones and gristle of his knee blown apart into a bloody-petalled flower of torn skin.

Chrysius fell back. He ordered his body to move in for the kill-stroke, but his body refused to obey him, shocked into disobedience. The Iron Warrior turned to Myrdos and the snarl of its deformed faceplate seemed to sneer as it levelled its bolter barrels at the Imperial Fist.

A massive volley of fire ripped into Myrdos, laying his ribcage open in a bloody mass. One of his arms was blown clean off and another shot punched through his eyepiece, splitting the back of his head open and spilling his brains across the black stone of the altar.

I will mourn later, Chrysius told himself. Time seemed to slow down, leaving him the moments he needed to follow his thoughts. I will weep for him among the shrines and statues of the *Phalanx*. But not yet.

Hanging above the altar was one of the specimen cages – this one containing another genestealer. Chrysius had fought them before, and knew them to be creatures of such viciousness that to take one down, one on one, in close combat was worth a badge of honour that Chrysius had yet to earn. They could be taken down at a distance with no loss, provided they were spotted and targeted in time. Up close, they were a horror.

Chrysius drew his bolt pistol, not moving from his position on his back. He aimed up at the chain holding the cell above the altar.

The Iron Warrior must have assumed Chrysius was trying and failing to aim at it. It blasted off a few bolter shots into the advancing Imperial Fists, then turned back to Chrysius. In the moment that gave him, Chrysius loosed off half his pistol's magazine, and the top of the cage was shredded in a burst of silver shrapnel.

The chain parted and the cell plummeted down. It landed just behind the Iron Warrior, who turned to see what had missed it.

The four clawed limbs of the genestealer inside reached out between the bent bars and grabbed the Iron Warrior by the neck. The alien's head was a mass of tentacles that splayed apart, revealing a beak-like mouthpart. The genestealer dragged the Iron Warrior against its cell, and lashed its tentacles around its helmet.

The beak punched out through the back of the Iron Warrior's face. The Traitor Marine convulsed, bolters firing randomly.

Chrysius forced himself to stand, his ruined leg threatening to buckle under him. There was no pain, even though there should have been too much for his armour's painkiller reserves to mask. He had no room for pain in him now.

The rest of his bolter's magazine was blasted point-blank into the feasting genestealer's head, shattering its alien skull and leaving it slumped in its cell with the dead Iron Warrior still held close.

Part of Chrysius wanted to pick up the remains of Brother Myrdos, carry him far from that battlefield and give him the funeral rites of a brother. He wanted to take Brother Vryskus, too, and bear the two sundered halves of him to the *Phalanx* where they might lie in state as heroes. But that part of Chrysius was a whisper compared to the hate rushing through him – now he was hollow, a desert valley worn smooth by a screaming wind. Everything was scoured away but the will to do violence to the Weaponsmith who had created all this.

Chrysius ran on, leaping down from the blood-slicked altar into the labyrinth. His vision swam with tears as he forced his way through the heaps of skeletons and wreckage. A red glow was ahead of him, and he recognised the heat and colour of molten ceramite. In the forges of the *Phalanx* it was melted down to create new armour plates. He caught the smell of it, breaking through the stench of bodies and boltgun propellant that had made it through the filters of his faceplate.

The forge at the centre of the temple was a structure of barricaded archways. Hundreds of skulls were mounted on spikes on the walls. Gunfire was blasting chunks from the barricades of wreckage the Iron Warriors had set up – the battle had already reached this far into the temple, the Imperial Fists following in the wake of Chrysius's charge and engaging the Iron Warriors from every direction.

The Weaponsmith must be here, in the forge.

In front of one of the barricades was Brother Hestion, the last member of Chrysius's squad. Hestion had charged through the hail of bolter fire to the foot of the barricade. Chrysius watched as he dragged an Iron Warrior over the barricade, flinging it to the floor and pounding a fist into its faceplate.

Another Iron Warrior mounted the barricade and vaulted down. He wielded a power axe with both hands and struck down at Hestion. The blade bit into Hestion's arm and almost cut right through it. Hestion grabbed the Iron Warrior by the throat with his good arm and, with a strength that even a Space Marine could rarely muster, hurled the Iron Warrior into the barricade. Chunks of wreckage and steel beams tumbled down.

Chrysius ran to his battle-brother's side. The Iron Warrior on the floor was trying to get up – Chrysius lanced it through the spine with his chainblade, putting all the momentum of his charge into the sword-thrust. The blade bit deep but did not penetrate far enough to kill the Iron Warrior, who turned and blasted at point-blank range with a bolt pistol.

Chrysius felt the armour over his abdomen dent and shear, but not give way. The bolter round had not penetrated. The next shot would.

Chrysius put a foot against the Iron Warrior's neck, feeling the spikes of pain bursting from his shattered knee. He drove down as best he could, forcing the Iron Warrior's head down, twisted the chainblade and put all of his weight behind it. This time the blade bored through the Iron Warrior's back. Chrysius pulled it almost all the way out and stabbed down again and again, each thrust bubbling up a torrent of gore from the well of blood.

Chrysius looked up to see Hestion and the second Iron Warrior duelling, axe against chainblade. The axe swung in a low arc, aimed at taking out Hestion's legs. Hestion blocked the blow with his weapon but in a flash of light the axe's power field discharged and the chainblade was ripped apart. Loose metal teeth spattered against Chrysius, embedding themselves in his armour like tiny daggers.

Hestion, unarmed now, put both hands around the Iron Warrior's neck. Chrysius fought to get his own chainsword out of the downed Iron Warrior's back but it had jammed tight against the breastplate of fused ribs. Finally it came loose and Chrysius lunged forward but his knee gave way, folding the wrong way underneath him.

The Iron Warrior drove the head of the axe up under Hestion's ribs. The Imperial Fist fell back, the breastplate of his power armour laid open. The Iron Warrior drew up its axe and buried the blade up to the handle in Hestion's exposed chest.

Chrysius cried out wordlessly. The Iron Warrior brought up the axe again and swung it down with such force it split Hestion's torso from shoulder to waist.

Chrysius grabbed the fallen Iron Warrior's bolt pistol from

the floor. He dragged himself forward a couple of paces so the shot would be point blank. He unloaded the pistol's remaining ammo into the back of the Iron Warrior, blasting apart the power plant of its armour.

Hestion was still alive. He was the strongest man, Space Marine or otherwise, that Chrysius had ever known and his last act was to grab the Iron Warrior's helmet and wrench it off, before falling to the ground.

The last round of bolter ammo went into the back of the Iron Warrior's head. It blew the back of the traitor's skull apart, throwing brain and skull against the fallen barricade.

Chrysius knew what he would see even before the Iron Warrior tumbled back, its head tilted so that Chrysius looked into dead eyes. He knew what the face would look like. He had seen it earlier, when he had killed the Iron Warrior in the fuel depot. The image had burned into his brain.

And this Iron Warrior was the same.

Chrysius was looking into a human face. Not a monster's face, not the face of a daemon or an inhuman fusion of man and machine. Just a man's face, like a Space Marine. No, not like any – Chrysius himself, with his gang tattoos, looked far more monstrous than this Iron Warrior.

They were men. Space Marines, just like him. Whatever made them the enemy of mankind, it was not the fact they were monsters, debased and savage creatures disfigured by the marks of their heresy. What made them traitors was something inside, something that waited inside every Space Marine.

There was nothing that Chrysius had seen in his life so hateful as a normal, human face on this enemy.

Chrysius struggled across the wreckage to Hestion's body. His battle-brother was dead – his innards were open to the air and Chrysius could see his hearts and lungs motionless amid the gore.

Chrysius pulled himself upright against the ruins of the barricade. Beyond it he could see molten ceramite pouring in sheets, like waterfalls, from above. Here, in the forge, was where the Weaponsmith waited.

Chrysius clambered over the fallen barricade. He reloaded his bolt pistol with hands that shook with pain and physical shock. It did not matter that he was hurt. When he was so full of hate, when it drove him on with such force, he could ignore that. He would suffer later. Now, there was one last kill to be taken.

In the centre of the forge, kneeling beside a black iron anvil, was the Weaponsmith.

The pain all caught up to Chrysius at once. He slumped down, supporting himself with one hand. He wanted to pitch forward onto the floor and let unconsciousness take over, but refused to allow himself such respite.

The Weaponsmith was three-quarters the height of a human, half the height of a Space Marine. It was roughly humanoid, though its limbs were too long for its body and its oversized feet had multi-jointed prehensile toes. Its hands had similarly long fingers, so dextrous they curved back on themselves like snakes. It was covered in red-brown fur. Its face was flat, almost simian, with an underdeveloped nose and wide mouth. It wore no clothing but had a pair of welding goggles clamped to its face and a bandolier of tools strung across its chest.

The anvil beside it was covered in tools and components. As Chrysius watched, it assembled a few into another creation, a spinning armature like a clockwork toy for the amusement of a child. The Weaponsmith let the device fall whereupon it took flight, catching the updraft of hot air from the forge and flitting towards the ceiling like an insect. The Weaponsmith watched it with curiosity, paying no attention to Chrysius at all.

There was no one else in the forge. The Iron Warriors were dead or fighting the main Imperial Fists force outside. Chrysius had been certain he would see the multi-armed servo-harness of Gurlagorg, the steam that belched from the engines and reactors mounted on his archaic armour, the pallid mask of synthetic flesh he wore as a face. But none of those were here, just the strange furred creature beside the anvil.

Another of the barricades fell in, shoved down by the combined weight of two members of Kholedei's Deathwatch kill-team. Kholedei himself followed them in.

'Kholedei!' shouted Chrysius. 'What is this? Where is Gurlagorg?'

Kholedei walked forward slowly. 'Step back, brother, This battle is over.'

'Where is Gurlagorg?' demanded Chrysius again. 'My squad died to get to him. Where is he?'

'Gurlagorg was never here, Brother Chrysius,' said Kholedei.

'But you spoke of the Weaponsmith! We heard you! That was why you were here!'

'And we were,' replied Kholedei, his voice level and calm. 'But I never spoke of Gurlagorg. This creature is of a species possessing a rare technological skill. The Iron Warriors were using it to manufacture wargear for them. It might reasonably be called a weaponsmith. That is what we were here to find.'

'You… you knew we would hear you,' said Chrysius. 'Over the vox. You knew we would believe it was Gurlagorg we were hunting, and you let my squad sacrifice themselves to kill him!' Chrysius aimed his bolt pistol at the alien, which again did nothing to acknowledge any of the Space Marines around it. 'And perhaps I will!'

Kholedei held up a calming hand, but the Space Marine beside him, who wore the golden livery of the Scimitar Guard beside the black of the Deathwatch, had his bolter up and aiming at Chrysius.

'The kraken rounds my kill-team use can punch through even the ceramite of a Space Marine's armour,' said Kholedei. 'Including yours, Brother Chrysius. Though you may not be familiar with the brain stem grafts of the Scimitar Guard, be assured that Brother Shen here can shoot you dead before your finger has finished pulling the trigger. We are here for the alien and we will take him alive. That is our mission, and we will complete it even if we have to go through you. I do not say this lightly, Chrysius. That we bring this alien back to the Inquisition is a matter outweighing either of our lives.'

Chrysius slumped and let his pistol drop. 'We were brothers, Kholedei. At Hive Mandibus you pulled Gruz from the rubble of that blast, and you debated with Vryskus for hours! They were your brothers! You were my brother! You knew we would die for the chance to kill Gurlagorg and you let us believe it anyway.'

'The Iron Warriors were trying to get this alien off the station,' said Kholedei. 'We had to take this position as quickly as we could. That meant spurring the Imperial Fists on to storm this place with all haste, more than combat doctrine would allow. We told you no lies and we fought as sternly as any of you, and for the same end.'

Kholedei knelt beside Chrysius and put a hand on his shoulder, and for a moment Chrysius saw in him the same White Scar who had once fought alongside him. But then that face was gone, replaced with another – the face of a Space Marine sworn to the Inquisition, and not to the battle-brothers at his side. 'And this xenos is a powerful asset to the Inquisition. Even among its own kind, it is a genius. It is responsible for arming whole Black Crusades and now that skill will be used for the good of the Imperium. You may not understand all that we have achieved here, but if you have ever trusted me, trust that it is a greater victory than killing a hundred Gurlagorgs.'

Kholedei waved the Praetors of Orpheus Techmarine forward. He placed cuffs on the alien's wrists and ankles. The xenos did not resist. One of the Techmarine's servo-arms was equipped with a syringe – this injected the alien, which slumped unconscious. The Techmarine picked it up and slung it over his shoulder.

'We must leave,' said Kholedei. 'I will pray for your fallen.'

'They are your fallen, too,' said Chrysius.

With that the kill-team left the forge, moving rapidly back towards the boarding rams. When the main Imperial Fists force breached the barricades, they found nothing but Assault-Sergeant Chrysius, slumped beside the anvil, exhausted and beaten.

* * *

Chrysius watched the science station explode and be scattered in the void, shattered by a few demolition charges placed at strategic points. Behind him, on the observation deck, were the bodies of Brothers Hestion, Vryskus and Myrdos, covered in shrouds, for they were in no condition to be viewed. Here they would lie until the Imperial Fists force had loaded their wargear and wounded onto their strike cruiser for the journey back to the *Phalanx*. The dead would be buried there, and their gene-seed would be extracted to be implanted into another generation of battle-brothers. It should have been a consolation.

Chrysius's helmet sat on the workbench in front of him. He had a little time before the force had to leave this place. He had found some paint and a brush among the workmen's tools on the fuel depot. Before he started work he glanced through the viewport again and caught his own face, illuminated by the ruddy light of the dark Euklid IV, covered in the gang tattoos that were far more monstrous than anything he had seen on the faces of the Iron Warriors. There had been nothing monstrous on the face of his friend Kholedei, either, but perhaps it had been there, exploited by the Inquisition to fulfil their mission at any cost – even the cost of fellow Space Marines' lives.

Perhaps Kholedei had been justified. Perhaps the Inquisition's mission had outweighed any Imperial Fist. Chrysius realised now, for the first time, he did not know.

As dawn broke on the far edge of Euklid IV, igniting the planet's atmosphere anew, Sergeant Chrysius began to draw the black stripe down the centre of his helmet. Brother Myrdos had never avenged his shame of losing at the Tournament of

Blades. Chrysius doubted he would never avenge his shame, either. But until he did, or more likely until he died, this would be the face he would wear.

THE VORAGO FASTNESS

DAVID ANNANDALE

'To be seconded to the Deathwatch is a great honour,' Captain Vritras had said. 'For the warrior, and for the entire Chapter.'

There had been just enough irony in the captain's tone for Teiras to feel he could respond freely. So he had. 'For an Ultramarine, certainly.'

'And for a Black Dragon?'

'This must be a joke.' He had never heard of any brother from a Chapter of the Twenty-first Founding serving in the Ordo Xenos's force of Adeptus Astartes.

Vritras's smile had been tight-lipped, grim and bitter. 'Of course it is a joke,' he had said. 'The Inquisition is famous for its sense of humour.'

Sense of humour? Perhaps not, Teiras thought now as he approached a massive set of doors aboard the Inquisition battle cruiser *Iudex Ferox. But a sense of the perverse? Ah, that's a different story.* And still he looked for the joke.

Beyond the doors was a small theatre. The curving rows of seats descended to a proscenium stage, where a marble lectern was flanked by rows of pict screens and, to the left, a hololith table. There were four other warriors present. They turned to look at him as he worked his way down to take a seat. He ran his eyes over the insignia on their right shoulders, and it seemed to him that here, perhaps, was the punch line. He started to grin.

'Do we amuse you?' growled the Flesh Tearer sitting in the front row.

Teiras shook his head. 'Your pardon, brother. I meant no offence. It is the situation that makes me smile.'

'What do you see that we don't?' the Relictor demanded. He sounded no more friendly than the Flesh Tearer, but had none of the other's defensiveness. There was a haughtiness to his tone.

'He sees a pattern, as now do I.' The speaker sat on the far right and at the rear of the chamber, as far as possible from the dim light of the single lume-strip that ran down the centre of the ceiling. He was the only Space Marine present who wore his helmet, and his right pauldron had no insignia. His livery was of the Deathwatch alone. He was anonymous.

'So do I,' said a soft voice. The Son of Antaeus sat a few rows back from the front, and he was a head taller than any of the others. He was one of the biggest Space Marines that Teiras had ever seen. Only Volos, a fellow Dragon Claw of the Second Company, was larger. Teiras nodded to the Son of Antaeus and took a seat beside him. 'Teiras,' he said. 'Well met.'

'Jern,' said the other, nodding back. He pointed to the others. 'The Flesh Tearer is Utor, and the Relictor is Kyral.' He jerked a thumb over his shoulder. 'And our shadowy friend tells us his name is Gherak.' His gaze focused on Teiras's forehead. 'You'll want to be careful. Our sponsor might decide a head like yours should have a place of honour atop a column.'

'Beauty like mine *is* a rare thing,' Teiras agreed, and showed his fangs. From the centre of his head grew a single horn, the gift of an overproducing ossmodula zygote. Like the other mutated battle-brothers of his Chapter, Teiras had moulded the bone protuberance, teasing out the shape it suggested and sheathing it in adamantium. It was conical, and curved to a lethal point. 'I plan to keep my head where it is,' he said, and as he held up an arm and flexed his fist down, a bone-blade suddenly jutted out from his wrist. The flash of pain as it emerged was so familiar, he didn't even wince.

'I shouldn't worry,' said a new voice. 'Your head is of far more use to me attached to your shoulders.'

Teiras faced forwards as Lord Otto Dagover stalked towards the lectern. The Black Dragon had known the name of the inquisitor whose orders he would be following, but little else. As monstrous as Teiras knew he looked to most mortals, and to more than a few Space Marines with his horn and stone-grey flesh, he was a physical ideal next to the creature that now stood before them. Dagover had so many bionic modifications, he might have passed for a member of the Adeptus Mechanicus were it not for the ostentatious morbidity of his remaining flesh. His ornate power armour was night-black, with silver spines rising along the shoulders and back. He was accompanied by a constant hum of servo-motors, and Teiras wondered how much of Dagover's original being was encased in ceramite, and how much of the ceramite encased anything at all.

Both of his arms, certainly, were artificial. They were longer than a human's, had several joints and ended in iron-clawed fingers that twitched at the air as if searching for prey. Above his shoulders, Dagover's head emerged from his gorget like a malignant tumour. There had been no juvenat treatments for the inquisitor. He wore his centuries and his battle scars like badges of honour and masks of horror. A few strands of grey hair hung like coarse spider's webs from a scalp that flowed like molten wax off his skull. Oversized lenses replaced eyes in something that was not so much a face as it was a hanging curtain of wrinkled, savaged flesh. Hooks pulled back the cheeks to reveal an almost lipless mouth. Teeth poked through, but they weren't genuine fangs like those of Teiras and Utor; they had simply been filed to cruel points.

Draped over the inquisitor's armour, pierced by its spines, was a cloak. It was a meticulously crafted leather patchwork, the different shades of hide suggesting the colours of a noble house. It took a moment for Teiras to realise the cloak was composed of flayed xenos skin.

Dagover's arms reached out and tapped at the screens and table. Picts of a planet appeared on the former, while the table generated a hololith of an immense fortification with a towering spire at its centre. 'Your mission,' he began without preamble, 'concerns the planet Discidia.' His words were amplified by a speaker in his gorget, but his natural voice was still audible, its cancerous rasp overlaid by the electronic scrape. There was just enough delay to create a sepulchral reverberation; the sound was redolent of all the nuances of pain both given and received. 'Your target,' Dagover went on, 'is the Vorago Fastness.' He gestured at the hololith.

Teiras took in just how many structures were contained within the walls displayed before them. There was a sprawling, disorganised quality to the layout, as if the buildings had sprung up over time and been built without regard for anything except the convenience of the moment. There was nothing liveable about the fortification, and it was far too large to be barracks. Judging from the scale of the buildings, the Fastness covered thousands of square kilometres. The meaning of the tower and the height of the walls registered. 'A prison,' he said.

Dagover nodded. 'A most profitable one, thanks in part to its quarries. One in particular also has a certain xeno-archaeological interest. My *colleague*,' he said with weary loathing, 'Inquisitor Salmenau has been overseeing a dig site at this location,' a light began to blink near the north-east wall, 'and his team has found a xenos relic of considerable importance.'

Kyral sat forwards. 'What kind of relic?'

To Teiras's surprise, Dagover answered. 'Early reports point to a cyranax weapon.'

There was a pause. The cyranax watchers were a xenos race that existed somewhere between myth and rumour. Teiras had heard whispers that the creatures possessed world-destroying technology, but he didn't know anything verifiable about them, not even whether or not they still existed. Teiras wasn't sure what was more startling: the nature of the information, or the fact that Dagover had revealed it so readily. The inquisitor smiled, and seemed to chill the air by several degrees. *A sense of humour, by the Throne,* Teiras thought.

Utor broke the silence. 'And the problem is?'

'Other than the fact that Inquisitor Salmenau's judgement makes him an unfit guardian of that weapon? An enemy force has arrived before us to claim the prize.'

'What enemy?' Teiras heard Utor's temper flare at Dagover's tease.

'The ruling council of Discidia has no idea. But their fragmentary intelligence strongly suggests the necrons.'

Teiras fought back a snort of disbelief. A single kill-team against an enemy about which so little was known beyond its utter implacability? Was there more information available than he suspected? 'What connection do the necrons have to the cyranax watchers?' he asked.

'Unknown, if indeed there is one.'

Better and better, Teiras thought. 'Are we really an adequate response to–'

'You are more than adequate,' Dagover interrupted. 'The necron force must be a small one, or all of Discidia would already have fallen, and Inquisitor Salmenau, of all people, has been able to stand up to the siege for a week. Furthermore, it is the will of the Inquisition that Discidia and its resources be preserved intact, not turned to so much glass and cinder by a large-scale war.' He began to shut down the pict screens. 'We will reach Discidia in a week.' He turned to go.

'How long can Inquisitor Salmenau hold out?' Teiras asked.

'His supplies should last for another five days.' The inquisitor's carrion flesh smiled again. 'If we get there too soon, there will be no incentive for him to leave his refuge, now will there?' Then he left the stage, metal and death disappearing back into the shadows.

'Well,' said Jern after a few moments. 'He told us a lot more than I was expecting.'

'But not the important thing,' Teiras observed.

'Which is what?' Kyral asked.

'Why us?'

Black Dragon. Son of Antaeus. Relictor. Flesh Tearer. Two fell results of the Cursed Founding, one member of a Chapter that was dancing on the edge of outright heresy, and one warrior whose genetic makeup was so corrupted that madness was not just a risk but a destiny. And if Gherak felt the need to keep his Chapter allegiance anonymous in *this* company, then his secrets were dark indeed. They were all from Chapters that were, at best, regarded with suspicion by the Inquisition and the more orthodox Adeptus Astartes. At worst, they were the targets of outright ostracism and investigation. The situation was more than bizarre. Not one of them should be in the Deathwatch. Teiras had no idea what game Dagover was playing, but he knew now that he was a long way from seeing the punch line to the inquisitor's joke.

Why us?

The feudal lords of Discidia were a forward-thinking aristocracy. Centuries earlier, the Vorago Fastness had been built with room for a near-infinite prison population. Larger than any one city on the planet, it had been conceived as a means of political control at least as much as a dumping ground for the criminal element. Discidia had the highest incarceration rate of any world in the Maeror subsector. It also had the lowest crime rate. Justice there was rudimentary to the point of being meaningless: any infraction, or even the mere perception of one, resulted in the accused being thrown into Vorago and forgotten. The abysmally short life expectancy in the prison hive kept the population density to merely hellish, rather than impossible.

Faced with such a surplus of space, the wise and benevolent regents of Discidia did the only logical thing: they imported prisoners. They let it be known to all neighbouring systems that here was a location where undesirables of whatever description could be sent and held for a suitable remuneration. And so, for generations had come a flood of inconvenient heirs, rivals and political malcontents, men and women who, for one reason or another, could not simply be assassinated, or whose continued existence was more profitable than their deaths. Those were the prisoners over whom an actual watch was kept, to make sure that they stayed alive for as long as was useful. Over time, the Vorago Fastness had become a profitable enterprise, feeding the wealth of Discidia's growing leisure class, and financing its exploding prison bureaucracy.

But the prison was a source of riches not only for what it held, but also for what it exported. It was built – by design – over many of the planet's richest deposits of benthamite. The stone was hard and smooth as marble, yet had the gloss and shine of obsidian. In its pure state it was as translucent as glass, but when other minerals were introduced it took on colours of extraordinary richness and hue. Its beauty and strength made it highly sought after for the construction of monuments. Very little struck awe into the heart of the masses with quite the same power as the sight of a sunset filtered through the beyond-royal blues and reds of a benthamite triumphal arch. And very little gladdened the hearts of Discidia's nobility quite like the quarrying of one of the subsector's most valuable resources by slave labour.

All of this Teiras learned on the journey to Discidia. A surprising amount he heard from scarified lips of Dagover himself, who seemed to be everywhere in the lead up to mission launch. Teiras asked him only once why he had put together a kill-team with such a roster. Dagover had only smiled in response. He had tilted his head, and the black lenses of his bionic eyes had flashed with the reflected light of a lume-strip. Teiras was sure the effect was deliberate.

And on the seventh day, the Thunderhawk gunship *Merciless* flew Dagover and the kill-team over the capital city, Carcera Lucrosus, towards the Lord Governor's palace. On Dagover's orders, the pilot came in low, skimming the rooftops. At first, Teiras had thought the approach was strategic, but there was no sign of conflict. The war they were heading for was confined within the walls of Vorago. What he was granted through the viewing block was a thorough perspective of the city. He glanced at Dagover. The inquisitor was watching him closely. *There's something he wants me to see,* Teiras thought. He looked down again, absorbing and evaluating.

Carcera Lucrosus was vast, and its regions varied between forests of glittering spires and shantytown swamps. But the slums were far more sparse, and took up far less real estate than Teiras was used to seeing in a city this size. He also saw none of the ant-like activity he would have expected. The slums were half-empty, some of them wholly deserted, their ramshackle structures collapsed into rubble.

The more affluent areas, on the other hand, were teeming. Sky-reaching needles of ambition and cathedrals of wealth sprouted in enclave after enclave of privilege and entitlement. Architectural follies fought to outdo each other in size and luxury. But the palace, centuries older than any of the buildings that surrounded it, was the grandest monstrosity of them all. Nestled beside the equally monumental outer wall of the Vorago Fastness, it sprawled for blocks, a tasteless concatenation of domes and minarets built beside and on top of each other like a cluster of gold-plated mushrooms. It was an unrestrained explosion of wealth and power. There was no tempering by faith; as evening fell and the *Merciless* lowered itself to the landing pad, Teiras saw a few devotional figures worked into friezes along the bases of some of the domes, but these gestures seemed hollow, mere artistic fillips.

'This is a corrupt city,' Gherak muttered.

Teiras agreed.

Dagover met with Lord Governor Pallens alone. His accompanying servo-skull sent a real-time hololith back to the Space Marines on the Thunderhawk. Teiras studied the updating images closely. The meeting room struck him as simply a throne room with variations. Even though the flicker and the grain of the hololith, the ostentation of the chamber was glaring. Floor-to-ceiling panels alternated between riotous mosaics of gold and benthamite, and enormous mirrors. Wealth and light reflected each other and turned the room into a narcissistic paroxysm. The work tables and pict screens almost disappeared beneath the visual weight of the ornamentation.

Pallens sat on a throne in the centre of the hall. The designs on the floor radiated out from the throne's dais, as if the Lord Governor were the fount of all knowledge in the room. But Pallens was not looking happy. He was a short, heavy-set man draped with too much finery, and he shrank from the sight of Dagover. Now the rays from the dais were so many accusatory fingers, pointing at the callow little man in the big chair. That he was flanked by the other members of the ruling council didn't seem to comfort him much. They were cowering just as badly. But all of them, despite their fear, still had an arrogant glint in their eyes. They resented the necessity of outside intervention, Teiras saw. They wanted a dirty job done so they could get back to the business of accumulating wealth. Over the vox transmission, Teiras heard all sorts of references to piety and worship of the Emperor, and he believed not a one.

Dagover consulted a data-slate. 'These floor plans are entirely accurate?' he asked the functionary who stood before the table. 'There has been no deviation from them at any time during or since the construction of the tower?'

'Those are the amended versions, lord,' the other man said. 'They illustrate the control room as it was built, not as it had been planned.'

Dagover nodded. 'And the power supply?'

'Prepared to your specifications.'

Dagover turned to go.

'When will the Fastness be able to resume normal operations?' Pallens asked. His voice shook, but his greed and arrogance overrode his fear.

'You are asking when Discidia will be free of the vile xenos taint?' Dagover's tone would have stopped the heart of a more intelligent man.

'Yes, yes,' Pallens said. 'Of course. But Vorago has been closed to all traffic in and out since the incident began, and every day that goes by, our economy–'

'Will stagnate and rot until, by the Emperor's good grace and my good will, I say otherwise,' Dagover snarled. He stormed from the hall.

There was nothing useful in that briefing, Teiras thought, as the hololith blinked out. *It was all for show. Why does he want us to see this?*

Teiras examined the bolter shell before inserting it into the magazine. The kraken penetrator round came to a solid adamantium tip. It was a thing of beauty.

The kill-team was loading up before leaving the *Merciless* for the generatorium. Dagover had distributed the equipment they would be deploying against the necrons. Along with the specialised shells, the bolters were Mark IVs with range finders, and the grenades were haywire variants. The weapons were impressive, but they were also, Dagover explained, best guesses. The hope was that the kraken rounds would tear through the enemy's armour, and that the grenades would disrupt the creatures' eldritch energy. The hope, not the certainty.

'We know one thing with absolute certainty about the

necrons,' Dagover said as the Deathwatch loaded up. 'And that is that we know *nothing* with certainty. Remember that. Be surprised by nothing. You will be fighting a foe who seems to be composed of nothing but armour. What would incapacitate a man or an ork is a mere inconvenience to a necron. We do not even know if they can be truly killed.'

'Why is that?' Teiras asked.

'They vanish,' said Kyral.

'You've fought them before?'

The Relictor nodded. 'Once. With my Chapter brothers.' He tapped his bolter's magazine. 'Let us hope these are more effective than standard arms.'

'What do you mean "they vanish"?'

'Just that. You'll see. Instead of dying, they simply disappear. They leave no corpses.'

'Nothing to study,' Jern realised. 'Any advice?'

'Hit them as hard and as quickly as possible.'

'Disrupt, paralyse, then exterminate,' Dagover supplied. 'And beware their weapons. As far as we have been able to determine though battlefield observation, their beams flay matter in molecular layers. Organic or inorganic makes no difference. It is simply sliced away to nothing.'

Teiras grimaced. The concept of the xenos weapon was distasteful. It lacked the directness, the brutal truth, of Imperial guns. He loaded the last of the kraken rounds, murmured a prayer of benediction over the magazine, then slammed it home in the bolter. Teiras liked these weapons. He left the *Merciless* eager to put them to the test.

* * *

The generatorium was vast. Its massed ranks of immense turbines marched into the distant gloom of the hall beneath a vault whose frescoes depicted the heroic rise and rise of Discidia's ruling caste. The particular blessing of the Emperor that they laid claim to was depicted as nothing less than their due. The walls and floor vibrated with the white-noise hum of the turbines. Here, power for the entire city was produced. Dagover was about to steal all of it for a few crucial seconds.

In an open space before the turbines was the teleporter that had been brought down from the *Iudex Ferox*. It was ancient. There was an artisanal touch to the ornate pylons that surrounded the pad, in the brass keys of the bulky cogitator, and in the inlaid mosaic of runes on the pad itself. This was a relic. A survivor, Teiras suspected, from the Dark Age of Technology. One of the treasures that the Inquisition held for its own particular use.

'It's glorious,' Kyral said. The Relictor ran a gauntlet over the surface of the cogitator. The machine gleamed with the patina of enormous age.

Jern seemed more concerned with the implications of its presence. 'How are we using this?' he asked.

'To teleport into the control room of the Fastness.'

'Control *room*?' Utor protested.

Jern exchanged a look with Teiras. 'Which I am sure,' the Black Dragon said, 'is located at the top of that centrally located tower, just as I am sure that there is no teleport homer to keep us from phasing into the floor or walls.'

'Quite,' Dagover said.

'This is madness,' said Utor.

Teiras looked at Gherak. The other Space Marine said nothing. He stood motionless, waiting, his posture suggesting indifference, as if he had seen this game of the inquisitor's many times before. 'All right,' Teiras said to Dagover. 'What's the trick?'

'Data,' Kyral said, still hovering over the cogitator.

'Very good.' The mask of ravaged flesh beamed, and the effect was obscene. 'Given enough information and power, this teleporter has a flawless precision of beam.' He held up the data-slate. 'Hence my insistence that the floor plans be accurate.'

Teiras felt himself grinning. However magical this equipment, there was a lunatic recklessness to the mission that spoke to him. It held a violent promise, one into which he could sink his fangs. He strode onto the pad. 'Brothers,' he said, 'the xenos foe awaits. Shall we go meet it?'

Reality blinked. The continuity of existence was severed as two spaces conjoined. There was the infinitesimal, but all-encompassing, moment during which the self ceased to be, and then Teiras had being once again.

The teleporter performed as Dagover had promised. The kill-team materialised in a circular chamber about twenty metres in diameter. Armourglas windows, overlooking the full prospect of the Vorago Fastness, ran around the entire periphery. Below them sat banks of cogitators, control panels and pict screens. In the centre of the floor, what looked like an extremely thick pillar was, in fact, an elevator.

Most of these details Teiras did not take in consciously until later. What registered in the moment were the half dozen metal skeletons that stood before him. They did not wear armour because they *were* armour. They were life of a kind, but their shape was death, their faces as unchanging and unforgiving as the bone they resembled. There was little in the eyes of these warriors beyond a driving hatred for anything that did not share their inorganic half-life. And there was no surprise. They raised their weapons and fired.

Teiras threw himself down. A gauss beam struck where his head had been a moment before. It glanced against his helmet, and warning runes lit up in his retinal display. The merest touch of the beam had damaged the ceramite. The light of the beam was the green of corruption and disease. A death ancient, merciless and incomprehensibly alien had found its expression in that light.

The space was too confined for the haywire grenades. Teiras returned fire with his bolter. The kraken rounds punched into the necrons, some going all the way through to the wall behind. A ghoul jerked and stumbled from the hits, its gun bucking up and the beam shearing away the rockcrete of the ceiling.

But the necron didn't fall. It stepped forward. It had been damaged, but it showed no pain. The lack of expression on its face was chilling, because what looked like a helmet was the creature itself, unflinching before the hail of destruction; and still the eyes glowed with that cold, immovable hatred.

Disrupt. Teiras rolled forward and came up like a battering ram against the undead thing's chest. He knocked it to the ground. *Paralyse.* Kneeling on the torso, he snapped out a bone-blade and plunged it into the necron's neck. With a vicious thrust, he severed the thing's head, and yet its hands reached up, seeking to pull off his helmet. *Exterminate*. He brought a fist down, pulverising the skull. There was a spine-grating electronic wail of agony. Then it cut off, and the necron was gone. Its vanishing was another reality blink. Existence cracked and reformed, taking the necron with it. Teiras felt himself twitch, as if he had been violently woken. Around him, there was nothing but a dispersing afterglow of rotted green.

There were other wails, a choir of the damned, as Teiras stood up. His kill-team brothers had destroyed the other machinic ghouls, but even in their passing, the creatures left behind a taint. There was something wrong with the atmosphere of the control room, as if a cemetery had learned rage. Jern's opponent still struggled. The Son of Antaeus, his armour bearing deep scrapes where a flayer beam had touched him, had shot the necron's limbs off, but the thing still tried to squirm forwards to attack him. The five of them watched for a few moments more before Jern dispatched the abomination with a shot to the head.

'A good start,' Utor said.

Kyral snorted. 'We've done little more than alert the main force to our presence.'

'So we strike quickly,' Gherak said. It was the first time he had spoken since they had arrived on Discidia.

'Agreed,' Teiras said. He examined the control room's screens. 'The mining rail network is still running.'

'No doubt being used by the enemy,' Jern said.

Utor grunted. 'Then we can reach them all the faster.' Even through the tone-deadening distortion of the Flesh Tearer's helmet speaker, Teiras heard a false note in Utor's eagerness.

It wasn't bravado he was detecting – the Space Marine worried about the prospect of battle did not exist. This was something else. Utor was working hard to hold himself back, Teiras realised. It wasn't battle that worried him: it was his ability to restrain his fall into the Black Rage. His eagerness and surliness were conscious performances, as if by acting the thuggish berserker he could stave off becoming the real thing.

And Dagover probably selected you precisely for that propensity to madness, Teiras thought.

He traced a finger over a hololith map of the prison's rail system. 'This line passes directly in front of the north face of this tower and crosses the dig site.'

Gears engaged and there was a steady mechanical hum as the elevator suddenly began to ascend. The kill-team faced the doors, bolters up. Gherak stepped forward with a heavy flamer. When the doors of the enclosed metal box opened, he flooded the interior with ignited promethium, bathing the group of necrons within with purging fire. The warriors did not feel pain, and they advanced into the control room, but the flame corroded their bodies. Their legs collapsed within a few steps. The Space Marines crushed the flailing skeletons beneath their boots and watched the bodies vanish in a flare of sickly green. Already, Teiras was growing used to their death wail.

The kill-team piled into the smoking elevator. The walls of the cage were scorched black, and a bas-relief frieze at its rear had been melted to ruin. Kyral pulled the lever that operated the lift. There were only two destinations: the base and the control room. The cage dropped with a rattling groan.

Teiras and Jern took up positions at the doors, and burst

through them as soon as they opened, into the night and open air of the Vorago Fastness. They unleashed a stream of bolt-fire as they charged, their kraken shells hammering into the ranks of necrons on the rockcrete platform before them. The others followed, and the kill-team hit the enemy with concentrated punch and momentum. Multiple bolters hit one target then the next, and with the sheer volume of fire, the kraken rounds were lethal this time. Kyral threw a haywire grenade at the end of the platform, catching the necrons in its disruption field. It did not paralyse them, but their movements became jerky and their guns would not fire. The ghouls marched forward out of the field. They were even more ghastly as they twitched. They were creatures from the galaxy's nightmares for whom death had become both meaningless and their only calling.

But the few seconds that the grenade bought were enough, and the bolter-fire did the rest. The necrons went down and vanished, leaving behind the echoes of their hate-filled electronic wails and the uncanny flicker of ghost light.

The kill-team moved forward. Teiras knew they hadn't been properly tried yet. The opposition was still organising. Even so, the assault had been a model of its kind. Every member of the team had fought as if amongst his Chapter brethren. There had been no need for verbal communication, barely even a gesture passing between the Space Marines. A good omen, he thought.

The platform ended at the rail line. The trains of the Vorago Fastness were not designed with passengers in mind. With very few exceptions, anyone travelling through the Fastness did so on foot. The trains were for the far more valuable cargo of benthamite. They were crude maglev affairs, long links of shallow freight wagons with the most basic locomotive imaginable. It was a car just large enough to hold a control unit as simple as the cable-lift's. The lever pulled down would set the train in motion. It would travel to the next stop on the line, where sensors would trip the lever back up, releasing the train from the magnetic field and bringing it to a stop.

The kill-team jumped onto the forward freight wagon. Kyral stood on the locomotive car and held the lever down. The wagons were empty, and the train accelerated rapidly.

'We're under way,' Teiras voxed Dagover back on the *Merciless*.

Maglev or not, the train rattled and shook as they plunged through the monstrous landscape of the Vorago Fastness. Over the centuries, a metropolis of improvised structures had risen. It made Teiras think of a collapsed hive. Shacks of sheet metal and primitive hab-blocks constructed from roughly chiselled slabs of stone tumbled over each other. There was no order, no thought to the assemblages, just a desperate grab for whatever space and materials could be had. Many structures had fallen, returning to the rubble from which they had sprung, crushing the souls that had sought refuge inside them.

Between the ruins and tottering agglomerations that would soon be ruins, the ground was hard-packed dirt and stone. The paths were a twisting labyrinth of switchbacks, random forks and dead ends. Some passed through perpetual night as buildings leaned together to form crumbling roofs over the passageways. The ground rose and fell. Some of the higher elevations ran past sunken windows, evidence that the denizens of the Fastness had built over whatever fell. Beneath the surface, geological strata held the record of imprisonment and death. Above the paths, running at the level of the upper floors of the taller buildings, were the maglev tracks. They were a metal web stitching the space of the Fastness together, the trains transporting the native wealth of the earth over the imported squalor of man.

Down those paths, through the windows and doors of the misery expressed in stone, and in the squares of subsiding wreckage, the human population of the Vorago Fastness swarmed and eddied like a blanket of maggots. The movement was desperate. It was a perpetual clawing for survival. Rotting food, weapons of stone and pipe, shelter or the means to build it, blood clans and shifting alliances – these were the currency that paid for another hour of life, another hour of fighting for the means to fight for another hour.

As the mining train raced through the vistas of the prison, Teiras saw moments of collective effort alternate with blood-soaked riots. The resilience of dignity adjoined the plunge into the bestial. He knew that there were good men and women in the cauldron. From Dagover's description, he understood that the political wealth of the prison meant that far more of the inmates were innocent of anything that he would recognise as a crime than were guilty. But wolves and lambs were both represented in the bubbles of hope and vortices of violence. The nature of such a place permitted no alternative.

The train entered the mining zones of the Fastness, where quarries broke up the chaotic squalor of the habitation sectors. Centuries upon centuries of benthamite extraction had created abysses from which rock was hauled by endless cable. Into them, men descended to an existence of slavery in depths so profound that the sky was lost. As the line ran deeper into regions rich in benthamite, the quarries became more numerous, canyons of darkness yawning beneath the train, while overcrowded towers of stone teetered on narrow plateaus between.

The attack came as the train was going to pass under another track. Teiras saw them lined up on the upper rail, waiting, motionless as armed statues. A dozen warriors, three larger and bulkier than the others. They opened up with a constant barrage of gauss energy before the Space Marines were even in range. The beams sliced the maglev track apart.

Teiras glanced down. They were passing over a quarry. The blackness looked eager to receive them. Ahead, on the other side of the gap in the line, was one of the narrow plateaus. 'Too late to stop,' Kyral warned. Teiras leaned over the rear of their cart, bone-blade out. He hacked at the link between carts. Iron parted before adamantium. He cut the rest of the train away just as they hit the gap.

The necrons' flayer beams had not warped the line. They had simply removed any trace of what had been there, reducing ten metres of track to floating atoms. The train rode air and dropped. The front cart, lighter now than the rest of the train, flew a little bit further as it fell. It missed the canyon by metres, slamming into the plateau on a hard diagonal. The kill-team was catapulted from the cart. Teiras curled into a ball and hit the ground like a meteor. He came to a stop when he smashed into the wall of a shack. The unmortared stone collapsed around him. He rose, shrugging off the debris and blinking away the amber warning runes before his eyes. His armour was damaged, but still functional.

The kill-team gathered in the street beside the cart. The landing had killed a dozen prisoners. Their deaths were unavoidable; there was no space in this anthill of humanity for anything to come down without harm. Teiras did not look back at the demolished hab behind him. He turned his attention instead to the street. It was barely four metres across, and moved uphill in a relatively straight line for several hundred metres before taking a sharp bend to the right. Vorago's haphazard architecture leaned over it. The roofs of some of the buildings almost touched each other, sealing the street in permanent night.

'They'll be coming soon,' said Kyral.

'Good,' Utor snarled.

Jern said, 'These structures are a gift.'

'Agreed.' *Ambush paradise,* Teiras thought.

Gherak pointed to a pair of buildings on opposite sides of the street near the top of the hill. 'There,' he said. They looked as stable as anything here was, and they had windows facing each other and looking back down the street.

The Deathwatch charged uphill. Desperate humanity parted before the Space Marines, looking at them with neither hope nor fear, only the feral calculation of survival. Teiras and Jern took the building on the right. There were no stairs between floors. Instead, there were holes cut on alternating sides of each ceiling with a large block of stone placed underneath. An ordinary human could climb to the next floor without too much struggle. The Space Marines leaped. They zigzagged from floor to floor until they reached the top. There were perhaps twenty

Fastness denizens here. As Teiras and Jern ran to the windows, a woman approached them. She had short grey hair that looked as if it had been shorn with a knife. Her age was difficult to guess – all the faces here had the worn look of lifetimes of hard experience – but she carried herself with a commanding bearing born of sheer determination.

'My lords, are you here to kill us or save us?' she asked. Her tone was respectful, but unafraid.

'Neither,' said Teiras. 'I'm sorry.' He was.

'And those creatures?'

'They have not come here to kill you specifically, but they will, all the same.'

She nodded. 'Then, my lords, I pray you: do not leave this place unchanged.' Then she stepped back. Other prisoners clustered around her, as if for protection.

What must not go unchanged? Teiras thought. *Us, or the prison?*

With Jern in position, Teiras climbed out the window and up onto the top of the building. He checked the lower end of the street. Nothing yet. There was time to refine the ambush. He loped from rooftop to rooftop, until he was about halfway down the slope. Opposite him, Gherak kept pace. They dropped at the same moment, lying flat on the roofs. The necrons had arrived.

The xenos ghouls had descended from their perch on the maglev line and were now moving up the street in a wedge formation. The spaces between them were so regular, their steps so precisely synchronised, that they could have been a single machine. But the aura of death that radiated from them had nothing to do with the unfeeling and the inorganic. It was as livid as the green of the gauss rifles. As mechanical and emotionless as the actions of the necrons appeared to be, they were motivated by an ineradicable hatred, older than human civilisation.

The necrons sought out the Space Marines through a process of brutal elimination. They simply killed everything in sight. Their gauss beams played over the prisoners, flaying them to the bone in agonising instants. The street erupted with a cascade of fragmented screams and violently shed flesh. The necrons swept the beams back and forth, slicing away the supports of the surrounding structures. The patchwork city collapsed in their wake, stone and blood spilling with a roar to close the street behind the marching abominations.

Teiras looked through his bolter's range finder. He zeroed in on the skull of the leading necron. It was one of the larger ghouls. Invisible beams bounced between the scope and the target, and the precise distance to the xenos appeared as a readout in the sight. Teiras adjusted his aim and fired. He held the gun steady as he pumped a stream of penetrator rounds into the necron's skull. It was like sniping with a bolter. The head disintegrated. The necron phased out in mid-step. Gherak took out another in the next rank. The perfection of the wedge was shattered.

The necrons retaliated. They charged forward and brought their beams to bear on the rooftops. But Teiras and Gherak had already moved on, leaping to the next building down and firing again. Two more ghouls uttered their electronic scream and vanished. The necrons spread their fire wide and low, and all the lopsided, deathtrap piles of stone for a hundred metres on both sides of the street now fell. Teiras saw the destruction coming to his position, and he jumped, dropping ten metres to the ground. He stuck the landing, and felt the jar of impact shoot up his spine. Gherak was also down and at his side in a moment. They were now behind the necron wedge, and they unloaded their clips into the ghouls at the same time as their brothers in the forward positions began shooting. A haywire grenade joined the enfilading fire, and the necrons were stitched with mass-reactive devastation. More were sent back to the hell from which they had crawled.

The ghouls staggered forward, as if against a strong wind, and emerged from the grenade's disruptor field. Beams raging, they toppled the buildings at the head of the street. Kyral, Jern and Utor jumped from the windows and outran the destruction, closing with the necrons and firing still. Teiras and Gherak advanced, and now they were a pincer snapping shut on the enemy.

The remaining necrons split into two groups and charged forward and rear, matching the Deathwatch's aggression, but not the kill-team's speed. The Space Marines came at the ghouls in sudden doglegs and diagonal sprints, keeping their movements unpredictable.

The street was a shrunken space, filled with rubble and smashed bodies. The two forces were in close quarters now. They were seconds from clashing together.

Utor leapt forward, reckless. A beam sideswiped his midsection. The Flesh Tearer fell forward, but then rose to a crouched firing position. His anger roared from the barrel of his gun.

'Brother Utor?' Jern voxed.

'Stupid,' Utor rasped. His breathing was laboured. 'Fine. Fine. Come on, then. Fight.' He spoke with the staccato of strain, but not, Teiras thought, from pain. He was holding back his rage with a slippery grip.

They had all taken glancing hits, but their armour held. Utor had suffered serious tissue loss in his midriff, but his Larraman cells' rapid formation of scar tissue was compensating. His breathing was a constant sub-vocalised growl. He fought with increasing savagery. It was as if every violent gesture was a blow against the madness that promised a deeper violence. But despite the toll it must have been taking on him, Utor's brutal energy was infectious. Teiras felt himself exhilarated by battle. The fury of the Emperor was upon him, and nothing could stem its charge.

The Space Marines moved as one, the genetic insanity of Utor's blood transmuted into an infusion of strategic savagery in his brothers.

Brothers.

Brothers.

Teiras felt the spirit of battle granting them the blessing of unity, turning them into the fingers of a single fist.

They raced over the final metres, taunting fate and lethal weaponry. Crimson runes flashed in Teiras's retinal lenses as a flaying beam glanced against his arm. But the contact was brief and shaken as he unleashed a torrent of bolter shells into the necron's face. Then he was moving forward through the skeleton's shriek and vanishing flash. In his peripheral vision, his brothers were moving with the same grace of perpetual killing.

Ahead of him, the last of the larger, more powerful ghouls

levelled its gauss blaster at his chest. Teiras threw himself to one side. The air shrieked with destructive energy and slashed at his armour's flank. The necron adjusted its aim. Teiras tucked himself into a roll underneath the barrel of the gun. Bone-blade unsheathed, Teiras slashed upwards, cutting through the fuel line. The weapon disappeared in a flash of disordered energy, and took the top half of the necron with it.

Teiras stood up. To his left, Jern knocked the barrel of a ghoul's blaster aside with his bolter. The necron countered with inhuman speed, reversing the gun and smashing its stock against the side of Jern's head. The blow would have staggered Teiras, but Jern's only reaction was to slam his bolter down on the necron's crown with such force that the machine head seemed to implode. Then it was gone. The last of the other necrons were also nothing more than the crackle of dissipating energy.

Utor stood over the spot where his foe had been. The growl in his breathing had ratcheted up. He was shifting his weight back and forth from foot to foot, a hunter looking for a reason to spring. Gherak stood in front of him, close enough to get his attention, far enough not to be an immediate threat. His bolter was mag-locked to his thigh, his arms at his side. 'Brother Utor,' Gherak said. 'Are you with us?' His tone was even, measured, neutral. When Utor didn't respond, Gherak repeated the question.

There was a brief pause in the rattling breath.

'We stand with you,' Gherak said. 'We stand in the Emperor's light. Can you feel it? Can you feel His blessing? It is upon our mission, it is upon this action and it is upon you.' He raised his right arm, hand open, palm up. 'Draw strength from His light, brother. Draw focus and clarity. He calls you to our mission, and it is far from over. We still have need of your strength, and of the gift that is yours alone.'

Teiras would have pledged his oath that he *heard* Utor blink. The Flesh Tearer stopped his rocking. 'Brother Gherak,' he said. He clasped forearms with the other Space Marine.

'We are close,' Kyral said. He was consulting the map on his data-slate. 'The target is on the other side of this plateau. A few thousand metres.'

They set off at a quick march. As they passed the wreckage of the building where Jern had been stationed, Teiras saw that the woman who had spoken to them had survived the collapse. She was helping dig for other survivors. She looked up, and Teiras nodded to her. She gazed back, impassive.

The kill-team moved beyond the destruction. Though the road turned at the top of the hill, it was faster to climb over the low houses and move straight towards their destination.

Teiras joined Gherak and opened a private vox-channel. 'You handled Utor well, brother,' he said.

Gherak shrugged. 'The true madness was not upon him.'

'But he was teetering on the edge. You brought him back. I thought your approach demonstrated an unusual understanding.'

'You mean I didn't call for his immediate execution?'

Interesting, Teiras thought. It was the first flash of emotion he had heard from Gherak. 'I meant that to view the call in his blood as in any way a gift takes a rare insight.'

'Do you regard your own mutation as a curse?'

Bless the curse. The refrain of the Black Dragons' holy communion came back to Teiras. 'My Chapter's creed is not that crude,' he answered; *and neither, it seems, is yours*, he thought. He waited for Gherak to speak again, but the other had fallen silent.

The train had taken them north and west from the tower, and by now the kill-team had travelled most of the way to the outer wall. They were, Teiras calculated, approximately level with the Lord Governor's palace. There were no more houses now as they entered mining territory again. There was a rise in the terrain ahead, and from the other side came a pulsing green glow and the *crump* of explosions.

At the crest of the rise, a quarry came into view. This one was not a vertical gulf, more a narrow box canyon. It had been dug into the hill, creating ragged, oppressive cliffs on either side of a steep, uneven slope. From its depths came the unholy flashes and echoing energy crackles of xenos warfare.

The kill-team descended the slope. The broken surface gave the Space Marines plenty of cover. They moved from boulder to boulder. On the other side of a large tumble of stone, they saw the siege. There were ten necron warriors. Before them was a monstrous face fifty metres high, and they were assaulting it with a relentless, untiring, mechanical rhythm. The face bore the disfigurements of a week of unceasing assault. Its features had blurred and crumbled, and what its true character had been was now impossible to determine. It had never been human, that much was sure. Teiras could see the vague suggestion of scales, and its eye sockets were much too far apart, as if the being represented had possessed 180-degree vision. More disturbing yet was that it did not appear to be carved from the rock. At first, Teiras thought that it looked as if it somehow had been *formed* by the rock, as natural an extrusion as a crystal. But that too was wrong. He had the process reversed, he realised. The rock had been formed by the face. Strata exposed by the dig showed the record of metamorphism radiating out from it. Benthamite and all its glory were the mere by-product of the face's creation.

Whatever its composition, the face had withstood days of incessant necron fire. So had the door in its roaring mouth. It was made of the same mysterious stone as the face itself, but its strength, too, was failing at last. It was pitted and crumbling. It had the visual consistency of sponge, even though it was still standing. The necrons eroded it further by the second.

The skeletal warriors were as rooted as turrets, moving only to play their gauss beams over a resisting part of the door. They were directed by a lone figure. It carried a staff that to Teiras resembled a cross between an ecclesiarch's sceptre of office and a spear. He caught a glimpse of the creature's face. It was the expressionless skull of its race, but it had only one eye in the centre of its forehead. The emerald glow of the orb was brighter and more piercing than those of its fellows. Its gaze was one of eternal, unblinking observation, analysis and judgement.

'There is much here to destroy,' Kyral said. He pulled out a melta bomb.

Teiras did the same. The canyon was very narrow, only a few dozen metres wide. The necrons were bunched close together. The invitation was impossible to ignore.

'Let us purge them from the Emperor's sight,' Teiras said.

He and Kyral leaped over the crest of the rubble. They raced down the slope. Halfway down, they were within range, and threw their bombs. The cyclopean necron noticed them and brought its staff to bear at the same moment. It fired. A blistering, shrieking beam slammed into Kyral's chest. The Relictor flew backwards, enveloped by howling light. Then the bombs landed, and there was a different light. This was the light of the Emperor, beyond molten, silver-white as blindness. It swallowed the necrons and their glow of the plague. There was a satisfying unity to the death shrieks. The one-eyed necron was caught at the outer edge of the bombs' radius of effect. Its lower half was liquefied by the heat. Its staff exploded, disintegrating its right arm. It dragged itself forwards a few metres before phasing out, and Teiras was sure he saw hatred in the fading glow of its eye.

Teiras turned to help Kyral, but the Relictor was already on his feet. His chest plate was badly damaged, but whatever the extent of his injuries, he strode on as if they were beneath notice.

'Brother,' Teiras began.

'I require no assistance,' Kyral snapped. He marched the rest of the way to the stone door.

Jern muttered, 'Aristocrat,' as he went past, drawing a snort from Teiras.

They gathered before the ravaged door. The melta bomb attack had damaged it still more, but it had not fallen.

'We are at the door, inquisitor,' Teiras voxed to the *Merciless*.

Dagover opened a general channel. 'Salmenau,' he said, 'let them in. You know you have no choice.'

Several seconds went by, pregnant with resentment. Then the door opened. There was no sound. The unknown stone split into six wedges that withdrew into the sides of the face's mouth. The kill-team moved inside.

The interior was surprisingly small, given the monumental façade. It extended for about thirty metres, was the same in width, and half that in height. The walls, floor and ceiling were smooth and rounded, like the interior of a bubble. Rows of lume-strips had been installed on the ceiling. Along the right-hand wall was a large cogitator and a panoply of excavation and analytical equipment fussed over by a clutch of tech-priests. Power was supplied by a large cable, almost as thick as Teiras's torso. It snaked into the cavern from an opening in the rear wall, near the ceiling. It must have been fed in through the top of the hill, and linked to a power source via the maglev tracks.

The weapon crouched in the middle of the floor. It was fifteen metres long, and two thirds of that comprised a monstrous barrel wide enough to take metre-thick shells – if indeed those were what it fired. Teiras couldn't begin to guess whether it was a projectile or energy weapon. Its body was articulated, and it rested on four insect-like legs. Teiras's lip curled. The cannon was an utterly and disgustingly alien object. There was also something about its design, its machinic mimicry of life, that reminded him of the necrons' guns. There was a connection, he realised. The nature of the link between the necrons and the cyranax watchers was as obscure as the watchers themselves, but the fact of the link was clear. There was a dark logic behind the necrons' presence here, and their pursuit of this gigantic weapon.

Facing the Deathwatch were Inquisitor Salmenau and the survivors of his team. Salmenau had clearly not been expecting serious combat. He was flanked by an Imperial Guard veteran, a man whose facial scars were so extensive that his face had become two eyes glaring out from a mass of thick, leathery tissue, an angry pink in colour. He had also been injured. His combat fatigues hung oddly on his left side, as if chunks of his body were missing. He was soaked in his blood. It seemed to Teiras that standing beside his master was all that the man could still do. The others were scholars, not fighters. They held lasrifles, but would be lucky not to shoot off their own heads.

Salmenau stood in marked contrast to Dagover. They were, Teiras knew, close to the same age, but Salmenau had undergone aggressive juvenat treatments. He seemed much younger, though there was a brittle tautness to his youth. His clothes were torn from combat, but after two weeks of being besieged, he didn't have a hair out of place. The cut of his breeches and coat was severe but stylish. His hand rested on the pommel of a power sword. He was no less grotesque than the massively armoured vulture that waited back on the Thunderhawk.

Dagover's voice crackled from multiple speakers. 'You aren't going to be difficult about this, Armand, are you? There really wouldn't be any point.'

'You cannot have it, Otto.'

'Why not? You don't appear to be doing anything useful with it. If you were going to use it, you would have done so days ago.'

Salmenau paled. 'Such xenos obscenities are to be studied, then destroyed. I would die before risking such a taint to my soul.'

'Which you were about to do. You Amalathians are so hide-bound, I'm surprised your pious caution hasn't led you to extinction.'

'You must not take the weapon.'

'Are you going to stop us?'

The scholars were trembling. One of them moaned, but they did not drop their guns. Teiras respected them for that.

Salmenau turned to the kill-team. 'You are being led down the path to heresy and treason,' he said. 'Step off it, for all our sakes.'

Teiras remained still. Dagover's enthusiasm for xenos technology disturbed him, but he had no wish to cast judgement, not when the Black Dragons were often denounced as abominations. And the oath he had sworn on his and the Chapter's honour was to serve the Inquisition in the person of Otto Dagover. The other Space Marines made no move, either.

Salmenau stepped directly in front of the weapon's barrel. 'You will have to kill me,' he said.

'Spare us the melodrama,' Dagover began.

He didn't finish. The room erupted with green light as a barrage of gauss beams blasted through the open door. Teiras hurled himself down and to the side, out of the direct line of fire. Jern hit the ground hard, smoke pouring from his damaged power unit. Salmenau ducked under the weapon, which the necrons' shots avoided, but his retinue was taken apart in seconds, bodies stripped and anatomised.

Teiras crawled forward with his brothers. He was able to stand once he reached the raging 'O' of the stone mouth, staying in cover on the right-hand side. He took a quick look outside.

The necrons were coming in force. He saw dozens of warriors, many of them the hulking variants they had fought on the street. At the head of the army came a figure whose tattered robes could not disguise a terrible majesty. It wielded a massive war scythe and towered over its troops, a monarch of death and machinic night. Its skeletal jaw parted, hurling a stream of alien curses as it closed in.

Salmenau scrabbled to the cogitator and turned some dials. There was a hum of power. The chamber glowed faintly and the door began to close. It was sluggish, and the necron fire ate at the wedges. The door stopped dead, leaving an oval about the size of a man. Gherak and Jern took up positions at the gap. Gherak crouched, Jern stood, and they loosed a steady stream of bolter-fire at the advancing ghouls, staggering reloads so the mass-reactive hell never stopped.

Teiras gave them further support. Warriors vanished in crackling glows, but the advance barely slowed. The door continued to erode. The arithmetic was unavoidable. The kill-team only had so many bolter clips. Not nearly enough.

'Ambush,' Gherak growled. 'They gave up part of their force so we would give them access.'

Teiras could almost admire the strategic precision of the necrons' sacrifice. They had abandoned just enough of their number to make that force convincing. It had never occurred to him that he had been gunning down bait.

'This barrier will not last,' Jern said.

Ducking just under the barrel of Jern's bolter, Teiras directed his fire at the approaching noble. The necron didn't even acknowledge the attack. The shells bounced off its form. Teiras thumbed a krak grenade from his belt and hurled it through the gap. The explosion immolated the two foot soldiers on either side of the lord, but the leader marched on without pause. It was less than thirty metres from the door.

Teiras looked back. Kyral was huddled over the back of the weapon. 'Brother Teiras,' he called.

Teiras dropped another warrior, then joined the Relictor. Utor took his place at the door.

Kyral pointed at the power cable. 'That links to the main generatorium for the Fastness. That should be enough power. I think I can connect the weapon. I see enough parallels to other relics of my experience.'

Use the xenos weapon? Teiras thought. The concept was disgusting. And yet...

'This is not done lightly,' Kyral said. He pointed to the disintegrating door. 'Or shall we die in purity and leave this to the necrons?'

Salmenau glared, but drew a laspistol and went to engage in symbolic defence of the entrance.

'I should be able to keep the power connected and flowing,' Kyral began.

'And I must pull the trigger,' Teiras finished. It was midway down the enormous barrel, shaped as if for a handheld weapon, but on a cannon the size of a major artillery piece. Teiras wrapped both arms around the firing mechanism. He watched the door.

The malevolent green intensified. The barrier did not glow so much as become translucent. The gap widened. Teiras's proximity to the weapon was the only thing that saved his life.

Salmenau reeled back from the opening, clutching at the perfectly sheared stump where his right hand had been. Utor, Jern and Gherak kept up the fire, even as their armour lost layers to the stray hits they did not move fast enough to avoid. Teiras listened to Utor's breathing. As if sensing he was monitored, Utor announced, 'Do not fear, brothers. If we are to meet the Emperor this day, I shall do so with a clear spirit.'

There was a flash of energy and green corruption. The door vanished. The necrons surged forward, led by their lord. It swung its scythe at Jern with blinding speed and shattered his pauldron. He fell, but was not cut in half. Teiras's eyes widened at Jern's strength. It was as if he wore a second suit of armour.

Utor had pulled his chainsword and was decapitating the warriors almost as quickly as they crossed the threshold to the chamber. Almost. The tide was pushing him back. A group of three converged on Gherak. He roared and threw himself into their midst. Others joined the attack. Individually, they were weaker than a Space Marine, but they fought with a terrible collective precision. Gherak sank under the attack.

Then he threw the attackers off and swung a chainaxe. And as he did so, he burst into flame.

At first, Teiras thought that Gherak had been hit by a flamer. Then he saw that the Space Marine himself was the source of the fire.

Teiras felt a moment of astonishment at the depths of Dagover's game. A Flame Falcon. The most cursed Chapter of the Cursed Founding, the most ill-fated of the Black Dragons' cousins. Declared Excommunicate by the Inquisition, they had, Teiras had always believed, been exterminated, and yet here was one, no doubt existing at the pleasure of Dagover.

What agenda am I aiding by fighting for this man? Teiras thought. But then Kyral shouted '*Now!*' and Teiras thought, *I fight for my brothers.*

The Deathwatch warriors threw themselves back and down.

The necron lord had reached the cannon and it swung its scythe at Teiras.

Teiras heaved back, and fired the gun.

It was as if he had personally triggered a nova cannon. The world vanished in a flash of quasar silver streaked with infernal red. Energies he could not begin to fathom sprang into being. Microseconds merged with eternity. Creation was the negation of all that stood in its path. There was a silent roar so huge it buried all sound except, deep within the core, something that sounded like a hissing whisper.

The light and the sound of otherness faded. In their wake came the almost reassuring rhythm of massive but conventional explosions. And in a straight line from the weapon: nothing. The necrons had vanished. So had a large section of the slope. A wake of pure destruction stretched as far as Teiras could see.

Behind him, Kyral, dazed, was picking himself up. The power cable was a twisting, burning wreck. Teiras imagined the immense recoil of the weapon transformed into annihilating feedback.

He had to know. He tore out of the chamber and scrambled up the cliff wall, punching handholds into the rock face where none presented themselves. It took him less than a minute to reach the top of the rise, and he was in time to see the last of what had been wrought. He had been right. The energy of the recoil had travelled back over the entire power network of the Fastness. The maglev web flashed orange and white, molten tracks dropping down like burning logs. Power nodes were exploding all over the Fastness, bright spheres of light and death in the night. In the distance, the tower swayed. It was the centre of the grid. The generatoria at its base were massive in power, and now massive in death. There was a huge flash. God-flames engulfed its entire height, and moments later the sound arrived, hammering the air and ground with a hollow blast of doom. The tower collapsed straight down, folding again and again in on itself.

Then there were only glows and echoes, and the anticipation of aftermath.

'You are a Recongregator,' Teiras said. Helmet under his arm, he was standing in Dagover's study aboard the *Iudex Ferox*. Gargoyles and the statues of martyred saints lined the walls.

The inquisitor was seated behind a massive desk. Its surface was covered in books whose titles Teiras was content not to examine. Crouched in his armour, his long bionic arms flicking through papers, Dagover reminded him of a scarab. 'And?' Dagover asked. He did not sound displeased that Teiras knew of his radical faction within the Inquisition.

'I want to know what we just did.'

Dagover snorted. 'It is not your place to ask.'

'I realise that. Nonetheless.'

Dagover nodded, that ghastly smile forming once again. 'Why don't you tell me what you think we accomplished.'

'We destroyed a necron raiding force. We also managed to shut down all power, and thus all security measures, of the Vorago Fastness, punch a large hole through its outer wall, and do considerable damage to the city beyond, including bisecting the Lord Governor's palace.'

'Quite,' Dagover said, the grin becoming even wider and more hideous. 'And...?'

'And the prison population has flooded into Carcera Lucrosus. We have effectively unleashed a civil war on Discidia.'

Dagover nodded. 'Would you say that the existing political order on Discidia was worth preserving?'

'No.' Teiras was surprised at how easily the answer came.

'So the wealth of the planet has been preserved, and a regime that was unworthy of the Emperor's light has fallen,' Dagover summed up.

'And this is how it is replaced?' Teiras asked, incredulous.

'You and I agree that the Lord Governor and his cronies were corrupt, but they kept well within the letter of Imperial law. They paid their tithes. They violated no edicts. And their political friends were many. I could not act directly.'

Teiras noticed Dagover's use of the first-person. 'You planned this from the beginning?'

'You flatter me. I took advantage of the opportunity that the necron attack provided.' The inquisitor leaned forward. 'But now, matters have changed as an unintended consequence of a necessary action.' He became deadly serious. 'Creative destruction is necessary for the salvation of the Imperium, Black Dragon,' he said. 'Do not doubt it.'

Teiras thought of the grotesque spectacle that the capital city had presented to him, and found that, indeed, he could not doubt what Dagover said. 'You plan to control the outcome?'

The smile again. 'Whatever faction wins will know that deviation from the good of the Imperium will be met with a most terrible judgement. In the end, a new, more pure order will arise. And so we have another small step towards galactic renewal.'

'That weapon is unlikely to fire again.' It lay in the hold of the *Iudex Ferox*. The back half had been turned to slag.

'No one on the planet will know that.'

The rest of the kill-team was waiting for him outside the study. Gherak had removed his helmet. Teiras looked from one Adeptus Astartes to the next. *We are the damned,* he thought, *fighting for the redemption of the Imperium.*

'Well?' Jern asked.

'Our missions will not lack for interest.'

'Was his visitor present?' Gherak asked.

'Visitor?'

'The ship that docked beside ours while we were on the surface. It sent a shuttle over about an hour ago.'

Teiras shook his head. 'There was no one else there but Dagover.'

'Well, old friend?' Dagover asked.

One of the statues moved. Shadows pulled away from grey armour. Canoness Setheno did not remove her helmet, but Dagover felt her gaze behind it. It was a sensation of discomfort that never faded. 'Your evaluation of the Black Dragon was correct,' Setheno said.

'I understand Inquisitor Lettinger is about to descend upon his company.'

'Then so shall I.'

The pitiless cold of her voice lingered long after she was gone.

FEARFUL SYMMETRIES

BY ROB SANDERS

'Fidus Kryptman,' the inquisitor spoke into the identi-vox. 'Three thirty-two thirty-four. Ordo Xenos.'

The security lamps in the passage flashed an urgent amber.

'Kryptman,' the tinny voice of the logic engine returned. *'Inquisition. Clearance: Tetra-Denticus. Admission granted.'*

The adamantium security gate to the dungeon vivisectorum scraped slowly to one side. The young Kryptman waited. Taking off his spectacles, the inquisitor proceeded to clean their infrared lenses with the edge of his hooded cloak. 'After you, arch-genetor,' Kryptman offered. 'After all, this is your world.'

Behind him, garbed in rich carmine robes, stood the master of the Opus Ersaticus forge-world – Arch-Genetor Zillicus Vandrasarc, also a celebrated organicist, who had long maintained working relationships with the holy ordos and the Adeptus Astartes as well. The genetor's scalp was threadbare and his cantankerous mask of a face gnarled and ancient. Kryptman spied the faces of liver-spotted cherubim peeking out from miniature hoods in the ample folds of Vandrasarc's robes. It was these homunculi familiars, growing from the arch-genetor's own flesh, which kept Vandrasarc alive, assuming for him some of the cancers and dilapidations of his extreme old age. Each pair of eyes fixed the inquisitor with their withered gaze; Kryptman couldn't begin to imagine what the venerable priest made of his ear-bauble, brow studs and eyeglasses.

'And of course, this is *your* facility, magos,' Kryptman acknowledged as a female tech-priest followed the arch-genetor into the vivisectorum. Magos Lisbex Orm was Kryptman's ordo contact on the forge-world. A magos xenobiologis of great skill, Orm had been invaluable to Kryptman in his recent investigations. From the back of her augmented skull hung slender mechadendrites that slithered about her like protective serpents.

'And this, your highly irregular request, inquisitor,' Vandrasarc carped back in a chorus of voices, from the many mouths adorning his ungainly body. 'We do not ordinarily sanction the vivisection of living xenos specimens here on Opus Ersaticus. It's reckless! You won't be satisfied until you've infected us all.'

'This is a maximum security compound, and the subject has been transported in perfect stasis. Magos Orm has taken every precaution, I assure you.'

'You can assure me of no such thing,' Vandrasarc replied crabbily.

'I can,' Kryptman returned, 'and I can say with confidence that despite the dangers inherent in this xenological research, there is no facility safer, nor more secure, in this entire sector.'

'We shall see, sir,' the arch-genetor cautioned, 'we shall see. What you fail to appreciate is that I am responsible for every one of the Omnissiah's subjects on this planet, and–'

'And I for the God-Emperor's across the Imperium,' Kryptman told him. 'Your concerns are duly noted. You are welcome to observe this procedure, as your rank and responsibility allows, but I must now give my full attention to my work. So, if you will excuse me...'

Kryptman entered the high security vivisection pit. The large chamber had been partitioned into two concentric sections: a sealed outer observatorium dominated by pict-recorders, auspectra, gun servitors and thick armourglas screens providing views of a secured inner section. Though the secure section was empty, the walls were adorned with arrays of servo-arms, mechadendria, automaton restraints and surgical toolery. Sentinel weaponry watched over the chamber. Armour-plated flooring and a vaulted roof section of darkened lancet ports, constructed from the same tinted armourglas as the observatorium screens, rose over and above the pit.

'All security protocols observed,' Orm reported. 'All countermeasures employed. Containment is ready for us, inquisitor.'

Donning a vox-thief headset, Kryptman spoke with confidence. 'Confirmed. All pict, vox and auspex set to archive. Magos, you may begin the procedure.'

The observatorium trembled as a floor section of the inner chamber parted to admit a rising platform from the containment-tomb below. The platform supported four crackling colonnades, between which a large organic specimen resided.

Kryptman felt the bile rising at the back of his throat.

The xenos organism was a living testament to revulsion: a large, bulbous pod, alien in its fleshiness and oozing a mucous coating. Shaped like a fat, tapering bullet, the thing was raw and repulsive.

'Subject is Specimen Phi-Delta two-seven-four-five-six,' Kryptman narrated into the headset. 'Recovered from the orbital path of the planet Tyran, on the Eastern Fringe; classification Rho, tithe grade Aptus Non. Cross reference Technis file zero-zero-one-zero-one-zero.'

Kryptman nodded at Orm, and the sizzling colonnades shimmered before settling to an inert stillness. The stasis field – the integrity of which the colonnades had maintained – collapsed through its chronometric dilations until, finally, the xenos organism became one with actuality. Mucus dribbled and glopped to the pit floor. The pod-flesh began to move, rippling and bubbling beneath its membranous surface.

'Specimen is rated as Inquisition clearance Beta-Major and a Class-Four threat,' Kryptman continued. 'Designated as "Mycetic Spore", specimen was recovered by the explorator supply tanker *Gorgus* en route to Tyran Primus and placed in stasis-quarantine. The *Gorgus* failed to deliver its promethium shipment, because the research outpost on Tyran had been destroyed. The ocean world itself has suffered a catastrophic event. Every microbe of life – floral and faunal – has been wiped from the face of the planet, including the benthic and atmospheric medium. The *Gorgus* found a dead world. A sterile ball of rock. My own investigations on the devastated planet revealed a data-codex secreted deep below the outpost by explorator personnel. It detailed not only a pattern of other dead worlds on the Eastern Fringe, presaging the progress of an extragalactic invasion fleet, but also the outpost's record of Tyran's own alien invasion. It seems that these spores were instrumental in bringing a new and previously undocumented xenos species down to the surface – an organic drop-pod, if you will. To honour the first known casualties of this alien threat, I have designated these monstrosities *Xenos horrificus* and their breed "the tyranid".'

'Permission to simulate aerodynamic heating, inquisitor?' Orm asked.

'Initiate,' Kryptman replied.

Two hydraulic servo-arms extended from their wall-anchors to present the scorched nozzles of mounted flamer appendages. Fat tanks of promethium percolated at the servo-arm's base as the pilots were ignited. Under the deft control of the magos's tendril mechadendrites, the pit appendages bathed the mycetic spore in chemical fire.

'The data-codex demonstrates the tyranids to be a highly hostile and adaptable race – an alien swarm made up of many different forms, each engineered for a specific purpose. Their aggression seems not to proceed from cultural prejudice or territorial concerns. They exist only, it seems, to assimilate encountered life into their bio-matrix. The building blocks of such life are then employed to propagate the tyranid species further. The gene-harvesting of victim-species assists in the engineering of further organism types and convey upon the alien swarm various environmental and aggressive advantages. A genetic arms race, if you will, in which the tyranid grows stronger with each new conquest.'

As the flamers withdrew and the inferno dwindled, the roasted, steaming surface of the pod was revealed: gone was the mucous layer, and in its place was a blackened shell.

An awful cracking sound filled the chamber and the spore – still burning in places – began to morph into a different shape. As the organism's muscular carapace proceeded to reorganise itself beneath the cauterised shell, splits and seeping cracks appeared. The thing changed from streamlined ghastliness to the foulness of a ruptured organ.

'Mucus film removed,' the inquisitor continued, one finger on the headset's earpiece. 'Spore appears to have changed its outward form, perhaps to reduce aerodynamism and slow what it senses to be atmospheric descent. Augur scans confirm the presence of multiple life forms within the spore.' Kryptman looked up, watching thin wisps of smoke rising towards the darkened gallery above. 'The first thing that always strikes me about the tyranid is the efficiency of their design and economy of their purpose. They waste nothing, not even energy. It is my belief that the creatures, demonstrated to be so hyperactively hostile in the data recovered from the Tyran Primus outpost, remain in a dormant state until primed. Heat generated by rapid descent through a planetary atmosphere might act as a trig–'

Even Kryptman was shocked by the speed of the attack.

Tentacles erupted from the scabbed pod and whipped their sinewy lengths around the flamer-equipped servo-arms. Orm attempted to retract the arms but the spore had entwined its barbed tendrils through their gears, pistons and fluid lines. The remote appendages groaned as the cogs in their motorised joints fought and slipped. If anything, the spore's grotesque appendages seemed to be winning the tug of war.

'Do you want me to use the incinerators?' Magos Orm asked Kryptman, who remained fascinated by the conflict. 'Inquisitor?'

The pod suddenly relaxed its grip, allowing the servo-arms to lurch back towards the wall. As they did, the ripper hooks on the tentacles slipped through both the fuel and hydraulic lines, spilling promethium and fluid onto the pit floor and turning the weaponised appendages into shuddering, sputtering wrecks. The tendrils writhed and coiled across the metal floor about the pod, sampling the featureless decking before being steadily retracted into the disgusting blob.

'Hostilities re-established with an attack on the apparatus,' Kryptman related calmly into the vox-thief. Stepping to one side, he briefly took in the runescreen bank in front of Magos Orm. 'Scans still show dormant life-signs within. Hypothetical diagnosis: the spore could be defective, carry a genetic design flaw or simply may have been mis-launched. This could explain the limited payload and the location in which the wayward spore was discovered.' Kryptman nodded to himself. 'Let's reduce the magnitude of the threat. Lisbex, you may begin Stage One of the surgical vivisection.'

Moving in past the twitching flamer appendages, a surgical mechadendrite closed with the fleshy surface of the pod. The prehensile limb was adorned with heavy-duty clamps and retractors, within which a selection of surgical saws, las-scalpels, suction lines and a plasma torch resided. Anchor-clamps thudding into the rippling surface of the pod, the arm proceeded to cycle through its toolery and ignite the blinding tip of the torch.

'Orm has selected the major axis, about the equatorial bulge of the oblate spheroid,' Kryptman identified. 'This being a site of previous appendage eruption, we might reasonably expect to incise between protective layers of sub-dermal carapace.'

As the plasma torch cut a sectional path down through the spore's surface, flesh bubbled and spat. Retractors moved in and prised the thick membrane aside with hydraulic determination. At this, twin surgical saws closed in to slice and burn their way through the alien sinew beneath.

Ichorous fluids of different colours and consistencies began gushing down the side of the spore as Orm's handiwork ruptured something within. Suction lines siphoned off the worst of the bleeding ooze but still a clotted pool of discharge began to collect on the floor beneath the pod.

With the same sudden reflexive rush, tentacles shot out from the incised area and grappled the mechadendrical toolery. Magos Orm even flinched at her control-bank.

'Magos. Initiate safeguards,' Kryptman ordered.

The vivisection pit flashed briefly with the crackle of electricity. Bolts of energy arced between the surgical tools and across the metal of the mechadendrite arm. The alien tendrils recoiled and shot back into the body of the pod, trailed by steam and smoke.

Kryptman regarded the thing coldly for a moment. 'Introduce prey specimens.'

The floor at the opposite end of the chamber began to part and another platform rose in its place. Tethered to the platform with ankle chains was an adult grox, with a juvenile cowering between the thick, reptilian legs of its mother. A gossamer net of wires trailed from needles in the grox's tough hide, monitoring the animal's biological functions. All horns and scaly hide, the beast of burden let its forked tongue slither out to taste the air.

The response was instantaneous. The grox let out a fearful snort before bellowing and heaving its rugged head, legs and swollen belly away from the mycetic spore – a deep and primal fear. Two of the restraints snapped immediately, leaving the beast to heave against the remaining manacles. The juvenile, knocked around between the adult's straining legs, sensed its mother's panic and began to wail.

The final two chains snapped and the grox ran at the reinforced screens, and Arch-Genetor Vandrasarc gasped with all of his mouths before backing away. The grox struck the screen with bestial force, but the thick armourglas held, forcing the animal to slink its knotty flank along the screen in dazed fright.

'Fear not, arch-genetor,' Kryptman reassured the Adeptus Mechanicus overlord. 'Magos Orm has built us a facility which is completely specimen-proof.'

A trill of pure animal terror drew their attention back to the pit: the juvenile grox had been following in its mother's thunderous footsteps, only to be seized from the rear by the explosive tentacled grasp of the spore. The mother grox stamped its feet and snorted, refusing to approach the alien horror even in the face of its infant's struggles. The juvenile's awful cries were suddenly silenced as the pod's writhing tendrils enveloped it.

Mummified in the slick sinew of the feeler swarm, the animal was dragged rapidly across the length of the vivisection pit. The mycetic spore petalled open like a germinating pod, forming a horrified semblance of a fleshy, dribbling mouth which swallowed the struggling creature whole.

'Fascinating...' Kryptman murmured.

With the mother grox's terrified bellows filtering through the section wall, Kryptman watched as the spore once again assumed a spasmodic throbbing. Rather than muscular morphage, the movement appeared more like hatchlings swarming within the stomach of a pregnant serpent.

'I see that our guests are no longer dormant,' the inquisitor murmured to Orm. The magos didn't respond. She didn't need to.

The thrashings of grox butchery within the mycetic spore soon moved to the spore itself. The floor about the disgusting thing had become a small lake of acidic ichor which blistered the deck. Criss-crossed slashes started to blotch the pod's fleshy dermis, while the blob itself seemed to shrivel and contract like a piece of giant fruit rotting at speed. The spore husk rocked this way and that. Something was fighting within. Fighting to be free.

'Any time now,' Kryptman spoke into the vox-thief.

Moments passed. The mycetic spore withered and died.

Without warning, scraps of carapace, sinew and flaccid flesh were sprayed in every direction by an internal jolt. Like a lurid blur, a succession of vicious organisms launched from the pod's remains at the mother grox – spindly, chitinous horrors, visited one after another upon the beast of burden and latching onto its hide.

The animal roared its fear and ran for its life, stomping its way around the exterior of the vivisection pit and running its scaly side along the screens and wall in an attempt to dislodge them. Orm was forced to raise some of the larger mounted servo-arms as the animal crashed around the chamber perimeter in raw terror.

Everything about the things upon its back was predatory: their arachnoid speed and mantid gait; their frenzied limbs; their whipping tails; the glistening reach of their scything talons and their rows of needle-like fangs. They were at once gristle-boned and powerful, ungainly athletic and raptorial. Things of loathsome perfection.

The grox crashed to the pit floor, the bone-blades of the attacking horrors slipping effortlessly through the animal's thick, scaly hide and plunging straight through its innards. The creature emitted one last high-pitched cry as the killers drooled and thrashed their stabbing appendages through its ruined torso.

'Assimilation of first prey specimen is complete,' Kryptman began again, without taking his eyes off the latest attack. 'The tyranids are a highly economical species. Nothing is wasted. Everything is biologically reinvested and reassigned. The spore has delivered its payload and has been sacrificed to fuel the hostilities of a vanguard xenoform – a sub-species I recognised from the Tyran Primus data-codex, although the tyranids seem to be immeasurably varied and in a state of constant hyper-evolution. This particular genus I have designated *Gaunti* and this sub-genus *Gaunti gladius*. There are many strains but I think it fair to indicate that, despite their abundant lethality, the gaunts are one of the smaller and less powerful tyranid forms. They are swarming predators that attempt to overwhelm their prey, with a combination of numbers, relentless aggression and almost surgical artistry.'

Kryptman watched as the xenos went to work on the grox carcass. The three monsters buried their chitinous heads in the beast's flank, the raw musculature of their bodies twisting and arching as they rent and gobbled prey-flesh in a chugging, instinctual motion. It was disgusting to behold.

'From observing the attack on the second prey specimen, we can confirm that each strike – although appearing mindless – is in fact precisely targeted. All major organs required for life have been punctured or ruptured, with the exception of the rather primitive brain. Predator specimens are now attempting to ingest tissue and complex proteins to drive their demanding metabolism.'

Gore-smeared, the beasts started to wander from the decimated carcass, their movements twitchy and inquisitive. Their tongues swung from their skulls like obscene, slimy eels and their dead alien eyes were everywhere. One approached the screen and seemed to regard Kryptman, who stared back at it through the transparency of the viewport.

'It is... worse than I had initially thought,' the inquisitor confessed. 'The information from the data-codex was suggestive of a single driving consciousness directing the invading tyranid swarm. Reports seemed to indicate that certain larger monstrosities – acting as a form of cellular node – prompted the lesser creatures to attack in disciplined patterns and powerful concentrations. Without these synaptic nodes, localised swarms were less effective and prone to discombobulation.'

Kryptman watched the beast as it tongued the armourglas. It wasn't thinking. Something far more alien was taking place in the creature's mind. The inquisitor felt its bottomless desire, simultaneously empty like the void yet more intense than the light from the brightest star.

It didn't just want to kill him; it wanted to *assimilate* him. To absorb his flesh and craft atrocity from it. To become one with his essence, the building blocks of his existence, and rob him not just of his life but of the future of his entire race.

'This construct, not unlike the documented xenos species *Corporaptor ymgarli*, demonstrates a congregative brood-communion. Here in the vivisection pit, having no synaptic contact with their tyranid kindred, these gaunts are operating on a pre-engineered, aggresso-cooperative instinct. This makes them perfectly designed for front-line, advance deployment, making the gaunt sub-species the most likely encountered in the early stages of a tyranid invasion. The data-codex confirms this.'

While the beast continued to watch the inquisitor, its kindred had wolfed down the remains of the grox. Now they proceeded to systematically test their confines, picking at the metal and armourglas with their scythes. They lashed out at the servo-arms and mechadendrites, and tore the stasis field colonnades out of the floor.

'The tyranids employ a myriad of biological weaponry,' Kryptman resumed his commentary. 'Reports show that the *Gaunti* alone has been engineered to deploy both ranged and close combat armament. This includes symbiotic ballistic weaponry that launches live, parasitic organisms. Conversely, a typical *Gaunti gladius* – if such a thing exists – favours the simplicity of face-to-face killing with razor-edged claws. More than a match for plasfibre, carapace or even power armour. Add to this the powerful bounding motion and flesh-tearing jaws and you have a lethal xenos predator.'

Kryptman turned from the screens. The gaunt still peered through the armourglas at him.

'Magos Orm, please begin Stage Two.'

The xenobiologos manipulated the controls, guiding robust servo-arms and restraint-appendages at the monsters. They began to retreat with skittish suspicion, hissing and spit-snarling at the cage of heavy-duty claws and hydraulic pincers closing in on them, bounding off the walls, screens and floor plates in an effort to remain out of reach.

'Initiate a threat protocol,' Kryptman instructed.

Orm brought the largest and most threatening servo-claw aggressively in on one of the beasts, prompting the monster to slash out with its own scything talons. Leaping up between the closing pincers, the gaunt perched on the claw and began slashing at the compression pistons and power lines.

'Increase.'

Two smaller adamantine grapplers came at the attacking beast, clamping it about the fore-scythes. At the gaunt's furious glottal hissing, its kindred killers launched themselves at the mechanical restraints. Mounting the reinforced arms on the tips of their claws whilst anchoring themselves with their whip-like tails, the horrors began to snag the servo-appendages with their needle-filled maws.

'Maximal threat, magos, if you please,' the inquisitor said to Orm, prompting the tech-priest to manoeuvre a tertiary set of mechadendrite restraints out from the nearby wall.

Snatching the three beasts from one another, the remote arms dangled the xenos above the pit floor and soon supported them by auxiliary servo-shackles and clawed fetters. Kryptman watched as the magos expertly rearranged the purchase of the restraints and spread each of the alien beasts out above the vivisection pit floor.

The tyranids heaved with all their alien might but the armature held them in place. As they rasped and spat their inhuman frustration, cranial block restraints moved in to keep their thrashing heads still.

Kryptman resumed his narration. '*Gaunti gladius* operates on the individual instinct to hunt and kill, although brood methodology dictates that this instinct yields greater dividends when employed in large numbers. The data-codex suggests that under certain circumstances, individuals might cooperate or even "strategise". Presumably, this effect is further enhanced at the level of a full swarm in the presence of the larger synaptic relay organisms.' He nodded to Orm. 'Magos, commence Stage Three: the surgical vivisection.'

'Proceeding, inquisitor,' Orm replied as her machines went to work. 'Also, deploying ballistics for ranged weapons testing,'

With the predator specimens splayed, a servo-arm bearing a multi-barrelled apparatus moved into place above the first. A targeter on the arm zeroed in on the beast's exposed shoulder carapace.

'Ballistics in three, two, one. Mark.'

With a brief flash, the automaton weapon fired its foremost barrel upon the restrained monstrosity. A las-bolt ricocheted off the shell-like carapace, prompting the gaunt to hiss its displeasure. The servo-arm descended to almost point-blank range and fired again, resulting in a small explosion of burned chitin and a squeal from the tyranid creature. The servo-arm retreated above the beast to reveal that the second shot had barely penetrated the creature's organic armour plating.

'Having already detailed the construct's devastating physical capabilities, it seems ranged combat is our best option against these xenos beasts,' Kryptman extrapolated. 'By far the most common weapons available in the Imperium are las-based in their technology, but as we can see, strikes in the nineteen to twenty-two megathule range struggle to penetrate the fused, chitinous plates sported by many bio-constructs. Even successful penetrative blasts would be fortunate to hit an essential organ in *Gaunti gladius*'s sparse physiology.'

As Kryptman spoke, the weapon-arm cycled to present one of the chunkier barrels in the attachment. The targeter guided the automaton in on the snapping beast's other shoulder.

'More effective is the 0.998 calibre boltgun. Standard issue within the Adeptus Astartes, although rarely employed elsewhere within the Imperial military. Observe.'

The attachment on the servo-arm blazed away, chugging mass-reactive shells at the creature. They impacted and shredded the gaunt's talon arm from its body almost as an afterthought; the scything blade-limb clattered to the deck as the alien obscenity screeched in instinctual fury rather than pain. Its shoulder was nothing more than a ruined stump of spurting gristle.

'Beyond the greater penetrative and overall stopping power of bolt weaponry, the large bore explosive ammunition has the advantage of being able to amputate – and therefore neutralise – the tyranids' integral weaponry. Recent advances in the development of bolt ammunition have led to variants that prove even more effective against such engineered breeds.'

Kryptman watched the barrels cycle once more and reposition above the monster's straining abdomen. The servo-arm bucked as it put a single high-velocity bolt into the beast's abdomen. There was no detonation, yet the screeching intensified.

'Hellfire rounds, in which the uranium core of a standard shell has been replaced with a mutagenic acid found to be effective against certain xenos species.'

The ragged hole left behind by the shot continued to grow as the edges melted away to create a cavernous crater in the thing. Its cries became choked gargles.

'Still, we may note, the predator specimen lives.'

The servo-arm cycled back to the previous barrel, which cleared and locked with an automated click. The targeter brought the boltgun attachment in above the creature's spitting maw, and it fired once, blowing the monster's ugly head from its carapaced shoulders.

'Kill-shots with standard mass-reactives should therefore be restricted to the cranial casing.'

Another mechadendrite manoeuvred in past the weapon-arm and positioned itself above the gnarled chest of the second test subject. Instead of barrels, the automaton limb mounted an arrangement of thick needles and helix-hypodermica.

'Proceed,' Kryptman ordered.

Rather than rotating, the arrangement shot forward with hydraulic force, ramming the nest of reinforced needles down through the creature's breastplate. Plungers and siphons pumped various liquids and gases through, and Kryptman waited a moment but the gaunt continued to snap and seethe in its restraints.

'We have tested a wide range of state-diverse toxins, Adeptus Mechanicus-engineered poisons and over one hundred naturally occurring venoms. Almost all have demonstrated little or no effect on the tyranid corpus-chemistry.' Kryptman took a step back from the armourglas screens. 'Magos, you are authorised for the deployment.'

Warning klaxons blared, and green lights on the hypodermica arm changed to red.

A larger needle shot out from the centre of the arrangement on a pneumatic carriage. It brutally punctured the gaunt's chest, prompting it to shriek.

The effect on the creature was instantaneous – it began to tremble within its restraints but the tremors soon turned to spastic jerking. Venting steam from its cracked dermis, chunks of the beast dropped to the floor, its macabre organics disintegrating into both gaseous and liquefied residue that splattered to the pit floor in a sludge-pool of wasted flesh.

'The only real success we have enjoyed was with the introduction of the Inquisition's own biological weapons. This is a weakened derivative of the Life-Eater virus, typically deployed during a planetary Exterminatus order – a tactic that even the holy ordos do not employ lightly. Not even the xenos can withstand the Life-Eater.'

While Kryptman had directed the ballistics and toxicological experimentation, a multi-attachment surgical limb had been busy at work on the third predator specimen, under Orm's expert control. Las-scalpels, surgical saws and field blades had worked up through the tyranid creature, amputating limbs and harvesting internal pseudo-organs before depositing the remnants in stasis caskets for further study. Magos Orm had worked swiftly with her remote toolery to excise and dismember the bio-construct from its clawed feet all the way up to its truncated neck. With the rest of the creature variously in pieces and in stasis, somehow it still managed to work its needle-fanged jaw in an instinctual snapping motion.

'The living surgical vivisection of the third xenos subject has been a success,' Kryptman announced, producing a data-slate and scanning down it, 'with the complete specimen recovered for further analysis, documentation and testing. The creature has demonstrated... a considerable resilience to shock and biological commitment to its genetically-engineered purpose. The chitin-carapace and skeletal structures stand up well to conventional blades, necessitating the use of chain- and power-tools.' The inquisitor grinned. 'The close combat *equivalents* of these tools would be expected to stand the best chance of wounding tyranid constructs at close quarters on the battlefield.'

Orm brought a rotary bone saw up behind the gaunt's head, cutting open the cranium from the rear. The beast's maw continued to snap even as she cranked open the skull and went to work on different parts of the thing's horrid brain.

'Psi-occulus augury has previously revealed dissipating fields of a psychic presence,' the inquisitor narrated, 'suggesting that certain parts of the brain might be responsible for the synaptic connection indicated earlier. This might be our first evidence of a grand insect-style agglomeration or gestalt consciousness, connecting all tyranid creatures by way of a single "hive mind".'

The beast's eyes burned with the blankness of alien hatred. As Orm removed the final and most primitive part of the brain, the monstrosity's jaws fell slack.

'One final surprise was the discovery of a birthing tract,' Kryptman noted with a mixture of technical enthusiasm and despair. A bionic appendage holding an open stasis casket rose to display a collection of fleshy, vein-threaded sphericles. 'This means that the predator subjects are able to reproduce independently once they have made planetfall, replacing expected losses and fortifying the vanguard swarm. We shall endeavour to raise these specimens to adulthood under laboratorium conditions in order to facilitate further testing.'

He placed his palm upon the slate, imprinting and closing the file.

'This concludes the investigation.'

Kryptman turned to find Arch-Genetor Vandrasarc looking at him with unbridled horror. Screwing up his ancient face, the priest shook a trembling finger at the vivisection pit.

'Get those specimens off my world,' the arch-genetor said bluntly, before trudging from the chamber.

Kryptman looked to Magos Orm, who merely shrugged.

'Amphitheatre lights,' the inquisitor muttered.

Above the secured inner chamber, lumen strips snapped into life, illuminating a crowded observation terrace that looked down upon the vivisectorum. The lancet screens were filled with rows of power armoured figures – hundreds of them, helmetless, standing in sombre silence. Space Marines, all, in battle plate of midnight black, polished to light-swallowing oblivion. Each bore the Chamber Militant symbol of the Deathwatch upon their pauldron.

A grim officer with scarred face and a neat, silver beard stepped forward and activated the observatorium vox-hailer.

'Very educational, inquisitor,' the veteran said in a voice of stone. 'Now you have shown us the specifics of this xenos contagion, tell us where we may find this foul species so that we can end them.'

'Here,' Fidus Kryptman replied, with equal gravity. 'Soon.'

The Deathwatch officer nodded in solemn satisfaction. Kryptman clasped his hands behind his back and stared up at him.

'But captain – understand that should you fail to halt the tyranid advance, they will soon be *everywhere*.'

'The Deathwatch do not fail, inquisitor.'

A SANCTUARY OF WYRMS

PETER FEHERVARI

-BEGIN RECORDING-

We walk blindly along a knife-edge slicing into oblivion. If we misstep we fall from our path. If we walk true we fall with our path. Perhaps there is a difference, but I have come to doubt it. Nevertheless, I will honour the Greater Good and allow you to draw your own conclusions from the facts.

I have little time, but even in extremis one must observe the correct protocols. That is what it means to be a tau amongst savages. Whatever else I have lost to this diseased planet, I will not lose that. Therefore know that I am Por'ui Vior'la Asharil, third-stream daughter of Clan Kherai. Though I hail from a Sept of worlds where the wisdom of the water caste is eclipsed by the ferocity of the fire caste, my family has served the Tau Empire with grace since the dawn of the first colonies. As I serve with this, my final account.

And so I shall offer you a beginning. Let it be the grey-green murk that is the perennial stuff of Fi'draah, my new world. As I stepped from my shuttle the planet seized me in a stinking, sweltering embrace and wouldn't let go. Blinking and choking in the smog, I heard harsh voices and harsher laughter; then someone thrust a filtrator mask over my face and I could breathe again.

'The first time is like drowning,' my saviour said. 'It gets better.'

I don't recall who the speaker was, but he lied: breathing this world never got any better.

'You have evidently made powerful enemies for one so young, Asharil,' the ambassador said without preamble, peering down from the cushioned pulpit of his hovering throne drone. His voice was soft, yet vibrant. It filled the spacious audience chamber like liquid silk, the weapon of a master orator. His summons had followed directly upon my arrival and I was mortified by my dishevelled state.

'I do not understand, honoured one,' I blustered, stumbling between respect and revulsion for the ancient who presided over our forces on this remote planet. O'Seishin's authority was a testament to the excellence of our caste, but he reeked of years beyond the natural span of the tau race. His flesh had aged to deep cobalt leather, barely concealing the harsh planes of his skull, but his eyes were bright.

'This is a terminal world,' he continued, 'a graveyard for broken warriors and forgotten relics like myself, not a proving ground for the hot blood of youth. Who did you offend to get yourself posted here, Asharil?' He smiled, but his eyes belied it.

'I walk the water path,' I answered, seeking the natural poise of our caste. 'My blood runs cool and silent, so that my voice may weave–'

O'Seishin's snort cut me short like a physical blow. 'I am too old for wordplay, girl!' He leaned forward and a strand of spittle escaped his lips. 'Why have you come to Fi'draah? Who sent you?'

'Honoured one…' I stammered, struggling to avert my gaze from the lethargic descent of his drool. 'Your pardon, but I requested this posting. I have made a study of the language and customs of the *humans*' – I deliberately used the gue'la word for themselves – 'and Fi'draah offers most excellent opportunities to deepen my insight.'

He appraised me with a distrust so candid it was almost conspiratorial, as if we were both willing players in a game of lies. A game that he was used to winning…

'So you wish to test yourself in the field, Asharil?' He smiled again and this time I saw humour there, though no humour I cared to share. 'Then I shall not deny you. Indeed, I believe I have a most suitable commission for you.'

I will never know why O'Seishin became my enemy in that one brief meeting, but he proved to be the least of the blights awaiting me on this world.

Of the long conflict between the Tau Empire and the gue'la Imperium for mastery of Fi'draah I shall not speak. Mysteries shroud the war like whispering smoke, but I learned little of them before O'Seishin dispatched me to oblivion. Of the planet itself I could say much, for I travelled its wilderness for almost five months, but I will content myself with a single truth: whatever you are told in your orientation, it will not prepare you for the reality of this place. To classify Fi'draah as a 'jungle world' or a 'water world' is to garb a corpse in finery and call it beautiful. Eighty per cent of its surface is drowned in viscid, lethargic oceans that blend into the sky in a perpetual cycle of evaporation and drizzle, wreathing everything in a grey-green miasma that seeps into the flesh and spirit. The continents are ragged tangles of mega-coral choked with vegetation that looks – and smells – like it has been dredged up from the depths. Stunted trees with fleshy trunks and bladder-like fronds vie with drooping tenements of fungi and titanic anemone clusters, everything strangling or straddling or simply growing upon everything else – fecundity racing decay so fast you can almost see it.

Whether Sector O-31 is the worst of Fi'draah's territories I cannot say, but it must surely rank amongst them. The gue'la call it *'the Coil'*, a name infinitely more fitting than our own sober designation, for there is nothing remotely sober about that malign wilderness. A serpentine spiral of waterlogged jungles, it is the dark heartland of Fi'draah's largest, most untamed continent. The war has left it almost untouched, but rumours haunt it like bad memories: of regiments swallowed whole before they could clash… Of lost patrols still fighting older wars than ours… And of ancient things sleeping beneath the waters…

Naturally, I dismissed such nonsense. My task was to cast the light of reason across this enigma and 'unravel the Coil' (as O'Seishin so artfully sold it). I was to accompany Fio'vre Mutekh, a distinguished cartographer of the earth caste on his quest to map the region. Fool that I was, I believed myself honoured! It was only later, when I saw how the Coil twisted in upon itself, that I realised the absurdity of our endeavour. I have often wondered whether O'Seishin is still laughing at me.

It says much about the nature of the earth caste that Mutekh approached his impossible assignment without rancour. A robust tau in his autumn cycle, he had a pompous manner that exasperated me, but he was utterly rigorous in his work. His assistant, Xanti, was a placid *autaku* (or data tech) who spoke rarely and never met my gaze. I believe he preferred the company of his neo-sentient data drone to his fellow tau.

The fourth and final person of note was our protector and guide, Shas'ui Jhi'kaara. A fire warrior and veteran of Fi'draah, she regarded the jungle with the tender distrust of a predator who knows it is also prey, and like many alpha predators she commanded her own pack: a dozen gue'la janissaries equipped with flak-plate and pulse carbines. They were all Imperial deserters, lured from the enemy by the promise of better rations rather than ideology, and despite the trappings of our civilisation they remained barbarians. Every night they gambled, quarrelled and brawled amongst themselves, but never in Jhi'kaara's presence. Had they known I spoke their native tongue they would have guarded their words more closely. Listening in on their crude passions and superstitions, I marvelled that their stunted species had ever reached the stars.

Together we entered the Coil: earth, water, fire... and mud, travelling its strange waterways in a pair of aging Devilfish hover transports. Every few days Mutekh would spot a 'notable feature' and call a halt. Then we would spend an eternity recording some obscure geological phenomenon or ancient indigene ruin. As the cartographer updated his maps and the janissaries patrolled, the jungle would press in, watching us with a thousand hungry eyes that belonged to a single beast.

'It hates us,' Jhi'kaara said once, surprising me as I stared back at the beast. 'But it welcomes us in the expectation that we will grow careless.'

'It is just a jungle, Shas'ui,' I said, squaring up to the warrior. 'It has no thoughts.'

'You are lying, waterkin,' Jhi'kaara said. 'You see the truth, but like all your kind, you fear it.'

'My kind?' I was shocked. 'We are the *same* kind. We are both tau.'

Her face was hidden behind the impassive, lens-studded mask of her combat helmet, but I sensed her sneer.

As our expedition stretched from weeks into months I came to detest every one of my companions, but Jhi'kaara most of all. While I recognised the place of the fire caste in the Tau'va, there was a coiled violence about her that disturbed me. Perhaps it was her hideous facial scarring or her playful contempt… But no… I believe it was something deeper. Like O'Seishin, she had become tainted by this world.

Taint. Such an irrational term for a tau to use; surely one better suited to the Imperial fanatics who condemn otherness for otherness's sake? Perhaps, but lately I have come to wonder whether the fanatics may have it right.

It is time I told you of the Sanctuary of Wyrms.

'What is it?' I asked, trying to decipher the dark shape through its veil of vegetation. Squat yet vast, it rose from the centre of the island ahead, evidently a structure of some kind, but unlike any other we had encountered in the Coil. Despite the obscuring vegetation, its harsh, angular lineaments were unmistakable, suggesting an architectural brutality at odds with the flowing contours of our own aesthetics. Even at a distance it filled me with foreboding.

'The Nirrhoda did not lie,' Mutekh said, lowering his scope.

The Nirrhoda? I recalled the feral, mud-caked indigenes we had encountered some weeks back. Technically 'indigene' was a misnomer since the native Phaedrans were descended from gue'la colonists who had conquered this world millennia ago and then, in turn, been conquered by it. Squat and bowlegged, with huge glassy eyes and yawning mouths, they were primitive degenerates who wandered the wilderness in loose tribes. All were unpredictable, but the Nirrhoda clan, who followed the chaotic arrhythmia of the Coil, were notoriously belligerent. Yet Jhi'kaara had known their ways and won a parley for Mutekh, who had traded trinkets for shreds of truth about their deceitful land. One such shred had led us here.

'They certainly did not lie about the wyrmtrees,' the fire warrior observed sourly. 'That island is infested with them.'

I had taken the gentle undulation of the towering anemone-like growths encrusting the island to be a product of the wind... *Yet there was no wind.* Now I watched their swaying tendrils with fresh eyes: at the base, each was thicker than my waist, tapering to a sinuous violet tip that tilted towards us, as if tasting us on the air.

'Are they dangerous?' I asked.

'Their sting is lethal,' Jhi'kaara said fondly, 'but they grow slowly. These must be over a century old. That structure–'

'Evidently predates the war,' Mutekh interrupted with relish. 'We must evaluate this discovery thoroughly.' Something like avarice swept across his broad face, revealing another shade of taint: the hunger to *know*. 'You will clear a path please, fire warrior.'

Jhi'kaara turned the rotary cannons of our Devilfish upon the forest, shredding the rubbery growths into steaming slabs that seemed more meat than vegetable. The trees shrieked as they died, their warble sounding insidiously sentient.

'It proved a poor sanctuary,' Xanti said with peculiar sadness. I glanced at Mutekh's assistant in surprise. He shrugged, embarrassed by my attention. 'That is what the savages called this place: the Sanctuary of Wyrms.'

Then the janissaries went amongst the detritus with flame-throwers, laughing as they incinerated the flailing, orphan tendrils. One brute grew careless and a whip-like frond lashed his face as it flipped about in its death spasms. Moments later the man joined it in his own dance of death. It was the first time I had seen violent death, but I was unmoved. Fi'draah had already changed me.

Unveiled, the building was almost profound in its ugliness. It was a squat, octagonal block assembled from prefabricated grey slabs that were as hard as rock. The walls tilted inwards to a flat roof that looked strong enough to withstand an aerial bombardment, suggesting the place might be a bunker of some kind. Circling it, we found no apertures or ornamentation save for a deeply recessed entrance wide enough to accommodate a tank. A metal bulkhead blocked the path, its corroded surface embossed with a stark 'I' symbol. Despite its simplicity, the sigil had an austere authority that deepened my unease.

'I am unfamiliar with this emblem,' Mutekh mused, running a hand over the raised metal. 'Your thoughts, Por'ui?'

'It looks like a gue'la rune,' I answered. 'Linguistically it translates as *'the self'*, but in this context it probably has a factional connotation.'

'So the gue'la built this place?' Xanti asked.

'Oh, I would most definitely postulate an Imperial provenance,' Mutekh said, clearly enjoying himself. 'Though it lacks the vainglorious ornamentation typical of their architecture, the configuration and construction materials are manifestly Imperial.'

'Why would there be Imperials on Fi'draah before the war?' Xanti seemed confused by the notion.

'Why *wouldn't* there be?' Mutekh proclaimed. 'Throughout the ages there have been Imperials almost *everywhere*. They are an ancient power that coveted the stars millennia before the Tau'va was revealed to us. There is no telling when they first came to this world. Or why.'

'This place has the strength of a fortress, but not the logic,'

Jhi'kaara offered, speaking for the first time. 'The walls are solid, but there are no emplacements or watchtowers.'

'Perhaps they are hidden,' I suggested.

'No, remember this is a *pre-war* relic,' Mutekh chided. 'It was not constructed to keep an enemy out, but to keep a secret within.'

'What kind of secret?' Xanti asked loyally.

'The kind that was worth hiding well!' There was a glint in the cartographer's eyes at the prospect. 'The kind that is worth learning for the Greater Good.' He slapped the bulkhead. 'Open it!'

There was no obvious access mechanism, but Xanti's data drone detected a biometric scanner embedded in the bulkhead.

'For the gue'la it is a sophisticated system,' the *autaku* murmured, his face lost in the dancing holograms projected by his drone. The small saucer-like machine hovered by the hatch, interfacing the mechanism with its datalaser and mapping it into territory its master could negotiate.

'I doubt I could deceive this,' Xanti said, 'but it appears the seal has *already* been broken… and crudely reset.' He looked up with a frown. 'Someone has trespassed here before us.'

Despite the damaged seal, night had fallen by the time Xanti had synthesised the correct trigger. Dead cogs ground into life and the bulkhead rose, groaning at this second desecration. A sour fungal fetor seeped from the dark maw, so dense it was almost visible. Some of the janissaries chuckled as I retched and fumbled for my filtrator mask, but their faces were pale. Jhi'kaara silenced them with a sharp gesture, but I felt no gratitude. Her sealed helmet spared her the stench we suffered. Where was the equity in that?

We entered the cavernous chamber beyond in a practiced formation, with Jhi'kaara's hovering gun drone taking point and the janissaries fanning out to either side. Our torch beams thrust back the darkness, but it clung to every corner and crevice like black cobwebs. The burned-out hulks of amphibious transports and machinery loomed on all sides, casting shadows across a graveyard of barrels and crates.

'The invaders closed off the escape route,' Jhi'kaara said, gauging the devastation. 'They destroyed the vehicles and sealed the exit in case anyone slipped past them.'

'Why did no one fight back?' I wondered. 'There are no bodies here.'

'A good question, waterkin.'

Across the chamber the inner hatch lay amongst the detritus, shredded and torn from its recess. Jhi'kaara knelt and ran her fingers over the wreckage. The edges were curled into serrated whorls of tortured metal.

'Chainswords,' she said.

'How can you be sure?' I asked.

'The teeth leave a pattern.' She paused and looked over her shoulder, staring right at me. 'Their mark is... unique.' It was almost a challenge.

'Unique?' As if by their own volition my eyes were drawn to the ghost of a scar running down the faceplate of her helmet, a wound that echoed the rift in her own face. And suddenly I understood why she knew these weapons so intimately.

* * *

The destruction petered out in the corridor beyond, but the sense of oppression did not. It shadowed us as we passed through one deserted chamber after another, closing in as we moved deeper into the outpost.

'Smaller teams would cover more ground,' Mutekh protested. 'Your caution is illogical, Shas'ui. This place is long dead.'

But the fire warrior would not split our force, and I was struck anew by the differences between the castes. We worked together for the Greater Good, yet our natures were discordant. Mutekh and Xanti were creatures of reason, while Jhi'kaara was pure instinct. What did that make me?

I brooded over the question as we pressed on, passing through guardrooms and storerooms, the hollow tomb of a dormitory and a mess hall where food still waited on the table, fossilised and forgotten.

'It took them unawares,' Jhi'kaara murmured, 'and it took them swiftly.'

'It?' I asked. 'You mean the invaders?'

'No...' For the first time she sounded troubled. 'No, I think this was something else.'

We found the first corpse in the communications room, propped up against the vox-console. Shrouded in heavy crimson robes, the mummified cadaver looked more machine than man. Its face was an angular bronze mask studded with sensors, seemingly riveted to the skull. A pistol was clutched in a bionic claw, the barrel shoved through the broken grille of its mouth. Its cranium had ruptured into a crown of splintered bones and circuitry.

'He shot himself before the intruders reached him,' Jhi'kaara judged.

'Or because they reached him too late,' I offered uncertainly. She glanced at me, waiting as I tested the intuition. 'He's the only one we've found. Perhaps that makes him different.'

'He was certainly different,' Xanti said eagerly. 'Judging by his extensive bionics he was a Mechanicus priest, probably an important one. Unlike ourselves, the data techs of the Imperium aspire to become one with their machines.'

The *autaku*'s passion surprised me. Abruptly, I realised how little I knew about my companions. We had travelled so far together yet we were still strangers. Was it our castes that divided us, or merely our personal flaws? Uneasily, I put the question aside and concentrated on the facts.

'Perhaps he summoned the invaders,' I suggested.

Jhi'kaara considered it. 'Perhaps he did, waterkin.'

And perhaps I am not the fool you took me for, I thought.

The elevator to the lower levels had been demolished and the hatch to the stairwell was welded shut from within, but that was no obstacle to our plasma cutters. Beyond, a metal staircase wound down into darkness.

Jhi'kaara's gun drone led the way, levitating down the stairwell as we followed on the spiralling steps, its searchlight diving ahead into the abyss below. As we descended, the walls became brittle and powdery, sucked dry by silvery seams of fungus. In places the filth had erupted into cancerous fruiting bodies, but they were all desiccated husks, seemingly petrified in the moment of blossoming. The stench was dreadful and I kept my filtrator firmly in place. Mutekh and Xanti soon followed suit, but the janissaries suffered stoically, unwilling to show weakness before Jhi'kaara.

They are like dogs trying to impress their master, I thought.

At regular intervals we passed access hatches to other levels, and I realised the bulk of the outpost lay beneath the ground, like a buried mountain riddled with tunnels and caves. Some hatches were sealed, others gaped open, but we ignored them all. Exploring the entire complex would take days and none of us cared to linger here. Instead we pressed on, drawn by a collective sense that the answers we sought lay below. But when the drone's light finally found the bottom of the stairwell we froze.

'Emperor protect us!' one of the janissaries gasped, but nobody reprimanded him for his atavism.

Our path terminated in a charnel pit. Dozens of cadavers were piled up below, mangled and contorted by violent death. The walls around them were pitted with deep craters, suggesting heavy gunfire, but it was impossible tell whether it was bullets or chainswords that had cleansed these dead.

Cleansed. It is another term that sits uneasily with the Tau'va, yet it is the right term, for these creatures were *unclean*. Despite their wounds and decades of decay, it was obvious they were only superficially gue'la. Their withered flesh was stretched taut across misshapen bones, thickening to gnarled plates at the ribs and shoulder blades. Many had double-jointed legs and scythe-like appendages jutting from their wrists. Their faces were atrophied relics in elongated, almost bestial skulls, the jaws distended by hardened, stinger-tipped tongues. Some still wore shreds of clothing, but most were naked.

They shed their clothes like redundant skins when the change came over them...

'We should go back,' I said with utter conviction. For once I suspected the janissaries were with me, but to my surprise they weren't the only ones.

'Asharil is right,' Jhi'kaara said. 'This tomb is best left buried.'

Mutekh hesitated. He was as repulsed as the rest of us, but leaving a mystery unsolved was anathema to him.

'Unacceptable,' the cartographer declared. 'It is our duty to assess, quantify and record this anomaly. The Greater Good demands courage. Has yours failed you, fire warrior?'

Jhi'kaara stiffened. The tension passed through the janissaries in a sympathetic wave and I saw their weapons twitch reflexively towards the cartographer. Even Xanti noticed it, looking back and forth between the opponents with a confused expression that was almost comical. Only Mutekh seemed oblivious to his own peril.

'I will continue alone,' he pushed, 'if you are afraid...'

I thought she would kill him then. I tried to intervene, to rise to my calling and smooth over the discord, but the words slipped away before I could marshal them. Instead, Jhi'kaara found a reserve of discipline I had not credited her with.

'Fire always walks at the fore,' she said. Without another word she stepped down amongst the corpses. And sealed our fate.

We followed the intruders' trail of devastation through a maze of laboratories and workshops that soon became unrecognisable. The fungal veins riddling the walls had grown ripe here, erupting into groping, ropey strands like calcified viscera. Before it froze, the stuff had entwined itself about everything, melting the rigid Imperial architecture into soft organic shapes.

We are crawling through a diseased corpse, I thought, *but what if it's not dead, just forever dying?* I fought to suppress the absurd notion, grasping for the clarity of the Tau'va, but in this cesspit it seemed a flickering, false hope.

The blighted dead were everywhere, snarled up in the weave where they had fallen. Shredded, pulverised or charred, they had died in droves as they swarmed against the incursion, and I found myself wondering at the lethality of their slayers. What kind of creature could carve a swath through such horrors?

We found the answer in a ravaged infirmary where the invaders had suffered their first casualty. The fallen warrior was almost buried beneath a mound of mutants, but there was no mistaking his stature. Alive, he would have been almost twice my height and countless times my weight. *Could it really be?*

'Space Marines,' Jhi'kaara said with something like reverence. 'And where there is one, there will be others.'

My breath caught as she confirmed my suspicion. I had studied accounts and pictures of the Imperium's elite warriors, but they had seemed a distant, almost mythical peril. They were the stuff of nightmares, bio-engineered giants bred to be utterly merciless in the service of their dead Emperor. It was rumoured that a hundred of these monsters could conquer a world.

'What were they doing here?' I wondered, staring at the dead Space Marine in fascination. A helmet with a sharp, almost avian snout hid his features, but I could imagine the face beneath: it would be pugnacious and broad, with skin like toughened leather and a fretwork of scars and tattoos – a face not merely honed by war, but *rebuilt* for it.

Jhi'kaara gestured to the janissaries and they heaved the mutants aside, exhuming the warrior's void-black power armour. Peculiarly, his left arm looked as if it were cast in silver, its shoulder pad carved into a stylised 'I' sigil inset with a skull. More incongruous still was the bright yellow of the opposite pauldron. For all his ferocity, this warrior's grasp of aesthetics had been woeful.

'I recognise this heraldry.' Jhi'kaara tapped the angular fist inscribed on the yellow pad. 'The Imperial Fists are old foes of the Tau Empire, but this…' She indicated the silver pad. 'This I have not seen before. And the Imperial Fists wear *yellow* armour, not black.'

'Wait,' I said, 'this second symbol… Isn't it like the one we found at the entrance?'

'It *is* similar,' Mutekh said, peering at the device, 'but the inset skull is a significant deviation. There may be a connection, but careless assumptions are dangerous...'

'Does it matter?' Xanti asked. 'The gue'la fanatics are all insane. Nothing they do makes sense.'

'Know your enemy as you would know yourself,' Jhi'kaara said, doubtless quoting some fire caste credo. 'There is a mystery here.'

There was certainly no mystery about the Space Marine's death: his breastplate had been cracked open like a shell and one of the mutants had virtually crawled inside his chest as it disembowelled him.

'The Imperium sent its finest warriors to purge this crisis,'

Jhi'kaara murmured thoughtfully.

'All the more reason for us to leave,' I insisted.

'No, we cannot.' She stepped away from the dead giant. 'Space Marines do not leave their fallen behind.'

'I don't see the relevance...'

'Do you not? *Think*, waterkin.'

'I...' The realisation struck me like ice water. 'You believe they failed.'

'Whatever happened here...' she said, sweeping a hand over the mutated horde, 'we must be certain it is over.'

The trail ended at the uppermost tier of a subterranean amphitheatre. Our torches struggled to make sense of the vast space, picking out details but unable to capture the whole, leaving me with the impression of a gargantuan hive woven from grey strands. Hunched in a depression at the centre of the chamber was a pale mound. Thick cords of fungus sprouted from its base, multiplying and tapering as they spread out to insinuate themselves into every surface.

As we descended, it became apparent the mutants had made their last stand here, throwing themselves between the invaders and the heart of their hive, but one-by-one the Space Marines had also fallen. The first lay two tiers down, still gripping his chain-sword though his head was missing. Like his comrade he wore black and silver power armour, but his right pauldron was completely different.

'A White Scar,' said Jhi'kaara, pointing out the crimson flash on the white pad. 'They fought honourably on Dal'yth.'

'There were Space Marines on Dal'yth?' I was appalled by the idea of the Imperium penetrating so deep into tau space.

'They almost *took* Dal'yth, waterkin.' She chuckled dryly. 'Among your caste some truths are left unspoken lest they wither your faint hearts.' Despite her words there was no malice in her voice. We had achieved an understanding of sorts, she and I. Of more concern was the possibility that my own caste had lied to me. Was that really possible? Remembering the ancient manipulator O'Seishin, I found little comfort.

As we continued our descent Jhi'kaara paused beside each of the fallen Space Marines and examined his insignia solemnly: a blue raptor against white... A white buzzsaw against black... She recognised neither of them, but she paid her respects regardless, for each had died hideously and heroically, surrounded by sundered enemies.

'Why would they bear different cadre badges?' I said, seeing how the riddle of their mismatched fraternity troubled her.

'*Cha'ptah* badges,' she corrected. 'Space Marines call their factions *Cha'ptahs*.'

I frowned at her awkward pronunciation of the gue'la word '*Chapter*'. 'And to answer your question, waterkin: I do not know. This co-fraternity contradicts everything I was taught about their kind. Space Marines adhere rigidly to their own clans.'

'Perhaps they were forced to fight together,' I suggested. 'Maybe it was a penitence for some transgression. Or an honour.'

Neither theory was reassuring, especially since the dead mutants were growing more fearsome. Some bore no resemblance to the gue'la at all, looking more like the spawn of an entirely different, utterly aberrant race. A few actually dwarfed the Space Marines, their bulk covered in spiny exoskeletal plates that looked strong enough to withstand a pulse-round. All were mottled with a fur of silver-grey mould, but it was impossible to tell whether the fungus had grown upon them or from *within* them.

Abruptly Jhi'kaara stopped, gazing at one of the larger beasts. 'I know what they are,' she said quietly.

'They are mutants,' Mutekh declared, 'evidently the product of some ill-conceived Imperial dabbling...'

'They are Yhe'mokushi, beasts of the Silent Hunger,' Jhi'kaara said. The reference meant nothing to me and the others looked equally mystified. She nodded, unsurprised. 'A predatory species the Tau Empire has only recently encountered. These differ from the bioforms depicted in our orientation sessions, but diversity is in their nature. They are living weapons that can steal form as well as substance, becoming whatever suits their purpose.'

'And they are hostile to the Tau Empire?' Xanti asked uneasily.

'They are hostile to *all* life save their own. Like locusts they exist only to consume and multiply, leaving nothing but dust and shadows in their wake. It is said the Imperium has suffered greatly from their depredations.'

We were silent. Here was another ugly truth hidden in the name of the Greater Good. Over the last few months my certainties had eroded away, revealing deception, obsession and horror. *What else had been kept from me?*

Down... further down... More dead Space Marines... First a golden beast's head set against midnight-blue, then another raptor, this one red against white.

'You respect these warriors,' I said, watching Jhi'kaara carefully.

'I respect their strength, Asharil.'

But I sensed her admiration ran deeper. Jhi'kaara was an outsider amongst her own kind, closer to Fi'draah's wilderness than the wisdom of the Tau'va. She was drawn to these warriors for their brotherhood as much as their strength.

By the time we reached the lowest tier we had found eight Space Marines. The last had succumbed at the periphery of his objective, his armour pierced in a dozen places by scything claws. Bizarrely he was still standing, his body wedged on its feet by the mass of corpses pressed against it. Even amongst his brothers he was a giant, but there were other differences. While the rest had painted their left arms silver, both his arms *were* silver – or more likely some stronger metal. Each was an angular augmetic, one terminating in a slab-like fist, the other in an intricate claw whose purpose was probably manipulation rather than combat. His personal heraldry was black, its symbol a stylised white gauntlet.

'Iron Hand,' Jhi'kaara declared. 'Another old enemy.'

'These would appear to be specimen containment units,' Mutekh said, pointing out a pair of toppled glass cylinders that looked big enough to hold the largest abominations. Ropes of fungus were wrapped around them, squeezed so tight the reinforced glass had fractured.

'The fools brought the Silent Hunger to Fi'draah,' Jhi'kaara hissed. I was surprised by the fury in her voice. She sounded like her *own* world had been threatened.

'So this place was some kind of prison?' Xanti asked.

'Not a prison,' Mutekh said as he followed the web of pipes running from the cylinders to a corroded bank of consoles.

'Remember the laboratories we passed through? No, this is a research facility. The Imperials were experimenting on these creatures. Perhaps they were seeking a means of communication…'

'The Imperium does not seek communion with its enemies,' Jhi'kaara said. 'They were looking for a weapon.'

'But why here?' Xanti wondered. 'Is it just a coincidence they came to Fi'draah?'

'Many of the indigenous fungi are lethal,' Mutekh speculated. 'Perhaps they were attempting to synthesise a pathogen.'

'Then they failed,' Jhi'kaara said flatly.

'We do not know that,' Mutekh protested. 'The techniques of the gue'la are riddled with superstition, but…'

'The Yhe'mokushi strain was too strong,' I said, surprised by my own conviction. 'When the Imperials infected it… it devoured the fungus…'

Intuition, I realised. *I am neither entirely a creature of reason nor instinct, but something subtler than either.*

'It *became* the fungus,' I finished. 'And then the fungus devoured them.'

My comrades stared at me, then their eyes wandered to the infested expanse around us. Jhi'kaara broke the silence: 'Search the Space Marines,' she ordered the janissaries. 'Gather their grenades.'

'What is your intent, fire warrior?' Mutekh demanded.

'We will complete our enemy's mission.' She indicated the monolithic puffball. 'Sometimes the enemy of your enemy is the greater enemy.'

'You will do no such thing!' Mutekh was appalled. 'We must

ascertain what the Imperials discovered here.' He looked to Xanti for support, but the young data tech avoided his gaze. *'Autaku!'*

'I am sorry, Fio'vre,' his assistant muttered unhappily, 'but whatever the Imperials found here... it did them no good.'

'I will search this one,' I said, heading for the nearest Space Marine.

'I trust you know what a grenade looks like, waterkin?' Jhi'kaara mocked gently. Then she was gone, heading for the upper tiers.

'Cowards,' Mutekh called after us. 'You are all betraying the Greater Good.'

No, we are serving the Greater Good, I thought fiercely. *Even if some of us have come to doubt it.*

Biting down my disgust I dragged a corpse away from my chosen warrior, intent on reaching his utility belt. That was when I noticed the hum. It was faint, but its source was unmistakable: *this Space Marine's armour was still powered.* Unsettled, I peered up at his archaic helmet. A flat visor covered the right side of his face, but the left was a tangle of bionics clustered around a jutting optical sensor. Up close he seemed more machine than man.

Iron Hand, Jhi'kaara had called this one...

'Fio'vre, wait!' The voice was Xanti's, its urgency irresistible. I glanced round and saw Mutekh standing beside the puffball, a laser scalpel in one hand and a sample container in the other.

'Wait!' I echoed, but the scalpel was already descending towards the mottled surface. 'Don't–'

The puffball exploded like a bomb.

And that's precisely what it is, I realised, *a spore bomb, dormant but not dead.*

There was no fire or fragmentation in the blast, but the concussion threw Mutekh across the tier, slamming him against the consoles with bone-breaking force. I saw his body rebound a heartbeat before everything was smothered in swirling grey smog. Clutching my mask tightly, I screwed my eyes shut and crouched, sheltering beneath the Iron Hand. The scattered janissaries cursed as the spore cloud rolled over them, then the curses turned to choked screams as their lungs drowned in filth. I heard them stumbling about as they fought to escape their torment. Someone opened fire blindly, his pulse-rounds sizzling as they ripped through the congealed air. Someone else screamed his last as a wild round struck him.

That was a mercy. The only kind remaining to these men...

I risked a glance as one of them fell to his knees alongside me. The toxic whiteout reduced him to a vague, flailing silhouette, but I could see his entire body heaving violently, as if in the grip of some bone-deep tremor.

Not bone-deep. This quake ran much deeper than that.

I heard his flesh seething as its muscles contorted into new shapes, stretching his skin taut in the struggle to contain the chaos beneath. Suddenly he screamed, spewing blood and spores as his back arched inwards at an impossible angle. The spine broke – then snapped back into a sleek, predatory curve. Vicious spikes erupted along its length, racing to catch up with his rapidly elongating cranium. His arms shot out in a welter of shredded fingers, propelled by the bone scythes surging from his wrists. He tried to scream again and his tongue burst free, thickened and barbed, like a stinger-tipped snake.

It looks like there is a wyrmtree growing inside him, I thought wildly. Any moment now, the newborn hybrid would turn and see me…

'Fio'vre! Where are you?' Xanti called as he came stumbling through the mist, his faithful drone hovering beside him. He saw me and raised a hand in relief. 'Asharil! Did you see–'

The hybrid leapt. Propelled by powerful, double-jointed legs it streaked through the air and was upon the *autaku* before he saw it coming. The bone scythes slashed down, impaling him through the shoulder blades and pinning him to the ground. His shriek was cut off as the beast's tongue shot out like a spring-loaded blade and punched through his filtrator mask. His legs kicked about spastically as it wormed its way down his throat, stinging and seeding him with spores. The abandoned data drone twittered in confusion and a scythe flailed out and sent it spinning my way. I covered my head as the saucer smashed into the Iron Hand and toppled beside me with a forlorn squawk.

The smog had thinned out, the spores settling over the chamber like softly luminescent dust. By their pallid light I saw that none of the janissaries had escaped the change. Some were still going through the final trauma, but five were racing towards a solitary figure on the topmost tier. Jhi'kaara was kneeling, tracking the approaching hybrids with her pulse rifle. She fired, but her chosen mark darted aside with shocking speed. I imagined her cursing then, angry but not afraid. *Never afraid…* She fired again, then once more in quick succession, the first shot tricking her target into the path of the second. The round struck the hybrid mid-leap, throwing it to the ground in a writhing heap. Before it could right itself, a third shot sheared through its skull. A kill, but it had cost her precious time.

With a chittering yowl one of the creatures leapt onto Jhi'kaara's tier, but she ignored it, intent upon a more distant mark. Before I could shout a warning, her gun drone swooped from the shadows and lanced her aggressor with its twin-linked guns, almost tearing it in two. Whirling round, the saucer sped towards another hybrid, spitting fire, but the beast danced about in ragged avian bursts, bounding between the floor and the walls as it charged. At the last moment it rolled low and sprung up beneath the saucer, latching on to its rim. The drone spun about, firing furiously as it tried to dislodge its attacker, but the beast was too strong. I imagined the machine's primitive logic core assessing probabilities and weighing up options. It found its answer within seconds and self-destructed, incinerating the hybrid from the waist up.

I had no more time to spare for Jhi'kaara's battle. Done with its prey, Xanti's attacker sat up on its haunches, sniffing the air while its victim writhed beneath it in the throes of change. I looked around, hoping for a fallen firearm… cursing myself for refusing to carry one… desperate for a clean death…

'Power…' The voice sounded like the wheeze of a dying machine. *A machine that spoke Imperial Gothic…* I looked up and saw the impossible: the Iron Hand had inclined its head towards me, its optic glowing a dull red, like a doomed sun. Beneath that merciless blaze water turned to fire and I became a creature of instinct. Grabbing Xanti's battered drone I hauled, staggering under the weight as I raised it to the giant like an offering to some primal god. The burden was as much philosophical as physical, yet my path seemed clear.

The galaxy was tainted and taint had to be cleansed…

A metal tendril uncoiled from the warrior's helmet, swaying about like a blind snake. Then it struck, its sharpened tip drilling through the drone's casing with a whine of ruptured metal. A moment later the snake became a leech, burying itself inside the broken machine's innards and sucking it dry of power. Power to reignite its master's hatred.

Honest hatred!

I heard Xanti's assailant rise behind me, but my world had narrowed to the awakening Iron Hand. I knew my sanity had gone, unravelled by O'Seishin's lies and Fi'draah's truths. All that remained was horror and the will to face it.

For the Greater Good…

The rest was a blur. The hybrid howled behind me and its kin answered from all sides. I spun round as it leapt, its virulent tongue extended towards me. The Space Marine's fist met the beast in midair like a turbotram, punching clean through its ribcage. He cast the corpse aside as the others fell upon him in a chittering, screeching mob. There were four in all, fully transformed and almost mindless in their need to rend and tear and infect.

The first came head-on and died in a heartbeat, its skull pulverised by a pneumatic punch to the face. His armour grinding like rusted cogs, the warrior swung at the waist and grabbed another by the throat, squeezing until bone and cartilage collapsed into paste. In the same instant he rammed his manipulator claw between the jaws of a third. Its head convulsed violently as the claw became a whirling rotary blade inside its mouth. He yanked the tool free in a storm of shattered bones as the final hybrid vaulted onto his back, scythes poised to hack down. Before it could strike, a bolt of energy punched through its skull, throwing it from its perch. I glanced up and saw Jhi'kaara kneeling a few tiers above us, her rifle levelled.

Cleansed, I thought, *every one of them.*

'Asaaar...haaal...' The voice made my name sound like something dredged up from a polluted ocean. I turned as Xanti hauled himself up, using his malformed scythes like crutches. His movements were clumsy, crippled by the capricious mutation of his muscles, as if the fungus was baffled by tau physiology. His face had stretched into a death mask, the lower jaw almost touching his belly, but his eyes were unchanged, staring at me with agonised recognition. *Pleading...*

'Asaaar...' Xanti's barbed tongue surged towards me. The Space Marine shoved me aside, but the stinger lashed my shoulder as I fell. A terrible numbness seized my arm before I even hit the ground. Dimly I saw Jhi'kaara vault from the tier above. She raised her rifle to her shoulder and advanced on the abomination, firing as she came. She didn't stop until it was a charred ruin. Then she turned her wrath on Mutekh's broken, spore-saturated body. The cartographer never stirred beneath the barrage. Perhaps he was already dead, but I doubt Jhi'kaara cared. The last thing I saw before consciousness slipped away was the dimming red light in the Iron Hand's optic.

'Power...' he whispered. And then we both faded to black.

* * *

'You were fortunate,' Jhi'kaara said when I awoke. The numbness in my arm had faded, leaving behind a dull ache. 'Its sting did not carry the infection.'

Then by unspoken consent we fed the Iron Hand, gathering the janissaries' weapons and power packs and offering them up to his ravenous mechadendrite. Our ritual was without sense for the enemy of our enemy was destroyed, leaving only the enemy, yet we never hesitated. We were both creatures of instinct now, bound by an imperative stronger than the Tau'va.

'How long have you waited?' I asked the giant when we were done. The Imperial Gothic came easily to my tongue. It always had.

'How...? **Long**...?' His voice was slurred and electronic, the syntax broken. '**Very** – long...'

'How did you survive?'

He turned his optic on me, weighing me up like an iron god. Abruptly the visor covering the right side of his face slid aside. In place of flesh and bone I saw a formless grey tangle riddled with electronics and corroded rivets.

'The **Flesh** – betrays,' he said, though he had no lips, 'but the **Machine** – is faithful.'

I saw his doom then. His body had succumbed to its wounds, but his depleted augmetics had endured, cradling his consciousness as life slipped away. Half-corpse, half-machine he had stood frozen in this chamber for untold decades, burning with impotent rage as his dead flesh was consumed. Denied neither sleep nor the deeper oblivion of death, he had watched as corruption blossomed within and without. I saw him descending into madness, then clawing his way back in the hope of redemption… then falling again. How often had that cycle repeated? And where did it stand now?

'Your mission is complete,' I said carefully, indicating the tattered spore bomb. 'We destroyed the taint.'

'**You** did – **Not**. This was – **Nothing** – just another **Tendril** – of the **Corruption.** I watched it grow – then grow stale – over the long – **Long** – long…' He faltered as his splintered mind strove for coherence. 'The **Root** – survives...'

He stepped towards the centre of the chamber, moving with surprising grace. We followed and saw the pit for the first time: a dark slash in the ground where the mega-fungus had bloomed. On closer inspection I saw it wasn't a pit at all, but a steeply inclined tunnel, its walls resinous with fungus, like the aperture of a titanic blood vessel. Or a stalk…

The spore bomb grew from here, I realised, *and the corruption is still down there, rooted deep in the ground.*

'The mission is – **Incomplete**.'

Like the Iron Hand's mission my story is incomplete, but that is of no consequence. My purpose is not to entertain you, but to warn you. Jhi'kaara will carry this log out of the Coil and ensure that it is heard and heeded. This undying tomb must be quarantined lest we fail to destroy its voracious legacy. *We?* Yes, I have chosen to accompany the Iron Hand on his final duty. I am no warrior, but I can carry grenades and we will bear many into the unclean bowels of this place. Jhi'kaara argued against it, of course, telling me it was her duty to make the final descent.

'You should bear the word and I the fire,' she said, but it could not be.

You see, I cannot return. Jhi'kaara was wrong: Xanti's sting did carry the contagion. Though his touch was fleeting I can feel the taint stirring in my blood like the promise of lies. I don't know how long I have, but I will not hide in the darkness until the blight takes me. Besides, my corruption is more than blood-deep, for I have fallen from the Tau'va. I am no longer a creature of water or fire, nor indeed of sanity, but I can still serve. I shall descend into the pit alongside my enemy and purge the unclean... For the Greater Good.

- END RECORDING -

EXHUMED

STEVE PARKER

The Thunderhawk gunship loomed out of the clouds like a monstrous bird of prey, wings spread, turbines growling, air-brakes flared to slow it for landing. It was black, its fuselage marked with three symbols: the Imperial aquila, noble and golden; the 'I' of the Emperor's Holy Inquisition, a symbol even the righteous knew better than to greet gladly; and another symbol, a skull cast in silver with a gleaming red, cybernetic eye. Derlon Saezar didn't know that one, had never seen it before, but it sent a chill up his spine all the same. Whichever august Imperial body the symbol represented was obviously linked to the Holy Inquisition. That couldn't be good news.

Eyes locked to his vid-monitor, Saezar watched tensely as the gunship banked hard towards the small landing facility he managed, its prow slicing through the veils of windblown dust like a knife through silk. There was a burst of static-riddled speech on his headset. In response, he tapped several codes into the console in front of him, keyed his microphone and said, 'Acknowledged, One-Seven-One. Clearance codes accepted. Proceed to Bay Four. This is an enclosed atmosphere facility. I'm uploading our safety and debarkation protocols to you now. Over.'

His fingers rippled over the console's runeboard, and the massive metal jaws of Bay Four began to grate open, ready to swallow the unwelcome black craft. Thick, toxic air rushed in. Breathable air rushed out. The entire facility shuddered and groaned in complaint, as it always did when a spacecraft came or went. The Adeptus Mechanicus had built this station, Orga Station, quickly and with the minimum systems and resources it would need to do its job. No more, no less.

It was a rusting, dust-scoured place, squat and ugly on the outside, dank and gloomy within. Craft arrived, craft departed. Those coming in brought slaves, servitors, heavy machinery and fuel. Saezar didn't know what those leaving carried. The magos who had hired him had left him in no doubt that curiosity would lead to the termination of more than his contract. Saezar was smart enough to believe it. He and his staff kept their heads down and did their jobs. In another few years, the tech-priests would be done here. They had told him as much. He would go back to Jacero then, maybe buy a farm with the money he'd have saved, enjoy air that didn't kill you on the first lungful.

That thought called up a memory Saezar would have given a lot to erase. Three weeks ago, a malfunction in one of the Bay

Two extractors left an entire work crew breathing this planet's lethal air. The bay's vid-picters had caught it all in fine detail, the way the technicians and slaves staggered in agony towards the emergency airlocks, clawing at their throats while blood streamed from their mouths, noses and eyes. Twenty-three men dead. It had taken only seconds, but Saezar knew the sight would be with him for life. He shook himself, trying to cast the memory off.

The Thunderhawk had passed beyond the outer picters' field of view. Saezar switched to Bay Four's internal picters and saw the big black craft settle heavily on its landing stanchions. Thrusters cooled. Turbines whined down towards silence. The outer doors of the landing bay clanged shut. Saezar hit the winking red rune on the top right of his board and flooded the bay with the proper nitrogen and oxygen mix. When his screen showed everything was in the green, he addressed the pilot of the Thunderhawk again.

'Atmosphere restored, One-Seven-One. Bay Four secure. Free to debark.'

There was a brief grunt in answer. The Thunderhawk's front ramp lowered. Yellow light spilled out from inside, illuminating the black metal grille of the bay floor. Shadows appeared in that light – big shadows – and, after a moment, the figures that cast them began to descend the ramp. Saezar leaned forward, face close to his screen.

'By the Throne,' he whispered to himself.

With his right hand, he manipulated one of the bay vid-picters by remote, zooming in on the figure striding in front. It was massive, armoured in black ceramite, its face hidden beneath a cold, expressionless helm. On one great pauldron, the left, Saezar saw the same skull icon that graced the ship's prow. On the right, he saw another skull on a field of white, two black scythes crossed behind it. Here was yet another icon Saezar had never seen before, but he knew well enough the nature of the being that bore it. He had seen such beings rendered in paintings and stained glass, cut from marble or cast in precious metal. It was a figure of legend, and it was not alone.

Behind it, four others, similarly armour-clad but each bearing different iconography on their right pauldrons, marched in formation. Saezar's heart was in his throat. He tried to swallow, but his mouth was dry. He had never expected to see such beings with his own eyes. No one did. They were heroes from the stories his father had read to him, stories told to all children of the Imperium to give them hope, to help them sleep at night. Here they were in flesh and bone and metal.

Space Marines! Here! At Orga Station!

And there was a further incredible sight yet to come. Just as the five figures stepped onto the grillework floor, something huge blotted out all the light from inside the craft. The Thunderhawk's ramp shook with thunderous steps. Something emerged on two stocky, piston-like legs. It was vast and angular and impossibly powerful-looking, like a walking tank with fists instead of cannon.

It was a Dreadnought, and, even among such legends as these, it was in a class of its own.

Saezar felt a flood of conflicting emotion, equal parts joy and dread.

The Space Marines had come to Menatar, and where they went, death followed.

'Menatar,' said the tiny hunched figure, more to himself than to any of the black-armoured giants he shared the pressurised mag-rail carriage with. 'Second planet of the Ozyma-138 system, Hatha Subsector, Ultima Segmentum. Solar orbital period, one-point-one-three Terran standard. Gravity, zero-point-eight-three Terran standard.' He looked up, his tiny black eyes meeting those of Siefer Zeed, the Raven Guard. 'The atmosphere is a thick nitrogen-sulphide and carbon dioxide mix. Did you know that? Utterly deadly to the non-augmented. I doubt even you Adeptus Astartes could breathe it for long. Even our servitors wear air tanks here.'

Zeed stared back indifferently at the little tech-priest. When he spoke, it was not in answer. His words were directed to his right, to his squad leader, Lyandro Karras, Codicier Librarian of the Death Spectres Chapter, known officially in Deathwatch circles as Talon Alpha. That wasn't what Zeed called him, though. 'Tell me again, Scholar, why we get all the worthless jobs.'

Karras didn't look up from the boltgun he was muttering litanies over. Times like these, the quiet times, were for meditation and proper observances, something the Raven Guard seemed wholly unable to grasp. Karras had spent six years as leader of this kill-team. Siefer Zeed, nicknamed Ghost for his alabaster skin, was as irreverent today as he had been when they'd first met. Perhaps he was even worse.

Karras finished murmuring his Litany of Flawless Operation

and sighed. 'You know why, Ghost. If you didn't go out of your way to anger Sigma all the time, maybe those Scimitar bastards would be here instead of us.'

Talon Squad's handler, an inquisitor lord known only as Sigma, had come all too close to dismissing Zeed from active duty on several occasions, a terrible dishonour not just for the Deathwatch member in question, but for his entire Chapter. Zeed frequently tested the limits of Sigma's need-to-know policy, not to mention the inquisitor's patience. But the Raven Guard was a peerless killing machine at close range, and his skill with a pair of lightning claws, his signature weapon, had won the day so often that Karras and the others had stopped counting.

Another voice spoke up, a deep rumbling bass, its tones warm and rich. 'They're not all bad,' said Maximmion Voss of the Imperial Fists. 'Scimitar Squad, I mean.'

'Right,' said Zeed with good-natured sarcasm. 'It's not like you're biased, Omni. I mean, every Black Templar or Crimson Fist in the galaxy is a veritable saint.'

Voss grinned.

There was a hiss from the rear of the carriage where Ignatio Solarion and Darrion Rauth, Ultramarine and Exorcist respectively, sat in relative silence. The hiss had come from Solarion.

'Something you want to say, Prophet?' said Zeed with a challenging thrust of his chin.

Solarion scowled at him, displaying the full extent of his contempt for the Raven Guard. 'We are with company,' he said, indicating the little tech-priest who had fallen silent while the Deathwatch Space Marines talked. 'You would do well to remember that.'

Zeed threw Solarion a sneer, then turned his eyes back to the tech-priest. The man had met them on the mag-rail platform at Orga Station, introducing himself as Magos Iapetus Borgovda, the most senior adept on the planet and a xeno-heirographologist specialising in the writings and history of the Exodites, offshoot cultures of the eldar race. They had lived here once, these Exodites, and had left many secrets buried deep in the drifting red sands.

That went no way to explaining why a Deathwatch kill-team was needed, however, especially now. Menatar was a dead world. Its sun had become a red giant, a K3-type star well on its way to final collapse. Before it died, however, it would burn off the last of Menatar's atmosphere, leaving little more than a ball of molten rock. Shortly after that, Menatar would cool and there would be no trace of anyone ever having set foot here at all. Such an end was many tens of thousands of years away, of course. Had the Exodites abandoned this world early, knowing its eventual fate? Or had something else driven them off? Maybe the xeno-heirographologist would find the answers eventually, but that still didn't tell Zeed anything about why Sigma had sent some of his key assets here.

Magos Borgovda turned to his left and looked out the view-spex bubble at the front of the mag-rail carriage. A vast dead volcano dominated the skyline. The mag-rail car sped towards it so fast the red dunes and rocky spires on either side of the tracks went by in a blur. 'We are coming up on Typhonis Mons,' the magos wheezed. 'The noble Priesthood of Mars cut a tunnel straight through the side of the crater, you know. The journey will take another hour. No more than that. Without the tunnel–'

'Good,' interrupted Zeed, running the fingers of one gauntleted hand through his long black hair. His eyes flicked to the blades of the lightning claws fixed to the magnetic couplings on his thigh-plates. Soon it would be time to don the weapons properly, fix his helmet to its seals, and step out onto solid ground. Omni was tuning the suspensors on his heavy bolter. Solarion was checking the bolt mechanism of his sniper rifle. Karras and Rauth had both finished their final checks already.

If there was nothing here to fight, why were they sent so heavily armed, Zeed asked himself?

He thought of the ill-tempered Dreadnought riding alone in the other carriage.

And why did they bring Chyron?

The mag-rail carriage slowed to a smooth halt beside a platform cluttered with crates bearing the cog-and-skull mark of the Adeptus Mechanicus. On either side of the platform, spreading out in well-ordered concentric rows, were scores of stocky pre-fabricated huts and storage units, their low roofs piled with ash and dust. Thick insulated cables snaked everywhere, linking heavy machinery to generators supplying light, heat and atmospheric stability to the sleeping quarters and mess blocks. Here and there, cranes stood tall against the wind. Looming over everything were the sides of the crater, penning it all in, lending the place a strange quality, almost like being outdoors and yet indoors at the same time.

Borgovda was clearly expected. Dozens of acolytes, robed in the red of the Martian Priesthood and fitted with breathing apparatus, bowed low when he emerged from the carriage.

Around them, straight-backed skitarii troopers stood to attention with lasguns and hellguns clutched diagonally across their chests.

Quietly, Voss mumbled to Zeed, 'It seems our new acquaintance didn't lie about his status here. Perhaps you should have been more polite to him, paper-face.'

'I don't recall you offering any pleasantries, tree-trunk,' Zeed replied. He and Voss had been friends since the moment they met. It was a rapport that none of the other kill-team members shared, a fact that only served to deepen the bond. Had anyone else called Zeed *paper-face*, he might well have eviscerated them on the spot. Likewise, few would have dared to call the squat, powerful Voss *tree-trunk*. Even fewer would have survived to tell of it. But, between the two of them, such names were taken as a mark of trust and friendship that was truly rare among the Deathwatch.

Magos Borgovda broke from greeting the rows of fawning acolytes and turned to his black-armoured escorts. When he spoke, it was directly to Karras, who had identified himself as team leader during introductions.

'Shall we proceed to the dig-site, lord? Or do you wish to rest first?'

'Astartes need no rest,' answered Karras flatly.

It was a slight exaggeration, of course, and the twinkle in the xeno-heirographologist's eye suggested he knew as much, but he also knew that, by comparison to most humans, it was as good as true. Borgovda and his fellow servants of the Machine-God also required little rest.

'Very well,' said the magos. 'Let us go straight to the pit. My acolytes tell me we are ready to initiate the final stage of our operation. They await only my command.'

He dismissed all but a few of the acolytes, issuing commands to them in sharp bursts of machine code language, and turned east. Leaving the platform behind them, the Deathwatch followed. Karras walked beside the bent and robed figure, consciously slowing his steps to match the speed of the tech-priest. The others, including the massive, multi-tonne form of the Dreadnought, Chyron, fell into step behind them. Chyron's footfalls made the ground tremble as he brought up the rear.

Zeed cursed at having to walk so slowly. Why should one such as he, one who could move with inhuman speed, be forced to crawl at the little tech-priest's pace? He might reach the dig-site in a fraction of the time and never break sweat. How long would it take at the speed of this grinding, clicking, wheezing half-mechanical magos?

Eager for distraction, he turned his gaze to the inner slopes of the great crater in which the entire excavation site was located. This was Typhonis Mons, the largest volcano in the Ozyma-138 system. No wonder the Adeptus Mechanicus had tunnelled all those kilometres through the crater wall. To go up and over the towering ridgeline would have taken significantly more time and effort. Any road built to do so would have required more switchbacks than was reasonable. The caldera was close to two and a half kilometres across, its jagged rim rising well over a kilometre on every side.

Looking more closely at the steep slopes all around him, Zeed saw that many bore signs of artifice. The signs were subtle, yes, perhaps eroded by time and wind, or by the changes in atmosphere that the expanding red giant had wrought, but they were there all the same. The Raven Guard's enhanced visor-optics, working in accord with his superior gene-boosted vision, showed him crumbled doorways and pillared galleries.

Had he not known this world for an Exodite world, he might have passed these off as natural structures, for there was little angular about them. Angularity was something one saw everywhere in human construction, but far less so in the works of the hated, inexplicable eldar. Their structures, their craft, their weapons – each seemed almost grown rather than built, their forms fluid, gracefully organic. Like all righteous warriors of the Imperium, Zeed hated them. They denied man's destiny as ruler of the stars. They stood in the way of expansion, of progress.

He had fought them many times. He had been there when forces had contested human territory in the Adiccan Reach, launching blisteringly fast raids on worlds they had no right to claim. They were good foes to fight. He enjoyed the challenge of their speed, and they were not afraid to engage with him at close quarters, though they often retreated in the face of his might rather than die honourably.

Cowards.

Such a shame they had left this world so long ago. He would have enjoyed fighting them here.

In fact, he thought, flexing his claws in irritation, just about any fight would do.

* * *

Six massive cranes struggled in unison to raise their load from the circular black pit in the centre of the crater. They had buried this thing deep – deep enough that no one should ever have disturbed it here. But Iapetus Borgovda had transcribed the records of that burial; records found on a damaged craft that had been lost in the warp only to emerge centuries later on the fringe of the Imperium. He had been on his way to present his findings to the Genetor Biologis himself when a senior magos by the name of Serjus Altando had intercepted him and asked him to present his findings to the Ordo Xenos of the Holy Inquisition first.

After that, Borgovda never got around to presenting his work to his superiors on Mars. The mysterious inquisitor lord that Magos Altando served had guaranteed Borgovda all the resources he would need to make the discovery entirely his own. The credit, Altando promised, need not be shared with anyone else. Borgovda would be revered for his work. Perhaps, one day, he would even be granted genetor rank himself.

And so it was that mankind had come to Menatar and had begun to dig where no one was supposed to.

The fruits of that labour were finally close at hand. Borgovda's black eyes glittered like coals beneath the clear bubble of his breathing apparatus as he watched each of the six cranes reel in their thick polysteel cables. With tantalising slowness, something huge and ancient began to peek above the lip of the pit. A hundred skitarii troopers and gun-servitors inched forward, weapons raised. They had no idea what was emerging. Few did.

Borgovda knew. Magos Altando knew. Sigma knew. Of these three, however, only Borgovda was present in person. The others, he believed, were light-years away. This was *his* prize alone, just as the inquisitor had promised. This was *his* operation. As more of the object cleared the lip of the pit, he stepped forward himself. Behind him, the Space Marines of Talon Squad gripped their weapons and watched.

The object was almost entirely revealed now, a vast sarcophagus, oval in shape, twenty-three metres long on its vertical axis, sixteen metres on the horizontal. Every centimetre of its surface, a surface like nothing so much as polished bone, was intricately carved with script. By force of habit, the xenoheirographologist began translating the symbols with part of his mind while the rest of it continued to marvel at the beauty of what he saw. Just what secrets would this object reveal?

He, and other radicals like him, believed mankind's salvation, its very future, lay not with the technological stagnation in which the race of men was currently mired, but with the act of understanding and embracing the technology of its alien enemies. And yet, so many fools scorned this patently obvious truth. Borgovda had known good colleagues, fine inquisitive magi like himself, who had been executed for their beliefs. Why did the Fabricator General not see it? Why did the mighty Lords of Terra not understand? Well, he would make them see. Sigma had promised him all the resources he would need to make the most of this discovery. The Holy Inquisition was on his side. This time would be different.

The object, fully raised above the pit, hung there in all its ancient, inscrutable glory. Borgovda gave a muttered command into a vox-piece, and the cranes began a slow, synchronised turn.

Borgovda held his breath.

They moved the vast sarcophagus over solid ground and stopped.

'Yes,' said Borgovda over the link. 'That's it. Now lower it gently.'

The crane crews did as ordered. Millimetre by millimetre, the oval tomb descended.

Then it lurched.

One of the cranes gave a screech of metal. Its frame twisted sharply to the right, titanium struts crumpling like tin.

'What's going on?' demanded Borgovda.

From the corner of his vision, he noted the Deathwatch stepping forward, cocking their weapons, and the Dreadnought eagerly flexing its great metal fists.

A panicked voice came back to him from the crane operator in the damaged machine. 'There's something moving inside that thing,' gasped the man. 'Something really heavy. Its centre of gravity is shifting all over the place!'

Borgovda's eyes narrowed as he scrutinised the hanging oval object. It was swinging on five taut cables now, while the sixth, that of the ruined crane, had gone slack. The object lurched again. The movement was clearly visible this time, obviously generated by massive internal force.

'Get it onto the ground,' Borgovda barked over the link, 'but carefully. Do not damage it.'

The cranes began spooling out more cable at his command, but the sarcophagus gave one final big lurch and crumpled two more of the sturdy machines. The other three cables tore free, and it fell to the ground with an impact that shook the closest slaves and acolytes from their feet.

Borgovda started towards the fallen sarcophagus, and knew that the Deathwatch were right behind him. Had the inquisitor known this might happen? Was that why he had sent his angels of death and destruction along?

Even at this distance, some one hundred and twenty metres away, even through all the dust and grit the impact had kicked up, Borgovda could see sigils begin to glow red on the surface of the massive object. They blinked on and off like warning lights, and he realised that was exactly what they were. Despite all the irreconcilable differences between the humans and the aliens, this message, at least, meant the same.

Danger!

There was a sound like cracking wood, but so loud it was deafening.

Suddenly, one of the Deathwatch Space Marines roared in agony and collapsed to his knees, gauntlets pressed tight to the side of his helmet. Another Adeptus Astartes, the Imperial Fist, raced forward to his fallen leader's side.

'What's the matter, Scholar? What's going on?'

The one called Karras spoke through his pain, but there was no mistaking the sound of it, the raw, nerve-searing agony in his words. 'A psychic beacon!' he growled through clenched teeth. 'A psychic beacon just went off. The magnitude–'

He howled as another wave of pain hit him, and the sound spoke of a suffering that Borgovda could hardly imagine.

Another of the kill-team members, this one with a pauldron boasting a daemon's skull design, stepped forward with boltgun raised and, incredibly, took aim at his leader's head.

The Raven Guard moved like lightning. Almost too fast to see, he was at this other's side, knocking the muzzle of the boltgun up and away with the back of his forearm. 'What the hell are you doing, Watcher?' Zeed snapped. 'Stand down!'

The Exorcist, Rauth, glared at Zeed through his helmet visor, but he turned his weapon away all the same. His finger, however, did not leave the trigger.

'Scholar,' said Voss. 'Can you fight it? Can you fight through it?'

The Death Spectre struggled to his feet, but his posture said he was hardly in any shape to fight if he had to. 'I've never felt anything like this!' he hissed. 'We have to knock it out. It's smothering my... gift.' He turned to Borgovda. 'What in the Emperor's name is going on here, magos?'

'Gift?' spat Rauth in an undertone.

Borgovda answered, turning his black eyes back to the object as he did. It was on its side about twenty metres from the edge of the pit, rocking violently as if something were alive inside it.

'The Exodites...' he said. 'They must have set up some kind of signal to alert them when someone... interfered. We've just set it off.'

'Interfered with what?' demanded Ignatio Solarion. The Ultramarine rounded on the tiny tech-priest. 'Answer me!'

There was another loud cracking sound. Borgovda looked beyond Solarion and saw the bone-like surface of the sarcophagus split violently. Pieces shattered and flew off. In the gaps they left, something huge and dark writhed and twisted, desperate to be free.

The magos was transfixed.

'I asked you a question!' Solarion barked, visibly fighting to restrain himself from striking the magos. 'What does the beacon alert them to?'

'To that,' said Borgovda, terrified and exhilarated all at once. 'To the release of… of whatever they buried here.'

'They left it alive?' said Voss, drawing abreast of Solarion and Borgovda, his heavy bolter raised and ready.

Suddenly, everything slotted into place. Borgovda had the full context of the writing he had deciphered on the sarcophagus's surface, and, with that context, came a new understanding.

'They buried it,' he told Talon Squad, 'because they couldn't kill it!'

There was a shower of bony pieces as the creature finally broke free of the last of its tomb and stretched its massive serpentine body for all to see. It was as tall as a Warhound Titan, and, from the look of it, almost as well armoured. Complex mouthparts split open like the bony, razor-lined petals of some strange, lethal flower. Its bizarre jaws dripped with corrosive fluids. This beast, this nightmare leviathan pulled from the belly of the earth, shivered and threw back its gargantuan head.

A piercing shriek filled the poisonous air, so loud that some of the skitarii troopers closest to it fell down, choking on the deadly atmosphere. The creature's screech had shattered their visors.

'Well maybe *they* couldn't kill it,' growled Lyandro Karras, marching stoically forwards through waves of psychic pain, 'But *we* will! To battle, brothers, in the Emperor's name!'

* * *

Searing lances of las-fire erupted from all directions at once, centring on the massive worm-like creature that was, after so many long millennia, finally free. Normal men would have quailed in the face of such an overwhelming foe. What could such tiny things as humans do against something like this? But the skitarii troopers of the Adeptus Mechanicus had been rendered all but fearless, their survival instincts overridden by neural programming, augmentation and brain surgery. They did not flee as other men would have. They surrounded the beast, working as one to put as much firepower on it as possible.

A brave effort, but ultimately a wasted one. The creature's thick plates of alien chitin shrugged off their assault. All that concentrated firepower really achieved was to turn the beast's attention on its attackers. Though sightless in the conventional sense, it sensed everything. Rows of tiny cyst-like nodules running the length of its body detected changes in heat, air pressure and vibration to the most minute degree. It knew exactly where each of its attackers stood. Not only could it hear their beating hearts, it could feel them vibrating through the ground and the air. Nothing escaped its notice.

With incredible speed for a creature so vast, it whipped its heavy black tail forward in an arc. The air around it whistled. Skitarii troopers were cut down like stalks of wheat, crushed by the dozen, their rib cages pulverised. Some were launched into the air, their bodies falling like mortar shells a second later, slamming down with fatal force onto the corrugated metal roofs of the nearby storage and accommodation huts.

Talon Squad was already racing forward to join the fight.

Chyron's awkward run caused crates to fall from their stacks. Adrenaline flooded the wretched remains of his organic body, a tiny remnant of the Astartes he had once been, little more now than brain, organs and scraps of flesh held together, kept alive, by the systems of his massive armoured chassis.

'Death to all xenos!' he roared, following close behind the others.

At the head of the team, Karras ran with his bolter in hand. The creature was three hundred metres away, but he and his squadmates would close that gap all too quickly. What would they do then? How did one fight a monster like this?

There was a voice on the link. It was Voss.

'A trygon, Scholar? A mawloc?'

'No, Omni,' replied Karras. 'Same genus, I think, but something we haven't seen before.'

'Sigma knew,' said Zeed, breaking in on the link.

'Aye,' said Karras. 'Knew or suspected.'

'Karras,' said Solarion. 'I'm moving to high ground.'

'Go.'

Solarion's boltgun, a superbly-crafted weapon, its like unseen in the armouries of any Adeptus Astartes Chapter but the Deathwatch, was best employed from a distance. The Ultramarine broke away from the charge of the others. He sought out the tallest structure in the crater that he could reach quickly. His eyes found it almost immediately. It was behind him – the loading crane that served the mag-rail line. It was slightly shorter than the cranes that had been used to lift the entombed creature out of the pit, but each of those were far too close to the beast to be useful. This one would do well. He ran to the foot of the crane, to the stanchions that were steam-bolted to the ground, slung his rifle over his right pauldron, and began to climb.

The massive tyranid worm was scything its tail through more of the skitarii, and their numbers dropped by half. Bloody smears marked the open concrete. For all their fearlessness and tenacity, the Mechanicus troops hadn't even scratched the blasted thing. All they had managed was to put the beast in a killing frenzy at the cost of their own lives. Still they fought, still they poured blinding spears of fire on it, but to no avail. The beast flexed again, tail slashing forward, and another dozen died, their bodies smashed to a red pulp.

'I hope you've got a plan, Scholar,' said Zeed as he ran beside his leader. 'Other than *kill the bastard*, I mean.'

'I can't channel psychic energy into *Arquemann*,' said Karras, thinking for a moment that his ancient force sword might be the only thing able to crack the brute's armoured hide. 'Not with that infernal beacon drowning me out. But if we can stop the beacon... If I can get close enough–'

He was cut off by a calm, cold and all-too-familiar voice on the link.

'Specimen Six is not to be killed under any circumstances, Talon Alpha. I want the creature alive!'

'Sigma!' spat Karras. 'You can't seriously think... No! We're taking it down. We have to!'

Sigma broadcast his voice to the entire team.

'Listen to me, Talon Squad. That creature is to be taken alive at all costs. Restrain it and prepare it for transport. Brother

Solarion has been equipped for the task already. Your job is to facilitate the success of his shot, then escort the tranquilised creature back to the *Saint Nevarre*. Remember your oaths. Do as you are bid.'

It was Chyron, breaking his characteristic brooding silence, who spoke up first.

'This is an outrage, Sigma. It is a tyranid abomination and Chyron will kill it. We are Deathwatch. Killing things is what we do.'

'You will do as ordered, Lamenter. All of you will. Remember your oaths. Honour the treaties, or return to your brothers in disgrace.'

'I have no brothers left,' Chyron snarled, as if this freed him from the need to obey.

'Then you will return to nothing. The Inquisition has no need of those who cannot follow mission parameters. The Deathwatch even less so.'

Karras, getting close to the skitarii and the foe, felt his lip curl in anger. This was madness.

'Solarion,' he barked. 'How much did you know?'

'Some,' said the Ultramarine, a trace of something unpleasant in his voice. 'Not much.'

'And you didn't warn us, brother?' Karras demanded.

'Orders, Karras. Unlike some, I follow mine to the letter.'

Solarion had never been happy operating under the Death Spectre Librarian's command. Karras was from a Chapter of the Thirteenth Founding. To Solarion, that made him inferior. Only the Chapters of the First Founding were worthy of unconditional respect, and even some of those...

'Magos Altando issued me with special rounds,' Solarion went on. 'Neuro-toxins. I need a clear shot on a soft, fleshy area. Get me that opening, Karras, and Sigma will have what he wants.'

Karras swore under his helm. He had known all along that something was up. His psychic gift did not extend to prescience, but he had sensed something dark and ominous hanging over them from the start.

The tyranid worm was barely fifty metres away now, and it turned its plated head straight towards the charging Deathwatch Space Marines. It could hardly have missed the thundering footfalls of Chyron, who was another thirty metres behind Karras, unable to match the swift pace of his smaller, lighter squadmates.

'The plan, Karras!' said Zeed, voice high and anxious.

Karras had to think fast. The beast lowered its fore-sections and began slithering towards them, sensing these newcomers were a far greater threat than the remaining skitarii.

Karras skidded to an abrupt halt next to a skitarii sergeant and shouted at him, 'You! Get your forces out. Fall back towards the mag-rail station.'

'We fight,' insisted the skitarii. 'Magos Borgovda has not issued the command to retreat.'

Karras grabbed the man by the upper right arm and almost lifted him off his feet. 'This isn't fighting. This is dying. You will do as I say. The Deathwatch will take care of this. Do not get in our way.'

The sergeant's eyes were blank, lifeless things, like those of a doll. Had the Adeptus Mechanicus surgically removed so much of the man's humanity? There was no fear there, certainly, but Karras sensed little else, either. Whether that was because of the surgeries or because the beacon was still drowning him in wave after invisible wave of pounding psychic pressure, he could not say.

After a second, the skitarii sergeant gave a reluctant nod and sent a message over his vox-link. The skitarii began falling back, but they kept their futile fire up as they moved.

The rasping of the worm's armour plates against the rock-crete grew louder as it neared, and Karras turned again to face it. 'Get ready!' he told the others.

'What is your decision, Death Spectre?' Chyron rumbled. 'It is a xenos abomination. It must be killed, regardless of the inquisitor's command.'

Damn it, thought Karras. I know he's right, but I must honour the treaties, for the sake of the Chapter. We must give Solarion his window.

'Keep the beast occupied. Do as Sigma commands. If Solarion's shot fails…'

'It won't,' said Solarion over the link.

It had better not, thought Karras. Because, if it does, I'm not sure we *can* kill this thing.

Solarion had reached the end of the crane's armature. The entire crater floor was spread out below him. He saw his fellow Talon members fan out to face the alien abomination. It reared up on its hind-sections again and screeched at them, thrashing the air with rows of tiny vestigial limbs. Voss opened up on it first, showering it with a hail of fire from his heavy bolter. Rauth and Karras followed suit while Zeed and Chyron tried to flank it and approach from the sides.

Solarion snorted.

It was obvious, to him at least, that the fiend didn't have any blind spots. It didn't have eyes!

So far as Solarion could tell from up here, the furious fusillade of bolter rounds rattling off the beast's hide was doing nothing at all, unable to penetrate the thick chitin plates.

I need exposed flesh, he told himself. I won't fire until I get it. One shot, one kill. Or, in this case, one paralysed xenos worm.

He locked himself into a stable position by pushing his boots into the corners created by the crane's metal frame. All around him, the winds of Menatar howled and tugged, trying to pull him into a deadly eighty metre drop. The dust on those winds cut visibility by twenty per cent, but Solarion had hit targets the size of an Imperial ducat at three kilometres. He knew he could pull off a perfect shot in far worse conditions than these.

Sniping from the top of the crane meant that he was forced to lie belly-down at a forty-five degree angle, his boltgun's stock braced against his shoulder, right visor-slit pressed close to the lens of his scope. After some adjustments, the writhing monstrosity came into sharp focus. Bursts of Astartes gunfire continued to ripple over its carapace. Its tail came down hard in a hammering vertical stroke that Rauth only managed to sidestep at the last possible second. The concrete where the Exorcist had been standing shattered and flew off in all directions.

Solarion pulled back the cocking lever of his weapon and slid one of Altando's neuro-toxin rounds into the chamber. Then he spoke over the comm-link.

'I'm in position, Karras. Ready to take the shot. Hurry up and get me that opening.'

'We're trying, Prophet!' Karras snapped back, using the nickname Zeed had coined for the Ultramarine.

Try harder, thought Solarion, but he didn't say it. There was a limit, he knew, to how far he could push Talon Alpha.

Three grenades detonated, one after another, with ground-splintering cracks. The wind pulled the dust and debris aside. The creature reared up again, towering over the Space Marines, and they saw that it remained utterly undamaged, not even a scratch on it.

'Nothing!' cursed Rauth.

Karras swore. This was getting desperate. The monster was tireless, its speed undiminished, and nothing they did seemed to have the least effect. By contrast, its own blows were all too potent. It had already struck Voss aside. Luck had been with the Imperial Fist, however. The blow had been lateral, sending him twenty metres along the ground before slamming him into the side of a fuel silo. The strength of his ceramite armour had saved his life. Had the blow been vertical, it would have killed him on the spot.

Talon Squad hadn't survived the last six years of special operations to die here on Menatar. Karras wouldn't allow it. But the only weapon they had which might do anything to the monster was his force blade, *Arquemann*, and, with that accursed beacon drowning out his gift, Karras couldn't charge it with the devastating psychic power it needed to do the job.

'Warp blast it!' he cursed over the link. 'Someone find the source of that psychic signal and knock it out!'

He couldn't pinpoint it himself. The psychic bursts were overwhelming, drowning out all but his own thoughts. He could no longer sense Zeed's spiritual essence, nor that of Voss, Chyron, or Solarion. As for Rauth, he had never been able to sense the Exorcist's soul. Even after serving together this long, he was no closer to discovering the reason for that. For all Karras knew, maybe the quiet, brooding Astartes had no soul.

Zeed was doing his best to keep the tyranid's attention on himself. He was the fastest of all of them. If Karras hadn't known better, he might even have said Zeed was enjoying the deadly game. Again and again, that barbed black tail flashed at the Raven Guard, and, every time, found only empty air. Zeed kept himself a split second ahead. Whenever he was close enough, he lashed out with his lightning claws and raked the creature's sides. But, despite the blue sparks that flashed with every contact, he couldn't penetrate that incredible armour.

Karras locked his bolter to his thigh plate and drew *Arquemann* from its scabbard.

This is it, he thought. We have to close with it. Maybe Chyron can do something if he can get inside its guard. He's the only one who might just be strong enough.

'Engage at close quarters,' he told the others. 'We can't do anything from back here.'

It was all the direction Chyron needed. The Dreadnought loosed a battle-cry and stormed forward to attack with his two great power fists, the ground juddering under him as he charged.

By the Emperor's grace, thought Karras, following in the Dreadnought's thunderous wake, don't let this be the day we lose someone.

Talon Squad was *his* squad. Despite the infighting, the secrets, the mistrust and everything else, that still meant something.

Solarion saw the rest of the kill-team race forward to engage the beast at close quarters and did not envy them, but he had to admit a grudging pride in their bravery and honour. Such a charge looked like sure suicide. For any other squad, it might well have been. But for Talon Squad…

Concentrate, he told himself. The moment is at hand. Breathe slowly.

He did.

His helmet filtered the air, removing the elements that might have killed him, elements that even the Adeptus Astartes implant known as the Imbiber, or the multi-lung, would not have been able to handle. Still, the air tasted foul and burned in his nostrils and throat. A gust of wind buffeted him, throwing his aim off a few millimetres, forcing him to adjust again.

A voice shouted triumphantly on the link.

'I've found it, Scholar. I have the beacon!'

'Voss?' said Karras.

There was a muffled crump, the sound of a krak grenade. Solarion's eyes flicked from his scope to a cloud of smoke about fifty metres to the creature's right. He saw Voss emerge from the smoke. Around him lay the rubble of the monster's smashed sarcophagus.

Karras gave a roar of triumph.

'It's… it's gone,' he said. 'It's lifted. I can feel it!'

So Karras would be able to wield his psychic abilities again. Would it make any difference, Solarion wondered.

It did, and that difference was immediate. Something began to glow down on the battlefield. Solarion turned his eyes towards it and saw Karras raise *Arquemann* in a two-handed grip. The monster must have sensed the sudden build-up of psychic charge, too. It thrashed its way towards the Librarian, eager to crush him under its powerful coils. Karras dashed in to meet the creature's huge body and plunged his blade into a crease where two sections of chitin plate met.

An ear-splitting alien scream tore through the air, echoing off the crater walls.

Karras twisted the blade hard and pulled it free, and its glowing length was followed by a thick gush of black ichor.

The creature writhed in pain, reared straight up and screeched again, its complex jaws open wide.

Just the opening Solarion was waiting for.

He squeezed the trigger of his rifle and felt it kick powerfully against his armoured shoulder.

A single white-hot round lanced out towards the tyranid worm.

There was a wet impact as the round struck home, embedding itself deep in the fleshy tissue of the beast's mouth.

'Direct hit!' Solarion reported.

'Good work,' said Karras on the link. 'Now what?'

It was Sigma's voice that answered. 'Fall back and wait. The toxin is fast acting. Ten to fifteen seconds. Specimen Six will be completely paralysed.'

'You heard him, Talon Squad,' said Karras. 'Fall back. Let's go!'

Solarion placed one hand on the top of his rifle, muttered a prayer of thanks to the weapon's machine-spirit, and prepared to descend. As he looked out over the crater floor, however, he saw that one member of the kill-team wasn't retreating.

Karras had seen it, too.

'Chyron,' barked the team leader. 'What in Terra's name are you doing?

The Dreadnought was standing right in front of the beast, fending off blows from its tail and its jaws with his oversized fists.

'Stand down, Lamenter,' Sigma commanded.

If Chyron heard, he deigned not to answer. While there was still a fight to be had here, he wasn't going anywhere. It was the tyranids that had obliterated his Chapter. Hive Fleet Kraken had decimated them, leaving him with no brothers, no home to return to. But if Sigma and the others thought the Deathwatch was all Chyron had left, they were wrong. He had his rage, his fury, his unquenchable lust for dire and bloody vengeance.

The others should have known that. Sigma should have known.

Karras started back towards the Dreadnought, intent on finding some way to reach him. He would use his psyker gifts if he had to. Chyron could not hope to beat the thing alone.

But, as the seconds ticked off and the Dreadnought continued to fight, it became clear that something was wrong.

From his high vantage point, it was Solarion who voiced it first.

'It's not stopping,' he said over the link. 'Sigma, the damned thing isn't even slowing down. The neuro-toxin didn't work.'

'Impossible,' replied the voice of the inquisitor. 'Magos Altando had the serum tested on–'

'Twenty-five... no, thirty seconds. I tell you, it's not working.'

Sigma was silent for a brief moment. Then he said, 'We need it alive.'

'Why?' demanded Zeed. The Raven Guard was crossing the concrete again, back towards the fight, following close behind Karras.

'You do not need to know,' said Sigma.

'The neuro-toxin doesn't work, Sigma,' Solarion repeated. 'If you have some other suggestion...'

Sigma clicked off.

I guess he doesn't, thought Solarion sourly.

'Solarion,' said Karras. 'Can you put another round in it?'

'Get it to open wide and you know I can. But it might not be a dosage issue.'

'I know,' said Karras, his anger and frustration telling in his voice. 'But it's all we've got. Be ready.'

Chyron's chassis was scraped and dented. His foe's strength seemed boundless. Every time the barbed tail whipped forward, Chyron swung his fists at it, but the beast was truly powerful and, when one blow connected squarely with the Dreadnought's thick glacis plate, he found himself staggering backwards despite his best efforts.

Karras was suddenly at his side.

'When I tell you to fall back, Dreadnought, you will do it,' growled the Librarian. 'I'm still Talon Alpha. Or does that mean nothing to you?'

Chyron steadied himself and started forward again, saying, 'I honour your station, Death Spectre, and your command. But vengeance for my Chapter supersedes all. Sigma be damned, I *will* kill this thing!'

Karras hefted *Arquemann* and prepared to join Chyron's charge. 'Would you dishonour all of us with you?'

The beast swivelled its head towards them and readied to strike again.

'For the vengeance of my Chapter, no price is too high. I am sorry, Alpha, but that is how it must be.'

'Then the rest of Talon Squad stands with you,' said Karras. 'Let us hope we all live to regret it.'

Solarion managed to put two further toxic rounds into the creature's mouth in rapid succession, but it was futile. This hopeless battle was telling badly on the others now. Each slash of that deadly tail was avoided by a rapidly narrowing margin. Against a smaller and more numerous foe, the strength of the Adeptus Astartes would have seemed almost infinite, but this towering tyranid leviathan was far too powerful to engage with the weapons they had. They were losing this fight, and yet Chyron would not abandon it, and the others would not abandon him, despite the good sense that might be served in doing so.

Voss tried his best to keep the creature occupied at range, firing great torrents from his heavy bolter, even knowing that he could do little, if any, real damage. His fire, however, gave the others just enough openings to keep fighting. Still, even the heavy ammunition store on the Imperial Fist's back had its limits. Soon, the weapon's thick belt feed began whining as it tried to cycle non-existent rounds into the chamber.

'I'm out,' Voss told them. He started disconnecting the heavy weapon so that he might draw his combat blade and join the close-quarters melee.

It was at that precise moment, however, that Zeed, who had again been taunting the creature with his lightning claws, had his feet struck out from under him. He went down hard on his back, and the tyranid monstrosity launched itself straight towards him, massive mandibles spread wide.

For an instant, Zeed saw that huge red maw descending towards him. It looked like a tunnel of dark, wet flesh. Then a black shape blocked his view and he heard a mechanical grunt of strain.

'I'm more of a meal, beast,' growled Chyron.

The Dreadnought had put himself directly in front of Zeed at the last minute, gripping the tyranid's sharp mandibles in his unbreakable titanium grip. But the creature was impossibly heavy, and it pressed down on the Lamenter with all its weight.

The force pressing down on Chyron was impossible to fight, but he put everything he had into the effort. His squat, powerful legs began to buckle. A piston in his right leg snapped. His engine began to sputter and cough with the strain.

'Get out from under me, Raven Guard,' he barked. 'I can't hold it much longer!'

Zeed scrabbled backwards about two metres, then stopped.

No, he told himself. Not today. Not to a mindless beast like this.

'Corax protect me,' he muttered, then sprang to his feet and raced forward, shouting, '*Victoris aut mortis*!'

Victory or death!

He slipped beneath the Dreadnought's right arm, bunched his legs beneath him and, with lightning claws extended out in front, dived directly into the beast's gaping throat.

'Ghost!' shouted Voss and Karras at the same time, but he was already gone from sight and there was no reply over the link.

Chyron wrestled on for another second. Then two. Then, suddenly, the monster began thrashing in great paroxysms of agony. It wrenched its mandibles from Chyron's grip and flew backwards, pounding its ringed segments against the concrete so hard that great fractures appeared in the ground.

The others moved quickly back to a safe distance and watched in stunned silence.

It took a long time to die.

When the beast was finally still, Voss sank to his knees.

'No,' he said, but he was so quiet that the others almost missed it.

Footsteps sounded on the stone behind them. It was Solarion. He stopped alongside Karras and Rauth.

'So much for taking it alive,' he said.

No one answered.

Karras couldn't believe it had finally happened. He had lost one. After all they had been through together, he had started to believe they might all return to their Chapters alive one day, to be welcomed as honoured heroes, with the sad exception of Chyron, of course.

Suddenly, however, that belief seemed embarrassingly naïve. If Zeed could die, all of them could. Even the very best of the best would meet his match in the end. Statistically, most Deathwatch members never made it back to the fortress-monasteries of their originating Chapters. Today, Zeed had joined those fallen ranks.

It was Sigma, breaking in on the command channel, who shattered the grim silence.

'You have failed me, Talon Squad. It seems I greatly overestimated you.'

Karras hissed in quiet anger. 'Siefer Zeed is dead, inquisitor.'

'Then you, Alpha, have failed on two counts. The Chapter Master of the Raven Guard will be notified of Zeed's failure. Those of you who live will at least have a future chance to redeem yourselves. The Imperium has lost a great opportunity here. I have no more to say to you. Stand by for Magos Altando.'

'Altando?' said Karras. 'Why would–'

Sigma signed off before Karras could finish, his voice soon replaced by the buzzing mechanical tones of the old magos who served on his retinue.

'I am told that Specimen Six is dead,' he grated over the link. 'Most regrettable, but your chances of success were extremely slim from the beginning. I predicted failure at close to ninety-six point eight five per cent probability.'

'But Sigma deployed us anyway,' Karras seethed. 'Why am I not surprised?'

'All is not lost,' Altando continued, ignoring the Death Spectre's ire. 'There is much still to be learned from the carcass. Escort it back to Orga Station. I will arrive there to collect it shortly.'

'Wait,' snapped Karras. 'You wish this piece of tyranid filth loaded up and shipped back for extraction? Are you aware of its size?'

'Of course, I am,' answered Altando. 'It is what the mag-rail line was built for. In fact, everything we did on Menatar from the very beginning – the construction, the excavation, the influx of Mechanicus personnel – all of it was to secure the specimen alive, still trapped inside its sarcophagus. Under the circumstances, we will make do with a dead one. You have given us no choice.'

The sound of approaching footsteps caught Karras's attention. He turned from the beast's slumped form and saw the xeno-heirographologist, Magos Borgovda, walking towards him with a phalanx of surviving skitarii troopers and robed Mechanicus acolytes.

Beneath the plex bubble of his helm, the little tech-priest's eyes were wide.

'You… you bested it. I would not have believed it possible. You have achieved what the Exodites could not.'

'Ghost bested it,' said Voss. 'This is his kill. His and Chyron's.'

If Chyron registered these words, he didn't show it. The ancient warrior stared fixedly at his fallen foe.

'Magos Borgovda,' said Karras heavily, 'are there men among your survivors who can work the cranes? This carcass is to be loaded onto a mag-rail car and taken to Orga Station.'

'Yes, indeed,' said Borgovda, his eyes taking in the sheer size of the creature. 'That part of our plans has not changed, at least.'

Karras turned in the direction of the mag-rail station and

started walking. He knew he sounded tired and miserable when he said, 'Talon Squad, fall in.'

'Wait,' said Chyron. He limped forward with a clashing and grinding of the gears in his right leg. 'I swear it, Alpha. The creature just moved. Perhaps it is not dead, after all.'

He clenched his fists as if in anticipation of crushing the last vestiges of life from it. But, as he stepped closer to the creature's slack mouth, there was a sudden outpouring of thick black gore, a great torrent of it. It splashed over his feet and washed across the dry rocky ground.

In that flood of gore was a bulky form, a form with great rounded pauldrons, sharp claws, and a distinctive, back-mounted generator. It lay unmoving in the tide of ichor.

'Ghost,' said Karras quietly. He had hoped never to see this, one under his command lying dead.

Then the figure stirred and groaned.

'If we ever fight a giant alien worm again,' said the croaking figure over the comm-link, 'some other bastard can jump down its throat. I've had my turn.'

Solarion gave a sharp laugh. Voss's reaction was immediate. He strode forward and hauled his friend up, clapping him hard on the shoulders. 'Why would any of us bother when you're so good at it, paper-face?'

Karras could hear the relief in Voss's voice. He grinned under his helm. Maybe Talon Squad was blessed after all. Maybe they would live to return to their Chapters.

'I said fall in, Deathwatch,' he barked at them; then he turned and led them away.

* * *

Altando's lifter had already docked at Orga Station by the time the mag-rail cars brought Talon Squad, the dead beast and the Mechanicus survivors to the facility. Sigma himself was, as always, nowhere to be seen. That was standard practice for the inquisitor. Six years, and Karras had still never met his enigmatic handler. He doubted he ever would.

Derlon Saezar and the station staff had been warned to stay well away from the mag-rail platforms and loading bays and to turn off all internal vid-picters. Saezar was smarter than most people gave him credit for. He did exactly as he was told. No knowledge was worth the price of his life.

Magos Altando surveyed the tyranid's long body with an appraising lens before ordering it loaded onto the lifter, a task with which even his veritable army of servitor slaves had some trouble. Magos Borgovda was most eager to speak with him, but, for some reason, Altando acted as if the xeno-heirographologist barely existed. In the end, Borgovda became irate and insisted that the other magos answer his questions at once. Why was he being told nothing? This was *his* discovery. Great promises had been made. He demanded the respect he was due.

It was at this point, with everyone gathered in Bay One, the only bay in the station large enough to offer a berth to Altando's lifter, that Sigma addressed Talon Squad over the comm-link command channel once again.

'No witnesses,' he said simply.

Karras was hardly surprised. Again, this was standard operating procedure, but that didn't mean the Death Spectre had to like it. It went against every bone in his body. Wasn't the whole point of the Deathwatch to protect mankind? They were alien-hunters. His weapons hadn't been crafted to take the lives of loyal Imperial citizens, no matter who gave the command.

'Clarify,' said Karras, feigning momentary confusion.

There was a crack of thunder, a single bolter-shot. Magos Borgovda's head exploded in a red haze.

Darrion Rauth stood over the body, dark grey smoke rising from the muzzle of his bolter

'Clear enough for you, Karras?' said the Exorcist.

Karras felt anger surging up inside him. He might even have lashed out at Rauth, might have grabbed him by the gorget, but the reaction of the surviving skitarii troopers put a stop to that. Responding to the cold-blooded slaughter of their leader, they raised their weapons and aimed straight at the Exorcist.

What followed was a one-sided massacre that made Karras sick to his stomach.

When it was over, Sigma had his wish.

There were no witnesses left to testify that anything at all had been dug up from the crater on Menatar. All that remained was the little spaceport station and its staff, waiting to be told that the excavation was over and that their time on this inhospitable world was finally at an end.

Saezar watched the big lifter take off first, and marvelled at it. Even on his slightly fuzzy vid-monitor screen, the craft was an awe-inspiring sight. It emerged from the doors of Bay One with so much thrust that he thought it might rip the whole station apart, but the facility's integrity held. There were no pressure leaks, no accidents.

The way that great ship hauled its heavy form up into the sky and off beyond the clouds thrilled him. Such power! It was a joy and an honour to see it. He wondered what it must be like to pilot such a ship.

Soon, the black Thunderhawk was also ready to leave. He granted the smaller, sleeker craft clearance and opened the doors of Bay Four once again. Good air out, bad air in. The Thunderhawk's thrusters powered up. It soon emerged into the light of the Menatarian day, angled its nose upwards, and began to pull away.

Watching it go, Saezar felt a sense of relief that surprised him. The Adeptus Astartes were leaving. He had expected to feel some kind of sadness, perhaps even regret at not getting to meet them in person. But he felt neither of those things. There was something terrible about them. He knew that now. It was something none of the bedtime stories had ever conveyed.

As he watched the Thunderhawk climb, Saezar reflected on it, and discovered that he knew what it was. The Astartes, the Space Marines... they didn't radiate goodness or kindness like the stories pretended. They were not so much righteous and shining champions as they were dark avatars of destruction. Aye, he was glad to see the back of them. They were the living embodiment of death. He hoped he would never set eyes on such beings again. Was there any greater reminder that the galaxy was a terrible and deadly place?

'That's right,' he said quietly to the vid-image of the departing Thunderhawk. 'Fly away. We don't need angels of death here. Better you remain a legend only if the truth is so grim.'

And then he saw something that made him start forward, eyes wide.

It was as if the great black bird of prey had heard his words. It veered sharply left, turning back towards the station.

Saezar stared at it, wordless, confused.

There was a burst of bright light from the battle-cannon on the craft's back. A cluster of dark, slim shapes burst forward from the under-wing pylons, each trailing a bright ribbon of smoke.

Missiles!

'No!'

Saezar would have said more, would have cried out to the Emperor for salvation, but the roof of the operations centre was ripped apart in the blast. Even if the razor-sharp debris hadn't cut his body into a dozen wet red pieces, the rush of choking Menatarian air would have eaten him from the inside out.

'No witnesses,' Sigma had said.

Within minutes, Orga Station was obliterated, and there were none.

Days passed.

The only thing stirring within the crater was the skirts of dust kicked up by gusting winds. Ozyma-138 loomed vast and red in the sky above, continuing its work of slowly blasting away the planet's atmosphere. With the last of the humans gone, this truly was a dead place once again, and that was how the visitors, or rather returnees, found it.

There were three of them, and they had been called here

by a powerful beacon that only psychically gifted individuals might detect. It was a beacon that had gone strangely silent just shortly after it had been activated. The visitors had come to find out why.

They were far taller than the men of the Imperium, and their limbs were long and straight. The human race might have thought them elegant once, but all the killings these slender beings had perpetrated against mankind had put a permanent end to that. To the modern Imperium, they were simply xenos, to be hated and feared and destroyed like any other.

They descended the rocky sides of the crater in graceful silence, their booted feet causing only the slightest of rock-slides. When they reached the bottom, they stepped onto the crater floor and marched together towards the centre where the mouth of the great pit gaped.

There was nothing hurried about their movements, and yet they covered the distance at an impressive speed.

The one who walked at the front of the trio was taller than the others, and not just by virtue of the high, jewel-encrusted crest on his helmet. He wore a rich cloak of strange shimmering material and carried a golden staff that shone with its own light.

The others were dressed in dark armour sculpted to emphasise the sweep of their long, lean muscles. They were armed with projectile weapons as white as bone. When the tall, cloaked figure stopped by the edge of the great pit, they stopped, too, and turned to either side, watchful, alert to any danger that might remain here.

The cloaked leader looked down into the pit for a moment,

then moved off through the ruins of the excavation site, glancing at the crumpled metal huts and the rusting cranes as he passed them.

He stopped by a body on the ground, one of many. It was a pathetic, filthy mess of a thing, little more than rotting meat and broken bone wrapped in dust-caked cloth. It looked like it had been crushed by something. Pulverised. On the cloth was an icon – a skull set within a cog, equal parts black and white. For a moment, the tall figure looked down at it in silence, then he turned to the others and spoke, his voice filled with a boundless contempt that made even the swollen red sun seem to draw away.

'Mon-keigh,' he said, and the word was like a bitter poison on his tongue.

Mon-keigh.

THE ALIEN HUNTERS

ANDY CHAMBERS

To be Unclean
That is the Mark of the Xenos
To be Impure
That is the Mark of the Xenos
To be Abhorred
That is the Mark of the Xenos
To be Reviled
That is the Mark of the Xenos
To be Hunted
That is the Mark of the Xenos
To be Purged
That is the fate of the Xenos
To be Cleansed
For that is the fate of all Xenos

– Extract from the *Third Book of Indoctrinations*

In the empty vastness of the void, a tiny sliver of metal drifted with its crystalline gaze fixed on distant stars. If it were taken from its setting, this artificial satellite would seem large to a man. To a man it would appear as a gnarled tower of steel and brass at the centre of vast spreading sails of silver mesh, like the overgrown stamen at the centre of an unnatural flower. But here in the emptiness between stars it was less than nothing; a tiny and unnoticeable mote on the face of the universe.

Few men would ever see this lonely artefact as it kept its silent vigil down the years. Inside it dwelt only clicking cogitators and thrumming data-stacks. The tireless machine-spirits meticulously marked off the span of centuries as they watched for signs their masters would wish to know of. The tower was called Watch Station Elkin and served the organization known as the Deathwatch.

If the machine-cant of the unliving occupants of Watch Station Elkin could be eavesdropped upon at this juncture, it would have revealed a flurry of activity. Relays opened and closed with a rapid chatter analogous to excitement at the first brush of distant energies.

+Anomalous contact detected: Bearing/98.328. Azimuth/67. 201.+

Moments passed as a faint ethereal breeze caressed the far-flung sensor nets of the Watch Station. Weeks or months away in realspace, events had occurred that only now had crossed the intervening distance to reach the artificial eyes and ears of the Station. The spreading ripples betrayed much to the watching machine-spirits. Their brass-bound cogs and gears ground the information into powder, reconstituted it, and sieved it back through data-stacks filled with information on every known contact signature, human or alien. A match was quickly found, one that was disappointingly mundane.

+Contact identified. Analysis confirmed: Warp egress signature of Imperial Pilgrim-class transport vessel verified. Location: Teramus system. 38AU from star, 68 degrees above plane of the ecliptic.+

Lenses locked onto the origin point of the warp signature picked out tell-tale twinkles of light, ones racing far ahead of all tertiary emissions. The clattering cogitators suddenly sped up to fever pitch.

+High energy discharges detected. Spectral output gradient indicates xenos-specific origins.+

+Cogitators II through IV assigned to verify. Processing... Contact confirmed. Cogitators V through XXII activated for cross-correlation.+

+Institute automated blessing protocols.+

+"Blessed be the Omnissiah, blessed be his coming and going, blessed be his servants, blessed be their instruments. Grant us the wisdom of His clarity this day."+

+Automated blessing confirmed. Cogitators V through XXII now active. Begin analysis.+

+Confirmed. Data-stack inquiry confirms weapon signatures most closely match eldar lance parameters. Logged as high probability xenos contact. Activate all remaining idle cogitators. Institute automated celebratory catechism.+

+"Praise be to the Machine-God, through Him our purpose is found."+

The full attention of the Watch Station was now bent on

the distant Teramus system. Weeks or months ago, alien-built weapons had been fired in a system that should have no xenos within a hundred light years. Perhaps once in half a century, Watch Station Elkin might detect such an event and such was precisely the purpose for which it was constructed. Slower ripples of energy were arriving now, laggardly waves of electro-magnetism and tardy infrared that betrayed the complexities of the unfolding drama. Each nugget of information was dissected with infinite care and precision; all was logged and recorded by the watching machine-spirits in an ecstasy of purpose.

+Tertiary contacts detected. Engine trace analysis indicates estimated twelve plus unidentified system vessels on intercept course with primary contact.+

+Broadband high power transmission detected. Imperial standard gamma level encryption. Origin point: Pilgrim-class vessel. Recording.+

'...Repeat. This is the *Penitent Wanderer* Imperial transport out of Dhumres. Our warp drive is damaged. Unidentified vessels closing in. We're running but we can't stay ahead of them for long. For the love of Terra, any Imperial vessel in the area please assist. Repeat.'

+Voice print confirmed human origin. Conjecture: Captain of *Penitent Wanderer*. Speech patterns indicate heightened stress levels. Conjecture: Under attack.+

The doomed pleas of the long-dead captain were taken and preserved in crystal and silicon for later examination, assigned with a low priority. Charters and logs were cross-examined to confirm the existence of the *Penitent Wanderer*. Its five-hundred year history of hauling pilgrims and convicts between Dhumres and Vertus Magna were appended to the growing report as a minor footnote.

+Confirmed. Additional low power transmissions detected. Unknown sub-Alpha level encryption. Cogitators II through IV assigned to breaking encryption.+

+Unfocused plasma dispersal detected. Conjecture: Drive loss on Pilgrim-class vessel designated *Penitent Wanderer.*+

+Confirmed. Alpha level encryption defeated. Signal content as follows:+

'There she is, boys! Didn't 'ole Buke tell you there'd be a soft touch for the taking today? Aren't I good to you? Now run her down careful, mind. I don't want her all spread across the belt like last time. Get this right and there's a year's worth of red sacra in it for everyone, got it?'

+Voice print confirmed human origin. Conjecture: Leader of system ships. Speech patterns indicate non-dispersed non-militaristic command structure. Conjecture: Pirate.+

+Subsequent transmission source from *Penitent Wanderer* detected. Confirmed low power broad band signal.+

'Engines are out! Hull integrity at thirty per cent! Their weapons cut straight through the plating like it was nothing! Anyone in range, please help! This is *Penitent Wanderer* under attack in the Teramus system... Emperor's teeth they're coming aboard... Even if you can't get here in time just make sure these bastards pay, get them, I–'

+Subsequent transmissions terminated at source. Naval data cross-reference confirms pirate activity reported around Teramus system. *Penitent Wanderer* logged as overdue, believed total loss. Situation unresolved.+

The dispassionate crystal eyes of Watch Station Elkin observed the dying moments of the *Penitent Wanderer* as the pirates closed in on their prey. The lightning-flicker of xenos weaponry had died away and nothing now remained to excite the interest of their masters, but the machine-spirits faithfully continued recording every detail of the month-old attack. The *Penitent Wanderer* was boarded, gutted and left drifting in the void. The pirate ships vanished back into the slowly tumbling corona of rock around Teramus's star and beyond the reach of the Watch Station's most sensitive detectors.

A report was filed and flagged in the data-stacks alongside hundreds of other incidents. With their work complete, the cogitators subsided into endless slow matriculations once more. In a year, a decade, or a century, their masters would come for the knowledge accumulated by the Watch Station and decide whether to act upon this particular report. Perhaps the nameless captain and his crew would be avenged, perhaps not. To the machine-spirits, and to their Deathwatch masters, simple vengeance was an emotion of no consequence.

Far from Watch Station Elkin and months later, a group of its masters did indeed meet in conclave at the great citadel of Zarabek. A towering edifice orbiting a dying star, Zarabek had once been the last holdfast of the race of Muhlari, a xenos people of tremendous antiquity that had claimed to have walked the stars when mankind was still in its infancy. The Deathwatch had ended the Muhlari centuries ago, slaying their den mothers and burning their sacellum of knowledge in the Purgation of Zarabek. The mighty fortress was purged by promethium fires from top to bottom as the Deathwatch consigned the Muhlari to the Book of Extinctions.

Afterwards, seeing Zarabek as a place both strong and well-hidden, the Deathwatch took it as one of their own. Zarabek became a Watch Fortress, like and unlike a hundred other hidden places scattered across the galaxy and used by the alien-hunting Deathwatch to keep vigil. Generations of serf-artisans began the work of chipping away the obscene carvings of the extinct Muhlari and rendering the fortress fit for service. Centuries later, the ghosts of the unfortunate Muhlari would scarcely recognise their own holdfast. The sinuous, curving Muhlari script covering Zarabek's lofty halls had been completely obliterated with ranks of statuesque Imperial heroes and crowding lines of angular High Gothic creed; elegantly curved pillars and arches had become sharp and angular; vast open spaces once filled with light and life were now dark and sepulchral.

Now the sternly chiselled faces of past heroes overlooked a company of living warriors close to blows. A dozen different Chapter icons were displayed by the assembled Space Marines: fists, claws, daggers, wings, flames, skulls set against green, red, white, yellow, silver and more. Save for this single link back to their parent Chapters, all present wore their power armour repainted in unrelieved black and bearing the silver skull icon of the Deathwatch. Despite this symbolic unity, barely submerged Chapter rivalries were coming to the fore and threatening to break the company apart.

'How can you speak such words? Are we not the Emperor's chosen warriors? Are we not vowed to seize the enemy by the throat at every opening and tear him asunder? Your cowardice sickens me!'

Gottrand's words rang through the grim silence of the Hall of Intentions like a clarion call, arousing snarls and imprecations from his fellow warriors. A score of hulking figures armoured in ceramite and plasteel surrounded him. For Space Marines of the Holy Emperor of Mankind, accusations of cowardice are a matter to be expunged by blood.

Gottrand grinned back at them all without fear. His sharp teeth and long, plaited hair marked him as a member of the Space Wolves Chapter as much as his grey shoulder pad marked with the icon of the wolf rampant. Such wild talk was expected among the brothers of Fenris, where the youngest Space Marine warriors, Blood Claws as they are called, are measured in worth by their gusto and carelessness of danger. His present companions evinced little appreciation for his savage brand of courage.

'Curb your tongue, wolf-cub. Your childish jibes have no place here,' grumbled Battle-Brother Thucyid. His own shoulder bore the black mailed fist against yellow that was the icon of the Imperial Fists Chapter. Stoic and meticulous by nature, the Imperial Fists contrasted the headstrong Space Wolves as night contrasts day.

'While lacking in tact, Brother Gottrand's point is well-made,' offered Brother-Sergeant Courlanth, his shoulder marked by the quartered crimson and gold of the Howling Griffons Chapter. 'What purpose do we serve if not to fight the alien? Why come so far from our respective Chapters, only to sit idle in defiance of the sacred vows we've taken?'

Courlanth addressed these words not to the assembled Space

Marines, but to one who sat apart from them on a throne forged of shattered alien bones and broken xenos weaponry. Watch Captain Ska Mordentodt glowered down at his squabbling charges with undisguised contempt. No Chapter badge or icon was borne upon his armour except for the silver skull of the Deathwatch. Which Space Marine Chapter Mordentodt originally hailed from was as unknown and as unknowable as the man himself.

Centuries of devotion to the Deathwatch vigil had rendered the watch captain a distant and forbidding figure. When Mordentodt finally spoke, the company present quieted instantly, not out of fear – for Space Marines know no fear – but out of respect to one that has long sacrificed the fellowship of Chapter brethren for the lonely vigil of the Deathwatch.

'Your vows are ones of obedience and service – a sacred charge to stand vigil among the Deathwatch,' Mordentodt grated. 'The defiance you speak of is defiance only of my authority as captain of this fortress.'

'Such was not my intent, watch captain, as well you must know,' Courlanth said with contrition. 'I wished only to add my voice to Gottrand's that the reports from the Elkinian Reach are disturbing and bear further investigation. Xenos weaponry appearing in the hands of pirates must surely fall within the remit of the Deathwatch.'

'A great many things fall within the remit of the Deathwatch,' Mordentodt replied grimly. 'Hrud migrations, necrontyr tombsites, xenarch raids, malgreth sightings, genestealer infestations and more, much more, fall within the remit of this single fortress and the handful of battle-brothers your Chapter Masters permit to stand vigil here.

'In truth, a hundred battle companies would be insufficient for the task. The xenos swarm and multiply beyond the Emperor's Light in such numbers. Where would you have me pluck the brothers needed to chase these pirates into their holes? What should remain unwatched while some of you indulge yourselves in the pursuit of glory?'

Courlanth bowed his head. 'Such decisions are yours and yours alone to make, watch captain. Though this is not my first vigil in the Deathwatch, I am but newly arrived at Zarabek and know nothing of the other commitments you speak of. My apologies if I spoke out of turn.'

Mordentodt made no response to the Howling Griffons sergeant, only gazing stonily out across the faces of the assembled Space Marines for several long moments. At this, a young Techmarine bearing the icon of the Novamarines on his right shoulder quietly stood forward and calmly returned Mordentodt's basilisk glare when it was snapped onto him.

'What is it, Felbaine?' Mordentodt growled. 'Do the machine-spirits seek to usurp my command as well?'

'No, watch captain, I wished only to draw to your attention certain details in the reports I brought back from Watch Station Elkin.'

'I see – more advice. I have a veritable feast of it laid before me this day. Out with it then.'

'I wish to be specific in one regard. The weapons used in the attacks closely match the signature of those used by the degenerate eldar. My xenos-lore is feeble compared to some present, yet even I know that the eldar wield blasphemous technologies of the most potent kind. To find such technology in the hands of pirates is exceptional to say the least.'

Mordentodt's eyes glittered at the mention of the eldar. 'So these pirates found a wreck and looted it,' the watch captain murmured with less conviction. 'It remains a matter of small and distant import compared to many of the others confronting this fortress.'

The Techmarine shook his head regretfully, his single bionic eye and the complex swirl of electoos that marked his cheeks flashing in the gloom. 'With respect, watch captain, even the finest savants of the Adeptus Mechanicus have struggled to maintain eldar artefacts in operative condition. For mere pirates to use and continue to use these weapons, they must be getting help from somewhere or someone – and I believe that is what is truly significant about this matter.'

Mordentodt sat back in his throne, contemplating the Techmarine's words. The implications were clear to all present. Some bargain had been struck between human and alien in the Teramus system. In the eyes of the Deathwatch there was no greater crime. Mordentodt eventually nodded grimly.

'Good. Well done, Felbaine. You apply logic to the problem while others do battle to see only who can bark the loudest. Know also that the Elkinian covenant of Ordo Xenos has also demanded – *demanded* – action be taken in the Reach due to the virtual cessation of shipping between Dhumres and Vertus Magna because of these pirates. The damned inquisitors call upon us because the Imperial Navy is too weak to act and the Imperial Guard too slow... Courlanth, you spoke in favour of this mission – will you now fulfil your oath to accept it?'

'It is my sworn duty to do so, watch captain,' Courlanth

replied, 'and my honour to serve the Deathwatch in any way I can.'

'Spoken like a true Howling Griffon,' Mordentodt grunted. 'I meant what I said about other commitments – I can spare no more than five battle-brothers for the Teramus kill-team, including you. Choose now those you would have accompany you from among those here present.'

Courlanth's voice was strong and steady as he named his companions one by one without hesitation. Each came to stand beside him to be eyed jealously by those not chosen.

'I name Brother Maxillus of the Ultramarines for his sharp aim and his honourable role in shared dangers past.'

'I name Brother Thucyid of the Imperial Fists for his strength and stoicism in adversity.'

'I name Brother Felbaine of the Novamarines for his knowledge and wisdom.'

'I name Brother Gottrand for his fervour and to spare those who remain behind at Zarabek from his wailing if he were not permitted to come along.'

This last drew a chuckle from his companions, most of all from Gottrand himself. Mordentodt did not even crack a smile.

'Set aside thoughts of your Chapters,' the watch captain warned. 'All are as one in the Deathwatch. Your only concern should be whether your remains will be returned to your brothers garlanded with honour and success, or failure and ignominy. Get to the arming halls and ready yourselves, the strike cruiser *Xenos Purgatio* departs for the Teramus system within the hour. Do not fail me. Do not fail the Deathwatch.'

The arming halls of Zarabek had been rebuilt from the walled enclosures that had formed the Muhlari sacellum of knowledge. The inquisitors of the Ordo Xenos had pored over the contents of the sacellum for weeks before ordering its complete destruction, to the predictable dismay of some of the attending Adeptus Mechanicus representatives. The Deathwatch had attended to the matter with customary thoroughness, grinding the delicate crystal data repositories into powder, mixing it with the crushed bones of the Muhlari, and shooting into the heart of the dying star nearby.

Now brass cages filled with racks of armaments enclosed the sacellum where libraries of data crystals said to encompass the whole length and breadth of the known universe had been stored. The far end of the cavernous halls was the realm of the Forgemaster. These glowed with ruddy light and rang with a cacophonous hammering where a thousand servitors worked beneath the Forgemaster's direction, churning out munitions for the Deathwatch's endless war against the xenos in all its forms. Everything was made here, from the humblest bolt shell to hundred-metre long cyclonic torpedoes built for the ruin of worlds.

Maxillus emerged from the cages and greeted Sergeant Courlanth with a clenched fist salute. Dark-haired and square-jawed, Maxillus looked every inch the archetypical warrior of Ultramar – so much so that the black of Deathwatch looked incongruous covering his armour. The Ultramarine easily held the hefty weight of a slab-sided Crusade-pattern boltgun upright in his other hand, the weapon's pistol grip fitted so perfectly into his fist that it looked like an extension of him.

'Well met, Maxillus,' Courlanth said warmly, returning the salute before gripping Maxillus by the forearm and slapping him on the shoulder plate. 'Ready your bolter well, brother, we aren't out for a simple afternoon's gaunt-hunting this time.'

Maxillus grinned appreciatively. 'Don't worry, brother, I'll make sure to bring along enough shells for everyone this time.'

Maxillus and Courlanth had fought together before on the moons of Masali, an arid agri-world that formed part of the Realm of Ultramar. They had met as part of a Deathwatch kill-team hunting down the resurgent tyranid broods which could never seem to be fully expunged after the defeat of Hive Fleet Behemoth in the First Tyrannic War.

Courlanth had been on his first vigil with the Deathwatch and feeling acutely aware of the absence of the stalwart Chapter-Brothers of the Howling Griffons that he had fought alongside for decades. Maxillus had inspired his confidence by telling him that a simple afternoon's gaunt-hunting was nothing to get anxious about. In the event, Maxillus's confidence was proven ill-founded and Courlanth's concerns had emerged as being warranted, but both had at least survived to share the tale.

Courlanth found Thucyid in another cage methodically slotting oversized bolt-rounds into the flexible belt feed of his cherished heavy bolter *Iolanth*. The heavy bolter stood over half as tall as a Space Marine, a huge slab of metal any ordinary man could scarcely lift, let alone fire, unaided.

As he took up each shell, the Imperial Fists veteran rubbed it with sanctified oils and whispered a prayer to Dorn and the Emperor to guide it straight and true. Thucyid looked up as Courlanth entered, his practiced hands still blessing and loading the bolt-rounds even as he gazed curiously at the Howling Griffons sergeant. Thucyid was scarred, with blond hair cropped to little more than stubble across his thick-boned skull. Five long-service studs gleamed on Thucyid's brow, plentiful evidence if any were needed of his extensive experience and battle-craft. The Imperial Fist was the first to speak.

'Why choose me, sergeant?' Thucyid said mildly, his hands never stopping as they loaded shell after shell into the link-belt. 'You were right to choose the wolf-pup, I think, his kind are bad at waiting for anything – most of all a fit chance for glory. I think that's why they wind up getting killed chasing the unfit kind so often. But why choose me?'

'Because when you chided Gottrand for his hasty words it was without real anger or challenge, and he subsided at once. The others were ready to fight him on the spot, but you just told him to know his place and he accepted it. I need that kind of stability – and quite possibly heavy firepower too.'

Thucyid still seemed puzzled. 'I suppose you're right – he did quiet down after that, can't understand why myself.'

'I've heard that among the Space Wolves, their veteran warriors wield heavy weapons much as you do, Thucyid, as they have the wisdom to know that winning battles requires fire support as well as the courage to rush into the midst of things. They're called Long Fangs and hold high regard at the Wolves' feasting tables.'

'Ah, so you're saying that you think Gottrand will listen to me because I'm old?' Thucyid said with a twinkle in his eye. 'Old and too slow with *Iolanth* to go rushing off anywhere.'

Courlanth grinned. 'I'm sure *Iolanth* – or more accurately her many offspring – will close the distance for you quickly enough. What shells are you loading for her?'

'Three-to-one mix of mass-reactive to Inferno in this belt, mass-reactive and metal storm in another, all Inferno in a third, Kraken penetrator rounds in a fourth. It's hard to know what we'll need so I've found it's best to prepare for all eventualities.'

'I ask your forgiveness for that lack of knowledge,' the Techmarine Felbaine said as he entered the cage bearing an ornate casket. 'I did not anticipate that the watch captain would react by sending a kill-team without arranging further reconnaissance of the system first. I fear the confrontation among the brethren drove him into hasty action to seek resolution.'

'Don't underestimate Mordentodt's foresight,' Courlanth said reassuringly. 'Further reconnaissance might have simply scared the pirates away – or more likely their mysterious benefactors – and left us with nothing. A single kill-team is enough to investigate and deal with the threat at the same time.'

'Perhaps, perhaps not,' insisted Felbaine. 'I fear that if we are not strong enough we will only know when it is too late and we have failed.'

'Then we will be avenged,' said Courlanth with finality.

Courlanth found Gottrand emerging from the forges. The Blood Claw had a sour look on his face as he ruefully contemplated his long-bladed chainsword.

'What's wrong now, Gottrand?' Courlanth asked.

'The Forgemaster here hasn't even heard of kraken teeth. On Fenris the Iron Priests must learn to carve them before they can even dream of smelting iron.'

'Significance continues to evade you. What exactly is the problem?'

'This blade is *Hjormir*,' Gottrand declared with pride and a little chagrin, brandishing the weapon with its sharp rows of contra-rotating teeth before Courlanth. 'It has been borne by my Great Company since the days of Russ. The Great Wolf entrusted it to me when I began my vigil so that it might add some new stanzas to its saga.'

'And so?'

'I chipped three of *Hjormir*'s teeth in training, and now I find they cannot be replaced by the Forgemaster. *Hjormir* snarls and whines at me in complaint whenever he is woken, and I fear I will offend his spirit if I bear him into battle in such a state.'

'Gottrand, if your chainsword has truly been fighting since the days of your primarch, its spirit has survived far worse calamities than a few chipped teeth. *Hjormir* will simply have to be remembered for fighting this battle wearing a gap-toothed smile.'

The command bridge of the *Xenos Purgatio* was a cold, cramped, angular space filled with low bulkheads, struts and stanchions that was designed for solidity more than comfort. The ship's Lochos was a gaunt thrall wrapped in a cloak of trailing cables that connected his cranium directly to the ship's primary systems. Ranged around the walls, dozens of niches held more thrall-servitors, each connected to their respective stations. The air was thick with machine-cant as the Lochos guided the kilometres-long vessel out of its docking berth in Zarabek's lower reaches and set it on a course away from the citadel.

Sergeant Courlanth had assembled his kill-team to coordinate his plans with the Lochos of the *Xenos Purgatio* for the coming action. A strike cruiser was capable of carrying a whole company of a hundred Space Marines across the stars and delivering them into the heart of battle via Thunderhawk gunship, drop pod and teleportarium. It had enough firepower to defeat any vessel of its own size, and enough speed to outrun anything greater. The strike cruiser also carried Exterminatus-class weapons that could devastate a world from orbit and expunge all life from it if such were deemed necessary. This vast, world-destroying ship and its thousands of thrall crew members were now theoretically under Courlanth's direct and absolute control, a somewhat dizzying prospect for a mere sergeant like him.

Fortunately, its Lochos – a servant of the Deathwatch permanently bonded to the machine-spirits of his vessel – had centuries of experience to draw upon. He would understand the capabilities and limitations of his ship far better than Courlanth could ever hope to. Unfortunately, the Lochos appeared fully engaged with getting the ship underway for the Teramus system. Courlanth feared to disturb the man-machine from his matriculations in case they ended up making a warp translation into a star, or something worse, thanks to his impatience.

'Felbaine,' the sergeant said at last. 'What can you tell us about the Teramus system? How can we track down our quarry once we arrive?'

The Techmarine gestured to a holo-pit at the centre of the bridge. Skeins and jewels of light sketched an orrery of a star system. 'This is Teramus,' Felbaine explained. 'See here the old, red star at its centre? In some long age past it gradually expanded to its current size and most of the worlds in its orbit were torn apart. The rings of rocky debris you see were formed out of the bones of them.'

'Does anyone live there at all?' asked Thucyid. 'Aside from heretics and pirates I mean – are there no outposts or astropath stations?'

'There used to be mines in the asteroid belts,' said Felbaine, 'but they were abandoned centuries ago. There's really no reason for ships to go to Teramus at all. I confess I was surprised when the watch captain spoke of the Ordo Xenos demanding immediate action over the affair.'

'If I may interject, my lords?' The Lochos's voice was a parchment-thin whisper issuing from speaker-grilles all over the bridge. The lips of his cable-cloaked body standing at the command console did not move. 'Our course is laid in, a task easily done because Teramus is within what you might call a calm channel through warp space. To either side of it lie areas of more tumultuous flux, so a course through Teramus is frequently used. On the passage between Dhumres and Vertus Magna, most Navigators need to translate into the real at Teramus in order to check their bearings or they risk straying into the aforementioned tumult and becoming lost.'

'I understand your meaning, Lochos,' said Courlanth. 'While Teramus itself is of no consequence, it lies on a route of importance.'

'Dhumres and Vertus Magna support a combined population of over ninety billion souls,' Felbaine added. 'Any disruption to their trade and shipping will cause immense privation and eventually disorder.'

'That must be what these eldar are really after,' said Maxillus. 'In Ultramar they are known for being ever-full of trickery and misdirection.'

'We'll make sure we catch some live ones so we can ask them,' joked Gottrand.

'Not if they hear of our arrival. They'll disappear into their rat holes at the first sign of trouble,' said Thucyid.

'It's a fair point,' granted Courlanth. 'Lochos, will you be able to keep the ship undetected when we arrive?'

'Impossible to determine given the unknown capabilities of the enemy,' whispered the Lochos, 'but our translation in-system will be far from the usual arrival points, and I will refrain from using active sensor sweeps to avoid advertising our presence. By using limited manoeuvring thrusts I will keep us undetectable against the background radiation of the star, save by direct observation.'

'Good. And what about locating their base?'

'Again, impossible to determine at this time. Once in the Teramus system it is likely that there will be emissions too weak to register from a Watch Station that will become readily apparent from closer proximity.'

'Very well. We may need to act to draw them out if that doesn't work, but I'm loath to tip our hand if we don't have to. Surprise will be key to victory.'

'I have a question to ask of the Lochos with your permission, sergeant,' said Felbaine. Courlanth nodded curtly in response, wondering what was troubling the Techmarine now.

'Lochos, Watch Captain Mordentodt said that the Imperial Navy was too weak to act, and yet I see recent Navy reports appended to the holo-display of the Teramus system – what can you tell us about those?'

'Three Imperial Navy patrols have been routed through the Teramus system to search for pirates in the past five years,' the Lochos said tonelessly. 'Two found no sign of pirates, the third and most recent failed to report back and is listed as missing presumed lost. Further operations have been suspended until capital ships can be found to reinforce the effort.'

'Then we definitely need the element of surprise,' Courlanth said grimly. 'I will pray that you tread lightly enough to evade detection, Lochos.'

'Have no fear, my lords,' the Lochos replied, 'no effort will be spared to bring you to battle in the manner of your choosing. For now, however, it may be wisest to retire to your Reclusiam while warp translation is achieved. I ask you not to wander the ship; you will find most sections sealed off or hazardous while in flight.'

The *Xenos Purgatio* slid through the churning rock rings of Teramus on minimum power, no more than a sensor-shadow among the hurtling drift of asteroids. No burst of comm-chatter had met its arrival, despite the ship straining every receptor to listen for it. Either the arrival of the Deathwatch strike cruiser had gone unmarked or their enemies were preternaturally well-disciplined. The other possibility, Courlanth silently reflected, was that they had been expected and were blithely drifting into a trap.

The bridge of the strike cruiser was once again alive with quiet machine-cant and drifting clouds of sickly sweet incense from auto-thuribles. Ranks of monotask servitors had already been sifting the available data for hours as they tried to locate a veritable needle in a haystack. Without recourse to active sensor sweeps, they must perforce look for tell-tale emissions that stood out from the natural cacophony of background radiation. Meanwhile, there was little for Courlanth and his kill-team to do but watch and wait while the man-machines ferreted out their target.

In deference to his passengers, the Lochos had configured the holo-pit to project a view of the outside world. Even with this aid the kill-team could see nothing but rolling rocks the size of mountains all around them, jagged-looking and ruddy in the backwash of Teramus's star. After several hours of this unchanging landscape, Gottrand was becoming increasingly restless. Courlanth was beginning to regret his decision to convene the kill-team so early. The hunt could take days rather than hours.

'I still say we issue a challenge,' the Blood Claw declared for the hundredth time, 'and board the first ship they send out. We take a prisoner and make them tell us where their lair can be found.'

'A direct challenge from a Space Marine strike cruiser will only send them running, xenos weaponry or not,' Thucyid said, 'but a faked distress call might produce the desired result.'

'It's simply too risky,' Courlanth declared. 'We have to find their nest before we act or we risk losing our chance to act at all. Our best and probably our only chance to discover the xenos connection will be to infiltrate the interior of their base and strike from within. If we are discovered before that, we have failed before we have even begun.'

'Courlanth is right,' Maxillus said loyally. 'The pirates are alien-tainted scum that need to die too, but the important thing is to find the xenos themselves. If there is a connection here then their corruption may have spread to other worlds too. It's our duty to root out every last vestige of it.'

Gottrand muttered something and turned away, pacing the deck-plates like a caged wolf. Thucyid looked to Courlanth and shrugged, appearing little troubled by the delay. The Imperial Fists were legendary besiegers who knew the value of patience.

'Contact detected,' the Lochos announced. 'A high albedo anomaly, probably the remains of a shipwreck.'

The holo-view swung around to show an apparently entirely identical selection of tumbling rocks. In the shadows of one asteroid, Courlanth could pick out a tell-tale glitter of metal.

'Lochos, take us closer,' the sergeant said. 'As quietly as you can.'

Courlanth felt the gravity fluctuate slightly as the strike cruiser changed course, its giga-tonnage of mass shivering as it manoeuvred on limited power. As his view steadied he saw more gleams coming into sight on the holo-view. There were more wrecks drifting in this sector of Teramus's asteroid belts, a lot more.

'The sheer brazenness of them,' Thucyid muttered in disbelief. 'There must be a hundred wrecks out there. How could the Navy have missed this?'

'The last patrol didn't, and it's probably out there adrift with the rest of them now,' Courlanth replied. 'Lochos, can you gain any notion of the age of these wrecks or how long ago they were taken?'

'Yes, my lord. Plasma core remnants detectable on most of the vessels give an approximation of age through their heat signature degradation. The vast majority of the visible ships were destroyed within the last year, while the oldest wreck is more than a century old.'

'The xenos weaponry has tipped the balance and now the pirates are running wild like a pack of rabid dogs,' Courlanth said grimly. 'With any other predator I would expect to find the freshest carcasses close to the lair. Is it so, Lochos?'

'Allowing for drift there is an apparent nexus of activity,' the Lochos whispered. 'I will indicate it on the holo-view.'

Cross-hairs sprang into place within the holo-view, indicating an island-sized asteroid that at first glance appeared little different from its fellows. Deep cracks were visible in its surface, wide enough and long enough to swallow the *Xenos Purgatio* whole.

'Trace emissions indicate power sources and atmosphere present in some areas of the asteroid. Dispersed ion trails indicate vessels travel to and from it with some frequency. I could find out more through active scans or a closer approach, but either action would substantially increase the chances of our detection.'

'Then ready a Thunderhawk for immediate launch and it can take us quietly in for a closer look.'

'Landing a Thunderhawk gunship on the asteroid will create unavoidable emissions that will almost certainly be detected,' the Lochos warned. Gottrand brightened visibly at the prospect.

'Then we simply won't land the Thunderhawk,' Courlanth countered. 'We'll land without it.'

Courlanth sat in the hold of the Thunderhawk with his kill-team, each of them fully occupied with making final checks of their armour and weaponry in preparation for combat. Theoretically, up to thirty armoured Space Marines could have been carried within that long, narrow space but it seemed crowded holding just the five members of the kill-team. Prayers were murmured and catechisms recited over the thick carapace of ceramite and plasteel that protected their bodies. Their weapons were anointed with sacred oils and given abjurations to the ferocity of their spirits.

'Pay particular attention to your atmospheric seals,' Courlanth bade them, 'and your backpack air scrubbers. We must respect the environment we enter.'

'Ah, when you've fought through plasma storms and acid lakes a little hard vacuum is nothing,' Gottrand joked. 'Are we not Space Marines?' Maxillus and Thucyid groaned at the old joke. Felbaine, looking a little uncomfortable, brought out the ornate casket Courlanth had first seen him carrying in the arming halls.

'I received specific instructions before we left Zarabek,' Felbaine said apologetically, 'that every member of the kill-team was to be outfitted with one of these devices before potentially entering any combat.'

'Eh? What are you talking about, what are they?' Gottrand asked dubiously as Felbaine opened the casket. Inside were five palm-sized, finger-thick discs embossed with a design of skull against a cross.

'Teleport homers,' Felbaine said. 'Devices that allow the *Xenos Purgatio* to lock its teleportarium onto their unique signatures over a considerable distance and through all kinds of interference. With these we can theoretically be recalled to the ship at any time.'

'I don't like that,' Gottrand declared sullenly. 'I don't like that at all. It smacks of going into battle ready to be pulled out of it at the whim of another. I am no puppet to be dangled on a piece of string!'

'Calm yourself, Gottrand,' Courlanth snapped. 'Who gave you these specific instructions, Felbaine?'

'Watch Captain Ska Mordentodt. He said he wanted…' Felbaine paused in momentary discomfort at the implied insult he was about to deliver. 'He said if things went badly he wanted no one left behind under any circumstances – "no Deathwatch corpses for the xenos to despoil" were his exact words.'

'I see,' Courlanth said icily, trying not to show his anger at the implications for his command. 'The watch captain has commanded and we must obey without regard to our foolish notions of pride and honour. Go ahead, Felbaine, fit your damned devices and I will have words with the watch captain after our return with them unused.'

As Felbaine set about spot-welding the disk-shaped devices to the kill-team, Courlanth consulted his inertial map via his armour's autosenses. The Thunderhawk was sliding along unpowered and undetectable, its engines dark since their initial push away from the docking cradles of the *Xenos Purgatio*. Their course described a precise arc which would take them to within a few kilometres of the pirates' asteroid base.

Mountains of rock and tumbling wreckage were all around them, sometimes so close that Courlanth could have opened a hatch and trailed his fingers across them. Micro-gravity effects from the passing asteroids made the Thunderhawk buck and judder, meteorites occasionally rattling off the craft's thick armour plates like hail. The course had been precisely calculated to avoid any direct collision with larger bodies – or at least so the Lochos had assured him.

They would be at their closest approach to the target within just a few minutes. Felbaine was just finishing the last piece of welding. 'Helmets on,' Courlanth ordered before clamping his own into place. There was a momentary sensation of claustrophobia before the autosenses connected and his vision cleared into tactical view with its display of status icons showing reassuringly steady and green. He checked around the rest of the kill-team, receiving the traditional thumbs-up signal from each in turn.

Courlanth stepped to the rear hatch controls and triggered them. Warning lights flashed before the entire rear wall of the hold hinged downward to form a ramp. Beyond the open hatch a rushing blackness was revealed, where the asteroids around them were just barely visible as a turning kaleidoscope of vast interlocking shadows. Courlanth walked onto the ramp, acutely aware of the tenuous grip of his magnetic-soled boots. Below him a vaster shadow was rearing up, its highest peaks painted crimson as they flashed in the light of the distant red giant. The Deathwatch sergeant braced himself at the edge for a moment before quite deliberately hurling himself off.

One after another the kill-team flung themselves after him:

Gottrand, Felbaine, Maxillus and Thucyid dropped towards the asteroid, spread-eagled in a perfect echelon behind Courlanth. Above them the Thunderhawk plunged silently onward through the maelstrom of stone until it could reach a safe distance to make a course change and return to the strike cruiser undetected. Thousands of metres below them, the asteroid that was their goal swelled rapidly as it came up to greet them.

Arlon Buke, King Buke the third as he styled himself, chafed uncomfortably in the rich robes he had forced himself to wear. He was hurrying through the twisting, lamp-lit rock tunnels of his kingdom of Bukehall with the robes unceremoniously hitched up around his knees for speed. Some fat Ecclesiarch or adept had died inside the starched folds of silk and satin he wore – dried blood still clotted the rich fur of the collar. But it was the freshest and most impressive looking of the pickings from the space lanes. It would have to do.

His bodyguards clumped along at his back, big men with bigger guns, who Arlon Buke had deemed stupid enough to be intimidating and trustworthy. The bodyguards were being careful not to snigger but he could feel their knowing smirks behind him. Buke didn't like wearing fancy robes. He would much rather be roistering with his men, drinking red sacra and indulging his most base lusts with the most recent acquisitions. There was no time for such happy diversions now. A black bird had flown, the winged messenger had come with fresh demands that he pay up or be replaced. They came so often now it seemed there was no end to them.

In his father's day, Buke could remember the black bird had

been seen precisely five times before Arlon had grown big and strong enough to strangle Buke the Second and take his place. Now every month brought word of new gifts and new prices from the winged ones, and Arlon never had the guts to turn any of it down.

The bird had said the Crimsons were coming to collect the latest payment in person, something Buke had always dreaded. The Crimsons were such sticklers for protocol that they looked down on him and mocked what they called his oafish ways at every turn. It didn't stop them dealing with him any more than it had stopped them dealing with his father, or his father's father before him in the first days after the Discovery, but Arlon still hated it. He did feel oafish and stupid around the Crimsons and the hungry, avaricious glitter in their eyes reappeared in his nightmares all too often.

From past experience, Buke knew that dressing in finery shielded him from some tiny part of the Crimsons' disdain. He had a sneaking suspicion that it was because the different clothes made it easier for them to pick him out from among his men and address him directly. The Crimsons really saw them all as just meat, beasts in an enclosure they could cull at will. Buke and his men could only avoid a trip down the hell-mouth by staying useful. Otherwise they might end up being carried off like Buke's father's father had been.

Buke reflexively smoothed the robes down again at the thought, failing to notice the sweaty trails he left on the white satin as he hurried along. The Crimsons weren't due for hours but he had to get things going in case they decided to play games by arriving early. Starting the meeting off with the

Crimsons claiming to be insulted by his inattention would not end well for him. Ahead of him the great brass valve that was the main door of the audience chamber was coming into view. Buke slowed down and dropped the hem of his robes, ambling onward with an outward show of stately confidence that he really did not feel. He could hear strains of weird, alien-sounding music coming from within.

They had chosen an impact point a kilometre out from the widest crack in the asteroid, reasoning that would be the most likely location for the base. What had seemed a shadowed crevice through distant telescopes was now revealed as wide valley between twin peaks. As they dropped closer, metal could be seen glittering in the valley and Courlanth knew the pride of vindication. Closer still and details became apparent to his autosenses when boosted to maximum gain: the hunch-backed shapes of system vessels, a spider-web framework of gantries and platforms, sensor dishes and defence turrets pointing at the tumultuous skies. Light and heat plumes betrayed occupation below, but the distance was too great to spot any suited figures.

Courlanth rotated to bring his heels toward the asteroid and folded his arms to his chest. He released a blast of compressed gas from his backpack to give himself a single, hard push downwards and the rocky surface leapt towards him. Seconds later Courlanth crunched into the sloping surface with legs braced, the impact of his armoured boots gouging two craters into the brittle rock. Behind him, Gottrand, Maxillus and Thucyid struck with more or less the same skill. Felbaine unaccountably misjudged his descent and struck with a force his suit's gyro-stabilisers couldn't cope with, sending him tumbling out of control.

The Techmarine half-stumbled, half-skidded away in a cloud of dust and debris, his excess momentum sending him downslope towards a yawning chasm. Under the asteroid's weak gravity Felbaine was less in danger of falling than flying off the asteroid altogether. It was still a very real danger. The kill-team would lose precious time hunting for him and Felbaine could even become irretrievable in the asteroid belt. A member lost before the operation even began would be a particularly ill omen.

The thoughts raced through Courlanth's head in less time than it takes to tell it. He ached to give direction but he had ordered comm-silence from the outset and was loath to be the one to break it. This was Courlanth's first real test of trust for the kill-team. All of them were members of the Emperor's finest and should be able to resolve the crisis without any orders from him. He was not to be disappointed.

Maxillus was closest and lunged forward without hesitation. The Ultramarine grabbed Felbaine's flailing arm and planted both of his feet and his other hand in a three-point stance for maximum traction. With Maxillus anchoring him, Felbaine managed to bring his own momentum under control and get his own boots properly down on the surface just at the edge of the chasm. Thucyid and Gottrand took up immediate overwatch positions and left Maxillus to his work when they saw what was happening. In less than three seconds, the situation was under control again with nothing but a floating cloud of dust and grit to betray Felbaine's misstep of a moment before.

Courlanth snapped his own attention back towards the pirate lair, looking for any sign that their landing had been seen. No alarm signals rippled the airwaves, no alerted guards appeared above the lip of the chasm; everything seemed quiet. The sergeant released a breath he hadn't realised he had been holding, hearing it whisper away through the tubes of his rebreather. He held up his gauntleted hand with palm outward and fingers spread to order the team to spread out. The kill-team silently moved apart and began to advance with him in low, loping bounds across the rocks.

Within minutes they had reached upper gantries that led down into the valley. Courlanth now had a clear view of a dozen system ships berthed untidily around it. The smallest was no more than a dozen metres in length while the largest was more than a hundred. The ships had the appearance of a selection of haulers and luggers that had been converted for more nefarious activities. They were bedecked with auxiliary engines, covered in crudely painted skulls and had prows barbed with antennae. The landing platforms the ships sat upon dominated all of the other structures in view. Near each platform shutter-like metal doors were sunk into the rock, this last presumably being airlocks leading to underground tunnels.

Courlanth scanned around carefully but he could see no signs of life. Gottrand pointed to his own eye-pieces and then to a set of landing platforms on the far side of the valley. After a few seconds Courlanth detected movement there: an open hatch in the flank of a ship and moving shadows that indicated men at work just out of sight. Felbaine signalled for his attention and moved closer to touch helmets with him. By using direct resonance they were able to talk with no risk of detection.

'The spirit of my auspex-scanner was somewhat disgruntled after my terrible landing,' Felbaine explained, 'but I believe that we're safe to use our communicators. We've passed inside their sensor net and I've found nothing that would pick us up this close.'

'You "believe?"' Courlanth said warily. 'I need certainties, Felbaine, not to risk discovery because you've made another mistake.' He saw the Techmarine tense inside his armour and regretted his harsh words immediately. Courlanth had spoken to Felbaine as he would have done to a Chapter Brother of the Howling Griffons – short and direct, unafraid to offer challenge or criticism. But within the confines of the kill-team, where every battle-brother consciously or unconsciously felt himself to be representing the honour of his own Chapter, it had been too much.

'I am certain our communications won't be detected,' Felbaine replied stiffly, 'but there is always a risk. The decision is yours.'

Felbaine was already castigating himself over his mistake in the landing and criticism had only added fuel to the fires of martyrdom. Courlanth turned back to the squad, struggling to think of how to reassure Felbaine that he still had his sergeant's trust. After a moment the Howling Griffon pointed to the side of his helmet and spoke via communicator.

'Communications cleared for use. Report in.'

'Gottrand, ready.' A small wolf icon sprang into being within Courlanth's autosenses as the Blood Claw spoke.

'Thucyid, ready.' A clenched fist appeared beside the wolf.

'Maxillus, ready.' An Omega sign joined the row of icons.

'Felbaine… ready.' A small sunburst completed the row.

The icons flashed as the suit's communication systems tested their signal strengths and returned a positive green across all of them. When he was satisfied that all was well, Courlanth began rapidly issuing his orders.

'We're here and the enemy has no idea of our presence, so we still have the advantage of surprise. No guards are visible so we'll take ourselves across to the occupied ship on the landing platform and find some prisoners there to question about the rest of the complex. Felbaine, I want you to place melta bombs on the other ships we pass and set them to a forty-minute delay. Take Maxillus with you to guard your back. Gottrand, Thucyid, you're with me. Any questions?'

Silence.

'Move out.'

The five Space Marines split up and disappeared into the shadowy tangle of walkways and gantries. They were rendered almost invisible by their night-black armour and the airless asteroid rendered their progress silent, save for the internal hiss of their retreaters. It seemed as if ghosts of vengeance stalked into the pirates' lair, grim revenants called up to exact retribution for their victims at last.

Buke hauled open the main door into the audience chamber and rushed inside with his robes flapping. Beyond it a wide circular chamber rose in roughly-hewn tiers to a domed ceiling high above. The chamber was the largest open space in

Bukehall and many more entrances dotted the upper tiers. Once upon a time it had been the main mining hall, a central hub from which galleries had been cut seeking the rich metal ores of the asteroid. The remains of old mine machines still littered the floor of the chamber, while torn conveyor belts hung uselessly from the upper tiers.

The Discovery had changed everything about Bukehall, changed it completely from the failing mining colony it was then to the pirate den it was now. Directly opposite, Buke could see the open mouth of hell. It looked like just another gallery sunk into the rock from the floor of the chamber. A little wider than the rest perhaps, and maybe a little taller, but unremarkable in itself. There was no indication that tens, perhaps hundreds of thousands of people had disappeared down that innocuous tunnel and never returned, starting with the first unlucky crew of miners that had been digging it. The weird music was coming out of it, a broken, haunting melody that hovered maddeningly close to the edge of perception.

A dark shape fluttered down from the rocky tiers above to alight on curved claws in front of Buke. The black bird was taller than him and rake-thin, with long limbs that were as narrow as spindles. Magnificent, black-feathered wings extended from above its shoulders to scrape the floor. Dark, malevolent eyes glittered at him from a face dominated by a cruelly hooked beak. The voice that issued from the being was cool, clear and indescribably ancient.

'Buke, Arlon Buke, here to make sure all goes smoothly,' the black bird said, cocking its head to one side. 'You are a wise man, King Arlon Buke.'

'Ha-yes, all the others are coming and the offerings are being brought,' Buke stammered, feeling the sweat running down his face. 'Naturally I came as soon as I heard. We were ready for-for–'

'This one–' the black bird interrupted, pointing a claw to a crumpled, bloody mass on the floor of the chamber. 'This one ran from our presence before the message was delivered. It died horribly. Not all are as wise as Arlon Buke, it seems; not all remember our pacts.'

'I-I remember the pacts we've made with the Crimson Blossom in every detail,' Buke said quickly and succinctly, 'and I regret that my man did not greet you with the proper obeisance, the – ah, the magnificent terror of your appearance must have been too much for him to bear.'

The black bird made a sound but Buke couldn't decide whether it was a snort or a titter as it turned away, flexing its wings noisily.

'May I ask a question to better make preparations to full satisfaction?' Buke ventured tentatively. The predatory, beaked face swung back towards him, half-opened as if in silent laughter.

'Speak your question,' the black bird said.

'What is the music I can hear being played? What is it for?'

'Celebration. A paean to the arrival of one so great that it is necessary to bring beauty as his vanguard into this benighted realm.'

'That's– ah that's wonderful news,' Buke said quietly. 'But what does it mean? Who is coming?'

'Sad, silly king Arlon Buke not to know,' the black bird mocked. 'Rejoice, you are to be in the presence of an archon of High Commorragh within the hour. Pray to your gods and give thanks that you will be permitted to grovel in his presence.'

As Courlanth crept through the long shadows cast by the pirate ships he got his first good look at them from close quarters. What he had taken for being barbed antennae from a distance were obviously nothing of the kind up close. Felbaine had called them lances and the name was highly appropriate. The xenos weapons were extremely long and slender. They tapered down from a metre-wide bulb-shape at the rear to no more than a hand's-span in width at their tip. The greasy-looking metal they were made of seemed to shimmer oddly between black and olive-green as the light reflected from it. These clearly alien-built weapons were mounted in clusters of twos and threes on the prow plating of the ships, in some cases protruding from holes crudely cut straight through it.

'How are those charges coming along, Felbaine?'

'Almost done, sergeant,' Felbaine's voice replied after a nerve-wracking pause. 'I will not have enough charges to destroy all of the ships, but I have rigged all of the ones along our route satisfactorily.'

'Will the xenos lance-weapons be destroyed?'

'I've placed the melta-charges to cause reactor meltdowns on the ships. I pray that the fires will be intense enough to destroy the alien weapons – they should be by all accounts.'

Courlanth hesitated for a moment. Again Felbaine presented him with uncertainties instead of solid facts, but this time he quelled the urge to demand a more specific answer. The Tech-marine was no doubt simply trying to be as accurate as he could be under the circumstances.

'Good enough,' Courlanth replied. 'Rendezvous with us at the loading dock.'

There were six humans at work inside the ship's hold, although 'work' was a loose definition of their activity. Four stood around watching while two others struggled to free a cargo sled that had spilled part of its load and wedged itself firmly into the rim of the hatch. The four gawkers supplied unhelpful commentary on their comrades' efforts via crude, unencrypted radio.

'Told you – gotta unload the whole thing,' observed one.

'No way you're getting that outta there,' chirped another.

'I already said. Jus' leave it or we're gonna be late,' warned a third.

'...and that'll get us skinned alive for sure,' whined a fourth.

All of the pirates wore light vac-suits that amounted to little more than rubberised coveralls with bubble-like hoods. All were armed with a variety of pistols and vicious-looking knives that were obviously intended to make for a ferocious show. Courlanth surveyed the open hatch critically and decided it would be hard to fit more than one of his fully armoured battle-brothers through it at a time.

'Gottrand, take the lead, I'll cover your back. Remember, I want one alive. Everyone else: overwatch. Gottrand wait – damn it!'

The Space Wolf was already darting out of cover and pounding for the open hatch. Inside it one of the pirates looked up quizzically, some premonition warning him of the danger heading towards him. Gottrand made a powerful leap in the low gravity and slammed both boots full into the wedged cargo sled. His combined mass and momentum popped the sled free like a cork from a bottle and sent it hurtling across the cargo hold. Men scattered with cries of alarm but one was too slow to dodge the caroming sled. He disappeared behind it with a shriek terminated by ugly cracking sounds as it struck the far wall with bone-crushing force.

Gottrand crushed the skull of the first pirate to speak with the butt of his bolt pistol. A split-second later he shot another pirate as they reeled back in horror from the hulking figure that had sprung up in their midst. The mass-reactive bolt went off in the man's chest and burst it open with a spray of gore that blinded the rest. It was an unnecessary nuance. Panic had already gripped the pirates, sending them running and screaming in all directions as they tried to escape.

The Space Wolf's gap-toothed chainsword, *Hjormir*, licked out and slashed through two of the survivors in a single, gory sweep. The last pirate darted around Gottrand and towards the hatch, skidding to a halt as he saw the armoured bulk of Courlanth blocking his path. The pirate opened his mouth to speak – to plead for his life, or curse, or pray – Courlanth never found out. Gottrand's chainsword crashed down through the gore-slicked bubble-hood of the last pirate, its contra-rotating teeth flinging out twin sprays of blood and bone as it chewed through to the spine. Courlanth ground his teeth silently as he bit back anger. The sergeant tried to recall the lesson he had already learned with Felbaine.

'An approach worthy of your Chapter Brothers,' Courlanth grated. 'But what of the prisoner I sought?'

'Fear not, sergeant,' Gottrand replied smugly. 'I had not

forgotten.' The Space Wolf dragged the wrecked cargo sled back from the wall to reveal one crushed, mangled, but very much alive pirate behind it. Courlanth slapped aside the autopistol the pirate was trying to raise and seized him by the throat.

'You know that you will die,' Courlanth told the wretch. 'Only the absolution of death will cleanse you of your crimes against the Immortal Emperor of Mankind. You may ease your passing by answering my questions. If you do not, then Gottrand here will crack open your skull and ingest what we need to know from your still-living brain. Do you understand?

'Yes!' the wretch squawked past the grip of Courlanth's steel hard fingers. 'I-I'll tell you anything you want to know!'

'Where did the alien weapons come from? Who maintains them?'

'The Crimsons bring them up from the hell-mouth! When they stop working we take them back and get new ones!'

'Who are these "Crimsons"? Describe them to me.'

'Tall! Thin! Not men! Something older they say, old as daemons! They demand tribute and we give it to them. They give us the guns and lots of red sacra, tell us where to find ships to hit.'

'And what do they demand in return for their help?'

'P-people! All kinds of things, but people most of all! They want slaves to take back to hell with them.'

'You prey upon your fellow men and trade the survivors to xenos as slaves, you deserve a worse death than I have the time to mete out.' Courlanth's fingers tightened inexorably as he struggled to maintain control of himself. 'Now… Tell me where I can find these Crimsons.'

The pirate clan was gathering in the audience chamber in dribs and drabs. They were being slow enough to make Buke nervous and he sent some of his bodyguard off as enforcers to hurry things along. Each crew that arrived dragged along their own tithe for the Crimsons of a dozen or more prisoners chained together. The slave coffles were gradually filling the floor of the chamber in ragged rows. Their suffering generated a low whine of misery throughout the chamber. It had taken Buke some time to notice it, but the sound mingled seamlessly with the weird music emanating from the hell-mouth in a number of disturbing ways.

The black bird had flown up to the tier above the hell-mouth and squatted there, enfolded in its wings like a patient carrion-eater poised over a carcass. It fluttered its wings as the alien music dipped and then swelled suddenly, crying out in a voice modulated so that it cut across the buzzing audience chamber.

'He comes! Grovel before your true master, meat-slaves!' the black bird announced. 'Archon Gharax of the Kabal of the Crimson Blossom approaches!'

Purple light was growing in the hell-mouth, a darkling illumination that seemed to show nothing but shadows. Within it, Buke could see shapes moving, twisted inhuman shapes that were approaching up the tunnel. At the last moment he remembered himself and dropped to his knees, pushing his sweating face down on to the dirt floor. Around the chamber it was as if a silent scythe swept through the other pirates as they all followed Buke's example. The wailing and whimpering of the chained slaves grew more intense as they realised something was happening, the weird music swelling to match it before dropping away to a sudden silence.

'Look up, King Arlon Buke,' the black bird said in hushed tones. 'The archon orders you to meet his gaze.'

Buke looked up from the dirt to see that the hell-mouth was no longer empty. A sinister company of beings now filled it. Each was as inhuman as the black bird but in different ways. There were slender warriors in insect-like armour carrying rail-thin rifles like barbed stingers. There were exotic, half-naked females as alluring as visions from a drug-fuelled dream that bore cruelly hooked knives and a look of awful hunger on their beautiful faces. In the background a trio of hunched, iron-masked creatures clustered around an upright device like a glass-fronted, tube-covered casket at the sight of which Buke was filled with an unspeakable thirst. Beyond them, hulking, furred monsters twice the height of a man filled the hell-mouth with their bulk, their long claws twitching menacingly as they stood quiescent – for now.

At the centre of the horrid company stood two figures who dominated the others as a sun dominates the sky. One was the individual that Buke had dealt with on every occasion previously that the Crimsons had issued from the hell-mouth. This was Maelik Toir. His angular, bone-white face and human-skin robes were not usually a reassuring presence, but on this occasion Buke felt relief to see him. Maelik was the purveyor of many things, most of all the red sacra Buke relied on to maintain his hold over the pirate enclave. Of all the Crimsons Buke had encountered, Maelik was the one who seemed least disgusted at dealing with him, projecting an aura of amused disdain instead of withering contempt.

But Maelik Toir was standing to one side, leaving the centre stage for another that could only be Archon Gharax. The eldar physically stood no taller than the others in his presence, but seemed larger somehow. He was clad in armour like burnished ebony and cloaked with a material so black it seemed to drink light into itself. One hand rested lightly on the gem-encrusted pommel of the long, curving blade sheathed at his side, the other holding a spike-crowned helm evidently just removed. Buke met the gaze of the archon as ordered and found that he could not look away. The alien's pitiless black gaze gripped him like a vice, its crushing presence wringing a gasp from Buke's lungs.

'Impressive, isn't it?' Maelik Toir whispered in his precisely-accented Low Gothic. 'An inheritance from his mother's side – they say that the Lhamaen Yesyr could turn one to stone with the poison of her glance.'

Buke could feel his soul being laid bare beneath the archon's gaze. Every petty malice he had inflicted, every base betrayal he had committed, felt like open pages in the archon's presence. King Arlon Buke could feel himself being weighed and measured by an intelligence infinitely older and more wicked than his own, his fears, limitations and secrets being picked over and discarded as irrelevances. After what seemed like an eternity, Archon Gharax broke the contact by glancing up toward the higher tiers of the chamber with a faint smile on his face.

'The archon finds you… suitable… to remain in his presence,' Maelik Toir told Buke. 'He will not disgrace himself by giving tongue to slave languages and so will speak through me. Address your replies to me alone, your words will offend his ears.'

Buke grovelled, keeping his face away from the archon's terrible gaze. 'W-we have brought our tithing as promised, illustrious one,' the pirate king stammered. 'We have held up our part in the pact, w-will you uphold yours?'

The words were old, a formula dating back to the Discovery, otherwise Buke would never have dared to use them right now. Maelik Toir nodded approvingly. Men had died horribly for diverging from the words of the pact in the past.

'Yes, Arlon, we will give you what you call the red sacrament in exchange for the slaves you've brought. Let us begin.'

Relieved to have someone else to brutalise, Buke turned on the nearest group of quailing captives and began kicking them to their feet. Stung by a sharp sense of self-preservation other pirates quickly joined him, half-dragging and half-carrying the unfortunates toward the hell-mouth. Maelik Toir examined each captive briefly before sending most onward to be hauled off into the tunnel by the great clawed beasts. One captive was deemed unsuitable and consigned to the casket attended by Maelik's assistants.

Buke and the other pirates salivated to see the machine at work so early in the exchange. The gurgling, reddening tubes surrounding the casket were almost hypnotic as they pumped and purified, distilling drops of the precious red sacra. He had to slap and curse at several of his fellows to remind them to keep the other prisoners moving before they became fractious. Cowed, beaten and emaciated as the prisoners were, even the very dullest of them could see their fate laid out before them now. Many would fight back rather than face being given to the aliens.

The archon stood to one side, surrounded by his warriors and entirely aloof from the proceedings. Buke wondered why the archon had troubled to come as a lord surveying his estates, with no orders to give. He noticed the archon looking expectantly towards the upper tiers of the chamber again and glanced there himself. There was nothing to be seen up there but shadows.

'We can take them!' Gottrand's guttural sub-vocal whisper came over the comm carrying a thick tocsin accusation with it. Courlanth was failing them as a leader by skulking and hiding when their opponents stood before them. Courlanth was nothing but a contemptible coward.

The kill-team crouched out of sight near the top of the large, circular chamber they had found. Below them were the pirates and their captives. To their left was the contingent of eldar they had just witnessed entering the chamber from a connecting tunnel. The kill-team's view of events was narrow and fish-eyed, a by-product of the fact that Felbaine was using a sensor tendril to spy on them without risk of exposure.

Courlanth stared intently at the view Felbaine was communicating to his own suit's autosenses. By his count at least a dozen eldar were at the tunnel mouth with more behind, with thrice that number of pirates handling the hundreds of prisoners filling the chamber. It was true that the more he delayed the greater the chance they would be discovered became, and yet he hesitated to start a battle that would inevitably kill so many innocents in the cross-fire.

'This is only their meeting point, we have to track them to

their lair–' Courlanth began, just as the first wailing prisoners were dragged before the eldar. His heart sank as he saw one of them sent to the torture device the eldar had brought with them. Even now, cold tactical logic would have dictated that the prisoners and even the pirates were of secondary importance to the real goal – that of rooting out the alien. Some in the Deathwatch would sacrifice a million innocents to achieve such a goal without blinking an eye.

But tactical logic could not make it acceptable for Courlanth to sit still and witness aliens torturing and murdering humans at will. He knew the kill-team felt the same way and that only his command had held them back so far. They must act now, even when the logical choice was to wait. Honour demanded it.

Courlanth outlined his plan in a terse series of commands. Wordlessly, Maxillus and Thucyid moved away left and right along the ledge, creeping cautiously to positions where they could maximise their crossfire. Felbaine readied a thick-bodied plasma gun, checking its temperamental coolant rings before setting it to maximal power. Gottrand, for his part, squatted back on his haunches with *Hjormir* in his hands, watching Courlanth expectantly. The Blood Claw had removed his helmet without orders as soon as they had entered the atmosphere-filled tunnels of the asteroid base. Now Gottrand's long braids and coarse beard jutted free in the light gravity, fully lending him the barbaric aspect of his native tribesmen on icy Fenris.

Courlanth hefted his own chainsword and bolt pistol in his hands. He committed his soul to the Emperor with a silent prayer before issuing the final order to begin.

'Execute.'

Thucyid's heavy bolter roared instantly to life, the staccato beat of its fist-sized shells an accompaniment to all that followed. A split second later, Maxillus's bolter added its sharper bark to the thunder of heavy bolts ripping across the chamber.

Courlanth and Gottrand leapt down from the ledge and saw the chamber for the first time with their own eyes. The pale ovals of hundreds of faces stared up at them from the chamber floor, both prisoners and their guards frozen in shock. A few looked up with hope, but most with abject terror at the two black-armoured giants landing in their midst.

'Suffer not the alien to live!' Courlanth shouted, his enhanced voice cutting across the thunder of explosions. His bolt pistol kicked in his hand as it hurled flame-tailed meteors into the nearest pirate guards. Blood sprayed as the explosive bolts punched his chosen targets off their feet with deadly accuracy. Gottrand had already bounded ahead of him, the Blood Claw having leapt down the stepped ledges to the chamber floor with reckless abandon. Courlanth pounded after him, doing his best to avoid crushing the prisoners huddled at his feet.

The chamber was in bedlam, with groups of prisoners turning on their guards while others tried to flee in panic. Panicked pirates were firing indiscriminately in all directions and sometimes cutting each other down in their own crossfire. Even though he felt a few solid slugs rattle off his armour, Courlanth ignored them as he surged after Gottrand. Maxillus was tasked with eliminating the pirates from his vantage point; each bark of his bolter marked another one being pulped by a single bolt round.

The tunnel mouth where the eldar had been gathered was lit by a lurid mass of flames where Thucyid's Inferno rounds had been at work. In the uncertain, flickering light Courlanth briefly glanced lithe eldar bodies twisting and leaping. At that moment Felbaine's plasma gun spoke with a crack like thunder, its actinic blaze flashing down on the eldar torture device like a finger of judgment. The device exploded instantly at the touch of the plasma bolt and sent gobbets of molten matter scything through its attendants. An animalistic howl of pain rang through the chamber, twisting a grim smile onto Courlanth's lips.

Two huge shapes shouldered their way out of the tunnel mouth and rushed at Gottrand. Courlanth recognised the beasts instantly as donorian clawed fiends – alien monstrosities of near legendary size and ferocity. He shouted a warning to the Space Wolf, but giant claws were already sweeping down on him with eye-blurring swiftness.

Arlon Buke had nerved himself up enough to edge a little closer to Maelik's casket in readiness to collect the first harvest of red sacra. It was dangerous stuff to take undiluted – it could kill a man in frothing agony if he took too much – but Buke reasoned he had a good enough tolerance to stand a few drops here and now. He'd earned it, kept up his end of the bargain and dealt with the Crimsons, so he deserved a reward. His mouth, his whole body felt parched in a way that only the red sacra could refresh.

The first explosions surprised Buke so much that he thought some sort of accident had occurred. His instinct for self-preservation threw him to the ground before he had time to think about it. In an instant the scene changed from the more or less orderly handover of slaves to the Crimsons to a roaring, flame-spitting battle. Buke saw a stream of bolter rounds hose across the hell-mouth and splatter it with a wreathe of flames that made it truly worthy of its name. The eldar darted away from the stream of searching bolts with preternatural agility, twisting and leaping incredibly in the low gravity. Some were still caught by the bolts and brutally pounded into bloody, burning ruin but most escaped, scattering among the broken mining machinery in the blink of an eye. The archon swirled his black cloak about himself and vanished with all the alacrity of a stage devil in a morality play.

All around him screams and confusion reigned as the prisoners tried to get away: Curses and shouts among the roar of explosions, the panicky chatter of his clansmen firing their weapons at unseen foes. Buke kept his face in the dirt and crawled towards Maelik's casket, unaware that his rich garb of silk and satin kept him alive as Battle-Brother Maxillus of the Deathwatch methodically picked off the other pirates in the chamber.

Buke raised his face again just in time to see Maelik's casket immolated by a plasma bolt. The delicate structure of metal and crystal shattered outwards as its contents were explosively vaporised. In the same instant, unthinkable pain lashed across one of his eyes and blinded it. He fell back and howled like an animal with the hideous sizzling meat smell of his own burned flesh in his nostrils.

Half-blinded, Buke scrabbled in the dirt with clawing fingers searching for pieces, fragments, anything that might give him hope. Screams and detonations surrounded him but his own world had shrunk to the reach of his arms. His torn hands brushed something smooth and curved that was still hot from the fires. He twisted around trying to focus his one remaining eye on his discovery.

It was a piece of tubing from the casket that was still sealed at one end. His heart leapt to see the tiny puddle of thick red liquid settled in the bottom of it. Weeping and laughing, Buke raised the broken glass to his lips and tilted it back to let the red sacra drop on to his tongue.

Explosions of orgasmic pleasure rolled through his body at the touch of the first drop. The pain from his eye was swept away, lost in a sea of absolute ecstasy. Energy flowed through him, revitalising every part of him from his brain to his glands. Every sense became crystal clear and hyperacute. Buke's pulse pounded in his ears as he struggled to his feet and roared his defiance at the universe. He could feel his muscles rippling, ripening with rich, red blood. He felt strong, stronger than ten men, faster than the wind. Everything he'd experienced from the red sacra before was nothing compared to this.

Buke took a step forwards. Two Space Marines in black armour were in the audience chamber and were cutting their way to the hell-mouth. The Crimson's huge bear-like pets had rushed out of the tunnel to attack them. Bloodlust swept through Buke at the sight. To see Imperial Space Marines, such fearsome giants of legend, dwarfed and overborne by the monsters set his pulse racing even faster. He would join in the victory, tear the hated Space Marines apart with his bare hands and bathe in their blood...

King Arlon Buke sprang forward with his fingers hooked like claws. He rushed into the fray shrieking like a daemon, ducked under the swinging claw of one of his bestial allies and leapt onto one of the Space Marines. The hulking, black-armoured warrior all but ignored Buke, shrugging off his grasp as if the pirate king were nothing but a small and overly rambunctious child. Buke was sent sailing past to land flat on his back beside a ruined mining machine.

Buke roared in frustration and tried to spring to his feet, but at that moment his overwrought heart virtually exploded with the strain it had been placed under. The hyperawareness given to him by the tainted red sacra ensured his dying moments were riven by indescribable agonies that, subjectively at least, lasted a long, long time.

Gottrand attacked the towering fiends like a blood-mad wolverine. A slashing claw of the first fiend was half-severed at the wrist by his long-bladed chainsword, even as his bolt pistol sent round after round ripping into the torso of the second. Courlanth joined the fray, hacking and slashing at the mountainous bulk of the twin monsters. It was as if they hewed at stone, the tough alien flesh resisting blows that would have cleaved a man in two. What injury the Space Marines inflicted seemed only to redouble the monster's fury, putting them in a whirlwind of snapping jaws and reaching claws. They needed help to beat the things quickly.

'Give us supporting fire,' Courlanth ordered. It was a risk to order fire into a melee, but the fiends were big enough to make prominent targets. A split second passed and no supporting fire came in. Gottrand was struck by a blow that sent him reeling, the fiend's claws tearing ragged holes in the Blood Claw's armour.

'Support fire, NOW!' Courlanth snapped as he rushed forward to protect the staggered Space Wolf. Still no bolts came in support. The sergeant realised that Thucyid's heavy bolter no longer sang its song of death.

'Under attack!' Maxillus's voice shouted back urgently. 'Thucyid and Felbaine are down! Poison! They've got–' The comm went dead.

Courlanth's mind reeled as he tried to fend off the gigantic fiends. More than half his team down in moments, what horror had the xenos unleashed? Maxillus had shouted about poison but no toxin should be able to overwhelm a Space Marine's genetic-ally enhanced constitution so quickly. A glancing claw ripped at his shoulder plate and drove him down to one knee.

Courlanth's anger and frustration coiled through him as he surged back to his feet. His chainsword flashed down on the leering, dome-shaped head of the fiend as it leaned in to bite him. Churning monomolecular teeth snarled and spat as they tore their way through the monster's iron-hard cranium before pulping the grey matter inside to slurry. Even brain-panned the monster remained a threat, the reflexive jerk of its claws knocking Courlanth back a dozen metres.

The sergeant skidded to a halt, half-sprawled against a piece of broken machinery and tried to stagger upright. He felt as if he had been hit by a gunship, icons in his autosenses were flashing warning amber as they began to take stock of his armour's condition. He looked up to see Gottrand plunge his sword,

Hjormir, into the other fiend with an eviscerating uppercut.

Gottrand did not withdraw his blade, instead dropping his bolt pistol so that he could heave the whirling chainsword upward with both hands. The furred giant collapsed, gripping the Space Wolf with its claws in an effort to crush him against its chest, but only succeeding in driving the blade ever deeper. Gottrand staggered free covered virtually head to foot in foul alien ichor.

The sudden silence that enfolded the scene was broken only by the crackle of flames and the moans of the injured. Courlanth looked quickly up to the ledge where Maxillus and the rest of the kill-team should have been, but he could see only shadows.

'Grip like an ice troll,' Gottrand muttered unsteadily. Courlanth saw the Space Wolf's scalp was laid open to the bone, and blood had slicked his braids into a thick mass. There was also the hint of stealthy movements in the shadows, meaning the eldar had not fled. They were still here and they were stalking the two surviving members of the Deathwatch kill-team. An unfamiliar chill ran down Courlanth's spine at the thought.

'Gottrand, we have to get back to the others, I–' Courlanth began before a barrage of shots swept across them. Hypervelocity needles rang off their armour in a scatter of ceramite chips and plasteel fragments. Decades of training took over as both Space Marines moved instantly to attack their assailants. Lithe figures sprang up to bar their path, wild and half-naked eldar that fought with the ferocity of daemons.

Gottrand was rapidly surrounded by darting combatants, his two-handed swings with *Hjormir* too slow and cumbersome to connect with his opponents. As Courlanth turned to assist he barely saw a blade flashing in at his side and had to twist desperately to avoid it. He turned to confront an eldar that seemed to have sprung from nowhere. The alien was clad in polished, insectoid armour with a spike-crowned helm, a black cloak swirling about its shoulders as it wielded a curved blade with fearsome speed and precision.

'My archon wishes you to know that it is Archon Gharax of the Crimson Blossoms that delivers your doom,' a voice called out in precisely accented Low Gothic from another part of the chamber. 'You should feel honoured.'

'Alien scum,' snarled Courlanth in response. 'You will all die!'

'Never, and certainly not by your hand, *sergeant*,' the voice gloated.

Courlanth fought with every ounce of his fury and skill, but the archon quite simply outmatched him. The sergeant felt like a stumbling child as he struggled after the elusive figure, every slash and shot was evaded without seeming effort, while every riposte the archon made left a new gouge in Courlanth's armour. Warning icons were flaring amber and red at the edges of his vision. The alien was toying with him, Courlanth was sure, and the thought of it drove him to new heights of rage.

The sergeant unleashed a furious whirlwind of blows with his chainsword, forcing his opponent to skip backwards a few paces. In the momentary breathing space he snapped open a frequency to the *Xenos Purgatio*.

'Lochos! Immediate kill-team extraction,' Courlanth was sickened by the thought of retreat but his duty was clear. The kill-team had failed and now the Exterminatus weapons on the strike cruiser must be unleashed to obliterate the pirate's nest once and for all. Something dark, terrible and corrupt had taken root in the Teramus system and Courlanth felt shame that it was beyond his strength to overcome it.

Only the hiss of static could be heard through the link. Inhuman laughter rang through the chamber.

'My archon insists that you remain,' the taunting voice called, 'after so much trouble has been taken to bring you here.'

The archon darted forward, deflecting Courlanth's swing with a thrust that slipped inexorably in beneath his guard. The sergeant felt the impact of the point piercing his armoured shell and sheathing itself in his guts. He felt the blade grate against bone as it was withdrawn as quickly as insect's stinger. Courlanth had been injured in worse ways before but this felt completely different. Icy numbness spread out from the wound site and didn't stop spreading. Poison!

The speed of it shocked him. Within a few heartbeats his whole body was unresponsive. The ground lurched beneath Courlanth as his legs buckled and blackness rushed into his sight. His last impressions were of falling forever.

Sight returned, at first without colour, vague splotches of light and shade in a moving pastiche. Courlanth's fogged mind tried to make sense of the scene. He was on his side with his helmet gone and his arms locked somehow behind him. Near him other figures in black armour lay prone on the rocky ground and he could see that their arms and legs were manacled. The sergeant could vaguely feel blood oozing sluggishly from his gut-wound and decided that meant that only a short time had passed. Such a wound would have been fully sealed by his superhuman constitution otherwise.

More detail swam into focus. Nearby was a curious structure, a tall arch of twisted silver and bone that was filled with multicoloured mists. Courlanth recognised it as a warp portal, a gateway into the inter-dimensional pathways the degenerate eldar used to move themselves around the galaxy. Such artefacts were always a curse wherever they turned up. This one had no doubt been lost for millennia until the unwitting asteroid miners unearthed it. Loyal citizens would have reported their discovery but the temptations offered by the eldar had corrupted the miners, turning them into slavers and pirates.

Lithe eldar shapes were moving around the warp gate. One, noting Courlanth's movement, turned and came closer. The sergeant saw a bone-white, angular face as it bent over him with a triumphant grin on its narrow lips.

'Simply amazing, the recuperative properties of your kind,' it said with what seemed genuine affection. It was using the same precisely accented Low Gothic that taunted Courlanth during his battle with the archon. 'After centuries of study you can still surprise me on occasion.'

Courlanth did his best to spit into the face before him but he could only drool. The alien carried on as if it were talking to a pet.

'You're probably thinking this was all for you, aren't you? That we planned to trap some *Deathwatch* here – well, you would be right. Give out some weapons and it's only a matter of time, as I told dear Archon Gharax, before the alien hunters arrive. You see, in Commorragh we have an insatiable hunger for diversion and your kind, your perfect, genetically-enhanced, muscle-bound kind, make for some of the best diversions this tired old galaxy has to offer.

'You will be taken from here to fight and die for our entertainment in the arenas, save perhaps for one or two of you that I will take for my own experiments. My toxin was pleasingly effective on this occasion, but that's no reason to neglect perfect–'

A sudden explosion of white light half-blinded Courlanth and cut off the alien's gloating in mid-sentence. The continuous hammer of bolter-fire split the air in the aftermath, mass-reactive bolts pulping the angular bone-white face in a shower of gore. The sergeant looked up to see figures in black Terminator armour towering above him, the twin flames of their storm bolters stabbing relentlessly as they cut a swath through the shocked eldar. The silver skull of the Deathwatch gleamed on every shoulder. In their midst, the grim face of watch captain Ska Mordentodt cracked in a rare smile as he and his men ruthlessly purged the aliens.

When the bodies were counted Archon Gharax was not found amongst them. Maxillus was dead, killed by a reaction to the toxins brewed by the eldar haemonculus Maelik Toir, while Felbaine was paralysed from the waist down by a spinal injury. The other members of the kill-team responded well to the Brother-Apothecary's ministrations and could stand on their own feet before Ska Mordentodt.

'Remember this day, brothers, teleport homers work better to summon aid than retreat,' the watch captain began.

'You used us as bait,' Courlanth said. He could not keep the bitterness from his words.

'I saved your lives,' Mordentodt reminded him, 'and many others besides by locating the gate. One less hole for the eldar to creep in through and the universe becomes a better place.'

'But why not tell us we had help to call upon at need? Maxillus is dead and Felbaine crippled!'

'The alien has a thousand times a thousand ways to glean such knowledge from you; what chance then of them leading us straight to their most secret places? They had to believe you defeated, just as you had to believe yourselves defeated.' Mordentodt shrugged. 'You volunteered for the mission without any such promises – if I have lied to you it is by giving you help you had no right to expect.'

'So this is the way of the Deathwatch – secrets within our own ranks – never knowing why or when we may be sacrificed to further some other design?'

'This is the way of the Deathwatch,' Mordentodt agreed.

LAST WATCH

L J GOULDING

The creature had lain in wait for many days, such being the nature of its foul kind. Amongst the tangled flora of Phirus its lithe form was rendered as nothing more than a shadow, the pigmentation of its carapaced hide blending with the reddish hues of the undergrowth. Its alien metabolism slowed, concealing it from all but the most sophisticated of auspex scanners, yet its muscle and sinew remained coiled in preparation for that perfect, opportune whip-crack lunge.

Murderous instinct compelled it. That, and the need to feed.

Brother Felgir had been adamant that he would slay this last beast himself, and as befit the barbarous traditions of his Chapter, he had pledged to take its skull as a trophy. *Tyranicus Chameleo*. The lictor. A fine kill for one so keen to prove himself in the eyes of his absent battle-brothers.

His bare face daubed with runes of slaying, he had stalked

the succulent forests by the light of the twin moons, with his long-handled axe gripped tightly in both hands. Skill born of a lifetime as a feral hunter carried him through the undergrowth with barely a sound, even in his night-black power armour – such had been his stealth that not even the birds nesting in the low fronds were startled by his passing. He had thumbed the wolf's head totem upon the haft of his weapon, and mouthed silent prayers to his ancestors.

But he was so much more than a mere tribal huntsman, more even than *just* a noble warrior of the Space Marines. He was Deathwatch. Xenos-slayer. Sworn defender of mankind against the enemy without.

Nonetheless, he had gravely underestimated his foe.

The attack came without warning as Felgir stooped beneath a cluster of scarlet inkvines. Cast in shadow, he spun reflexively just as the lictor reared up to its full height, its scything forelimbs lashing out with blinding speed. He tried to block with his axe while dropping down to evade, but the beast launched its spiny bulk forward, gripping his armoured pauldrons with long, dextrous talons as it drew back for another strike.

Half-pinned on his knees, Felgir whirled the axe overhand into a single grip and brought the blade down hard on the creature's wrist. The lictor shrieked, its twitching feeder tendrils flaring in agony for just a moment before pulling back into its maw, and Felgir struck again and again at the wounded joint.

With a sudden twist of its body, it hurled him away into the rubbery trunk of a large stem succulent. He crashed to the ground, great gouges dug into the ceramite of his shoulder plates where the beast had clawed at him, and a spattering of alien blood across his face and chest. Felgir rolled back to his feet, and spat.

The lictor was favouring its bloodied wrist, but it stalked sideways through the undergrowth with blade-limbs extended, never once taking its predatory eyes from its quarry. It chittered and huffed, and snorted in agitation as it flexed the wounded carpus, its barbed tail whipping back and forth like an enraged serpent.

Felgir dived in once more with a savage bellow, his axe held high, but the beast lashed out again with those scything limbs and cleaved through the adamantium haft as though it were a twig.

Caught off balance, Felgir stumbled for just a moment, but that was all that the beast needed; a spasm wracked its torso and a dozen fleshy barbs shot from chitinous sheaths between its ribs, piercing the softer seals of Felgir's armour and embedding in his exposed flesh. His stifled cry of pain was cut short by the bio-venom that coated their tips, though he still managed to plant a solid fist into the lictor's mandible before it hoisted him from his feet, and the creature roared its bestial triumph.

The hunter had in fact been the *hunted* all along, and the tyranid monstrosity now dragged its stricken prey into a deadly embrace, feeder tendrils quivering in anticipation.

That was when I chose to put an end to the debacle.

The high angle afforded by my vantage point presented a relatively clear view of the beast's armoured nape. I had already identified the optimal kill-shot when it had first emerged from concealment – a single mass-reactive into either eye socket – but the flow of Felgir's combat had robbed me of all three subsequent opportunities. Instead I put the shell (mercury-slug Stalker pattern, single discharge) into the nerve cluster at the first branch of the lictor's spine.

The creature let out a single yelp, its forelimbs dropping slack while the rest of its body shuddered and buckled. As it fell forward, I feared that Felgir would be crushed under the dead weight, but in his feverish state he continued to struggle and moan weakly from beneath the alien carcass as his transhuman physiology worked to neutralise the bio-toxins in his system.

Brothers Mettius and Hadrovar descended to ground level with me, securing the perimeter and tending to Felgir. I should not have indulged him in his tribal pretentions, though in this instance I am glad to confirm that it did not affect the outcome of our original operation (all hostile xeno-forms purged).

Brother Felgir will wear the scars of his own hubris for the rest of his days, and in this I believe that the lesson has been learned.

My lords, submitted for your approval, I hereby present this full tactical report on the completed mission against the tyranids on Phirus. As the ranking Deathwatch officer, I, Brother-Sergeant Marek Angeloi – formerly of the Scythes of the Emperor Chapter, Adeptus Astartes – do declare my sacred oaths upheld and my part in this endeavour to be complete.

The xenos beasts of Hive Fleet Kraken are purged from the Veneros Sector, but the war rages on throughout the segmentum. With the permission of my esteemed and learned lords, I shall return to it now.

Not in the noble black livery of the order, but once again in the colours of my fallen Chapter brethren.

For the Emperor. For Sotha.

ABOUT THE AUTHORS

David Annandale is the author of the digital short story *Eclipse of Hope* and the novellas *Yarrick: Chains of Golgotha* and *Mephiston: Lord of Death* for Black Library. By day, he dons an academic disguise and lectures at a Canadian university on subjects ranging from English literature to horror films and video games. He lives with his wife and family and a daemon in the shape of a cat, and is working on several new projects set in the grim darkness of the far future.

Braden Campbell is a classical actor and playwright, currently living in Milton, Ontario. His theatrical work has seen him perform across not only across Canada, but in England and New York City. For the past five years he has also worked as a freelance writer, particularly in the field of role playing games. Braden has enjoyed Warhammer 40,000 for nearly a decade, and remains fiercely dedicated to his dark eldar.

Author of the Dark Eldar series, along with the novel *Survival Instinct* and a host of short stories, **Andy Chambers** has more than twenty years' experience creating worlds dominated by war machines, spaceships and dangerous aliens. Andy worked at Games Workshop as lead designer of the Warhammer 40,000 miniatures game for three editions before moving to the PC gaming market. He now lives and works in Nottingham.

Ben Counter is the author of the Soul Drinkers and Grey Knights series, along with two Horus Heresy novels, and is one of Black Library's most popular Warhammer 40,000 authors. He has written RPG supplements and comic books. He is a fanatical painter of miniatures, a pursuit which has won him his most prized possession: a prestigious Golden Demon award. He lives in Portsmouth, England.

Peter Fehervari slipped into the parallel surreality of television almost twenty years ago and never quite escaped. As a rogue editor, his life is an eternity of cuts and mixes to quench the dreams of thirsting producers while actually getting things on air. He has cut promos for many well known television shows, but winning a place in a Black Library anthology eclipsed it all. Since then his short stories have appeared in *Heroes of the Space Marines* and *Death Watch: Xenos Hunters*. Fire Caste is his first novel. He currently presides over a dormant Chaos Gate in London.

L J Goulding has written many stories for Black Library, including 'The Great Maw', 'Last Watch' and 'The Oberwald Ripper'. After collaborating on many similar projects, 'Mortarion's Heart' is his first audio drama. By day he works as a member of Black Library's editorial team, proving that an obsessive and encyclopaedic knowledge of the Horus Heresy can be a useful thing after all. He lives in Nottingham, UK.

Nick Kyme is the author of the Tome of Fire trilogy featuring the Salamanders. He has also written for the Horus Heresy, Space Marine Battles and Time of Legends series with the novels *Vulkan Lives, Fall of Damnos* and *The Great Betrayal*. In addition, he has penned a host of short stories and several novellas, including 'Feat of Iron' which was a *New York Times* bestseller in the Horus Heresy collection *The Primarchs*. He lives and works in Nottingham.

Born and raised in Edinburgh, Scotland, **Steve Parker** currently lives and works in Tokyo, Japan. In 2005, his short fiction started appearing in American SF/fantasy/horror magazines. In 2006, his story 'The Falls of Marakross' was published in the Black Library's *Tales from the Dark Millennium* anthology and his first Warhammer 40,000 novel, *Rebel Winter*, was published in 2007. He introduced readers to the Deathwatch kill-team known as Talon Squad in the short stories 'Headhunted' and 'Exhumed'. When he's not writing, he enjoys martial arts, heavy metal music and supporting wildlife conservation.

Anthony Reynolds's work for Black Library includes the Word Bearers trilogy, the Knights of Bretonnia series and the Horus Heresy short stories 'Scions of the Storm' and 'Dark Heart'. Originally from Australia, Anthony moved to the UK where he worked within Games Workshop for many years before returning to his homeland. He is currently touring the world, taking inspiration from natural wonders that he can twist into devious monstrosities to populate the 41st Millennium.

Rob Sanders is a freelance writer, who spends his nights creating dark visions for regular visitors to the 41st millennium to relive in the privacy of their own nightmares, including the novels *Atlas Infernal* and *Legion of the Damned*. He lives in the small city of Lincoln, UK.